# OVER THE LIMIT
## My Secret Diaries 1993-8

# OVER THE LIMIT
## My Secret Diaries 1993-8

Bob Monkhouse, O.B.E.

Century · London

First published by Century in 1998

Copyright © Bob Monkhouse 1998

Bob Monkhouse has asserted his right under the Copyright, Designs
and Patents Act, 1988, to be identified as the author of this work

First published in the United Kingdom in 1998 by

Century, 20 Vauxhall Bridge Road, London SW1V 2SA

Random House Australia (Pty) Limited
20 Alfred Street, Milsons Point, Sydney,
New South Wales 2061, Australia

Random House New Zealand Limited
18 Poland Road, Glenfield
Auckland 10, New Zealand

Random House South Africa (Pty) Limited
Endulini, 5a Jubilee Road
Parktown 2193, South Africa

Random House UK Limited Reg. No. 954009

A CIP catalogue record for this book
is available from the British Library

Papers used by Random House UK Limited are natural, recyclable
products made from wood grown in sustainable forests.
The manufacturing processes conform to the environmental
regulations of the country of origin.

ISBN 0 7126 7707 0

Typeset by SX Composing DTP, Rayleigh, Essex
Printed by Mackays of Chatham plc, Chatham, Kent

CHARMINSTER

This book is dedicated to my wife Jackie who endures my stupidity, takes care of me in sickness and in health, runs our home, does all the shopping and cooking, remains calm and lovely whatever the circumstances, and who even finds time to write the dedications for all my books.

# READ THIS FIRST!

Imagine owning an oblong apparatus, about the right size to fit into your pocket or handbag, a device which would be constantly ready for use without the need of switches, batteries, winding up or plugging in, able to go forwards or backwards, to stop and start as you wish, and fully equipped to provide you with immediate information and entertainment. Well, you're holding one right now. It's called a book.

Five years ago I wrote my autobiography, *Crying With Laughter*, to mark my sixty-fifth birthday. Had I then died at once you would have been saved the time you're squandering now. But that first book became incomplete as soon as I'd finished it.

## Please be warned!

Offering you my thoughts and memories and opinions in diary form is a bit like presenting you with a two-ton box of chocolates with no guide on the lid as to what's in the centres. Five or six at a time is the most one can enjoy.

I think these pages are best for dipping into now and then, skipping the ones that don't appeal.

It's unlikely that you'll share all my passions although I promise that I'll try not to witter on too self-indulgently. My basic instinct as a populist entertainer should inhibit my presumption of your interest in my private predilections: my two granddaughters, malt whiskies, B movies that only utter anoraks like, walking around cities, cartoon strips before 1960, food supplements, cooking by Nico Ladenis, unusual clocks, Californian wines, the silent films of Louise Brooks, every Tetris computer game, Phil Collins, fresh Canadian salmon, obscure videos, sci-fi and fantasy illustrations, museums and art galleries in Washington and Vienna, 78 r.p.m. records and gramophones, the country songs of Reba MacIntyre and the varsity songs of Rudy Vallee.

By now you'll have noticed that this book is slightly more than normal size and weight. It may have occurred to you to wonder how it is that, while my autobiography dealt with sixty-five years of my life in a single tome of average measurements, a mere five years can fill out a greater number of pages. Let me explain.

Firstly, when I wrote my history I had to leave out a heart-breakingly large number of funny stories, little-known facts about people other than myself and some actionable gossip about the good, the bad and the litigious.

When five years ago I went to the Sky News studios to promote my life story I was slightly taken aback by Selina Scott's observation that my autobiography included stories about famous people who were dead. 'Do you think it's fair,' she asked, 'to tell tales about people who are dead and can't answer back?'

'They're the best ones,' I told her, adding that I most certainly hoped that people who are dead don't answer back and if they ever did, I'd have a laundry problem. Selina regarded me more in sorrow than in anger.

On my way out I noticed the flat screen that served as a background for the weather forecasts had been freshly painted. The painter had leaned a placard against it saying WET PAINT under which an unknown hand had added, BECOMING DRIER LATER. I was gratified that a particle of wit could survive in that otherwise humourless zone.

Secondly, a collection of memoirs like this, strung along the chronological washing line of a diary, can allow itself to ramble a bit, change the subject at whim, express the author's opinions and generally present silly ideas, conversations with other minds, and other oddities with which I might hope to amuse dinner guests but which wouldn't have fitted easily into the more formal narrative of my existence.

Lastly, much of this volume is reminiscence. When you're seventy, reminiscing is a second chance at happiness.

Some recollections astonish even me. My memory continues to serve up daily surprises: driving past the Milverton Lodge in Dickenson Road, Manchester, for example, and so inadvertently conjuring up a long-forgotten scene from 1959 of Lady Sarah Churchill pursuing me round the private hotel wearing only fur slippers, brandishing a carving knife and threatening to cut off my 'meat and two veg'! Sir Winston's daughter was under the influence of proscribed substances and was irked that I, being in love with my leading lady at the time, had not succumbed to her widely distributed charms. If that seems scandalously unkind, I'm sorry, but it's true and such vivid memories do have a place in honest memoirs.

Again, the sound of Bing Crosby singing 'April Played the Fiddle' flashed up a sequence from the dim recesses of my mind. Bing was in London in the 50s and had agreed to record a 45-minute radio show for what was then called the Light Programme, the equivalent of Radio 2 today. I'd written the script and joined the BBC's department heads for lunch at the Criterion with Bing before the afternoon recording.

We arrived first and when Bing walked in with his musical director, John Scott Trotter, we hardly recognised him from his movies. The toupee had been left in its box and Bing was very bald.

Once the Americans were seated at our corner table, Ronnie Waldman, the Head of Radio Variety at that time, asked what Bing would like to drink.

'Bourbon, if you please.'

'A large one?'

'No, no, thank you. Just the regular-sized bottle.'

There was a pause while we all decided whether to laugh or not.

Ronnie saw something serious in Bing's gaze and ordered a bottle of American whiskey, hard to get in London in that austere post-war decade. Bing drank it steadily throughout lunch, pouring and gulping between mouthfuls of fried chicken with sweetcorn fritters. By the time we left the restaurant he was as drunk as any old derelict I've ever seen swearing at traffic in Kilburn. When the cold air of wintry Piccadilly Circus hit his lungs, his legs went boneless.

'He'll never be able to do the show,' whispered Johnny Stewart, the producer.

Trotter, who'd ignored Bing's boozing until that moment, answered, 'Just get him to where you want him.'

We held Bing up by supporting him under the arms and it took some effort to propel him along the icy pavement to the basement studio of the old Paris Cinema in Lower Regent Street. Manhandling him down the first flights of stairs was hard work and at the top of the final flight he slipped out of our grip and rolled down the nine remaining steps. Alarmed, we ran down after him but in his filleted state he was quite unharmed and seemingly unaware of what had happened. His blue eyes were unfocused and rolling sightlessly in their sockets.

'What the hell can we do?' demanded Ronnie.

Trotter helped to dump Bing onto a couch in the small continuity suite.

'When do we record?' he asked.

'In less than thirty minutes.'

'Is Paul all set?'

Paul Fenoulhet was conducting the orchestra.

Ronnie nodded. 'Yes, everything's ready except our star! He'll never sober up for hours.'

'No,' Trotter agreed. 'He's whacked OK. Let me know when you want him on stage and help me get him there.'

Trotter went off to speak to Fenoulhet and tell him what he wanted him to do. The studio audience arrived by coach and filed into the seats. At two minutes to showtime, Trotter and Ronnie lifted Bing from his seat and half carried him along the corridor to a door that led to a curtained-off area of the stage. I held it open as they went through and asked, 'What happens next?'

Trotter murmured into Bing's ear. 'Wake up, Mr C! Time to work!'

What I saw then seemed like a miracle.

As Trotter spoke those words and Fenoulhet cued a bell note from the pianist, Bing straightened, gave a light cough and stood alone.

An announcer at the centre stage microphone declaimed, 'Ladies and gentlemen, Bing Crosby!' and Bing, suddenly sober, stepped through the curtain. The audience applauded wildly and, without needing a second bell note to put him in the right key, Bing reached the mike and began to sing the first line of his theme song unaccompanied:

> *'When the blue of the night meets the gold of the day,*
> *Someone waits for me . . .'*

The orchestra came in smoothly and for the next three-quarters of an hour this extraordinary performer sang ten songs quite wonderfully. His memory of each lyric was exact and, even stranger to me, he was able to do the dialogue with the show's compere that I had written. Not only did he read the script clearly, he performed it with great charm and ease.

Now here's the weirdest part. Just as he had sobered up as soon as he got his cue, so the reverse now took place. The show ended, the audience cheered and clapped, Bing bowed, walked off the stage and the moment his feet were back behind the curtain, he stopped to look around him, seemed to shake himself slightly, sighed and collapsed into our arms, just as totally plastered as he had been before. We all looked in utter bewilderment at Trotter.

He shrugged. 'Man's brain is divided. He's two guys. I can't explain it. Could we have a car, please? I don't think we can carry him all the way to the Savoy.'

I've known Jekyll-and-Hyde talents before and since but never have I witnessed anything like the two Bing Crosbys that I saw that day.

Neither of those two anecdotes would really have suited my first book, which was essentially about me and not about those whose paths have crossed with mine so incidentally. Yet I have plenty more to tell so I'd best begin the proper job of setting out this diversion.

But the very act of starting needs consideration. Every writer knows how important it is to engage his readers' attention with the very first sentence. For advice I called on my friend, the best-selling author Freddie Forsyth. He told me of two thriller writers who, competing for the most attention-grabbing line, came up with:

> *It was nearly midnight before they had scraped Uncle William off the dining room table.*

and

> *'Was it necessary,' asked the judge, leaning over the bench, 'to produce this entire lake in evidence?'*

Take your pick.

Now I've started, I'm going to continue by answering a few questions.

After that, you can peep into my diaries. Go on, I don't mind.

# ANSWERS FIRST

As a radio and TV quizmaster I must have asked a hundred thousand questions over the past fifty years. Later on, somewhere in the journal section of this book, I'll be presenting you with questions for which I have no answers.

But first let me offer you my answers to actual questions which I've been asked by the press and public and, until now, haven't really had time to think about. Satirically, that is. And we all know how much more seriously comedy should be taken if it's called satire. Satirists claim the higher ground of social and moral comment without resorting to populism. Look how satire prevented the rise of German Nazism in the 30s.

The greatest of those cabaret satirists was Karl Valentin. His parody of Adolf Hitler was dangerously famous in the Third Reich. One of his most quoted witticisms originated on the night he told his audience, 'A funny thing happened on the way here. I saw a black Mercedes go by and there weren't any Gestapo in it!'

Valentin was arrested and spent several years in prison and in a concentration camp. After the war ended, he was fêted by his loyal fans at a comeback performance. As the welcoming applause finally faded, he told them, 'I was wrong about that black Mercedes – there were some Gestapo in it!'

**The five-year plan**
The bulk of this book is a journal of the five years that have passed since the publication of my autobiography, *Crying With Laughter*.

Obviously every day of those years hasn't been packed with incident so I've tried to be selective, assuming there would be a limit to your patience with or interest in my every journey, engagement, meal, shopping expedition, phone call and bowel movement. Where gaps of many days occur, you may assume that so did doldrums.

*What do you think of your job?*

They say laughter is infectious and laughter is what I offer you. As a comedian, I'm not unlike a prostitute. I'm available for nightly hire to give you what pleasure I can. I go away with your money, never knowing your name. If I ever see you again I doubt that I'll recognise you. And, as I've said, what I offer you is infectious.

The two greatest businesses in the world are comedy and prostitution. Doesn't matter whether you're a comedian or a hooker – you've got it, you sell it, you've still got it!

*Is Bob Monkhouse your real name?*

Yes, although I did consider changing it. Throughout history courtesans and jesters have something else in common – they adopt names that proclaimed their vocations. Whores were called Lulu, Zazi, Fifi and Fanny. Clowns took names like Coco, Chuckles, Little Titch, Charlot, Buster and Cheerful Charlie. If your parents christened you Bonzo, you're hardly predestined to become a royal mistress. Likewise, how many comics are called Camilla?

Parents can influence their children's entire life by the names they give them. Look at Alexander the Great – what a start his folks gave him. With a name like that he was bound to do well. So what sort of sadistic parents did Ivan the Terrible have? What cruel bastards. Unless, of course, their actual names were Mr and Mrs Terrible. But just imagine how the course of history might have changed if we'd had Attila the Honey.

*Are there any true stories you couldn't tell on TV or in print?*

Well, let's find out, shall we? If this stays in the book, no; if not, yes. When I was hosting 'Family Fortunes' we had some survey results we just couldn't use on a family show. We asked one hundred people to name the part of the body they found most sexually stimulating. Top answer from women was buttocks. Top answer from men was 'My right hand'.

*Can you recommend a diet?*

Yes, it's official. According to *Slimline* magazine a man having sex can burn 250 calories. Or 3,000 calories if she keeps her tights on. Hookers in King's Cross are now calling themselves 'horizontal fitness trainers'.

*What laws would you change and why?*

We live in a very unjust society with vast numbers of homeless in this country. And the fact of the matter is, a dog can wander around London or Manchester or any major city, not belonging to anyone, and you can call the RSPCA or any other humane society and they will come and get the dog. But a human being can wander around that same city, not belonging to anyone, and there's no one to call.

Now maybe I'm being a bleeding-heart liberal but I think we need a Royal Society for the Protection of Human Beings. I think that homeless people should be collected from our streets and given food and shelter for up to two weeks and then, after fourteen days, if no one has claimed them . . .

Oh, I can just imagine the dawning disbelief in your eyes. What? You don't really think I'm going to suggest that after fourteen days, if nobody claims them, homeless people should be painlessly put to sleep? Come on, you can't believe I'm that sort of monster. Of course I'm not suggesting they should be destroyed.

They're far too valuable for scientific experiments.

No, I mean to benefit veterinary research. Be fair: if we can use beagles to measure the toxic elements in cigarette smoke harmful to humans, then surely we should be able to use football hooligans to research mad cow disease.

You may think that I'm using satire to make a point, dear reader, but the real point is that the system doesn't work when we have thousands and thousands of people homeless. And the only solution is to topple the Government from power, chuck them all out; we need new leadership – forget Tony Blair, forget William Hague, forget Paddy Ashdown – oh, you'd already forgotten Paddy Ashdown – and elect me, me, me, make me your Dictator! I'll run Britain like a business – I'll burn it to the ground and collect the insurance.

*Who's your favourite real-life relative?*

My aunt Edith is eighty-eight years old, still driving. Not with me, I'm not quite insane. You wouldn't know anyone was in that car unless you looked in it up close. She's shrunk so much that she's too short to dunk a biscuit. People are in Sainsbury's car park yelling, 'Stop that old Vauxhall Viva, it's running away!' 'No wait, it's one of them Jeremy Beadle stunts!' All you can see – red knuckles and some white fluff.

She drives to an old persons' restaurant – they do a very nice large-print alphabet soup.

Eighty-eight years old and she still makes me laugh, mostly at the way she wears her stockings. She just rolls them up to her knees . . . and stops. She can't get them any higher, and besides, that was all the fashion back when she was a girl. Then her local shop stopped selling stockings and she had to start buying tights. And she still only rolls them up to her knees. Now there's a little hammock between her legs.

And she keeps *Reader's Digest* in there . . . with a selection of fresh fruit . . . and she's waddling around her flat . . . 'Would you like a grape?' No! I don't even want to touch *Reader's Digest*.

### *What year were you born?*

The year of the stock market crash, 1928. I was a little boy during the Great Depression, money was short. One Christmas there was a big fancy-dress party in our village hall. We couldn't afford costumes. We changed clothes with the neighbours – they went as us and we went as them.

1928, that makes me seventy. People say that when you reach seventy you're sure to notice yourself slowing down. But, honestly, I haven't noticed myself slowing down at all. But then – what if being seventy has slowed down my ability to notice?

I'm the same age as Sean Connery. Just last week I was talking to a woman in a singles bar in Smethwick – it could happen – and she chanced to remark that Sean Connery has sexy bedroom eyes. I said, 'What are those?' She said, 'Eyes that tell me he's thinking, "You will go to bed with me, you will go to bed with me."' I said, 'What kind of eyes have I got?' She said, 'Inquisitive eyes.'

And I was hurt at first but then I realised she was right because I was thinking, 'Will she go to bed with me? Will she go to bed with me?'

### *What's the greatest advance in entertainment in your lifetime?*

TV, I suppose. Twenty years ago we only had three channels. Today, twenty years later, thanks to that money you laid out for satellite, you've got dozens of channels where you can watch the same shows we saw on three channels twenty years ago.

But technically, TV's improving all the time. In our immediate future, there'll be cinema-size flat screens that can occupy an entire wall of your home with a picture of perfect clarity, every fine detail minutely reproduced . . . and you'll have to decide for yourself, is this the way you really want to watch Jo Brand?

*What is your view of life? Has yours gone too fast or too slowly?*

Of course life is too headlong a rush through the years. I found the first half of my life a bit like tennis scores – I seemed to go straight from zero to fifteen to thirty to forty.

But isn't it curious that we spend the first half of our lives picking up habits that will shorten the second?

*Is money important to you?*

Maybe money isn't the key to happiness, but, hey, if you've got enough money, you can have a key made. There may be many Golden Rules in life but one I know is true: that he who has the gold makes the rules.

Someone once said life is like a donut, 'You're either in the dough or in the hole.'

# PART I: MY DIARIES

*24 June 1993 – 23 August 1995*

## Thursday, 24 June 1993

It's done, it's gone, it's out of my hands. The manuscript of my life and times has been delivered into the hands of my publishers and I am once again a free man. Free to do what I have to do almost every day: read the newspapers and invent jokes based on topical events. Tonight I'm doing a cabaret at the National Exhibition Centre's Metropole Hotel for a major pharmaceutical group. There's a perfect headline for them in the news today – a 50 per cent rise in the price of Valium. So I write the joke, the final word to be delivered in a dazed and lifeless manner:

*The price of Valium is set to go up 50 per cent. When they told Valium users about this they said, 'Whatever.'*

So what else is new? I find news stories that suggest more gags:

*In a survey the majority of British women said they'd rather go shopping for clothes than go on a blind date – which makes sense in a way. With shopping, you get to try things to see if they're big enough for you.*

*Fashion designer Giorgio Armani confessed to bribing Italian tax officials. He was sentenced to wear brown shoes with a blue suit for six months.*

*Michael Jackson has agreed to pay Lisa Marie Presley three million dollars not to write a tell-all book about their marriage. Now there's another example of discrimination against women. She's a girl, she only gets three million – if she'd been a boy, it would have been twenty million.*

Then I remember that when Jackie and I were last in America, I found that they actually have a Michael Jackson chocolate bar on sale and – I'm not making this up – the ingredients are 'White chocolate with no nuts'.

And so the process goes on as it has over the past five decades or so. When I first started writing comedy for professional comedians in the late 40s they were mostly love/hate relationships. The comedian loves new material but hates the fact that he can't create it; *ergo*, he hates the writer. The writer loves the idea of delivering his own material but hates the fact that he's not funny on stage; *ergo*, he hates the comic.

To the comics of the 40s and 50s, scriptwriters were slave labour.

Most funnymen of the variety theatres wanted their audiences to believe that they invented their own patter. Some of them – Eric Barker, Richard Murdoch and Kenneth Horne, Charlie Chester – did dream up most of their own stuff and consequently they had a fellow feeling for me and other young writers. But the majority depended on underpaid lackeys like us to provide a constant stream of new ideas while otherwise ignoring our existence.

Al Read, a great radio star, relied entirely and exclusively on the words provided by a mild-mannered producer named Ronnie Taylor but liked to pretend that Ronnie was just his assistant, a 'gofer' on whom Al practised his routines.

Tommy Trinder, one of the superstars of the London Palladium, didn't even talk to his writers Max Kester and Con West but dealt with them through his agent, often instructing him to pay them in goods he'd been given when doing shop openings.

Bob Hope, always reluctant to pay the crew of writers who kept him so plentifully supplied, would make them wait at the foot of a high staircase while he stood at the top, dropping their pay cheques one by one so that they had to catch them as they floated by or pick them off the floor. It was degrading, but the price was right.

Although I still depend upon my knack for turning news items into comedy, those early years taught me to appreciate with gratitude the work of my collaborators today: Neil Shand, Rob Colley, Debbie Barham and most especially Colin Edmonds, more like a son to me and my wife, Jackie.

But a few sharp observations in the form of one- or two-liners won't hold an audience for the forty-five minutes of an after-dinner speech, or the hour or more spent on the cabaret floor. For this the comedian needs good routines and I'll always be grateful to the outrageous American Lenny Bruce for showing me how to get laughter from truth, however uncomfortable the procedure.

When Bruce came to London for the first time, he performed at the Establishment, a cabaret theatre at 18, Greek Street, Soho, where a strip joint called the Tropicana had previously enjoyed my unblinking attention. Founded by Peter Cook and friends at the start of the 60s, the club's clever scheme was to circumvent the insensitive scissors of the Lord Chamberlain whose censorship had been bowdlerising our plays and theatrical revues since the sixteenth century. Cook, Jonathan Miller, Alan Bennett, Dudley Moore and director Nicholas Luard had realised that no such proscription applied to entertainment in a private, membership-only place of amusement.

Five thousand subscriptions at two guineas each (£2.10), plus a bit of private capital, financed the venture which opened on 5 October 1961, with a riotous first night in its cramped and crowded upstairs room, providing two seatings for dinner at either eight-thirty or eleven, each followed by a performance by a resourceful gang that included John Bird, John Fortune and Eleanor Bron. The midnight show also featured extemporised additions from Cook, Miller, Bennett and Moore who would arrive breathless from that evening's staging of *Beyond the Fringe*. It was irresistible fun and an overnight sensation.

When the team read Kenneth Tynan's opinion of Lenny Bruce in the *New Yorker*, in which he praised 'the sharpest denter of taboos at present active . . . who breaks through the barrier of laughter to the horizon where the truth has its sanctuary', they sought out Bruce's albums and, knocked out by his iconoclastic fantasies, became determined to bring him to London.

Every young comedian and comedy writer had those albums too and, like me, could recite them by heart. We awaited Bruce's arrival with mixed feelings – mounting excitement as the day grew nearer and mounting resentment at the sniffy way the British press were representing him as a threat to our morals.

'Diarrhoea of the mouth,' warned the *Observer*. 'He is 36, small, stubbly, with a drawling voice. His mother was a burlesque actress (from whom he gets some of his jokes)' and told Britain to expect the 'farthest-out of all the American sick comics . . . A Vulgar Tasteless Boor'.

Bruce's first night was a conquest of the converted. The rest of his visit was an artistic triumph over the rudeness of the unenlightened. He appeared for thirty nights and I was there for twenty-two of them (even though his midnight show ran till two in the morning), relishing his uniqueness while suffering with him the stupidity of a crowd that had been brainwashed by hostile reports in the broadsheets.

Chinless wonders and brain-dead débutantes flocked to see him, not to be delighted by his breathtaking style but because it was the fashionable thing to do. 'They say he actually uses the f-word!' they'd gasp as they took their places. Then, as soon as Bruce began his more scandalous routines, they'd cover their ears and walk out as noisily as they could. One prosperously dressed man sat with his family giggling at the opening routines with which Bruce would assess the audience's speed and level of comprehension. Then when Bruce changed gear and started his brilliant piece about cancer, the man rose to his feet and shouted, '*Cancer*? That's quite enough!' and bustled his wife and companions from the room still shouting '*Cancer*?' in disbelief.

Heckling came from the ignorant of every class; I remember hearing him interrupted by cries of 'Yankee filth!' and 'Dirty Jew-boy!' On an evening when it was obvious that the crowd had only come for the thrill of hearing public profanity forbidden elsewhere, Bruce's handsome face assumed the most innocent expression. Very politely he asked, 'Are you waiting to hear me say fuck?' The silly audience hooted and clapped. 'Oh, I see. You're real sophisticated people. Nothing shocks you, is that right?'

More daft applause and whoops.

'OK, let's get rid of all those bad words that we pretend don't exist. Then we can relax and get on with the comedy. Shit. Balls. Tits and arseholes. Prick, dick, cock and schmuck. Clitoris, vagina, pussy and cunt. Everybody OK so far?'

They were loving it like naughty schoolchildren.

'Go on, Lenny!' called one. 'Britain can take it!'

'OK, you're all so hip, I think maybe you're ready for the big one. Here we go!'

Bruce feigned blowing his nose into his hand and wiping the result on the back wall.

'Snot!'

A stunned silence at first. Then a woman's cry of 'Shame!' And within a count of three, the crowd turned into a lynch mob. Amid the angry outcry, someone threw a glass at Bruce and it smashed on the stage. A fist fight broke out near me and I saw Bruce being ushered from the stage as the mob began to demand their money back.

Bruce had tested their brave new tolerance to destruction.

On another raucous evening the most celebrated actress from Ireland, Siobhan McKenna, kept yawning very loudly and then made a great display of walking out in disgust. Peter Cook stepped up to thank her for leaving and her burly escort punched him very hard on the nose. Distancing herself from the brutality, McKenna reached the door and turned to proclaim with a dramatic gesture, 'These are Irish hands and they are clean!'

Cook replied, 'This is a British face and it is bleeding!'

Bruce devised a cute strategy to deal with these difficult audiences. He'd always taped his performances and now he had the bright idea of playing back the worst behaviour of the previous night's bunch to that evening's assemblage. We stood condemned by the vicious heckling and the blind stupidity of a British mob as the embarrassing evidence poured out of the loudspeaker. Where Bruce talked about love, far too honestly for local tastes, we reacted with hate.

Robert Frost wrote, 'No tears in the writer, no tears for the reader.' Bruce showed me the trick of taking my worst moments and using them to amuse people, turning tears of despair into tears of laughter. It's a kind of therapy that's seen me get over a lot of woe by sharing it in the form of comedy.

Everyone can relate to it. Perhaps it's partly *schadenfreude*, we laugh because it didn't happen to us, or it might be that, when something that was once awful is recalled in happier circumstances, it seems funny because of its human commonality. We are bonded at a deep level by life's many tragedies and, as Lenny Bruce put it, 'Pain plus time equals humour.'

## Monday, 28 June 1993

Tonight I dine with Random House's hospitality, a dozen key executives in the book trade and some of Century's publishing personnel. As usual I check the morning papers for something topical to joke about:

*The biggest selling new product in China is a thing called Weight Loss Soap. They claim that you lose pounds in weight when you wash with this soap. Listen, if you're so filthy that, when you take a bath you actually drop pounds, then maybe weight isn't your biggest problem.*

*Finns and Scots are top of the Euro sperm count. A Scotsman in his prime can produce over 600,000 spermatozoa in a single ejaculation. I said to my wife, 'I wonder why it takes over half a million sperm to fertilise one egg.' She said, 'That's because they're men and they won't stop to ask for directions.'*

*In Holland police have arrested a man for posing as a 'qualified optician'. Difficult case to prosecute because none of the witnesses can identify him.*

Halfway through my after-dinner speech, Jackie enters the room. She's arrived a little early with Robert Purdie, our driver, to collect me for our journey home to Bedfordshire. Jackie's been to dinner with a friend and has enjoyed a few glasses of wine.

For the first and only time in her life, she heckles me. And the assembled company decides that she's a lot funnier than I am.

Afterwards they want to know when she's going to write *her* autobiography.

Yes, I know what Lenny Bruce said: 'Pain plus time equals humour.' Time hasn't kicked in yet.

## Saturday, 24 July 1993

We've arrived to spend five weeks in our Barbados Sandcastle and I'm excited at the prospect of seeing my autobiography in print. The publishers have promised to FedEx me a hardback copy hot off the press. Meanwhile I'm reading other people's life stories and they all seem to be much more interesting than mine.

One's a non-fiction book about serial killers and the one I just can't take to is an American mass-murderer called Jeffrey Dahmer. This man ate seventeen people. Seventeen! I mean, I can understand one or two but when you eat seventeen people, I'm sorry but you're just eating for eating's sake.

Isn't it amazing how our prisons and institutions are releasing unstable psychopaths who have no business mixing in normal society? There's another case in the book about this man who got so annoyed because his dinner was late that he killed his mother and father and girlfriend and then posted their body parts to the police. Now he's been released on condition that he takes pills to control his anger. True. How'd you like to be at a party with this guy when he starts slapping his pockets and going, 'Where the hell did I leave them?'

## Monday, 2 August 1993

Heavy rain didn't discourage Barbados from enjoying its colourful festival called Crop-over, traditionally celebrating the end of the sugarcane harvest, and Kadooment Day, when the entire island population involves itself in street parties, marching bands, fantastic floats, calypso concerts and a day-long televised parade in Mardi Gras style featuring dazzling and wildly inventive costumes that have been created and stitched together in the twelve months since the last grand procession. It's a glorious affair and the national enthusiasm is stupendously exhilarating.

The banks are closed today but I need cash so I go to the Barclays at Sunset Crest.

An old black lady is already ahead of me, looking quite breathless and flushed. As she slides her credit card into the slot, she turns to me.

'Been marchin' wid de parade,' she gasps, laughing and clasping her hand to her large bosom. " 'Scuse me, please.'

She slips off her right shoe and pokes about inside, lifting a moist insole and peering beneath it.

'Shoes pinching?'

'Oh, no, dese are fine shoes.'

She balances on one leg and, wobbling uncertainly, taps out her PIN number.

'See, I can't remember my number and de bank tell me not to write it on a piece of paper in case someone snatch it off me in de street.'

The machine delivers her money and she takes it.

'So, you see?'

She holds out the shoe for me to look inside.

'I wrote de number inside my shoe!'

## Monday, 16 August 1993

Today we went shopping in Bridgetown's newest supermarket and they had frozen venison! Look what we do with meat – we change its name so we'll feel better about eating it. We kill a deer but do we eat deer? No, we create a euphemism and call it venison. We always change the name of the animal after we kill it.

A bull becomes beef, a pig becomes pork, a horse becomes a burger.

Did you read that story that some cheapo junk food outlets put earthworms in their burgers? I didn't believe it. Then the other day I'm in a fast food joint, I cut my burger in half and watched both sides crawl off in different directions.

One paper claimed that some cheapo junk food outlets put kangaroo meat in their burgers. And my wife's been wondering why I keep waking up in the night for a quick jump.

## Wednesday, 25 August 1993

The heat is intense, too much even for native Barbadians, but I'm in celebratory mood so we're off to Holetown this evening to dine at the Mews with friends, Sue and Jeremy Beadle. We get the table on the balcony, where the evening breeze is scented by a nearby bush of Lady of the Night, and I order a bottle of Bollinger.

'What's the occasion?' asks Jeremy.

I explain: 'It's the date that Jac agreed to marry me exactly twenty years ago.'

My first wife left me in '66 and I remarried on 4 October '73. At first I lived alone between marriages but I didn't like it.

My first wife kept everything so I had to start from scratch in an empty house, even had to buy crockery.

I took along Joan Prichard, my agent's wife, to help me pick it out and it was a perfect example of how men think differently from women.

She said, 'You need dinner plates. You must definitely get eight place settings.'

'Eight? That's a great idea.'

'Yes, so you can have friends to dinner.'

That's a woman's thinking. What was I thinking?

'Eight meals in a row without washing up!'

## Thursday, 2 September 1993

This is a busy week for publicising my autobiography. Yesterday was spent at my Bedfordshire home talking to some extraordinarily attractive women – Corinna Honan of the *Daily Mail*, Elker Tullet of 'London Tonight', Natalie Graham of the *Daily Express* and Zoë Heller of the *Independent on Sunday*, the latter being my only hostile encounter of the campaign. Zoë's a looker and a smart writer but, despite my efforts to please, she doesn't take to me, my attempts to amuse or my prose style. She will report that I have the eyes of a 50s starlet and a writing technique too elliptic to be honest. My only other bad crit will come in press clippings from an anonymous wag doing book reviews for a Suffolk paper: '*Crying With Laughter*, an autobiography by Bob Monkhouse: poor choice of subject.'

Today I'm in London being interviewed by Radio 5, signing books at Hatchards, lunching with Andrew Duncan of the *Sunday Express*, meeting lovely Hannah Stevenson for a regionally syndicated piece and being a John Dunn guest on Radio 2. I've got severe toothache and John is very sympathetic, recommending his Harley Street dental surgeon.

'He uses Sodium Pentothal, Bob, you won't feel a thing.'

Out of politeness, I take the dentist's phone number from him but I've no intention of going to see the man. I'm not scared of dentists but I am wary of what might happen *at* the dentist's, which is why I never let them use Pentothal as an anaesthetic.

Sodium Pentothal is a truth drug: they used to give it to spies during the Cold War. If you fall under the influence of this drug you can't help blurting out the truth.

Now suppose your dentist is a very unattractive man.

Here he is with trays full of needles and hooks and drill bits and here you are, totally at his mercy.

I don't think this is the ideal moment to feel compelled to say, 'Goodness me, you have bad breath and thick nasal hair in addition to being ugly, bald and boring, you big-nosed sadistic bastard.'

Back in Leighton Buzzard in the evening my regular dentist makes time for me and my tooth-grinding problem is solved without much discomfort. I go to bed early because tomorrow will take me to have early morning fun with Chris Evans and Paula Yates on Channel 4's 'The Big Breakfast'.

When I arrive at the Thames-side location at 5.30 a.m. I'm greeted by the sight of a corpse floating in the docks. I hurry inside to report the horrifying news. The floor manager is sanguine.

'Don't worry about it, Bob, we get lots of floaters bobbing up here. They go in the water upriver and this is their first stop. A police patrol always checks it about eight o'clock and they fish 'em out. Come on, let's lighten up and laugh it off!'

Next on my agenda is a chat with plain-spoken Richard Littlejohn on LBC and the recording of some items for Radio 4 to be used on Ned Sherrin's 'Loose Ends', a rare concession from his famously live show. Ned's an old friend and knows me well so his questions are provocative in the friendliest way. One in particular brings out a heartfelt reply.

'As a lifelong movie buff, Bob, do you think you can answer almost any question about films?'

Not any question, no.

Is there someone in your life who asks questions that do not contain a single clue as to what the answer might be?

My wife does this, and I'm not exaggerating.

'What's the name of that film we saw about two years ago with the actress whose name always reminds me of that shop where you bought that awful thing you never wear, it just sits in the cupboard, she wore a dress like the one your sister had on the day I lost my purse at that shopping centre, oh, you know the one, we thought it was about a murder or something but it turned out to be about smuggling or spying, it had a short title like "Waterworld" or just one word like that, or maybe two or three short words, we saw it on TV the same day I had spoken to the garage about the missing car mats, I remember because this film had a car like ours, only it was American and a different colour but you argued with me and we lost track of the plot, only I think it's on again but I can't look it up because I don't know the title – what is it?'

At which point I turn to an invisible audience and I say, 'And that, ladies and gentlemen of the jury, is when I shot her.'

**Monday, 6 September 1993**

When George Gershwin died the great American novelist John O'Hara wrote, 'They tell me Gershwin's dead but I don't have to believe it if I don't want to.'

On one May morning about 13 months ago they told me Bernie Winters was dead. Not to me, he isn't. Not to his thousand friends or his million fans either. Bernie's still more alive in our hearts than most people who are still walking around.

Some people – most of them, really – are difficult to recall in totality. You make an effort of memory and you conjure up a detail here, a detail there, the way someone laughed or the way they walked, their eyes perhaps or some odd saying they had.

With Bernie no effort is required.

I just think of him and there's the entire man. I hear his voice and, more than that, I hear what he's saying. The huge, lovely presence of that personality is so strong that I can watch him walking up to me, feel his embrace, join in his laughter (of which there was a great deal) and share his tears (of which there were a great many).

Bernie's life force filled each minute of each day and imprinted itself on the minds of all who met him. You've heard the description 'larger than life'. Bernie's emotional and spiritual charge was just that: larger than life. That's why those who knew him know him still. He's going to be around as long as we are.

Great comedians are more than just funny. Mind you, Bernie was very funny indeed. Thirty years ago I remember watching him rehearse a couple of really rotten sketches for the ABC Television series he did with his older brother Mike. I went outside and walked around the studio in Didsbury, Manchester – actually the old Odeon cinema – thinking what a terrible show it was that week and wondering if it would affect the audience's reaction to my own comedy spot.

When the show went on the air what had seemed glum stuff was transformed as magically as the philosophers' stone was meant to turn lead into gold, and I watched amazed and tried to understand how Bernie was doing it. This clown who had fretted and frowned and, agonised with worry, drudged through that afternoon's rehearsals reciting and fluffing the witless lines – here he was, convulsing the crowd by making fun of the script, the show, the audience, his brother and himself. Mostly himself.

Bernie was stripping himself bare of all those vanities and pretensions that we humans tend to use in defensive situations. He made himself utterly vulnerable. Every look, every gesture, told the audience he was helpless – he didn't know how he'd got into this mess, and please would they show mercy. He was endearing and comical and, more than anything else, a real human being evoking a real human response. It was great comedy from a performer capable of more than he ever really knew.

To say that Bernie led a modest life without vanity is to deny his pride in his family and friends, his home and his appearance (no performer was ever more immaculate); but deep within was an insecurity that took the form of natural unboastfulness and a glorious capacity for self-mockery. Bernie's stories against himself, of his failures and mistakes, were – *are* – hilarious. On TV chat shows with the likes of Terry Wogan, Des O'Connor and me, he would tell tales of inadequacy that had us all weeping with laughter and affection. What made them so wonderful was that they came from the giant heart of Bernie – bitter humiliations and pain made jubilantly funny.

When he toured with Leslie Crowther in *Bud and Ches*, a musical about the legendary double act of Flanagan and Allen, the show played to full houses in towns like Brighton and Richmond but when they got to Glasgow, in Bernie's own words, 'Nothing, nobody, zero business! The doorman was arrested for loitering. They shot a stag in the dress circle. Jimmy Logan said to me, "For God's sake, why are you doing a show about Bud and Ches in Glasgow? They wouldn't come here themselves in their heyday. The only people coming to see you think you're Chas and Dave!"

'The business was just as bad when we got to the Liverpool Empire. Leslie, being very shortsighted – and I mean *very*, when his eyes were closed he couldn't see his eyelids! Many's the time he'd lie awake in bed wondering if he was asleep or not. Where was I? Oh, yeah, Liverpool. Leslie'd look out a crack in the curtains and just about make out two people sitting there and say to me, "It's a packed house! Wonderful! Not a seat to be had!"

'The Liverpool Empire holds 3,000 people, right? Saturday matinée we had twenty-three. And out of the twenty-three, seven were comps, free seats! Not even Leslie could kid himself we were full because twenty-three people don't make much noise and his ears weren't bad. And in the interval you could hear music from the street because there was a shop opening and they had a bit of a parade, you know, two horses and a truck with a couple of girls in swimsuits. Half of our audience went outside to watch the parade and never came back. So there we were, left with eleven. Eleven people watching us! So we ended up playing 'em at football and we lost six nil.'

When the very new, very raw comedian met a beautiful, very young dancer all those years ago their love affair could have been just one of those things. Somehow wisdom prevailed and Bernie became Bernie-and-Siggi.

Everyone who's been in British show business longer than five minutes knows Siggi. No performer's wife has ever been more fiercely loyal. My wife Jackie is loyal too but not as fierce. Siggi brought to Bernie's existence the strength and discipline it needed. She has seldom suffered fools gladly and, where Bernie was sometimes too conciliatory, it was Siggi who had to cut through the thousand kinds of nonsense that waste a popular entertainer's time and money and get the important things done. If Bernie was the one who loved to say yes, she was the one who took the responsibility of saying no. In this way Siggi was able to give Bernie what he may have needed most. He needed to be loved.

When Siggi asked me to join Jimmy Tarbuck in speaking a few words of tribute at Bernie's funeral, I lay in bed the previous night and silently asked Bernie what I should say.

He rolled his eyes to heaven in frustration and said, 'Listen to the man! Mr Words, doesn't know what to say! Bubbela, it's not an audition, the first of a series, the Palladium, is it? It's a freebie, you're doing it for friends, darling. I mean, if it was me having to speak at your funeral, we'd have a problem. I wouldn't 'ave a clue, hopeless! But you, you're a genius, you'll walk it, a doddle!'

And I went to sleep reassured, contented that my dearest of friends was still with me.

Siggi and their son Ray watched over Bernie's final months while keeping up a magnificent lie. What Bernie never knew was that, right from the time of his operation in September 1990, they had known he was going to die. The doctors had told them that the cancer had already spread from his stomach to his liver and that eventually it would kill him. They kept the secret. You don't tell a man who's going into battle that he's not going to win. If you have enough love to bear it, you stay in his corner and cheer him on right to the very end. That's what Siggi and Ray did, at God knows what emotional cost.

But for me and so many others, Bernie Winters cannot be gone. He's in the next room or on tour or in Spain or anywhere except right here at the moment. Physically absent, that's all.

I know what they say, that the man died on 4 May 1991, but, like John O'Hara wrote, I don't have to believe it if I don't want to. So today is Bernie's sixty-third birthday. Many happy returns, old friend.

## Wednesday, 8 September 1993

I'm in the Caledonian Hotel, Edinburgh, on the publicity trail to promote my autobiography. Yesterday was Manchester and tomorrow will be Birmingham. Already my suitcase is heavy with books I've bought for myself at every bookshop we've visited. Here I am plugging a single volume while simultaneously acquiring dozens. They will join a life-time collection.

There are hundreds – no, thousands – of books in my house. None of them belongs to my wife. Jackie gives or throws books away as soon as she's read them. I think she's missing the point. Once you've read a book its contents become part of you. Its story, its information, its message from the writer to you, all this enters your mind and stays somewhere in your memory. To part with a book you've read is to lose some of its influence, rather like parting with a friend. It belongs on a shelf in your home just as much as its thoughts belong in your mind. Of course you can return to a book just as you might call on a person for conversation but even if you never feel the urge to open that book again, its very presence is a comfort. Each book I own is treasured for its good company. A wall of books is more pleasing to me than an ocean view.

I wish that I had written more books myself. When I was in my twenties and churning out numberless radio and TV scripts in partnership with other neophytes, I'd work through the day and night without rest. By the time I was forty I knew a little better. Only a writer within range of genius can maintain a ceaseless output of work without stopping to absorb the ceaseless input of life. The ability to produce ideas depends upon the ability to assimilate the raw materials for their manufacture. Remember the story of the two men who chopped wood for a day. One never paused, chopping away non-stop. The other took a breath about once an hour, starting again after five minutes or so. When darkness began to fall the man who chopped wood without stopping saw that his pile of logs was much smaller than his companion's and asked, 'Why is your pile bigger than mine?' The other said, 'Every time I took a break I also sharpened my hatchet.'

The fact that the first bloke then buried his axe in the second one's skull has nothing to do with the moral of the story. Perpetual motion brings diminishing returns.

## Monday, 13 September 1993

After a weekend spent with Andrew and Madeleine Lloyd-Webber at Sydmonton, I'm a bit talked out. Having enjoyed a very fine dinner on Friday evening, we returned Saturday morning looking forward to the musical entertainment that was planned for the theatre in the garden. Bad news instead. The *Sunday Mirror* sent word that they intended to run a hideous story about me and the oldest of my three children, Gary.

Profoundly handicapped from his premature birth in 1951, Gary's cerebral palsy robbed him of the ability to hear, speak, stand, walk or use his hands or arms. Otherwise a bright, handsome and affectionate boy, he grew up at home but, as his condition worsened, he became a resident at his choice of centres for the disabled. While he was staying at one of these, a Spastics Society home in Essex, he expressed a fondness for another occupant, a young woman whose physical impairments were even greater than his own. Gary aspired to normality and in his view such devotions as he felt deserved to be celebrated in marriage.

Because the local clergy would not agree to conduct a wedding where it could not be certain that both participants fully understood the undertaking, we arranged for a church ceremony that would satisfy Gary's dreams, a blessing of the couple's friendship.

Both families attended and although, like many prospective grooms, Gary became very anxious at the last minute, we managed to get him dressed formally and a wheelchair procession made its way through the sunlit village. At a drinks reception afterwards, Gary expressed great satisfaction that his wishes had been fulfilled and posed as his sweetheart's family took snapshots.

It was these photographs that the *Sunday Mirror* was proposing to run over three pages together with a vicious story to the effect that I, by not recognising the occasion as a real wedding, was denying my son's friend her proper status as his wife.

With wholehearted support from Andrew and Madeleine and advice from their legal advisers, I argued away the entire morning on the phone in my efforts to get the untrue story spiked. It was in vain. The *Sunday Mirror*'s editor and proprietor were both unsympathetic and adamant.

On Sunday morning Jac and I skipped the church service attended by most of the Sydmonton guests and drove to a nearby supermarket to find the newspaper's entire front page taken up with my smiling face and the huge headline to the effect that I had callously broken the heart of my son's wife by ignoring her. Apart from the fact that this was so cruelly untrue, I was horrified to see the pictures inside which made Gary appear disfigured and foolish. While Jackie did her best to comfort me, I sat in the car and wept, not just for the insensitivity and injustice but also for all the years invested in protecting my son from any sort of exploitation.

A few weeks later the *Sunday Mirror* was to publish a full apology and retraction on the front page but it would do little to compensate me for their ruthless abuse of the facts or to reduce my contempt for the writer, her editor and the publisher.

So here we go, putting all that behind us, off to Liverpool to chat with the fabulously funny Pete Price on Radio City, moving on to an interview for the *Liverpool Echo* and a banquet at the Liver Building to raise funds for our principal charity, the SOS.

Every time I set foot in Merseyside, I think it's small wonder that Liverpool has provided us with so many comedians. It is, succinctly put, a witty city. It's a social requirement there.

I remember Norman Vaughan, hot from hosting the famous *Sunday at the London Palladium*, coming back from a week's engagement at the Wooky Hollow Cabaret Club, Old Swan, in shock. I told him I was due to play a week there. 'Don't pause!' he advised anxiously. 'Forget timing a gag – don't allow a moment's silence. Me, I always take a breath before I deliver the last few words of a joke.' He clasped his head in memory of the humiliation. 'And every time I did eight waiters shouted funnier punchlines than mine!'

At this evening's banquet Pete Price's hilarious but sincere introduction for my speech and the generous laughter of the quick-witted audience combine to blow away the sour experience with the *Sunday Mirror*. People who grow up alongside the Mersey find they've got to compete in natural everyday humour or become socially overlooked. As a result, the funny side of everything occurs to them immediately. I've heard ordinary members of the public ad-libbing better than most professionals.

Tomorrow will bring a spot on 'This Morning with Richard and Judy', my official opening of the SOS office in Liverpool and a leisurely drive home, but not before I've encountered another example of Scouse wit.

I offer my credit card in John Lewis's men's department but my purchases added up to a sum in excess of the normal limit. The salesgirl explains that she has to have the transaction approved by the manager. She calls out to him, 'Mr Stringer! I need approval.'

The reply is instantaneous. 'You're a deeply beautiful person, Doreen!'

## Sunday, 19 September 1993

A survey of readers in the *Sunday Mirror* says that 84 per cent of the British population lie to their parents, 75 per cent lie to their friends and 68 per cent lie to their spouses.

Now what makes anyone suppose that these people are telling the truth to the *Sunday Mirror*?

Why should they?

The *Sunday Mirror* doesn't do it for them.

## Thursday, 23 September – Sunday, 26 September 1993

Thursday has me at the Motor Cycle Museum speaking to a large audience of W. H. Smith employees about my book. We have a question and answer session and, among various queries, an attractive young woman asks me, 'Are you a flirt?'

'Why do you ask?'

She holds up a headline from a tabloid. It says, 'YOU LIVE LONGER IF YOU FLIRT' and she reads out more: 'FLIRTATION RAISES THE SPIRITS AND ADDS YEARS TO YOUR LIFE SAYS A REPORT ON HUMAN BEHAVIOURAL BENEFITS.' I answer that I think I used to be a pretty good flirt although I didn't get the hang of it right away. 'Another boy at school told me that you had to convey romantic interest by making eye contact – which is fine but for how long? Because a fine line separates eye contact and the piercing stare of a psychopath.

'And my blind dates never really worked out well. I mean, I was always up for it but, I don't know, somehow the last few words of the evening always seemed to be "That's him, constable!"'

I'm surprised how well these two ad-libbed gags register with the youngish gathering. From the Midlands I travel by car to Weetwood Hall Hotel on the Otley road out of Leeds. I'm doing a charity night cabaret in a marquee at the refectory of the university. On the journey I've been thinking about flirtation as a subject for comedy and a routine is beginning to take shape. I try some of it out this evening and it goes very well.

I say, 'I think one of the charms of flirtation is that it's short-lived. It's a prelude after all, the first part of the mating ritual during which men and women pretend they want the same thing which, of course, in the long run they don't. Because we're not just different, we're opposites. Whereas a woman longs for the *one* man who can satisfy her *every* want and need, a man longs for *every* woman to satisfy his *one* want and need.

'Women flirt better than men because they're in less of a hurry. Men are impatient: that leads to all we read today about women at work being sexually – what's the word, is it har*assed* or *har*assed? Har*assed*? OK. One of the programme secretaries at the BBC was complaining about being sexually Harrissed but she works on "Animal Hospital".' Rolf won't mind.

Friday evening takes me on to the BBC's 'Danny Baker Show' and my flirting routine has expanded still further so I use it. It's a midnight transmission so I can put in a naughty line.

'Is spring still the season for flirtation? And it must work because more women get pregnant in May than any other month – they say it must be something in the air. Their ankles, I expect.

'But attitudes are changing if you go by public surveys – do you believe in those things? In *Arena* magazine, most men surveyed overwhelmingly said that the number one thing that attracts them to a woman is . . . what do you think? Her personality! Well, that would explain the popularity of those blow-up dolls. Guys love their personalities.

'And 73 per cent of men surveyed said that at one time or another they have said "No" to sex. You know what doctors call these men? Convicts.'

This extension of the subject works well and it's rewarded with big laughs. Saturday and Robert, my regular driver, is still at the wheel, driving this time to the Paynesthorpe Co. Club, Criggleston, Wakefield, while I'm still in the back seat of the Merc developing the flirtation theme.

'Do people still call it flirting? Well, perhaps I haven't completely lost my touch at it. True story: yesterday in Kensington I just got to my car as a traffic warden was starting to write me out a ticket so I summoned up all my charm and said, "Oh, sweetheart, surely a glamorous young creature like you doesn't want to be cruel to a famous TV star who could get you into show business where you could flash your gorgeous eyes and long, lovely legs?" and, thank God, it worked.

'He let me go.

'Bless him, he made a pretty good omelette too.'

A nice-looking man at the front winks at me. I might drop that last gag.

Sunday brings a happy occasion for an old and valued friend although he's not expecting it.

James Moir is leaving BBC TV and his colleagues and friends have secretly prepared a surprise party in the form of a spoof 'This Is Your Life'. Everyone loves Jim, a portly and deeply humorous chap with bright eyes and a tiny nose. His years as Head of Variety, now known as Entertainment, were wonderfully productive and they've earned him a terrific turn-out of famous faces. We're all hiding in the back room of the City club while Jim's being toasted and back-slapped by the great and the good from the Television Centre's host of programme makers. Then Terry Wogan springs his trap and escorts Jim to the stage where, one by one, we're called forth to speak our piece.

Paul Daniels, Sir Jimmy Saville, Syd Little and Eddie Large, Moira Anderson, Noel Edmonds and Bruce Forsyth all make wonderfully comic speeches about Jim but the hit of the evening, thanks to Jimmy Tarbuck's encouragement, is Mike Yarwood.

Paralysed with stage fright just before his entrance is due, Mike is forcibly propelled on to the stage by Tarby and immediately recovers his composure, delivering a brilliantly extemporised address to roars of approbation. Afterwards Mike shows so much relief and pleasure that it seems his mental block about public appearances has been demolished. Tarby is to take him in hand and persuade him to impersonate Prime Minister John Major on 'Live from the London Palladium' and, although the evening's celebration is for Jim Moir, there's a mildly hysterical excitement among the performers because of Mike's apparent return to superb form.

But the talented man's psychological problem will return to inhibit him and our joy for him will be short-lived. He is so well liked and admired among his fellow professionals and we know what agony he's gone through in trying to face audiences without the help of vodka. Stage fright can prove fatal to careers like ours and we empathise. We've all been there.

Standing alone in the spotlight with no justification for your presence except the laughter you're expected to cause can be terrifying. You can accuse a comedian of many things but never cowardice. Public surveys confirm that the thing that frightens people more than the prospect of death itself is getting up in front of an audience and speaking. Yet night after night, year in and year out, the stand-up comic walks out to face possible disaster.

One night of rejection can undermine your confidence for months. No amount of approval helps to obliterate the memory of a cold crowd sitting in silent judgement, condemning you to struggle for their goodwill in vain. The suddenly unfunny funnyman stands alone at the microphone, mouth drying, sweat running cold, legs trembling. No one can help him. Nowhere can hide him. As a comedy writer once observed, 'That's why the first stand-up comedians were court jesters who usually were deformed. Nobody else wanted the job.'

Every comedian I know can recall with absolute clarity the times and places where their act died. I've died eleven times and I remember every painful detail, although three of the occasions are lightened by the memory of a wryly amusing coincidence.

The first was at the Piccadilly Hotel, Manchester, at a charity banquet for the Showman's Guild. Just before I went on to the cabaret floor the organiser quietened the room and announced the unexpected death from heart failure of the Guild's popular chairman. Two minutes' silence were observed, broken only by sobs, and then I was introduced and swiftly became the second corpse of the evening.

Unwisely, I soldiered on with jokes that now had the ring of horror about them. Every gag I knew was about to come out of my mouth next seemed to be about illness, hospitals or funerals. The more I failed to amuse, the faster I chattered until my words lost all their meaning. People stared at me bleakly or shook their heads at one another more in sorrow than in anger. My contract stipulated an act of not less than thirty minutes. It felt like thirty days' hard labour. I took refuge in my song parodies. At least with the piano, bass and drum thumping away behind me, the audience's hush was drowned. Eventually I concluded my seemingly endless half-hour at a point when I would normally have expected the applause to bring me back for an encore or two. This time the loudest sound in the hall was my footsteps as I left.

A tall, blond head waiter met me with a stiff malt whisky. I thanked him and he said in a mid-European accent, 'Not so good for you tonight I am thinking. In Switzerland we are hearing much about your British comedians but you are my first to observe. Tough job!'

About three years later I was booked to entertain after a sales conference for Kleenex at the NEC's Metropole Hotel. This time I couldn't lay the blame for my flopping so horribly on the announcement of someone's demise. This lot just didn't want to know about comedy, what they wanted to do was dance. They were enthusiastically exercising to a Beatles medley when someone important at the top table decided it was cabaret time.

The toastmaster stopped the band and as the customers on the dance floor looked around uncertainly, he announced me without attempting to settle them down. The rest of the people in the room were talking loudly and table-hopping and my three musicians weren't in position to play me on because the eight-piece danceband was still making its exit.

I walked through the stragglers, literally pushing my way to the microphone, and tried to take charge.

Forget it. I toiled through my allotted time but this time it was not in silence. Everyone was talking more noisily than I was. The louder I shouted, the higher went the room's decibel level of conversation. It was like trying to be funny on the floor of the Stock Exchange.

As I came off the floor, numb with the experience of being totally ignored, the tall, blond banqueting manager greeted me with a stiff malt whisky.

'Vell, vell, so ve meet again,' he said pleasantly. 'Not so good for you again tonight I am thinking.'

Five years pass and I'm engaged to provide a midnight show for the management and staff of a famous soft drink company at a large Brighton hotel. Unfortunately for me, soft drinks are not what the firm's management has put on the tables. Their managing director, keen to acknowledge everyone's contribution to a year of record sales, has decided that his workforce is entitled to a right old booze-up. Every table has jugs of beer, red wine, white wine on ice, plus bottles of gin, whisky, brandy and, quaintly, Bailey's Irish Cream liqueur. Dinner lasts four hours.

I don't know about this. The nervous sub-agent who's arranged this booking comes to inform me that my audience is roaring drunk but the reception clerk has given him the wrong room number and he can't find me. I put on my bowtie, a crisp dress shirt and my beautiful new choco-late brown dress suit and go like a lamb to the slaughter.

Forty-five minutes later I'm back in my bedroom, peeling off my dinner jacket and shirt over which an over-affectionate lady, resolved to embrace me during my opening song, has upchucked. My trousers are also decorated with pudding and cream caused by my collision with a waiter who, unable to weave his way through the drunks, was crossing the cabaret floor during my performance with a tray full of desserts.

The audience, which cheered my entrance uproariously for quite a long time, was then unable to understand anything I said to them. Their atten-tion span was such that they couldn't remember the first line of a two-line joke so the funny payoff held no meaning. I must admit they were mostly very jolly and anxious to call out encouragements while I was trying to amuse them, but when I once again resorted to music and led them in a singsong of music hall ditties, a couple of tosspots started to weep, a fist fight broke out at the back and a window was somehow shattered.

I'm about to shower when my phone rings. The porter asks if it's con-venient for the hotel's deputy manager to come up to apologise for the accident with the dessert tray. Before I can say that it's not necessary, there's a knock on my door. I call out, 'Just a moment!', put on the hotel bathrobe, turn off the water and go to open the door. Somehow, some part of my mind knows and yet it's also saying no, it couldn't be. But it is. Tall, blond and bearing a malt whisky on a silver salver.

'Remember me, Mr Monkhouse?'

'How could I forget you?'

'I offer deepest apologies for your clothes. Please send the dry clean-ing bill to us, the hotel will pay. These people, they have been drinking since seven o'clock and not eating the dinner. Their behaviour was very unfortunate.'

'Don't mention it.'

A pause, and then I almost say the words with him. 'Not so good for you again tonight I am thinking.'

'No, not so good.'

'Three times now I have seen you perform. Is it like this always for you?'

'Always.'

'Excuse me, but do the audiences ever laugh at you?'

'Never.'

'Do you not feel like giving it up?'

'I can't give it up,' I explain. 'I'm a star.'

## Tuesday, 5 October 1993

During a week of twice-nightly variety at The Grand Theatre, Wolverhampton, exactly thirty years ago, I performed alongside the most jubilant libertine I have ever known. Along with the looks of a Greek god, life had handed him access to all its carnal delights and he had the appetite, strength and energy to exploit them as prodigally as a handsomer version of the phallically advantaged Priapus.

David Whitfield was a young labourer from Hull who joined the merchant navy more from poverty and desperation than any call of the sea. In his mid-twenties he had grown into a supple muscularity that would have attracted women even without the appeal of his cerulean eyes, Hollywood profile and blond quiff.

At singalongs aboard ship or in coastal pubs, his untrained but powerful tenor developed ragged bravura qualities in imitation of the MGM film star Mario Lanza. He sang with spirit and dash. Timing was just right for his discovery. In the early 50s the British record industry was just beginning to enjoy the first signs of a post-war boom and popular tastes were changing. Dance band crooners were now regarded as Sinatra wannabees, as out of fashion as the 40s themselves, and pop singers with big lungs were becoming all the rage. These stentorian balladeers filled the air waves and the public cheered their sheer ability to be ear-splitting. Frederick Ferrari belted out Neapolitan canzones on Cheerful Charlie Chester's radio show, Lee Lawrence shook the rafters with pseudo-operatic arias, Malcolm Vaughan lent his shrill but thrilling warbling to a string of sentimental heartbreakers and the king of all the vein-poppers, Josef Locke, blasted Blackpool fans with Irish broadsides that surely must have cost them hearing aids in later life.

Fortunes were being made. For roving talent scouts to have missed Whitfield's obvious possibilities, they'd have needed to be deaf to the piercing volume of his top notes and blind to the excitement of teenage girls in the working men's clubs that were now paying him five pounds a night to hold forth with a dozen full-throated songs. Sure enough, Decca Records invited him to audition in 1953 and immediately issued his first big hits, 'Bridge of Sighs' and 'Answer Me', the latter going to No. 1 in the UK and creating instant national stardom for the unsophisticated fellow. He took to it like Aladdin to his cave.

When I introduced him on a Royal Variety Performance a couple of years later, his self-assurance was already remarkable. After thundering out his latest chartbuster 'Rags to Riches' he grinned up at the royal box, shouted, 'Story of my life, your Majesty!' and winked.

Throughout the 50s, his recording hits defied the onslaught of rock 'n' roll and took him around the variety circuit at a then unheard-of £950 per week. His phenomenal 'Cara Mia', accompanied by the Mantovani orchestra, dominated the UK number 1 position for ten weeks as it sold over three-and-a-half million copies and even reached the US Top Ten, a rare feat for a British singer in those days. Everywhere he went, women of all ages threw themselves at him and he never dropped one of them.

'Me and Michael Holliday, we were on a screwing binge, keeping score and rogering every bit of crumpet in sight,' he told me, referring to another popular recording star of the day, a fellow merchant seaman whose Bing Crosbyish tones also attracted female admirers. 'We were both in Scarborough all summer and the poor bloody theatre doctor, he damn near wore out his car driving between me at the Floral Hall and Mike at the Futurist, jabbing our arses with penicillin injections every other day!'

Topping the bill at the Blackpool Wintergardens, Whitfield's first floor dressing room was in use all day as a sort of sex therapy centre.

Eric Morecambe told me, 'I didn't believe all the stories so I called round to have a look for myself and, bless my soul, it was like a non-stop orgy going on there. Girls were hanging round the stage door but I didn't realise why. I'm innocent about things like that. I was pushing my way up the stairway, wondered what these giggling girls were queuing up for. I thought they just wanted autographed photos or at most a kiss! When I got to the doorway and looked inside, David and three of his mates were hard at it with about six half-naked teenagers. I suppose I'm easily shocked because I've never gone in for that sort of thing, more's the pity. Anyway, David spotted me and shouted for me to come inside and help myself. I said thanks very much but I'd already had some that day at the vicar's coffee morning.'

The final scene of the show's first half was typically opulent for a George and Alfred Black production. All the dancers and singers were dressed as nuns and monks.

Carrying candlesticks, they filed down the aisles toward the stage as the orchestra played Whitfield's inspirational hit 'Santo Natale'. Previously dark and unnoticed panels in the walls of the auditorium now brightened into vivid life as stained glass windows and the curtain rose on a cathedral setting. After the singers had delivered a medley of uplifting numbers and the lead soprano had disposed of 'The Holy City', Whitfield would enter to stand in front of the altar and sing 'Ave Maria' with such passion that only the interval could follow it. At one performance only, this routine changed in one small detail. On that single occasion, Whitfield stood not in front of the waist-high altar as usual but behind it. There was a good reason.

Our shared week in Wolverhampton some years later gave me the opportunity to check on the accuracy of the story I'd been told by the comedian Wally Harper.

'It's all true, every word of it,' Whitfield laughed with frank delight at the memory. 'See, I love the people I love with all my heart. My family is very precious to me. I'm a simple sort of man, I never lie, I've never stolen anything, I'd help out anyone in trouble. These aren't boasts, they're God's honest truth. But look at what happened to me. Like in my song, I went from rags to riches overnight. One day I had bugger all, the next I had everything a man could want. Another kind of guy, he might take it all in his stride and do things in moderation. You get chaps like that, they win a million on the pools and say it won't change their lives. Well, I'm not that sort. I grab my good luck and I squeeze it dry and I use it for all it's worth. Women? I love 'em. I can stop drinking after a few pints if I want to but I can never have enough shagging. I'd never want to hurt anyone, mind, I only want people to be as happy as I am. And there isn't a happier man alive. I love every moment of every single day and night. If I lost my cock I'd cut my throat. If I was a woman myself my knees wouldn't know each other. And, I'll tell you what, if I *was* a bloody woman, there's no one I'd rather have it off with than David Whitfield. I fuck like I sing, with all my heart and soul! That's what happened that evening. I was totally absorbed in what I was doing and oblivious to everything else.'

The object of his utter concentration had been a pretty youngster who'd been chosen from the throng of groupies twice before. She was hooked on backstage sex and knew how to slip unseen past the stage-door-keeper.

She reached Whitfield's door just as his dresser helped him on with his blue jacket over a crisp white shirt and solid maroon tie. David was wearing underpants, shoes and socks but had picked up the habit of leaving his trousers off until the last minute as a precaution against creases and wrinkles. As soon as he looked up and saw the girl, he grinned and checked his wristwatch.

'Just time to get one in!' he cried and, as the dresser sighed in peevish impatience with his star's wanton ways and flounced out full of pique, the excited lass flung herself backwards into an armchair and pulled her frock up to show that she wore nothing below the waist.

Whitfield's pants were off in the same moment that his ever-ready masculinity sprang into action and he moved into position between her waving legs, placing his hands beneath her buttocks and thrusting home. Her delighted squeals obliterated the sounds from the small loudspeaker on the wall so that Whitfield was blissfully unaware of the stage manager's voice speaking over the strains of 'Jerusalem, Jerusalem' to announce, 'Stand by, Mr Whitfield, please, two minutes.'

About ninety seconds later the door burst open and the dresser stood there in a screaming panic. 'You're on, David, you're *on*!'

'Jesus!'

Without missing a stroke, Whitfield swung both the girl and the armchair over to the wall of the neighbouring dressing room and thumped on it with his fist, yelling, 'All hands on deck!'

The room next to his was occupied by Buck & Buddy, a male comedy dance team who were part of Whitfield's gang and regularly shared the fringe benefits of his lovestruck following. They'd turned down the volume knob on their Tannoy to sit there in their underwear listening to the sounds of copulation and, though becoming quite stimulated by such noisy abandon, had started to grow anxious about Whitfield missing his cue. Now they heard the call to duty and immediately ran out of their room and into David's, Buck already in a state of readiness.

Still keeping up the rhythm of the coupling, the long distance lover gasped, 'Fall in on the count of five! One, two, three, four . . .'

With the timing of skilled professionals Whitfield withdrew and Buck replaced him. The girl gave a squeal of joy at such scandalous fun and Whitfield spun round and ran to the stairway, pounding down the stone steps to the wings of the stage below.

As the musical bridge that introduced his big number was played, he bent low so as to remain unseen and scuttled across the stage between the backcloth and the rostrum that bore the rear part of the cathedral setting. All the audience now saw was Whitfield's fair head and shoulders rising into view behind the cross-bearing altar, his fists gripping the edges of the table as he hauled himself up. With uncannily lucky timing he steadied himself and stood firmly at his full height as he hit his first note.

If ever the phrase 'you just had to be there' applied to any one theatrical event, this was it.

Only about fifteen people were privy to the sight from the two sides of the stage but none ever forgot it.

My comic friend Wally said, 'We didn't know whether to laugh or cry. Here was the biggest singing star in the country singing a hymn to the Virgin Mary naked from the waist down with a hard on!'

Of course the glossy tumescence slowly diminished as the aria went on, all eyes from the wings fixed upon the gently bobbing member as it gradually lost its grandeur and lowered its head nod by nod, beautifully lit from each side by purple pageants with a blush pink glow from fluorescent strips beneath.

Its final subsidence coincided with Whitfield's strident closing note. The audience cheered as always but the acclamation from the stageside witnesses had twice the fire. Whitfield had the humour and grace to bow to left and right in acknowledgement.

A certain kind of man can behave like a sexual predator without feeling responsibility or guilt and I could never condone such selfish behaviour but Whitfield wasn't like that.

He was a free spirit who was nevertheless true to life's important loyalties like family, friends and business partners, but these ties had nothing to do with his leisure activity.

He didn't pursue women as much as they pursued him. If he treated them casually, that was how he believed they regarded him; a bit of fun and no harm done.

Throughout his philandering he was constantly cheery, courteous and very generous.

By the turn of the 60s he was the last major pop star of his style and he wisely moved away from commercial heart-tuggers to operetta and Richard Tauber favourites.

That was what he'd been giving the passengers on a Chinese cruise ship touring the South Pacific when he had the first signs of a heart condition. Blithely, he pressed on with his tenth Australian tour and died in Sydney. His ashes were later scattered at sea off Hull, close to his birthplace. He was just two weeks away from his fifty-fifth birthday. When the news broke I believe a lot of women wept with fondness for the care-free troubadour of their youthful flings.

## Saturday, 16 October 1993

This evening I'm doing about an hour of stand-up and song parodies on the stage of the Palace Theatre, Appleton Gate, Newark. Twenty years ago I did the same but in those days my supporting bill was more than a trio and a pretty vocalist. And I had to work hard to follow the funniest old biddy ever to close the first half of a variety bill. To tell you about her, I have to go back even further, to 1948.

I was in the RAF and stationed in London and the unit's only male switchboard operator was Stan Tracey, destined to become one of the leaders in the composition and keyboard interpretation of progressive and classical jazz. Whenever I was engaged to appear on a radio show, Stan would provide the piano accompaniment for my songs. We got four guineas each, a total of about £8.40.

Although heterosexual himself, Stan was so fascinated by homosexual culture he'd adopted the Polari, an informal vocabulary yet to be made famous a decade or so later by Kenneth Williams and Hugh Paddick on radio's 'Round the Horne'.

'Varda the naff eke on that polone!' he'd scream, meaning look at the plain face on that girl, adding, 'Bona lallies though!' if her legs were good enough. He found Camp Coffee and Queen-size beds irresistibly funny and I couldn't see the joke.

I'd never had any experience of homosexuality, not even at Dulwich College where it must have had its adherents. All I knew was that you could go to prison if you got caught in the act. I found Stan's mock, limp-wristed posturing quite hypnotic.

'Do you know anyone who's actually that way?' I asked him.

'I'll take you down to the Shaftesbury Hotel in Seven Dials,' he winked.

We arrived about seven in the evening and the bar was already packed to overflowing with no woman there but the barmaid.

'Now, who's here to educate you?' said Stan, peering round the chattering crowd. 'Ah! Just the one I'm looking for! Over there, holding court by the window.'

We pushed our way through the throng to where an elf-like young man with pale skin was the centre of an admiring circle. He was concluding a story and all I heard of it was, '. . . so I told him, I said, if you want to give me something that goes in pink and hard and comes out soft, it'd better be bubble-gum.'

His small audience laughed inordinately and as Stan introduced me they dispersed.

'Bob Monkhouse, meet my old mucker, Rex Costa.'

'Jameson now, Rex Jameson. Sounds more butch,' he said extending a finely boned hand to me. 'I heard you on the wireless with Stan, what was it, a couple of Saturdays ago? That Edmundo Ros programme.' He gave me a very shy sideways look. 'Not bad at all. Some funny stuff. Make it up yourself, did you, or nick it off them Yank shows on that Armed Forces Network from Germany?'

He'd got me there. American comedy shows, intended for the US forces in Europe, could be heard in England through a barrage of medium-wave static. I'd pinched two gags from a New York comic named Henny Youngman and this laconic chap had spotted them.

'You talk as if you're in show business yourself,' I said and caused Rex's remaining companions to gasp in exaggerated horror.

Stan grinned at Rex and shrugged apologetically. Then he turned to me and said, 'Bob, Rex is Mrs Shufflewick!'

Well, the mere idea that this five-foot twenty-three-year-old with a face like the young Buster Keaton could have been the dirty old woman I'd seen on the stage of both the Windmill and the Metropolitan, Edgware Road, seemed incredible. Mrs Shufflewick was about forty with a big red conk and a gin-soaked wobble in her walk. She told us she had a weakness for the Navy. 'The last sailor I met was French, he kissed me on both cheeks. I was doing up my laces at the time.'

Rex had none of his creation's boozy self-assertion. He was as frail as a foundling, which he was. His real mum left him on the steps of Trinity College Hospital when he was two weeks old and he spent his childhood with a foster mother in Southend. In all the years that I came to know him, Rex carried the burden of rejection, always getting dumped by men he should never have loved in the first place. He was emotionally fraught and difficult to manage, although his loyal band of pals did their best to protect him through periods of insecurity and black depression.

But once the catalogue frock and the frizzy perm went on, Mrs Shufflewick was a wicked show-off. As his friend Molly Parkin once observed, 'It is as painful and personal as laughing at your mother when she has had one too many.'

And, of course, as far as Rex was concerned, his mother might have been in the audience, laughing unknowingly at her son.

Shuff was marvellous with posh audiences. He turned up for me at a distinctly up-market charity ball I helped to organise for the British Heart Foundation. The crowd had more titles than Waterstone's. Chandeliers were outshone by tiaras. It was the kind of upper crust that comedians fear because it has a united social attitude which can be both judgmental and dismissive.

When cabaret time came I went on to introduce the acts and struggled to get polite laughter for five minutes. A good magician's best tricks were received coolly and a fine folk singer had a rising buzz of conversation to contend with.

But then out shuffled Shuff and the difficult gathering became a pushover. One sniffy, disapproving gaze from that cartoon hag brought the first gale of laughter. Shuff hitched her shawl, poked at her pathetic hat and used the simplest jokes in her repertoire to convulse them. With eyes occasionally glazing over and a tottering stance, it seemed a brilliant, funny and accurate portrayal of an old biddy who's guzzled enough alcohol to strip the paint off the *QE2* – which, of course, Shuff had. He was just a gnat's breath the right side of being incapable.

This was the true phenomenon, just as described elsewhere in these memoirs in regard to Bing Crosby's transformation to temporary sobriety while in the midst of total intoxication for just as long as it took to do the job: the inexplicable compartmentalising process of the mind, a performer's automatic pilot.

After the cabaret came dancing and Shuff joined the charity committee's party as himself. Deeply inebriated, he accepted congratulations on his performance from an admiral in full dress uniform who had joined the function late from a state occasion at Buckingham Palace. Shuff registered a vague impression of the man's appearance. 'I love sailors!' he belched. Then his eyes focused on the admiral's ribbons, the brocaded sleeves, the gold braid. He peered woozily up at him and declared, 'No shit, dear heart, you must've gone down on Nelson to cop that lot.'

A favourite Shuff story comes from the later years when he often seemed too sloshed to get away with it. Lily Savage was yet to be created when her *alter ego* Paul O'Grady was part of a supporting bill at the Nashville, a pub managed by the stern John Gleason.

In those days Paul's drag work was as one-third of a singing group recreating the Andrews Sisters and sending up 1960s pop groups. He was already a committed fan of Shuff's: 'This drunken little old dear'd come out and sing "Bless This House" and tell the saga of being on the back of a bus with a sailor and a fishcake – mad, magical!'

Before showtime, already half cut but able to sense Paul's affection,

Shuff asked, 'Would you dress me, dear?' and tottered off to the tatty dressing room. Gleason had overheard. He added, 'Do it. Get that drunken old whore ready to work. Then I can lock her in till we need her.'

Once Paul had packed the star into the familiar outfit, Shuff rose to seek refreshment but found himself alone in a sealed room.

Paul remembers, 'He started to plead with me through the door, begging me to run to the off-licence. Well, I took pity on him. I brought back half a bottle of brandy. And there I'm stood holding it like a fool outside this locked door thinking how's he gonna drink this? But I reckoned without the true cunning of a boozer. He had me hold the open bottle against the lock and a straw came through the keyhole!'

Shuff drank the bottle in one go.

'When it came time to unlock the door poor old Shuff was lying on the floor, melted.' But, according to Paul, somehow he went onstage and his act was as funny as ever. I dare say you had to be there.

I have an old reel-to-reel tape of Shuff and, believe it or not, he got nine big laughs out of this venerable piece of material. See if you can guess the points at which the laughter broke out:

*I have been under the doctor for the past six months. On and off. And he's a big feller. And I like to go down, I do, I like to go down every Tuesday evening. I always go in the evening 'cause his hands are warmer then. And I sit in his insulting room and he's got all the magazines laid out for you to read. I was reading one last Tuesday and it's very sad about that Titanic. And there was a whole page devoted to the stars and the occult. It's written by a gypsy feller and he has got a glass eye and a crystal ball . . . what he looks into. He's a bit of an acrobat. There was one woman the other week, she wrote this letter, she said, 'Dear Gypsy Joe, my husband has just recently retired at the age of sixty-two and is pottering about the house and all he can think about is, um, you know. I cannot bend down to plug in my Hoover or do any low dusting . . . but what he takes advantage. The house is in a shocking state. And my nerves are shot to pieces. Please could you help?' And she signed herself 'Worried'. Oh, and then she'd put, 'PS: Please excuse the jerky handwriting.'*

### Wednesday, 20 October 1993

Comedy material doesn't write itself but its creation is constantly stimulated by paying attention to what people have to say. Still plugging my life story, I'm on Pebble Mill's TV morning show with Anne Diamond and Nick Owen and they bring up a story in today's papers in which a psychiatrist says that actors and entertainers are seeking the love denied them in childhood. Anne says that comedians always make fun of psychiatry and asks me if I believe in it.

'Yes, I'm trying a Freudian analyst but I don't completely trust him. I just found out he's been seeing other people. He said to me, "Bob, you're an obsessive, compulsive, repressive, aggressive, depressive repulsive" – and I still think he's keeping something back from me.

'Anyway, I've almost come full circle in therapy – now I forgive my father, I can relate to my mother, I'm in harmony with my children and I love my wife – but I can't stand my imaginary friend. His name's Vernon – he's a user. I'm getting bills from my analyst for sessions I've never had. Vernon is going without me. And he's mean. You know how we all have an inner child within us? My inner child is in traction. Vernon pushed him down a flight of stairs. But at least this analyst has been helping me get over my habit of being such a suspicious husband and I've been doing fine. And then last night my wife, in the heat of passion, called out someone else's name in bed. Doris.'

This evening Jackie and I call in at the RAC Building, 89, Pall Mall, to be interviewed by any interested party at a bookselling thrash called 'Books for Giving'. One such person is Emma Stone who tells me she's a freelance survey taker. I've never met one before so I ask her what surveys she's worked on lately.

'Sex surveys sell best. Do you think marriage is good for male health? Should lovers tell each other what pleases them best? You collect about 500 responses, work out your percentages of yes and no and offer them to the sort of magazines that run this kind of stuff.'

She tells me she actually carried a poll that covered this subject a few weeks ago and 63 per cent of men surveyed said it's annoying when women tell them, in the middle of sex, how to satisfy them.

I say, 'That's so typical of men, isn't it? They never want to stop and ask for directions.

'But I'm all for telling your partner what you want in bed although it isn't easy – how do you tell your partner after twenty-two years that, just once, you want somebody else?'

Emma laughs delightfully.

See what I mean? You listen to people, you find material.

## Tuesday, 26 October – Wednesday, 3 November 1993

Nine days during which my mind has been greatly exercised on the nature of who and what makes us laugh. No, I mean more than usual.

Here I am on Tuesday, clowning for a Sekonda wristwatch commercial, pretending to be a timepiece.

Wednesday afternoon, I go to Brinsworth House to visit with some of the elderly entertainers who are cared for there and I find myself discussing mime with one of the finest silent clowns of the variety years, George Truzzi, who once worked with his knockabout partner Laurie Lupino Lane for Charles Chaplin. In the evening I do cabaret for Colt Cars at the Tara Hotel, Kensington, and deliberately include some really silly mugging and funny walks to very satisfactory results. They like me acting daft even though they know I'm not. Interesting.

On Thursday I do some subtle, classy stuff at 1 p.m. for the IPM Conference in Harrogate, clever people who run head-hunting services. Their laughter is intelligent and selective. Back to Pebble Mill by 5.30 to record a Radio 4 programme on 'Stage Fright'. Then spend a great evening raising funds for Turning Point, the organisation that battles under-age drug and alcohol abuse. Dave Ismay collects Jackie and me from the Swallow Hotel and we join a few hundred Midlanders for dinner and speeches to mark the start of Birmingham Comedy Week and celebrate the success of the Tony Hancock Society. Hancock's prodigious scriptwriters, the towering team of Alan Simpson and Ray Galton, speak jointly. Then Ian Hislop displays his keen wit and I bat last. I fall into a deep discussion with Ian about the charms of simple comedy and its exponents versus the sophisticates. He says he believes in what he thinks is funny and not what an unquantifiable crowd might think is funny. In this way, he attracts his own kind.

Off to the Isle of Wight on Friday where Jackie and I check into Swainston Manor near Yarmouth where Maggie and Fred run a splendid guesthouse. I strut my stuff on Saturday evening at the Savoy Country Club for Maurice Lickens, experimenting with a performance of a broader style. It seems to make for a warmer response to some of my mock-angry rantings.

Home on Sunday to work on some TV scripts: I'm still thinking of how the British view their comedy merchants. Tuesday I'm talking about the great Chic Murray with his daughter, Mrs Annabelle Meredith.

And on Wednesday, 3 November, I'm at the British Film Institute watching black-and-white films of 50s TV comedy in company with veteran writers Brad Ashton, Denis Gifford and Dick Vosbrugh. Somebody remembers that today is the birthday of one of the sharpest comedians in the Western world, Dennis Miller. Miller is hardly known to the British but his zealous American admirers enjoy his high level of

sarcastic wit coupled with didactic prose. Few comedians seek acceptance by ranting but that's what Miller does, vociferating with unyield-
ing contempt for everything that deserves it, risking the alienation of the
less sophisticated majority in favour of intelligent attention from the
comparatively elite. I don't believe he'd do well in the UK, one of my
principal reasons being our national inclination to regard intelligence as
a suspicious, even dangerous attribute. It's part of our Anglo-Saxon
tradition.

Our forefathers commemorated this tendency in song and story. A
cursory glance through our literary inheritance will show that admiration for intellect has seldom been one of its instinctive splendours. By
the same token, the comedians we love uncritically are those who best
disguise their depth of thinking and expose their humanity.

Smart alec is an English insult; 'too clever by half' a disapproving
criticism. The British, more than any other great nation, have always
equated simplicity and goodness; smartness with trouble. Honour and
decency are best served by the innocent while mischief is the business
of the smartass.

To observe this distrust of intelligence in our literature, we need look
no further than to the greatest of our writers – Scott, Milton, Fielding,
Dickens, Thackeray or Shakespeare.

Shakespeare's brainiest characters are cunning, heartless or doomed.
The possession of such intellect as King Richard the Third's or that of
Iago or Edmund signals a breach with decency. Cursed with intelligence
and its inevitable evils are Cleopatra, Goneril and Lady Macbeth.
Prospero's sagacity is unreasonable and Hamlet is too contemplative to
live. We must seek elsewhere for moral conduct and, being British, we
know where to find it – among the dumb clucks.

Shakespearian probity is the province of stout-hearted simpletons
like Florizel, Bassanio and Duke Orsino.

The heroes of the great English novels are true-hearted duffers
almost to a man, artlessly blundering their way to the final chapter to be
saved by the grace of God rather than any trace of their own ingenuity
or thought. Their heroines are similarly air-headed, our affection for
their wholesome naïvety taken for granted by their creators, while the
female characters who exercise their minds are as wicked as Becky
Sharp and Beatrix Esmond can be.

Milton's version of the devil in *Paradise Lost* is a typically Anglo-
Saxon interpretation of the Book of Job. Whereas, in my reading of the
Bible, Satan is generally depicted as nothing more intelligent than a
troublesome body while God is seen as the source of profound and enig-

matic wisdom, Milton reverses the apportionment of intelligence. This just happens to accord with English prejudice.

He gives us a Satan with a super IQ who probes and challenges and a harshly oppressive God who doesn't, and whose angel warns Adam against questioning Heaven's laws.

Not only do Milton and his distinguished literary colleagues make these judgements about simple goodness and cerebral evil; they assume that we share them, and we do.

Dickens gives us lovably dimwitted but well-meaning heroes and heroines threatened by thinking villains, and he fills the stage with supporting characters who are both unsophisticated and amusing. They know where they are in the pecking order and we can view them with enjoyable superiority through the eyes of Dickens. They are splendid fools, often patient and loyal, occupying their proper place in British society. The same characters, transplanted to French literature, might inspire a similar respect for their staunch and noble qualities but it would be blended with compassion for their ignorant condition.

The convention survives in our fiction, on stage, film and TV. The poor but honest need not to be downright stupid to be endearing but they'd better not be too smart for their own good either. We may cheer on Sherlock Holmes in his ritual tasks of outwitting criminal genius but we don't love him. It's Hercule Poirot's weaknesses – his vanity, his splay-footed trot and his sexual neutrality – that render his little grey cells acceptable. The best-loved characters in every popular soap are those who are a few episodes short of a series; the more astute, the less cherished. If this bias applies to drama, so much more does it affect our attitudes to comedy.

Our national qualms about cleverdicks have influenced our selection of stars among each generation of comedians, particularly Americans who are perceived as too slick and tricky to begin with. In their own country, where intelligence among purveyors of fun is more generously respected, being sharp-witted is no obstacle to being loved by the public. Bob Hope's good-looking urbanity powered his rise to lifelong favour, likewise Groucho's deadly markmanship with a brilliant insult or David Letterman's late-night lapses into literacy.

All the greater then are the achievements of those comedians who, while making us laugh, have allowed their considerable mental abilities to be seen and yet won our hearts in spite of them.

Despite the lunacy of his body language and the generally irritable madness of his comic characters on screen, no one supposes John Cleese to be a dimwit in reality.

Most of us know that he went to Cambridge, that he's made a brilliant success of his training film company and that he wrote his own box-office smash, *A Fish Called Wanda*. So great is John's appeal, so intensely funny his work, that we don't resent his intelligence despite its rather haughty air. A more powerful emotional reaction is at work.

Talking with Cleese on several occasions in London and abroad, I've never felt comfortable with him and have concluded rather immodestly that this was because he wasn't comfortable with himself. Others have made similar observations, finding him at ease when working but socially less assured. The contrast between his most familiar professional comic mask – snooty, impatient over-confidence often disintegrating into hilarious panic – and his personal uncertainty when required to make ordinary small-talk with relative strangers offers promising material for the amateur psychologist. Setting aside such temptations, I believe the extra dimension of genuine vulnerability that lies behind the performances is what causes us to do more than laugh so deeply at Cleese. Along with the laughter comes caring. However mesmerised we are by his implacable return of a dead ex-parrot, Basil Fawlty's stunning rudeness, or Archie Leach's inhibited lust for Jamie Lee Curtis's jewel thief, Cleese involves us at a less conscious level. It's our intuitive concern for the man himself that works the magic which elevates amusement into affection. His daunting intelligence notwithstanding, we sense the lonely susceptibility of a person for whom we can feel sympathy, even love.

Born under Scorpio in 1939, Cleese was six feet tall by the age of twelve. He has described himself as a timid, weedy kid with no way of fading into the background, adding, 'being feeble, with weak muscles, I was bullied a lot and couldn't deal with it very well. I've always hated bullies.' It's ironic, maybe significant, that no one has portrayed them better, from the sadistic bossiness of John Otto Cleese in radio's 'I'm Sorry I'll Read That Again' to a memorable Petruchio for BBC TV.

By the time he joined the Cambridge University Footlights he was nineteen and six foot seven and he had equipped himself with ways of dealing with what other people thought of him.

A fellow student told me, 'John adopted a bored, uninterested air as if he didn't give a stuff but every now and again he'd let loose such biting sarcasm, really spot on and very funny, that everyone would laugh and then he couldn't conceal his pleasure at that. He'd keep a straight face but his eyes gave him away.'

While earning a law degree at Downing College, Cleese had shone in comedy sketches and, in the wake of *Beyond the Fringe*'s successes in

London and New York, he went to Broadway in 1964 as one of the stars of the revue *The Cambridge Circus*, remaining to appear there in *Half a Sixpence*. He returned to London to write and perform for radio and TV, notably 'The Frost Report' where he formed alliances that led to 'Monty Python's Flying Circus'. Python movies followed, together with roles in a dozen other films, but his creation of the magnificently paranoid Basil Fawlty remains his most astonishing work.

When a single character (seen in only twelve half-hour episodes) captures the public's attention with enough force to remain fresh in the mind twenty years later, it has to be extraordinary. That it inspired a generation of young comedians who couldn't withstand its effect on their own work is apparent from watching Rowan Atkinson, Rik Mayall, Adrian Edmondson, John Hegley and others, most obviously Michael Barrymore. Fawlty is the embodiment of manic depression, simultaneously a loathsome bully and coward, tortured into physical spasms by the push–pull of his ego and his inadequacy, all rendered joyous to behold by Cleese with more than just precise timing, energy and originality. The man invested more than his skills in bringing Fawlty to life: he put himself in. For all his comic ghastliness, the frustrated hotelier evoked a response of warmth in us, recognition and pity for his reality, that only the defenceless honesty of the actor could achieve. To differing degrees the same truth can be detected within Warren Mitchell's ignorant ogre, Phil Silvers's quicksilver con-man and Richard Wilson's hapless curmudgeon. Alf Garnett's despair and anger are fed by Mitchell's own despair and anger. Silvers, until mental illness robbed him of it, was vitalised by the same optimism and vanity that charged Sergeant Ernie Bilko. Wilson has admitted that Victor Meldrew is partly a repository for his own flaws.

Intelligent comedians who can't bring to life some fictional monster to please the public have a decision to make. Since they must offer a version of themselves for approval, should they let the people see how clever they are or attempt to conceal it? Are they lovable enough for us to forgive their superiority? You may think that Stephen Fry is so moist and delectable that his brains are no hindrance to our desire to cuddle him, whereas Mark Thomas's shameless exhibition of dazzling percipience denies him our sentimental devotion.

Brian Viner has written, 'We Brits love only the comics who seem dumber, dafter or deader than us, and preferably all three, such as Benny Hill and Frankie Howerd. Sharp as a tack, Ben Elton or Bob Monkhouse, we either grudgingly admire or can't abide.'

With what a dilemma then does John Sessions present his audience.

Here he comes, sharp as that same tack, burdened with a BA in Eng. Lit. and a doctorate on poetry, trained at RADA and acclaimed in drama, spinning mercurial patterns of verbal brilliance to out-Stoppard Joyce and vice versa. On BBC 2 his occasional series, 'Tall Tales' and 'Likely Stories', in which he's played all the characters while sustaining an imaginary series of settings, has won him a sufficiently large coterie of fans to fill the Haymarket Theatre for an impressive number of nights. After seeing the live show I wrote him a letter of sincere if voluble praise. Re-reading it before its dispatch, I decided it needed a touch of lemon juice to cut the syrup but could add nothing sharper than wondering whether or not the audience had missed just a few good jokes because they weren't bright enough to keep up. Sessions replied at once, blind to all the effusive compliments and homing in on my tiny cavil, writhing in guilt that he had stampeded through the show like a mustang in a cloud of hornets and totally abandoned the faithful crowd, or words to that agonised effect. Here was proof, if proof were needed, of the man's tenderness of self-esteem. Here too the reasons for loving him, over and above his labyrinthine sentences and vast knowledge. He's a lonely darling who needs us. Shy, self-effacing, peeping at us hopefully and sideways from under his curly cap of hair, his little mouth tucked up in an apologetic half-smile, he can show off as much as he likes, the forty-year-old scamp. Of course, if he weren't so erudite, he'd be more accessible to the masses. But, God love him, he can't help himself. Put him on 'Whose Line Is It Anyway?' and see how sulky he makes the rest of the team, relentlessly chasing the elusive butterflies of classical allusion up historical hills and down literary dales in a profusion of puns and accents and mimes. It's just as well he's so damn lovable or the others might lynch him.

As a solo writer/comedian, Sessions will never appeal to a large audience because most of his ingredients are too scholarly, even recondite. Stephen Fry and Hugh Laurie deal in arcane humour too but their appeal lies less in what they do than how they do it. They move, separately or together, through every kind of comedy, whimsical or ingenious, popping up in historical guise in the 'Blackadder' series, teamed as Jeeves and Wooster, almost divided in 'Peter's Friends', in tandem again for 'A Bit of Fry & Laurie', a drama for Laurie here, a Hollywood role for Fry there, a West End play for Laurie, a best-selling novel from Fry, countless commercials, but the sheer style remains consistently, effortlessly serene.

In their early appearances Laurie was familiar as the dupe or disciple, Fry as the patronising manipulator or mentor, attitudes they first paraded in – here it comes again – the Cambridge University Footlights Revue in 1981, a show which they took, or which took them, to Edinburgh and Australia. At Granada TV they joined Ben Elton, Robbie Coltrane and Siobhan Redmond and made a fair fist of a scrappy revue titled 'Al Fresco'. Caught up in the Alternative Comedy machine, Fry and Laurie appeared in all its varied products – 'The Young Ones'; 'Filthy, Rich & Catflap'; Happy Families' – catching most attention in five-minute duologues for Channel 4's 'Friday' and 'Saturday Live'. Their jointly written scripts quickly became less predictable, more often bizarre and quirkily intricate in defining their relationships, richly characterised and profoundly absurd.

When I was to meet Laurie on the first day of filming a three-part drama called 'All or Nothing At All', its producer cautioned me not to praise him. 'Hugh's never pleased with what he's done. If you tell him he's wonderful he won't believe you. He'll think that you're insincere.'

Rather overdoing the advice, I shook Laurie's hand for the first time and said, 'I've seen a lot of your work on TV and I don't think much of it.'

Laurie is a well-bred, circumspect man, unaccustomed to such conversational violence. His face froze and he focused on middle distance. I hastened to repair the damage.

'I heard you had a low opinion of your own performances so I thought you'd find it a bit of a relief to meet someone who shared your views.'

'Really.'

'Actually, you've caught me in a lie. I admire you immensely.'

He looked at me with curiosity but seemed mollified.

'People tend to misunderstand this modesty thing. It's just that I set myself foolishly high standards I can't possibly reach.'

On a later day in the filming, on location in West Hampstead, we posed in a garden for publicity shots and chatted about Fry.

'He's two years older than me – 1957, 1959 – and generally much happier. That is to say, I'm very happy and he's permanently ecstatic.'

I mentioned that, although I had met him only once and then fleetingly at a BBC press affair, Fry had written me a most charming letter after hearing me with Dr Anthony Clare on Radio 4's 'In the Psychiatrist's Chair'. 'He said how glad he was to hear from a comedian who isn't angst-ridden and racked with *Weltschmerz*, or English words to that effect. He was so pleased to hear me expressing joyful gratitude for my life in comedy. He even said, and this made me laugh a lot, that when he grows up he wants to be just like me.'

Laurie was unsurprised.

'He's very generous and kind. We've both had things rather easy really so we ought to be grateful. I don't think either of us has ever had any doubts about being able to do whatever we've set out to do.'

This was said without a trace of hubris and it's true that Laurie's life has been a pleasant one. His home was safe and his family well-off and supportive. Like his GP father, whose rowing won him an Olympic gold medal, Laurie was an accomplished athlete and model pupil, first at Eton, then joining the 1980 Cambridge rowing team for the narrowest of defeats. A fine, solid background for a decent professional man with none of the comic's traditional influences of deprivation, desperation or deformity. So why comedy?

'It's just that I find everything rather funny,' he said, disposing of the matter. It's apparent that Laurie isn't keen to analyse his irresistible urge towards comedy. Analysis might alter an essential compulsion.

Compulsion is the word that Fry uses. 'Hugh and I often become like adolescents,' he's reported to have said. 'Being funny is a compulsion really. Show business legitimises that compulsion . . . which is delightful.'

Where Laurie is a private man, Fry appeared to go public years ago. He emptied his cupboard of skeletons, declaring his gay celibacy, an adolescent suicide attempt, his trio of school expulsions, some shoplifting and a stolen credit card fiddle that earned him a three-month prison sentence. This a fact list of naughtiness behind which Fry's real privacy is preserved.

His public frankness aside, Fry's emotional core remains inviolate. We know that he was almost unfairly gifted from childhood and that he rebelled against authority with anti-social behaviour enabled by immature arrogance. His fear of his father, a daunting personality with musical and scientific talents, challenged him in a way he now appreciates. He explains that 'No doctor would advise bringing up a baby without any exposure to germs. It's the same with the trials of rivalry, hostility, dejection and rejection – if you don't go through these things when you're young you can't cope later.'

He's still finding it hard to cope with his physicality. He considers himself 'a hideous spectacle; tall, knobbly, squashy and unappealing'.

Today he leans on no one. He doesn't yearn to feel yearning. He has said that he would rather be needed than need. His friends adore him but, although the affection is mutual, he doesn't pursue them. Of sex, he has said, 'I prefer not to do things I cannot be good at.'

It seems to be one of the very few things he's not good at. You might expect a fair amount of envy of his swift mind and professional successes but such resentment withers with the simultaneous recognition of his lovely nature. Here's as close to a superbeing as comedy can offer us, wealthy, acclaimed, mock supercilious with it, and God packaged all of this in six foot four of uncoordinated self-loathing, a gangly workaholic who hates to be hugged – yet it's being so cheerful that keeps him going. If he can be happy with all this to deal with, what have we got to worry about?

(In the year of my 70th birthday and the publication of this book, Fry will at long last have found a companion with whom deep affection is mutual but, consistent with the observations above, he will continue to keep this part of his life as private as he can.)

In the examples of egghead comedians considered thus far – Cleese, Sessions, Fry and Laurie – their winning aspects as men have helped us to care for them despite their enviable advantages. If the denial of love for certain comedians, resulting from our detection of their high intelligence, is reversed by their vulnerability, what of smart comics who show no such frailty, displaying only confidence in their superior mental faculties without the mitigating qualities of human weaknesses?

Such a one is the American comedian Don Rickles whose act has always been a hilarious torrent of abuse, shouting at Orson Welles, 'Who makes your tents?' and to Joan Rivers, 'If Edison had seen you naked he never would have invented the light bulb!' Another was Sam Kinison whose death at thirty-nine robbed the US comedy scene of its most controversially brutal and sacrilegious bombast (risen again, Christ makes the bitter discovery that he's 'the only savior who can use his own hand as a whistle'). Neither Rickles nor Kinison enjoyed real TV success but a third hostile comic stylist has done so – Dennis Miller.

Hip, disdainful and iconoclastic, Miller's take-it-or-leave-it coolness clicked with sharp US city audiences and on campus but clunked in the less sophisticated comedy clubs of the Midwest. National fame came when he joined the New York-based 'Saturday Night Live' in 1985 and, in place of Chevy Chase's cuteness, presented a news monologue called 'Weekend Update' with what he called his 'low-key, non-threatening cynicism'.

Pleasant looking, with thick brown hair and a full-lipped and lop-sided sardonic smile, Miller's major contribution to the show, until he left the SNL team in 1991, was this round-up of topical events on which he could deliver such scornful jokes as:

*Subscribers to* Time *magazine might have noticed that this week's issue with its cover story on 'Women in the Nineties' was three days late.*

*And, boy, all of us guys were sweatin', uh?*

*News on the sexual front is unrelentingly bleak. I read this morning it's now believed that you can get AIDS from hoping you don't get it.*

*They say that when you sleep with somebody now, you sleep with everybody they've slept with for the last ten years. Well, they've amended that. It's even worse – they now believe you've also slept with everybody they turned down.*

*Last week a dying Palestinian's life was saved when he received a heart transplant from an Israeli soldier. Immediately following the successful four-hour operation, the patient awoke, thanked his doctors and beat himself about the face and neck with his own fists.*

– ending each routine by smacking the edges of his pages together and rising from his desk with the thank-God-that's-over catchphrase,

*And I am outta here!*

Seldom has a comedian seemed to need his audience less; no need for laughter, no need for approval. Yet, more than most, he is able to identify the earliest purpose of his professional comedy appearances as his response to a need, a need he disliked in himself.

'It was a neurotic phase that started making me feel sheepish about myself. I'd say to myself, "My God, you mean you *have* to go out there and load it up in front of all these people every night to get your esteem fulfilled?"

'I had to find out that it's subtler than a need. A need drives you. I don't want to be driven. So it became my choice. I like it.'

Perhaps an adult can make that distinction and, by deliberate thought processes, turn an involuntary hunger into the exercise of a preference, but when did the need begin? Peter Sellers said he never knew the itch was there until the first time someone scratched it for him. Miller says he can remember the moment too.

'I was in tenth grade, sitting in a study hall in high school. And sitting next to me was a football player, just about the coolest cat in the school. The seating chart just happened to fall out that way. And I was very small for my age, not particularly adept with women, and not good at sports. And I was always quiet but I always had funny lines in my head. And I can remember how this one day I just said what I was thinking, I just spoke the words, and here was this guy looking at me like, "I can't believe the little gnat said that" – and then he looked at me again and he laughed. He laughed like, "You're all right, I see you now and I like you." And God, it was amazing. The feeling of reward. For once I was the experimental rat that got the corn kernels instead of the electric shock. And I went, "Wait a second, I think he's just laughed at me – I'll do it again." And I started shooting these lines over at him and he's really laughing and listening to me. God, from that place on . . . that was the day.'

Over twenty years on, Miller can look back and appreciate his good fortune. An unexceptional Pittsburgh-born youth of slight build and few skills, he had found his Aladdin's lamp.

'I think everybody is given something, some way of endearing themselves to other people, and if they explore themselves they'll find it. I was so lucky I was given this. That might sound a little pretentious but, any time I've ever had to be with strangers, at a party or something, where most people are kind of self-conscious and scared, at least I can say something funny. You know, a remark that relaxes everyone, including me. After that, I can move on, get to know people more significantly maybe – but I do have that calling card.'

Finding a social identity as a witty person is one thing. Wanting to get up on stage and display it is another. For Miller, another revelation was required but he didn't know it at the time.

'When I first got out of Point Park College I was so lost. I had this journalism degree but no idea what I wanted to do. I was a janitor for a while, then I drove a flower truck, nothing I felt I really wanted to spend the rest of my life doing. And I was lucky that I went into a club one night, no special reason, and I happened to see a comedian doing his thing and he was really bad. Now if he had been great I would've sat there and thought, "God, I couldn't do that." But he just happened to be horrific and I thought, "Hey, I could be that bad, pal!" And I started doing it in little joints around Pittsburgh in the late 1970s and, lucky again, the next thing I know comedy in this country becomes like the new vaudeville. There's such a boom, the smallest town has two clubs, and I'm riding the wave. New York in 1980, then Los Angeles in '83.

'This new comedy thing, you know why it's such an intoxicant for kids. It's a chance to achieve something like rock star fame without having to learn to play guitar. They're saying like, I can just be a comic and get the same sort of heat!'

Early in Miller's bid for prominence as a comedian a certain disillusionment overtook him. He was quoted as saying that he had 'neurotic chromosomes swimming around in my head' and that 'with stand-up comedy you're putting your self-esteem into the hands of some 300 partially inebriated humans every night'.

'I was treadmilling on the comedy circuit and it's tough when the people in the room don't necessarily want to see you. They're going to be there regardless, much of it for social reasons. Or they've come in that night thinking, "I hope this guy is a juggler" and then you come out and start talking about political stuff. And half the people get pissed at you and the other half don't understand, it was just . . . some of those clubs were pretty brutal, the Kentucky Fried Chicken of comedy. If you couldn't serve up what they'd come for, they wouldn't swallow it.

'Now I've gotten older in this business and a bit better at it, I'm able to advertise myself at a theatre and I find it much easier to talk to 1,500 to 2,000 people who know who you are, aren't just coming there to have a drink, are coming there to hear what you say and have some expectation and some prior knowledge of what you're about.'

Among all comedians, Miller may be unique. His derision of world figures, expressions of contempt for the phoney and his exasperation with stupidity are not cosmeticised by a comedian's natural bag of tricks. His attitude suggests that we'd better come up to his speed, his level of thinking, or we're out of the game. Get it or go.

Apparent indifference to their audience's reactions, except for the occasional expression of reproach when the crowd is slow to pick up on a gag, has been a useful defence against rejection for such English exponents as Jack Dee and Paul Merton, but it's understood by all that this deadpan unconcern is a pose. Getting either of these performers to surrender to a rare smile is a moment of triumph for their fans. The frown breaks down and we witness a tiny tribute to the Les Dawson twinkle.

Nor do the comedians who affect such detachment as part of their technique allow it to be supposed that they truly believe themselves to be a cut above the rabble they survey. It's just part of the unspoken conspiracy that we permit the pretence in the cause of amusement.

Straight-faced comedy is nothing new. Sixty years ago the unsmiling droll was popular both on stage and on the wireless: Gillie Potter lectured in haughty tones, George Robey chided and warned, Naunton

Wayne drawled like an upper-class twit and Oliver Wakefield dithered quite poshly.

In later times, Alan King took aggravation to new heights of hilarity. When he first arrived in London in the 1950s as opening act for Judy Garland, his scowling stare and simmering fury were a comic sensation, only partly because his anger was rooted in truth. He'd stride on, cigar in hand, allowing the applause to die while surveying the spectators with a stony gaze, then say:

> *Well, I'm not crazy about you either.*
> *I am the most successful unknown in show business.*
> *I've been America's newest comedy star for nine years.*
> *For a while I was a film studio's newest comedy star.*
> *Put me down as a semi-finalist.*

Alan King is irritated but he doesn't irritate. Of all the entertainers who approach us in anything other than a friendly manner, none convinces us that he really means it. None, that is, but Dennis Miller. All he is is funny, you don't get anything else. No concessions.

'I don't think there's any truisms about comedy but . . . it's sort of an angry exercise. The things I find funny in life are the things I first find unfair. Comedy is some sort of reflex of effort to make them fair. So I'm cynical, at least comedically, because a lot of things in life don't make sense to me. They seem rather incongruous, no, *unfair* is the word, so to make sense of them, I do comedy.'

If his career thrives, we may see more comic sniping at bigotry, pomposity and ignorance from journalistic commentators turned stand up, following Miller's brand of 'low-key cynicism'. Meanwhile, for those who can swallow intellectual and moral superiority without much sugar to help it down, we have Ben Elton.

**Thursday, 18 November 1993**
When 'The Golden Shot' was attracting 12 million viewers with its live transmissions every Sunday, everybody with an axe to grind wanted to appear in the guest spots and it was difficult for me to refuse friends.

One such was the splendidly mustachioed Sir Gerald Nabarro, MP, who wanted to plug his autobiography. He was seventy years old when he died twenty years ago today.

He was such a great champion of the British motorist that it's surprising how often he managed to become lost even on motorways. He and his agent went astray on the way to ATV's Birmingham studios and pulled up in some tiny Warwickshire village. The agent called out to a passing villager, 'Where are we?'

'In your car,' came the surly answer and the man walked on.

'What a miserable bastard!' said the agent.

Sir Gerald disagreed.

'That was a classic parliamentary reply to your question. It was short, it was true and it told us nothing we didn't already know.'

## Tuesday, 30 November 1993

I go to Buckingham Palace today for my investiture. We who about to be honoured are gathered in the Queen's Gallery, a very grand hall hung with a hundred pictures by the likes of Sir Anthony van Dyck, Hans Holbein, Rembrandt van Rijn, Frans Hals, David Teniers, John Michael Wright, Sir David Wilkie and, of course, Antonio Canaletto who has more than fifty paintings in the Royal Collection. I don't want to leave.

However, a handsome equerry uses his powerful tones to address us with instructions and, having separated us into groups according to the honours we are to receive, guides us into the seating area from which we will be called one by one. First we have to queue up to have the hook fixed on to our clothing where Her Majesty will hang the medal. Moss Brothers must have a full-time left lapel mender.

Half an hour later I hear an officer of the household call out, 'Mr Robert Monkhouse!' and for a moment I don't recognise the name. Then I jump up and stand ready to approach my monarch. Although I've met her before at royal functions, I'm always amazed how small she is. Just the right size for a postage stamp.

I see the equerry murmur in her ear as each candidate walks up, tipping her off about who they are. God knows when he tells her about me but he had to refer to a sheet of paper first and when he read it, he shook his head in mild surprise.

'You've been at your job almost as long as I've been at mine,' says the Queen, expertly fastening my OBE to my chest.

'Yes, ma'am.' It has to rhyme with 'jam', we've been told.

'Are you planning to retire?'

'No more than you are, ma'am.'

'Ah. Well, that would be telling.'

She concludes our little exchange by briskly taking my hand and throwing it away.

Outside the Palace, I pose for press photos with Jackie, who looks glorious, and my agent Peter Prichard whose birthday it is. He's wearing his OBE with a superior smirk that says, 'I got one before you.'

We lunch at Chez Nico where the great chef provides a fitting banquet and all I can think about is the couple of seconds it took me to recognise my name.

I was christened Robert but I've always liked to be called Bob.

I had a girlfriend once who'd been christened Roberta but everyone shortened it, first to Bobbie, then to Bob. So we were the Two Bobs for a while.

Whenever we made love she'd call out, 'Bob! Bob! Bob!' and I was never quite sure which one of us she meant.

But I gave her the benefit of the doubt; I assumed she was calling out *my* name so I reciprocated by calling out her name. God, it must have sounded weird, gasping alternately, 'Bob!' – 'BOB!' – 'Bob!' – 'BOB!' – a bit like having sex in a Swiss valley.

I'm not crazy about my name. I prefer the way American Indians chose such descriptive names – Laughing Waters, Iron Eyes, Painted Eagle – but I haven't picked a name for myself yet.

I've been giving Indian-style names to other people, though. Only last week I ran into my first wife, Crazy Bitch. With her new husband, Nutless Wonder. On the way to visit her mother, Cow That Will Not Die.

I told my wife about it. She said, 'Very funny – have you got an Indian name for me too?' I said, 'Well, yes, Thighs of Thunder, I have.'

She said, 'That's very funny coming from you, Man Who Flies Kite On Windless Day.'

I said, 'A man who flies a kite on a windless day couldn't get it up.'

She said, 'That's my boy.'

No respect for an OBE, that woman.

## Friday, 3 December 1993

*I knew I'd met a rogue elephant when the ivory he sold me turned out to be bakelite.*

I wrote that joke when I was eleven years old. My mother had just explained to me the pachydermatous allusion in the title of Geoffrey Household's novel *Rogue Male* and I was on to its comic potential like the joke-obsessed child I was – still am, for that matter. (Bakelite was a kind of pre-war plastic.)

In those days I thought all animals were funny and most of my childhood jests and cartoons seemed to involve them. When the BBC's 'Zooman' on 'Children's Hour' talked about 'milking a snake', another entry went into my exercise book:

57

*Milking a snake can't be easy. How do you get the little bucket between its legs?*

Throughout my adolescence I continued to add to my handwritten collection, making up simple jokes about tired kangaroos being out of bounds, swimming elephants never forgetting their trunks, newly-wed rabbits going on a bunnymoon, ingrown hares, hyenas who saw nothing to laugh at, tarnished goldfish, teetotal newts, vertiginous lemmings and, as sexual sophistication dawned, female deer passing the buck and randy squirrels putting it in a nutshell.

Today I turn the dog-eared pages of my notebooks, look back upon my youthful self and marvel that I was ever so naïve as to suppose that animals were something to laugh about. Life was to teach me otherwise on this day in 1961.

The idea of 'owning' an animal had always seemed pretty barmy to me. Sam, the black family cat of my early youth, was the most independent creature I knew and, so far as I could tell, thought *he* owned *us*. As our proprietor he was very fair. As long as we provided him with food, drink and comfort, he allowed us complete freedom, right up until the day he used up all nine lives in one go, chasing a fieldmouse across Bromley Road, Beckenham, under the wheels of a 227 bus to Penge. He was his own moggie to the end.

Notwithstanding my inability to grasp the concept of anyone actually possessing Sam or any other living creature, my parents bought me a tortoise and told me it was mine to keep. Of course it wasn't. It never gave the slightest sign of my existence, let alone recognition of my sovereignty.

Its raisin eyes showed no awareness as it snapped liplessly at lettuce, released gnarled droppings from its other end and staggered off pointlessly to anywhere and nowhere. You could paint the name 'Valerie' on its shell in ochre enamel – and I did – but it made not a ha'porth of difference to the thing's real identity, which was about as interesting as that of a conker and not as much fun to play with.

Valerie was tucked up for the winter of 1938 in a shoebox full of straw and left to hibernate. We forgot all about her until the following June when my father and I were in the cupboard under the stairs searching for his tennis racket. He found the shoebox, brought it out into the hall to look under the straw and shouted, 'Robert! You don't deserve to have nice things!'

I watched him toss Valerie's more-or-less vacant shell into the dustbin and I felt sorry, not for Valerie but for myself. I had never asked to be a zookeeper. Thereafter no tortoise jokes appear in my schoolboy notebooks. There are no jokes about waxbills either.

The first I knew about them was the noise. I was just home from school and taking off my overcoat and cap in our hall when I heard a horrid squeaking and clattering from behind the open door of the sitting room. I peeked in and saw my mother beaming through her hornrims and poking a pinkly polished fingernail between the bars of a large square birdcage on the sideboard. Within their prison bustled four small and nasty-looking birds with swollen red beaks and hard claws that rattled on the perches and swings. I watched them flutter and collide and splash their drinking water over our biscuit barrel, their clowns' noses emitting tuneless staccato beeps.

'Look, Robert,' said my mother. 'Here are your new pets. They are yours to keep.'

I knew what that meant: that I was saddled with the jobs of cleaning, watering and spending my weekly pocket money on millet and cuttlefish for these hysterical intruders. Mine to keep? All the waxbills knew about me was my unwelcome proximity. I had only to enter the room for the little dunderheads to go into their regular frenzy, filling the cage with ear-splitting panic, feathers flying out everywhere while their high-pitched Morse code signalled gormless alarm.

On 3 September, 1939, Prime Minister Neville Chamberlain declared war and my father returned the rackety birds to the petshop, preparatory to evacuating the family to West Worthing in Sussex. I felt like writing Herr Hitler a fan letter.

In West Worthing I turned thirteen and my best friend at school presented me with three white mice in a wooden box with a glass front and a little wheel. I left its door open all night.

The next morning two of the stupid things were still in there. I put them in a paper bag and surreptitiously released them at the back of a hardware and grain store in the high street. Mixed emotions: I felt like Lincoln freeing the slaves as an expression of selfish vandalism.

Abandoning the white mice, however, had also been an act of self-definition. I knew now that I wanted nothing to do with captive creatures. I stuck firmly to this decision, politely refusing proffered gifts of puppies, budgerigars and hamsters.

But years, as they pass, tend to weaken resolve and I was to fall victim twice more to the burden of responsibility that is Animal Magic. That is, if you can apply those words to Jackson's Tri-horns.

I was twenty-eight by now, leading a sportive company of entertainers in summer season at the Winter Gardens, Blackpool. My dresser was a dear old man called Harry Butterworth who had a very special friend named Garth. One day Harry came to me in tears and told me that his special friend had gone off with another special friend who was apparently more special than Harry.

''E's scarpered with this lad 'alf 'is age, gone off with 'im just like that! Not a word, not a thank-you, not a kiss-me-'ow's-your-father. What am I to do with 'is pets? I can't give 'em a home, Mr Munt'ouse, I've not got the faculties at my 'ouse.'

Harry tugged at his nose, getting makeup on his thumb, and looked up at me coyly.

'So I was wondering if you could see your way to – er – well, they're no trouble, I promise. Very quiet and quite valuable to them as likes 'em. A bit of food, a bit of warm, and they amuse theirselves really.'

Feebly resisting, I found I'd given a home to two of the ugliest reptiles I've ever seen: triple-horned chameleons named Edward II and Gaveston. They were grisly lizards with swivelling eyes who moved hardly at all inside a huge glass cage which now rested on a low bench in my hired summer home on the seafront of St Anne's. The mid-1957 weather was blustery and cool on the Fylde coast and I'd been told that a constant temperature of eighty to ninety degrees was necessary for my unwanted guests. I bought a convection heater and left it permanently switched on in the spare room where the pair perched on their branches in implacable immobility, never even bothering to change their hue to match the wallpaper.

Apart from the cost of maintaining this stifling heat in the room, there was a sickly smell, not from the scaly namesakes of the gay English king and his bit of rough but from their essential food, the memory of which still brings an involuntary shudder of disgust.

I had to call in daily at a bait shop in Fleetwood for a tin of bluebottle maggots. Have you ever looked into a tin of bluebottle maggots? If you have, you'd certainly remember not to do it again; if you haven't, don't.

It's Dante's Inferno for the wrong end of the food chain, a writhing pandemonium of 300 off-white grubs with a single black dot at one end which may serve as maw or anus or both. Like simmering sour milk they squirm in unceasing agitation, horribly burrowing and surfacing under and over each other, vermiform souls in a frantic furnace, impelled by cruel nature to survive this foaming crucible in order to achieve their eventual glory and become bluebottles. It doesn't half put you off all that reincarnation malarkey.

Gaveston was a natural marksman. Inside the glass case the bluebottles were born and began to buzz about. One would alight within his range. His independently rotating eyes would fix upon it. His deadly tongue would thicken in his squamulose throat, then shoot out to its full nine inches, attaching a sticky globular tip to the insect, then reeling it in to be munched reflectively.

Edward II was a lousy shot and within three weeks he was lying on the bottom of the case having literally dropped off the twig. For the first time he changed colour. Still green but definitely pasty with it.

Gaveston stopped eating, a fatal loss of appetite which I at first attributed to grief but, as I later learned from the petshop proprietor who examined his corpse, was due to a fatal case of botweed. Good.

And so to my final, and I swear upon its finality, brush with the Wild and Wacky World of Wildlife. I adopted a chimpanzee.

Oh, I can sense your contempt. Here was I, aged thirty-three, a full-grown man with a history of pet-death, reneging on all I had determined. I've no real defence either since my purpose was low, a cheap – well, cheapish – grab for publicity. I was in the twelfth month of a play at the Prince of Wales Theatre in London's West End and business was flagging. A publicist named Ben Lewis said, 'We need picture coverage. Picture editors like monkeys. For a few quid you can adopt a monkey at Regent's Park Zoo, pay for its keep. A Monkey for Monkhouse! Bob in the Monkeyhouse! I don't know how I think 'em up.'

It turned out that all the primates in London Zoo were taken. 'Never fear, Chessington Zoo's got a pregnant chimp, going to drop it any day now. Bob's Bringing Up Baby Bonzo! I like it.'

I got to the zoo on the day the baby chimp was born. The two keepers responsible for the Chessington apes were both named Gus. They had removed the baby from its mother as a safety measure. The little creature was quite repulsive, lying unconscious in an oxygen tent as if drowned, its thin black hairs pasted to pinkish-grey skin.

'You can't pick him up yet, can he, Gus?' said Gus.

Pick him up? I felt ill just looking at him.

'But come back Saturday and you can help feed him, can't he, Gus?' said the other Gus.

The next weekend I posed for photographs holding the infant Kong, a name I'd offered in fun but which had been immediately adopted. I managed to manoeuvre a rubber teat into Kong's weak mouth and he ingested more milk and sugar water than he brought up. I felt proud.

The next day I drove to the zoo again and waited till Kong wakened so I could feed him again. I thought he looked a wee bit stronger. As I nursed him, I became aware of his mother looking at us from her cage about twelve feet away. She grinned at me and I felt encouraged.

Somehow I managed to find myself at a loose end most days over the following weeks and made the daily trip to spend a few hours with Kong. He was still sickly but there was a new shine to his eyes and he could lift his head and grasp the feeding bottle with a promising energy. My depression over sagging receipts at our theatre box office had lifted also and my stage brother, young Michael Crawford, remarked on my restored involvement in my role. Business picked up too.

Just a few weeks after Kong was born I drove to Chessington as usual. Caring for Kong was occupying most of my days and I was gratified that the little fellow was recognising me now and clinging to me while he slept after a feed.

His mother's grins from the neighbouring cage had become wider than ever. Her unwanted offspring had mysteriously become my most absorbing concern and I arrived with a small mixture of fruits – berries, seedless grapes, currants – which I hoped might tempt him.

Both Guses – should that be Gusses or, for Latin scholars, *Gi*? – met me at the gates with grim expressions. I got ready to summon up a joke to keep pain at bay. It wouldn't come and I was without defence.

My Kong was dead. On instructions from the zoo's director or some other, the little chap had been returned to his mother for nursing. She had killed him at once.

I thanked the keepers and drove away. I drove for hours and, for the first time in over a year, was late for curtain-up that evening. To this day I can't remember where I'd been or what I'd done.

Since then I've composed hundreds of thousands of jokes, many of them about various animals. It's unlikely that I'll ever come to love a rogue elephant or hate one either. I'm never likely to have an emotional involvement with a giraffe or a polar bear or a golden eagle. Jokes about these funny fellows are easy. I can do you a nice line in unicorn gags, for example. I just don't choose to joke about creatures – mammalian, reptilian or avian – with whom I have had personal contact but established no rapport whatsoever. They don't need me and I don't need them. The mere thought of their natural indifference robs me of the ability to laugh at them. You'll never hear me kidding about the total self-interest of tortoises, caged birds, tame mice or monochrome chameleons.

And I don't joke about chimpanzees either.

They can tear your heart out, these strange brutes. And if they teach you more about yourself than you ever knew, it's not intentional. They neither know nor care what you think about them. They're animals, that's all.

Brutal, dreadful, irritating, selfish, silly, exposed, frightened, forsaken, hopeless nuisances . . .

Just like me.

### Wednesday, 22 December 1993

We arrived by Concorde here in Barbados four days ago. Having no up-to-date British newspapers we get most of our international news from CNN. I don't know why we watch it. It's mostly either depressing or infuriating. Like today; just when you think that the French can't get any more annoying, they do.

This morning, officials in France have announced they intend to purge their language of what they call 'alien English words' like 'bull-dozer', 'chewing gum' and 'cheeseburger'.

They say these words are polluting the purity of the French language. But, if you've been to France, you know this isn't the first time they've done this.

The French have already got rid of a lot of other English words like 'please', 'thank you', 'excuse me' and 'sorry'.

### Saturday, 25 December 1993

Christmas Day is blessed with Barbados sunshine for us and three drenching showers of Barbados rain for the garden.

Tonight we dine with our friends, Nick and Veronica Hudson. Nick's a brilliant chef and restaurateur so the food is great. They are sincere Christians so I won't risk offending their sensibilities by repeating my observation to Jackie this morning.

I told her I feel sorry for Jesus because his birthday fell right on Christmas Day. So he probably only got one present for both.

'Here you are, Jesus, Happy Birthday *and* Merry Christmas! This is an expensive gift so it's for both!'

And he'd get some myrrh or something. That's a weird present. Do you know what myrrh is? It's a salve, an ointment like Vaseline.

You've got to know someone really well before you give them Vaseline for a present.

### Saturday, 1 January 1994

After a very late New Year's Eve at the invitation of Lady Bamford, I'm back down to earth with a bump today, being interviewed for one of the two daily newspapers here in Barbados, the *Nation*.

A beautiful lady with skin the colour of a new penny arrives at Sandcastle and comes straight to the point. Which is better, comedy or sex?

I tell her that I suppose there are obvious advantage and disadvantages with both.

With sex, you don't have to wear a bowtie – but then, with comedy, you haven't got to fiddle with those manacles.

In neither sex nor comedy do you want to hear someone yelling, 'Get off!'

I think comedy is probably better because, well, in comedy a one-man show can be great but with sex . . . very lonely.

In comedy, I've never had my microphone let me down.

In comedy, I've never had an audience close their eyes and pretend they're with another comedian who has bigger jokes.

And finally, in comedy, someone pays me, whereas in sex . . .

## Wednesday, 12 January 1994

According to the BBC World Service today, Michael Jackson says he'd like to live in Britain. Yes, that's just what our country needs – another ageing queen with children problems.

I switch on CNN and there are more American weirdos, more people claiming to have been abducted by aliens, subjected to experiments and then returned to earth. No one much believes them. Well, I do.

The way I see it, fish don't know that we're up here but we still keep pulling them out of the water for sport, then unhooking them and throwing 'em back.

I bet every time we catch a fish some other fish are swimming around going, 'Hey, wait a minute! Where did Keith go? No, I am not crazy, he was swimming right there a moment ago . . .' and you know that when we throw Keith back, the other fish aren't going to believe a word of his story.

## Wednesday, 26 January 1994

People often ask me what it's like living in our adopted West Indian home and I try to explain as best I can. What happened today has provided me with the perfect, true anecdote to explain one aspect of the island's lifestyle.

Just over a fortnight ago we had some house-painting done on the upper sundeck at Sandcastle but the workmen left a small patch unpainted. I'm not much use at DIY but I didn't want to recall the man to do such a small job. Besides, an empty tin of the paint he'd used was lying in a corner so I figured I could easily get some more.

Two days later I was in Bridgetown, the capital of Barbados. If you don't know the place you might imagine a bustling capital city, but nobody bustles on this island. Everyone takes it easy. I once saw a dog walking after a cat.

In the main builders' merchants I asked for a tin of the paint I needed. The sales assistant looked doubtful but strolled slowly to his stockbook to check its pages. After a few minutes of study he looked up.

'Well, now. We haven't got that particular kind in stock just now. Tell you what. We could order that for you and have it here in, oh, about a month.'

'That's too late. I'm leaving in a couple of weeks.'

'That's too bad. Here's what you do. You see a general store anywhere, you go in and ask for this particular paint on the off-chance they got some old stock on the shelf someplace.'

I thanked the man and forgot about it. Until today. Jac wanted to buy some flying fish for our dinner so we drove north along Highway One, the road that takes the shoreline route for most of the west coast. About fifteen minutes' drive from our home is the island's second-largest borough, Speightstown. It was asleep in the heat of the early afternoon.

While Jac was buying the fish from the permanent market stall, I crossed the quiet high street to enter the dusty darkness of the town's only general store. A grizzled old man with nothing to do sat behind the counter. He showed me a gold tooth and asked, 'I help you?'

'I hope so. Do you sell paint?'

'For sure we sell paint.'

There was a long pause.

'What kind you want?'

I told him the brand and the type and number.

He scratched his thin white thatch very slowly.

'No, we don't have dat one. But I can get it for you. De traveller, he be coming t'rough here pretty soon, pretty soon. I reckon I can get you a tin of that paint in, oh, say about eight or nine weeks.'

'Eight or nine weeks? I could get it in Bridgetown in a month!'

His grin spread gradually and he shook his head in amused disapproval of such impatience.

'I dare say you could but you see . . .' he chuckled, took off his spectacles, rubbed his eyes, and regarded me serenely. 'You see, we're not in de Bridgetown rat race here.'

**Wednesday, 2 February 1994**
Hmmm. I'm not too sure about the elegantly beautiful lady whom LWT
has assigned to produce 'An Audience with Bob Monkhouse'.

At our 11 a.m. meeting today she'd prepared her notes based upon
my autobiography. While the events she had listed were all true incidents in my life and had seemed quite suitable for the book, as comedy
material they lacked the strength needed to sustain an hour of laughter.

So I explained that I wasn't too keen on performing these stories
without being funny along the way.

She didn't appear to accept this, pointing out that the truth about me
was what she found interesting and she was sure the celebrity audience
would be equally diverted by it.

I said that, while an in-depth interview with Michael Parkinson might
require some truthful account of my life and times, this was more the
sort of show designed to be a vehicle for what I do best, which is stand-
up comedy.

She asked me if I didn't think they'd seen me do that sort of thing for
years and that a different approach would be refreshing.

I studied her list of subjects.

She had about two dozen headings, words like 'Boyhood – overweight', 'First Audition – failure' and 'Fatherhood – problems'. I tried
to clarify my views. While I could deliver a truthful lecture on these
topics, it wouldn't be all that comical and I believed my celebrity audience would expect strong comedy responses to their questions.

She felt honesty was important and would be appreciated more than
fictional jokes.

I pointed to one of her headings: 'Family – tragedies'.

'You see, if you give me a subject like that, I'm going to say something along the lines of . . .'

I tried to dredge up a joke she'd get.

'Well, let's see. Oh, yes. My Aunt Maud died last week. We had her
cremated. In fact, I think that's what caused it.'

I waited for her to smile but her eyes were full of sympathy and she
reached out to pat my hand and said, 'I'm so sorry, you must feel awful.
Would you like a glass of water?'

**Sunday, 6 February 1994**
Family snaps can be reminders of past pleasures. Souvenirs of visits
abroad, baby shoes and home movies often delight. But when you've
done a truly ghastly TV show which you pray is buried in the forgotten
past, be sure that your prayers will be unheard and its disinterment will

take place in public to shame you with hysterical howls of contumely.

This evening I was the sole guest on the very first TV outing for 'Room 101', formerly a well-received radio show in which celebrities are invited to name those things which so displease them that they want them banished for ever to George Orwell's hellish chamber.

I went like a lamb to the slaughter, armed only with my arguments for the eternal proscription of my *bêtes noires* which included the nation that originated that last expression. Apart from wanting the French consigned to oblivion, my other choices ranged from Cilla Black's singing ('like labour pains set to music'), Elvis Presley and the folk song 'Kum Ba Yah' to sandals with socks, impenetrable plastic wrapping on cheese and the hokey-cokey. Unwisely, I added 'The Big Breakfast' to the list, having suffered the task of presenting it for a week when gale force winds were making my ninety-minute journeys by car in the wee, small hours of the morning quite hazardous. Even more unwisely, my list of hates mentioned a TV series called 'Carnival Time' which I barely survived in 1967. I was utterly certain that no recordings had survived with me. Certainty, like pride, cometh before a fall.

Nick Hancock is cunning beyond belief. The tiny wiseacre who hosts the show has a hundred nifty one-liners pencilled into a notebook in front of him with which to puncture his guest's every pretension. And his production team is heartless in its dedication to unearthing embarrassing footage. No sooner had I mentioned my appearances on 'The Big Breakfast' than a clip was summoned up and here was I on the studio screens, looking whey-faced and senile, grappling the slowly collapsing heap of self-penned cue-cards on my lap as I sat on a toilet between two screaming Irish puppets named Zig and Zag.

Worse, my confidence that Anglia's 'Carnival Time' was more lost than Atlantis became a fragile dream cruelly shattered as I watched my thirty-nine-year-old self capering idiotically on a jerry-built stage somewhere in Gorleston on Sea singing a sub-Sinatra attempt at weaving East Anglian place names into a 'Come Fly With Me' parody, stimulating no apparent appreciation from the stony-faced Norfolk crowd in 1967 but provoking ear-splitting mockery from the mob in the 'Room 101' studio. Hancock offered the view that, over the years, I'd become a sort of cult. He stopped short of identifying the typographical error.

Truth to tell, only once was I involved in something that was destined to attract a cult following, so much so that its fanatical devotees respect me solely for my small contribution to it.

My friend Tony Hawes was chief writer on ATV's 'Des O'Connor Show', a mid-60s mixture of sketches and songs. Another popular half-hour, mainly for kids, was Gerry and Sylvia Anderson's 'Stingray', the adventures of a space age submarine manned by wobbly puppets. The opening sequence each week featured a giant fish which rose majestically from the sea and then returned in a slow parabolic dive.

'Wouldn't it be funny if Des were in the bath and the big fish did that leap right between his legs?' said Tony one morning in my St John's Wood garden.

'Gerry would love that. And he'd know how to do it too.'

A phone call followed and suddenly I was driving my friend westwards out of London to the Anderson film studio for lunch with the creator of 'Joe 90', 'Four Feather Falls', 'Captain Scarlet' and, most successfully of all, 'Thunderbirds'.

Gerry greeted us warmly but with an air of distraction. 'Tony, Bob, good to see you. Can either of you talk like an American?'

I have three American accents – New York, Tennessee and what passes for a rather camp San Francisco.

'Wonderful! You can look at the script over lunch and record the lines between two and four o'clock.' A thought struck him. 'You don't mind, do you? The chappie I booked has let me down a bit.'

I didn't mind at all. And so I joined Shane Rimmer and the other actors to record the soundtrack of what has become Anderson fandom's favourite feature film, *Thunderbirds Are Go*.

Years later the subject of this legendary movie cropped up in conversation with Alfred Marks. A versatile comedian in his early career, Alfred's basso profundo tones took him into films and stage plays where he became a distinguished dramatic actor, notably as the tyrannical father in the West End production of *Spring and Port Wine*.

'Oh, yes, I heard you did me out of a job on that Thunderbirds thing,' he boomed.

'Really? I'm sorry, Alfie.'

'Couldn't matter less. As a matter of interest, how much did he pay you? Or can't you remember?'

'I was just helping out. I did it for nothing.'

'You're an idiot. He offered me £200 for the day.'

'So what happened?'

According to Alfred, he'd looked at the script Gerry sent him and reconsidered. It seemed to him that the journey and the work involved was worth at least £400 so he'd sent a telegram to Gerry. It read rather brusquely, 'Double fee or count me out.'

Gerry's telegram in reply was equally to the point.

It said simply, 'One, two, three, four, five, six, seven, eight, nine, ten.'

**Wednesday, 9 February 1994**

Among the minor items in the news this morning is the discovery of more Cro-Magnon cave art in France. There are small engravings, statuettes in mammoth ivory and portraits in fine-grained rock depicting monstrous female figures.

Twenty thousand years ago the cavemen who painted their walls with representations of wild animals were gifted artists.

They understood the creatures they hunted and portrayed quite perfectly. Presumably they knew their women even more intimately.

Had they wished to create beautiful statuettes and drawings of their females, they could have done so with all the skill and grace they gave to their animal pictures.

So how can we explain the Ice Age figurines that depict women of the time as grotesque and repulsive? Well, it's obvious really.

They're the world's first mother-in-law jokes.

**Monday, 21 February 1994**

Sir Rex Harrison popped up again today. This is the third time in ten days. Two Fridays ago I was asked to play the Harrison role in new stage production of Noel Coward's *Blithe Spirit*. I used my age as an excuse to say no. Last Thursday I was invited to recreate Harrison's 'Doctor Dolittle' in a Radio 2 adaptation of the film musical and, although I love the songs, again I said no. There are few performers who wouldn't suffer by comparison with the original star and I'm certainly not one of them. Besides, I've already had an unsatisfactory brush with the colossal dud which almost ruined 20th Century-Fox studios.

I'm still thinking about that experience this morning as I arrive at LWT to make final plans for the taping of 'An Audience with Bob Monkhouse' next Sunday. In Reception I'm accosted by the palely loitering Nigel Lythgoe. Once an acclaimed dance director, this nimble chain-smoker with the eyes of a good-looking frog is one of the very few TV executives who understands show business and I've begged him to oversee the show I'm doing.

'Before we go into the meeting, Bob, could you do a passable Rex Harrison as Professor Higgins?'

'Probably not. Why?'

'I need a novelty spot for a charity concert. Could you do Eliza instead?'

On my way home from LWT I ought to be concentrating on the one-man show that lies only six days ahead but instead I can't stop thinking about that man and my memorable encounter with him in March 1972.

Rex Harrison had come to the ATV studios at Borehamwood to record a number for 'The Burt Bacharach Show'. I was working in next studio on a live edition of 'Saturday Variety' with Larry Grayson and June Whitfield. During a pause in our rehearsals I slipped across to watch Harrison performing 'If I Could Go Back', a rather awful Bacharach–Hal David song from the current and unsuccessful movie remake of *Lost Horizon*.

As always, his contribution was immaculate in delivery, timing and manner. After concluding a perfect take, he focused on me with his head cocked to one side in shrewd assessment. I was taken aback; even more so when he lightly stepped across the set and stopped a few feet away, tilting his left shoulder towards me as he wiped his hands with a makeup cloth.

'So. My unwitting pupil. I've wondered about you many times, you know.'

'No, I didn't know. I never imagined that you knew I existed.'

He exploded with laughter. 'Good God, a fellow can't turn on a television set in this country without you're there grinning at him.'

He threw the cloth to one side and extended his hand. As I shook it, I said, 'What did you mean by "unwitting pupil"?'

He called to the floor manager, 'Are we finished here, Richard?'

'Just getting a clear, Rex.'

'I'll be in my dressing room.' He took my arm. 'Come, let's have five minutes.'

Upstairs in the room he offered me a drink from a large silver-and-leather flask but I declined. As we sat, he sipped from the matching silver cup and explained.

'I don't for one moment suppose that you've consciously studied me. But I spotted my influence in something you did bloody years ago, some bedroom comedy with that Irish actress. Blonde, went to Hollywood in the 40s, nearly got to play the part of "Forever Amber" . . .'

'Peggy Cummins?'

'That's the woman.'

I had co-starred with Peggy in a live celebration of BBC Television's twentieth anniversary and, yes, the one-act play we did took place in a bedroom setting. But that had been sixteen years earlier.

'About that long ago I dare say. You did a couple of things that I discovered far, far before that, whenever I was playing in *French Without Tears* at the Criterion. That would be in 1936.'

'What things?'

'Oh, tricks. Do you know what Noel Coward said about me? He'd just seen me in his play *Design for Living*. He'd done it on Broadway and here I was, playing his part at the Theatre Royal, Haymarket. Well, he watched me in this no-win situation and then said, "If Rex were not the best light comedian in the business *after me*, he'd be a car sales-man."'

I laughed at the truth of it and then saw the point.

'Do you think I'm elegant enough to sell Bentleys?' I asked.

'You see, I knew you'd be like this. The same as you are when you're working, only of course the working version is you made larger than life. That's what I discovered. To be myself on stage but with greater strength, greater style, greater energy. All well harnessed, of course.'

'Yes, you're just like you are on film.'

'Right. When the cameras aren't on me, I relax, reduce the output as it were. Richard Burton said something in his diaries about my brand of acting and my offstage personality being bound together inextricably.

'The difference lies in the degree of projection. Richard's private-life voice is the same as his voice when he's acting, he simply enlarges it so as to be heard. I do that. So do you.'

I felt very flattered that he was comparing my efforts with those of himself and Burton and I said so.

'Why? It's all technique. You still use a little trick of timing I swear you picked up from me because I don't know any other actor who does it. On the very last two words of a sentence you switch from looking smart to looking innocent.'

'Yes, I do but I've never thought about it. It's instinctive.'

'As soon as you saw it worked, you mean. You may have absorbed it as thoughtlessly as a sponge does water, sucked it into your subcon-scious or whatever, but it didn't become instinctive till you'd tried it a few times, bet your bottom dollar on that. What are you doing?'

I had my script in my hand and now I'd turned it over and was scrib-bling on the back.

'Taking notes. I don't want to forget any of this.'

He chuckled and stood up to remove his jacket. Still an imposing figure at the age of sixty-four, tall and slender though developing a slight paunch, Harrison's movements seemed naturally graceful.

'I'm an amalgam of influences. I was lucky enough to see wonderful actors who specialised in comedy. Brilliant chaps like Sir Gerald Du Maurier, Ralph Lynn and Tom Walls in the Aldwych farces, Sir Charles Hawtrey and A. E. Matthews. And I learned never to let the audience catch me acting. These high comedians, they never forced it, made it all seem effortless. You never sensed that they were trying to make you laugh. It may well be that the throwaway manner that they mastered has passed down through me to you.'

'You never tried to imitate them, though?'

'Thank God I'm not good at imitations or my influences might have been too obvious to the public. Actually I did imitate Ralph Lynn.'

'But he was the silly ass type with a monocle and no chin.'

'Oh, not his character. I used to try to do his gestures. He had these wonderful hand movements, totally unique, terribly funny and *real*. That was what impressed me, the way he made his comedy seem naturalistic and unforced.'

He fluttered his fingers and gave a foppish shrug to suggest what Lynn had done but only succeeded in looking more like Rex Harrison than ever.

'What I sense you may lack is the dark side of a star. A drive for perfection that tolerates nothing less. I feel no anger in you. All great actors are angry a lot of the time.' He stretched like a cat on the chaise.

'Did you ever see me in *My Fair Lady*?'

'Yes, both in New York and London.'

'Oh, yes, Drury Lane. How did you like using my dressing room? I made them do it all up for me in 1958.'

I told him I'd been very grateful that, during the run of *The Boys from Syracuse* at the Theatre Royal, Drury Lane, the star dressing room had been opulently decorated.

'They cut out my best song, you know. Marvellous damn thing called "Come to the Ball".'

He had been lounging on the chaise but now he jumped up and paced the floor.

'It was part of an entire ballet sequence where Liza was coached on how to behave at her first society outing. We did it in New Haven, you know, when we were on the tour getting it right for Broadway. Well, it was cumbersome, they said. Unnecessary, they said. And poof, it was gone. A wonderful song. Listen!'

For the next four minutes or so I sat mesmerised as Harrison sang and acted the intricate lyric by Alan Jay Lerner, moving about the dressing room as totally absorbed in giving his performance as I was in witnessing it. I could hardly pay enough attention to this extraordinary treat for the sheer wonder of its occurrence. Had I watched it in a theatre with 2,000 others it would have been stunning. Imagine the effect of having Professor Higgins revived before my eyes to give this overwhelming private show for me alone. I could feel myself blushing with a strange kind of embarrassment and yet telling myself to take in every moment of this unique event. It was such a generous and charming thing to do that I could only succumb to it with the thought that such a man could have no dark side, his sole motivation being to beguile. His talent was so prodigious that he could afford to squander it in the interests of winning new friends and inspiring affection. He was all that was witty and wise, a kindly magician who was surely a stranger to the anger he found absent in me.

As he concluded, ending the song exactly as he would have done in the theatre, I broke into involuntary applause.

Harrison beamed with satisfaction and bowed deeply.

There was a knock on the door.

'Rex, that's a wrap. Burt asked if you wanted to see it played back.'

Harrison clapped the floor manager on the back and said, 'Lead on, good Richard!' and the three of us walked downstairs.

'My rehearsals will be starting again,' I said apologetically.

'We'll meet again! I feel very sure of it.'

We didn't. The last I saw of Rex Harrison was about an hour later. I was finished with my preparations for the Saturday show and paused on my way home to look in again on the Bacharach set, expecting the scenery to have been struck to make way for tomorrow's part of the production.

Instead I stopped short just inside the door. Harrison was standing in the middle of the same set creating hell.

All of the camera and sound crew and the lighting men looked downcast. The director stood facing Harrison, his hands raised in a placatory gesture. There was no mollifying the furious star. Harrison's voice cracked like a whip.

'I don't give a monkey's fart what you think! That camera shouldn't be where it is when I reach the turn. I turn this way now. Not the clumsy move you had me doing on the last three takes! And I want the light to catch my face as I tilt my head just like this, got it? And as for running out of time, let me tell you something. We're going to do the fucking song until we've got it right! Right?'

I crept away. I'd seen both sides of a star.

During that sole encounter I didn't get around to telling Harrison how close I had come to meeting him six years earlier during the filming of *Doctor Dolittle* in which he played the eponymous hero with support from Anthony Newley, Samantha Eggar and an underrated score by Newley and Leslie Bricusse. In 1966 Harrison and I shared an agent, a charming man named Laurie Evans who was my drama representative for five years and never managed to get me a single acting job. Evans phoned to tell me that director Richard Fleischer's film unit was shooting in England's most beautiful village, Castle Combe. Harrison felt that the scenes coming up lacked 'the crackle of wit' and had asked Evans if he knew any joke writers.

'Do you feel like a look-see?'

'You mean at the script?'

'No, the filming. Pop out to watch them at it. See what you think.'

What I thought was never expressed because nobody ever asked me. What I saw was a film crew and cast apparently in peril of their lives. A young English gentleman had decided to save the lovely village from the ravages of the Hollywood heathens. His chosen method of preserving that particular bit of our heritage as to blow it up. He and his equally misguided chums were planting bombs all over the area during the night, timed to explode just after filming began each morning. New arrivals like myself were being advised to go away again as rapidly as possible.

I took a walk through Castle Combe and it was just as enchanting as it was supposed to be, quite unspoilt except for one eyesore. Draped over the church gate was a banner crudely painted with the words GO HOME TWENTIETH CENTURY FOX.

A few minutes before I had come on the scene the police had managed to arrest the foolish crusader as he and an accomplice were on their way to hang the sign from the picturesque church tower. As I stood there a constable on a bike appeared, folded up the evidence, tucked it under his arm and cycled away.

Not wishing to be innocently sundered by a nutter's hidden gelignite, I drove back to London. Sure enough two bombshells blew up the next morning and the filming was disrupted for a day as the bomb squad searched for the others. Once the devices were rendered harmless, the required scenes were shot and the *Doctor Dolittle* circus moved off to film in St Lucia, unthreatened by dynamite and English eccentricity. The fellow who'd caused the rumpus was fined £500 for putting lives in danger, getting off pretty lightly really. Perhaps the good magistrate decided that the young man had suffered enough having to go through life with the name of Lieutenant Sir Ranulph Twisleton-Wykeham-Fiennes.

For a moment I consider telling that story next Sunday to the celebrity 'Audience with Bob Monkhouse'. But then I think no, it's one to save for my next book if I live long enough to write another.

## Sunday, 27 February 1994

It's been a frantic three and a half weeks leading up to this evening's taping of 'An Audience With . . .' My beautiful lady producer's sense of humour notwithstanding, I've prepared a mass of new comedy ideas which should provide appropriately funny answers to anything the famous faces in my studio audience can throw at me. Nigel Lythgoe, the LWT executive, has kindly and wisely stepped in to give my approach to the show his stamp of approval.

Meanwhile the lady has graciously surrendered her campaign for vaudevillian verity and done her professional part wonderfully well, having unearthed some archive film of me which has lain unseen in someone's vaults since the mid-50s and early 60s: a cinema commercial for Mars Bars that shows the young me as so revoltingly, eye-rollingly oleaginous as to be sure to provoke hilarity, and the classic car-with-no-engine sequence from the days when I hosted 'Candid Camera' while smoking a pipe.

I've had my agent put me about a bit to try out the new material and judge its value so I've spent my last fourteen evenings energetically, pounding around the stage of Bob Potter's Lakeside Country Club in Frimley Green near Camberley, entertaining the Antler Luggage personnel at the Belfry in Sutton Coldfield, being a surprise speaker for the staff of Safeguard Systems at the Hospitality Inn in Brighton, giving my all at Everest Double Glazing's Quality Club bash at London's Royal Lancaster, even testing my latest nonsense on sixty mobile phone salesmen at a prize-giving upstairs in Langan's where I originated the line, 'It's the first time I've seen a room full of men all arguing about who's got the smallest one.'

Now I'm to face up to the judgement of my peers with an audience that will include Stephen Fry, Denis Norden, Mandy Smith, Jeremy Beadle, Mark Lamarr, Billie Whitelaw, Phil Cool, Richard Digance, Claire Rayner, Mr Motivator, Little and Large, Sir John and Lady Mills, Michaela Strachan, Barbara Knox with Lynn Perrie and the stars of 'Coronation Street', Bill Treacher with Wendy Richard and the stars of 'EastEnders', Stephen Tompkinson with David Swift and the stars of 'Drop the Dead Donkey', Bob Holness, Ted Rogers, Sean Blower from 'London's Burning', Gaby Roslin, Lorraine Kelly with Eamonn Holmes, Michael Ball, Linda Robson with Pauline Quirke and Lesley Joseph, Lynda Bellingham, Bobby Davro, Pat Coombs, Gloria Hunniford, Bill Oddie, Pete Price, Katie Boyle, John Junkin, Anne Aston with Wei Wei Wong from 'The Golden Shot', Ruth Madoc, John Inman, Rod Stewart, Joan Collins, Michael Caine and many more. About 5 p.m. I have a sudden and unexpected attack of nerves, an excruciating wave of giddy panic that sweeps through my body like an earthquake tremor. Its aftershocks diminish over about ten minutes.

Nervousness is rare for me. I get anxious before Royal Variety Performances because the audience reaction is unpredictable and, on a single occasion, I remember the time fast approaching for my entrance on a live TV show in the late 60s when the entire studio began to swing around me as if I were riding on a merry-go-round. Luckily for me, the guest star spotted my confused condition, took my hands in hers and spoke to me reassuringly and firmly until the terror passed and I was able to walk out in front of the cameras calmly and on time. If I didn't love Anita Harris for many other reasons, I'd always love her for that.

Bobby Davro gets uptight about performing in certain places, his big hate being the Great Room in the Grosvenor Hotel, Park Lane. I'm not boasting when I say that I love that venue. When the sound system's good and the lighting right, with enough people to fill the 1,400 seater, there's no better spot for me to do my thing.

Considering he's a dazzling cabaret star who never fails to delight every crowd he meets, it's odd that Bobby has such a phobia. He's a worrier I suppose and I'm thoroughly ashamed of a trick I once played on him. I'm not one for practical jokes as a rule but as I arrived at the Grosvenor House to do a show in the Great Room there he was with his beautiful wife, chatting away to some friends in the reception area.

'Hello, Bob, working here tonight?'

'Yes, in a couple of hours.'

'Great Room? Don't know how you do it, mate. Take my hat off to any comic who'll walk out into that hell. Death, that bloody Great Room is. I'd rather pack the business in than play that torture chamber.'

Bobby was booked for a 10.30 cabaret in the Ballroom, smaller and more nightclubby than the huge chamber he hated. After some more friendly chat his companions dispersed and we went to our separate bedrooms in the hotel to prepare. I'd just finished a quick snack from room service and climbed into my dress shirt and suit when Satan whispered in my ear.

I phoned Bobby's room. The exquisite Mrs Davro answered. I assumed the thickest Spanish accent I could muster.

'Good evening, pliz escuse my troubleeng you, madame. I am Hernandez Delgado, the banqueteeng man'ger. Pliz may I spik weeth Mistair Davro?'

Bobby came on the line.

'This is Mr Davro. What's up?'

'So sorry to bother you, sair. We have a seetuation. Very few people have turned up for the function een the Great Room. And far too many guests have turned up for the function een the Ballroom. So we are switcheeng the two functions around and you weell be performeeng tonight in the Great Room. Hokay?'

I heard a thud as the phone hit the floor.

After a pause a female voice explained, 'My husband will be back in a moment. Please hold on.'

I couldn't continue the deception.

'Oh look, this was just a silly gag . . .' but she'd gone. I hung on for two long minutes, my remorse increasing. At last Bobby came back to the phone.

'Hello? I've had a moment to think. It's a question of what I'm contracted to do, you see.'

'Bobby, I'm sorry. This is Bob Monkhouse speaking. I was only kidding.'

'What?'

'It was a stupid joke.'

'Let me speak to the banqueting manager again.'

'There is no banqueting manager. That was me. You're still working in the Ballroom tonight.'

It took a few seconds for the truth to sink in. Then Bobby said in a low voice, 'You bastard, you made me shit myself.'

Bobby had no time to listen to my apologies, he had laundry problems to sort out and quickly too.

If I hadn't felt bad enough at the time, my fit of funk at the prospect of confronting so many fellow professionals and a possible failure this evening makes me empathise with Bobby as never before.

But he's long since forgiven me and, when I overcome my dread and make my entrance to a wonderfully warm welcome, he's one of my most enthusiastic supporters, laughing, cheering and clapping every gag.

The show is a triumph and at the party afterwards everyone is very complimentary. Billie Whitelaw's husband, the writer Robert Muller, asks me if I was scared before the show. I've known my intellectual friend for many years and I can't lie to him.

'Yes, I suffered a few pangs of trepidation this afternoon.'

'Fear can be useful if you harness it. Consider what danger does to the human system. When you're frightened the sympathetic nerves are excited and adrenalin is poured into the blood from your adrenal glands, two little triangles just above your kidneys. This chemical reaction is vital in energising your body to deal with an emergency. The mum who sees her child run into the road or the athlete gearing up for a race both have this sudden surge of adrenalin. It triggers those symptoms we know all too well – the pounding heart, rapid pulse, sweaty palms – but it's also mobilising sugar from the liver to provide instant energy.'

'I certainly felt that energy take over this evening.'

'Yes, fear was your friend tonight. It can sharpen your reflexes. Your nervous system with its countless switches, junctions and evaluation centres will use its incomparable skill to channel constant streams of nerve impulses toward the proper decision and action. So trust your stage fright. It's working for you. It's on your side. All you had to do to use these desirable effects was to take and keep control of the vitality they brought you.'

Robert downs the last of his drink and checks his watch.

'We must be off, Billie. By the way, Bob, did you know there's such a thing as a fear of fear itself? It's called phobophobia.'

My God, just the thought of getting it terrifies me!

## Saturday, 5 March 1994

Entering Studio One at the BBC Television Centre to do a guest spot on 'Noel's House Party' this evening, my mind goes back exactly ten years to a night at Catch a Rising Star, the once famous comedy nightspot in New York. I was presenting little-known American comedians on 'The Bob Monkhouse Show' on BBC 2 and producer John Fisher had picked only the best: Jim Carrey, Dennis Leary, Stephen Wright and Billy Crystal among them. Now Jackie and I sat at a tiny table with glasses of white wine and Jack Daniel's respectively and watched a parade of indifferent comics offering ten-minute sets that had our minds wandering. Then we sat up and paid attention. An elegant brunette had taken the stage, attractive and reserved in manner. We listened entranced by her gentle voice, impeccable timing and completely original material.

She told the audience that she'd had a few other jobs before trying to get this comedy career going.

*I was a stewardess for a while. On a helicopter. There were about five, six people tops. I'd say, 'Would you like something to drink? You would? Then we're going to have to land.'*

*I was a waitress for a while – in a revolving restaurant. And I had a bad memory for faces. I used to say, 'Just shut up and eat it.'*

*I had the most boring office job in the world. I used to clean the windows on envelopes.*

*Now I work for myself, which is fun – except when I call in sick, I know I'm lying.*

*I'm starting off in comedy here in New York. I lived in New York a long time in one of those brand new high-rise buildings. The walls were very thin. I remember one night my neighbours called me up and asked me, 'Rita, could you please stop eating pudding?'*

*It was right near Central Park. I couldn't actually see the park but if I concentrated I could hear the screams for help.*

*I moved to Los Angeles looking for someone to marry. I have a boyfriend but I love the idea of being married, I do. It's so great to find that one special person that you want to annoy the rest of your life.*

*He's younger than I am. In fact, he's two years younger than he thinks I am.*

*Well, the old theory was 'Marry an older man because they're more mature.' But the new theory is 'Men don't mature, marry a young one.'*

*Oh, I heard booing and my boyfriend hates that joke too. But he still gets angry when I bring cereal home that doesn't have a prize in it.*

Three months later she came to London at my invitation and did my show. It led to her own series on BBC 2. From this she got increased international status and an English husband and she's now a headliner wherever she appears in the USA. We saw her show in Las Vegas and every seat was sold. Jac and I felt a twinge of pride. We saw Rita Rudner first.

## Monday, 28 March 1994

We Concorded out here to Barbados on Saturday, dined last night at Sandy Lane with Gloria Hunniford, Christopher Biggins, Lesley Joseph, John and Melanie Rendell of *Hello!* and all looked forward excitedly to this evening's open-air performance of *A Midsummer Night's Dream* in the grounds of Holders Hill House. Our invitation is made out to 'Mr & Mrs Bob Muncus'.

No one in the UK seems to trouble with our surname but as soon as we set foot in foreign parts the mispronunciations abound. An Arab I met said it was the 'kh' in the middle that causes people to use a harsh 'cchh' sound at that juncture as in the Ayatollah Khomeini. But that doesn't account for some of the variations we get here in Barbados where we've been addressed as MacHowes, Marquess, Mughatch and even Manoosie.

In the mid-50s, when I and my family lived at 87, Hodford Road, Golders Green, our gardener was a Mr Hobbs.

He looked after four gardens in the area including that of our next-door neighbour, the poet Danny Abse, brother of the one-time Labour MP, Leo Abse.

Danny called round one day to return a book he'd borrowed and found me relaxing in a garden chair while Mr Hobbs worked in the flowerbeds.

'Afternoon, Mr Abs!' called out the gardener, mispronouncing the name to rhyme with Babs.

I looked questioningly at my neighbour.

'Oh, I know, he's always got it wrong.'

'Then why not put him right?'

'I don't like to embarrass him.'

'Don't be daft,' I said and called out to the gardener 'Mr Hobbs! My neighbour would prefer it if you called him Ab-sey!'

'Very friendly,' he replied with a gratified smile at Danny. 'Thank you, Absie! And you can call me Hobbsie!'

## Friday, 1 April 1994

Good Friday and Barbados is suitably overcast and quiet, the air still, the leaden sky apparently intending to hold its breath until it turns blue.

I've never paid much attention to this holiday. To me, Easter meant a seaside booking in some pier theatre or cabaret in a Jewish hotel in Bournemouth. That's why, forty years ago, I made the mistake of going to Israel for the Easter break.

My first wife and I arrived at our hotel in Tiberius to find the Yom Kippur, the Jewish Day of Atonement, just beginning. We sat miserably in the dining room, listening to Hebrew prayers and staring at what seemed to be two dishes containing a spring onion and some cement.

We ameliorated disaster by sightseeing and pursuing all available entertainment. Thus we saw Neil Sedaka's concert for a huge kibbutz and obtained tickets to a performance of the Israel Philharmonic at the magnificent Mann Auditorium.

We were admiring the architecture when I ventured the suggestion, 'They presumably named this building after the great author, Thomas Mann.'

An old gentleman standing close behind me put his hand on my arm. 'Forgive me but I couldn't help overhearing you. You're wrong. It's named after Frederic Mann from Philadelphia.'

'Never heard of him,' I admitted. 'Did he write anything important?'

'Yes. A cheque.'

## Friday 8 April 1994

At first glance the Rastafarians who sell coconut juice from their wooden stalls at the roadside may appear hostile. Their faces in repose seem to glower from beneath their dreadlocks. It's a false impression. In general the juice vendors are funny, carefree men who love to laugh.

They're also cricket mad. When England beat the West Indies in Barbados on this day in the fourth Test of the 1994 series by 208 runs, it was the first visiting Test team to succeed since R.E.S. Wyatt's fifty-nine years previously. As I went shopping in Speightstown, I walked a little taller.

'See da proud Englishman today?' cried one to another.

'He don't know!'

'Tell him!'

'OK, I tell him. See, man, we *got* to let you win once every few years or you too *terrified* to come back!'

The lads whose patch is nearest to our home make their own brand of Bajan booze by knocking out the 'eye' of the coconut, pushing the sour plum-like ackee fruit inside, adding sugar and very raw rum, then sealing it up to ferment until it's ready. I wondered how they could tell when it was ready. 'We make 'em seven at a time, man. When de first one explodes, de other six be ready!'

## Friday, 15 April 1994

I always bring a dozen or so video cassettes here to Barbados. This evening we'll watch again the programme made in tribute to the best-loved British clown of my lifetime, Tommy Cooper, who died during the transmission of *Live From Her Majesty's* ten years ago today.

Tommy had a brass neck with balls to match. Once, with West End streets at a standstill due to poll tax demonstrations, he persuaded me to travel with him on the Underground. I had argued that other passengers would surely recognise him even if they failed to spot me.

'Bob, it's London, mate. Anywhere else, yes, we'd get bothered. But I've lived all my adult life in this city and I'll tell you something you ought to know already. Only taxi drivers recognise you. No other bugger looks at you. And taxi drivers only clock you in case you do a runner.'

It's a curious fact but Tommy was quite right. Others with well-known faces concur; while most people in the rest of the country quickly identify celebrities and often react by claiming an autograph and sometimes offering opinions about their work, it's possible to walk about London all day without registering the slightest acknowledgement from the public.

Even Tommy with his great bumpy face and lurching height went unnoticed as we bought our tickets and rode the escalator down to a crowded platform.

'Being this tall I have to be careful on the Underground,' he confided as we boarded our train. He looked round cautiously. 'I live in fear of gay midgets strap-hanging.'

During the trip a beggar moved through the carriages. He was dirty and unkempt with a card on a string round his neck crudely lettered with the words NEED MONEY FOR FOOD.

His manner was both reproachful and threatening as he held out a stained plastic cup for donations while carrying an ugly mongrel which kept up a low growling murmur in the back of its throat.

He arrived at our seat and loomed over us. 'Money for food,' he muttered. Tommy looked up from our conversation and seemed to notice the beggar for the first time. 'Eat your fucking dog,' he suggested and carried on talking to me.

### Wednesday, 11 May 1994

Today Claire Gannaway of the *Daily Mail* interviews me on the subject of fame. The occasion is the fortieth anniversary of my very first TV series, 'Fast & Loose'. She asks me about the necessity for vanity as part of a performer's character. What I believe a comedian needs is what everybody needs whatever their situation in life: self-confidence. And that comes from self-knowledge. Playing a role in life to win approval from others, trying to be someone you're not, makes self-confidence impossible. You meet arrogant people who appear to radiate self-assurance but often their bluster and conceit are indications of inner uncertainty. They're faking themselves. Take time to think about who you really are and what you have within you. Be true to that self and all that you have to offer. The surer you are of your nature, the more confident you become. And with self-confidence comes serenity, freedom of mind and a clearer view of others.

That first television series of mine, the one that began on 11 May 1954, was well received in the press. I was very impressed by my success. Two nights later my wife and I went to the Cinemathèque Français in London to see a special showing of a silent feature made in 1928, *Show People* starring Marion Davies and a supporting cast of Hollywood celebrities. In fact, the whole film is about fame and its absurd illusions.

Due to my habitual unpunctuality, we arrived late but the house lights were still on as we entered the cinema. The stalls were thinly occupied by a handful of stalwart fans of the silent era and, as we moved down the aisle, every one of them turned towards us. Then they broke into spontaneous applause. I was overwhelmed. As we took our seats and the lights dimmed I thought, 'Wow! So this is the power of TV!'

After the film had been shown, the house lights came up and as the small audience began to leave, the manager of the cinema approached me. 'Well, you really saved the evening!'

'Oh, thank you. I was amazed and thrilled that everyone recognised me.'

He looked perplexed.

'I'm not sure what you mean. It's just that immediately before you arrived I'd announced that unless we had at least two more people in the cinema I wouldn't be showing the film.'

## Wednesday, 25 May 1994

Two days in succession have reminded me of Dame Gracie Fields.

Yesterday, during rehearsals for Emap Consumer Magazines Awards at Alexandra Palace, there was the great entertainer's photo on an office wall, waving and grinning at the camera as she introduced a new television programme called 'Picture Parade' in 1938. Then today at 11.30 a.m. I'm at the Dorchester Hotel in Park Lane to do a Littlewoods Pools cheque presentation and the company's representative shows me a photo of the first-ever such ceremony by a celebrity – it's our Gracie again, clowning with a three-foot dummy cheque.

She was a very down-to-earth lady. I saw her practical side in 1958 when we arrived at the Manchester Free Trade Hall for a midday broadcast of Christmas songs and verses. After an early morning rehearsal we walked round to the Midland Hotel for a bite to eat.

In those days they offered a full English breakfast – two eggs, bacon, tomato, fried bread, sausage, tea, toast and marmalade – for the inclusive price of one shilling and sixpence ($7\frac{1}{2}$p).

Gracie told the waitress, 'That'll do me, love, but I don't want the eggs.'

'If you don't have the eggs I have to charge you à la carte prices. It'll come to two shillings and ninepence.'

'Come again, love?'

'See, the full English is a sort of special offer, everything all in the one price, Miss Fields.' The waitress was becoming flustered. 'I'm ever so sorry but if you don't have the eggs I'm supposed to charge you separately for each item and it adds up to a bit more.'

'A *bit* more?' gasped Gracie. Then, seeing the girl's discomfiture, 'Ee, it's all right, lass. I'll have the full English breakfast for one and six.'

'Thank you, Miss Fields. And how would you like your eggs?'

'Uncooked,' answered Gracie, 'and still in their shells.'

When the two eggs arrived she wrapped them carefully in a handker-chief and tucked them in her handbag.

Later that morning the BBC producer in charge of the Christmas pro-gramme told Gracie that the show was running three minutes too long and asked her to cut one of her four songs. Gracie said, 'I'm doing all four songs as a special offer, love. If I cut one out I'll have to charge you separately for the other three and it'll cost you another fifty quid.'

The bewildered producer smiled as if he understood, wandered off and cut something else instead. Gracie winked at me.

'You're never too old to learn new tricks,' she whispered.

## Wednesday, 1 June 1994
Sixty-six years old today.

I'm now at the age when happiness is finding my glasses soon enough to remember what it was I wanted them for.

## Wednesday/Thursday, 15–16 June 1994
For two evenings I am once again at the mercy of an unknown quantity.

The video company VVL has hired Bob Potter's Lakeside showplace for the taping of my cabaret. Marcus Mortimer, one of the few TV pro-ducers who really understand comedy, will direct the show. The production will cost over £100,000 to make and, though we don't know it yet, it will eventually sell in excess of £1.3 million worth of video cas-settes. But that's not what I'm thinking about as the early evening sun deepens the shadows in my dressing room.

I've prepared everything I can. Together with Colin Edmonds I've polished up new material for months, trying it out on a dozen different audiences. I've written a new opening and closing song, new lyrics for a false exit three-quarters of the way through, I've got the marvellous Laurie Holloway and his musicians backing me, a new dress suit from my tailor, Geoff Souster of Luton, and the beautiful Spaniard, Eva Moore, is moonlighting from 'Des O'Connor Tonight' to do my makeup. There's only one thing over which I have absolutely no control.

If I get two unresponsive or dullwitted audiences in a row, I'm scuppered. And it could happen. I'm just praying that the people who will be coming to see me over these two nights are going to be here because they like me and my kind of comedy.

A crowd is not a community. Whether it's a mob of shoppers or passers-by observing an accident, the group has no history or unity.

When a star performer refers to the people gathered to watch him in a theatre as 'my audience' he identifies their only common concern. These strangers share a wish to see the star do his stuff. Nothing else brings them together. The crowd is composed of individuals who have assembled for a single purpose. It has a mind and a mood, but no ring-leader, no organisation, no policy, no neighbourliness. The entertainer may impose a temporary bonding upon such a throng but it vanishes as soon as the people disperse.

That's why it's exciting to us when the person on the stage makes us take part in some communal activity. Briefly, we can pretend that we are not just a collection of separate souls but a band of like-minded friends. When we act like a congregation and join in the songs, it's called 'community' singing.

If one of us is persuaded to go up on the stage with Buttons or the conjuror, we are hooked by the participation of 'one of us', a member of our short-lived family. There's a sense of danger too. Will a volunteer from the audience, our special representative, disgrace or do us proud? In our assemblage we may have a lord or a lunatic. The star is taking a chance. Is he so enchanted by the illusion of 'my' audience that he forgets that a crowd's components come in every sort and shape?

Some artists must make use of audience members due to the nature of the amusement they offer. Nightly, the stage hypnotist risks picking on another potential litigant who will take him to court alleging permanent mental damage resulting from being made to go cock-a-doodle-do.

Other performers dip into the crowd for years before hitting a booby-trap. After 5,561 performances of *Cats* on Broadway, Rum Tum Tugger chose the wrong woman to urge on to stage and she sued Lord Lloyd Webber for £7.5 million in compensation for 'violation of civil rights, assault, battery, invasion of privacy, negligence, intentional infliction of emotional distress and false imprisonment'. The incident lasted fifteen seconds.

In years long gone by, in pantomimes and seaside shows, I often brought children on to the stage. Little girls in birthday dresses have sat on my knee. Today I'd fear accusations of sexual harassment.

Lionel Blair, a much-loved friend for over forty years, is fearless with audiences. With sophisticated aplomb and wicked wit, he's dealt with every kind of heckler who's tried to bait him and every sort of drunk who's stumbled across the cabaret floor towards his glamorous dancing girls.

Such consistent success can breed over-confidence. Lionel went into the world of Christmas panto with his usual blithe enthusiasm. In the scene where his character invites children to join him on stage he felt he was in his element. He moved along the row of little boys and girls asking their names and various questions well calculated to produce amusing responses. At the end of the line was a ginger-haired, freckle-faced, six-year-old urchin in a stained jumper and wrinkled short trousers, just the sort of large-eyed ragamuffin to appeal to the hearts of every mum and dad in the theatre. Moreover, he looked appealingly anxious.

Lionel cocked his head at the lad and winked, then went down on one knee and put his arm around the boy's thin shoulders with a reassuring squeeze.

'And what have you got to say for yourself, young man?' he asked, holding the handmike to the boy's lips.

In a very clear voice the little chap gave a ringing answer.

'Touch my dick and you're dead!'

In my busiest cabaret years I made a point of breaking the imaginary barrier between performer and audience.

I felt the best psychological moment for this was after I'd been on stage for about fifty minutes. Then, just prior to singing the song that gave me my first exit, what's called 'false tabs' because one returns for an encore, I'd remark on how wonderful all the women looked and make a sudden move into the audience. This nearly always brought a sense of heightened excitement because I was unexpectedly entering their territory and inviting one-on-one personal contact at random.

As soon as I was amongst the crowd I'd begin asking the women's names, commenting on their clothes, hair and choice of companion.

While I have an encyclopaedic collection of laugh lines in my memory that I've invented for use in this routine, it's essentially extemporised with naturally occurring ad libs scoring the biggest reaction.

Although I'm at pains to be courteous and unthreatening, a spotlit comedian with a handmike moving towards you must appear slightly intimidating. Consequently my questions have received some dumbfounded responses.

At a nightspot called the Broadway in Failsworth, near Manchester, I'd prepared gags about all the nearby localities. I asked one reluctant woman 'And where have you come from?'

'The ladies' toilet,' she blurted.

Asked her first name, a well-upholstered matron in the Double Diamond, Caerphilly, told me, 'Mrs Morgan.'

'What's your *first* name?'

'Matthew.'

The people chuckled. 'Your name is *Matthew*?'

'That's right. Mrs Matthew Morgan.'

'Matthew's your husband, I see. And what does he call you?'

'A stupid cow.'

My second-worst experience with the rogue element in the crowd was in a rather smart nightspot, El Dorado in Glasgow. If what follows seems to you to be the least likely slapstick sequence ever, I would feel much the same except for the fact that I was there and every word of this account is true.

It all started innocuously enough.

A request was made before I went on: would I hand over a bunch of flowers to Sophia at table 12 during my act? The card read, 'Happy 27th Birthday to Darling Sophia from Your Devoted Hubby Andy.' It was explained that a cake would be presented at the same time so I told the manager that I'd do it just before my false exit in the audience participation routine.

Just how much booze had gushed down the throats at table 12 during the following hour or so I couldn't have known. The rowdy roar that went up when I announced the presence of the birthday girl should have warned me. But everything was going so well that evening that any twinge of caution I might have felt was numbed by the mass approval I was enjoying.

The trio played 'Happy Birthday To You' and I led the singing while stepping to the back of the cabaret floor to pick up the bouquet. Meanwhile two waiters made their way to the table with a large cake glittering with twenty-seven candles.

As I left the cabaret floor and approached the revellers I could see that Sophia was not quite the joyful centre of attention one might have expected. She was red-faced, sweaty and surly, her mascara running, lipstick smeared, her pink satin gown sagging off her shoulders to expose too much moist bosom and her orange hair oddly awry. Still no alarm in my subconscious. I went straight into my usual patter, a silly little joke about the fashionability of low necklines – 'Are they on the way out?'

'Well, you look lovely this evening,' I began. She grabbed my wrist and pulled the radio mike to her lips.

'My husband just told me I look like shit.'

Devoted hubby Andy rose unsteadily and shouted loud enough to drown the crowd's laughter: 'You *do* look like shit!'

With a fine show of speed and strength, Sophia snatched the mike from me and cracked Andy across the face with it. Andy side-swiped Sophia and her head went into the birthday cake.

I retrieved the mike as friends held Andy back and others helped Sophia back into her seat. It was a moment or two before I realised that the sharp contact with the bridge of Andy's nose had damaged the mike's delicate circuitry and my attempts at pleasantries were going unheard.

At this point a woman screamed and pointed at Sophia's untidy hair. It was smouldering from its contact with the burning candles on the cake and, even as we saw it, the smoke seemed to billow outwards in the spotlight.

The good news was that Sophia was wearing a wig; the bad news that it was a cheap wig and inflammable, not to say incendiary.

Andy, coming partly to his senses, caught up a glass from the table and threw the contents over Sophia's head. Whether it was neat brandy or some other combustible liquor I don't know but it flared up sensationally.

As the shrieking Sophia tugged off her incandescent coiffure and flung it away, this ball of hairy flame fell among the huge array of artificial paper flowers that decorated the sides of the stage.

Men trying to stamp out the resulting conflagration merely succeeded in filling the air with countless tiny pieces of floating, burning tissue. That was when the smoke detectors kicked in.

Within seconds every expensive hair-do, every elegant gown, every smart suit, in fact every damn thing in El Dorado was drenched by the most generous sprinkler system I've ever encountered. A veritable monsoon fell. The same audience that had so shortly before been screaming with laughter now screamed with panic as the teeming downpour made the floors slick under their shoes and people slithered into one another in their rush to escape.

The glamorous atmosphere had been instantly transformed into smoke, steam and the reign of St Swithin.

Me, I scooted after the musicians. Those buggers always know a safe bolt-hole. We wound up in the nightspot's cellar storeroom, wrapped in clean dry tablecloths and sipping the proprietor's whisky as a remedy for smoke inhalation.

It took all the next day to restore the place to a condition fit for an evening's business. My favourite line came from manager Alex Craigie, without a trace of humour intended.

'That wee woman has made trouble here before, I'm afraid,' he apologised. 'She's a bit of a hothead.'

Joan Rivers says the audience is her partner and if her partner won't play, the game should be called off. But she added, 'One night in Philadelphia the audience hated me and I walked off stage swearing that I'd get out of this business. The next night they loved me and I fell back into their arms like a baby.' That's a matter of group mood. Individual nutcases who disrupt the performance are something else. Ted Ray once told me that when he was singing a Bud Flanagan song on the stage of the Finsbury Empire a youth fired an air rifle at him. Jim Bowen had to dodge about a bit at Blackpool's Central Pier when some lunatic in the front row began throwing darts. And as the much-loved recording star Matt Munro strolled from table to table in the Kon Tiki, Wakefield, singing 'Please Release Me, Let Me Go' a paying customer rose from his seat, seized the singer, locked him in a professional wrestling grip and shouted, 'Get out of that!'

Phil Hyams, the impresario who built the State Cinema in Kilburn and the Trocadero at the Elephant and Castle, lived to be 102 in 1997 but only because he wasn't murdered sixty years earlier by a disgruntled patron who pursued him up an alley with a carpenter's saw because he hadn't enjoyed that evening's presentation of 'Mr Phil's Talent Contest'. Cornered, Phil fluently persuaded the madman that he wasn't Phil at all but Phil's brother Sid. 'I told him he'd find Phil in the cinema car park in half an hour's time. He went off to wait there and I told the police where to pick him up, saw and all!'

'Audiences are like a herd of animals,' Phil told me once. 'Sometimes they'll do anything for you, tame as anything. When I hadn't got enough seats to satisfy the demand, I actually persuaded every boy in the cinema to take a girl on his lap. The fire inspectors didn't like that but they liked my booze so they shut up.

'OK, but when people crowd together they can also form a mob. That unconsciously lowers the intellectual and moral level of every person in it. Jung said something like that. The dynamics of the collective man, the demons that lie dormant in everyone until they're part of a pack. I had a swarm baying for blood once.

'I'd put a girl singer on during an amateur talent night and somehow, after seeing two bad acts before her, they just decided to hate her. Within sixty seconds it had turned from normal booing and hissing to a really ugly roar, really dangerous. Men were standing, shaking their fists. Women were yelling horrible things. The poor girl was paralysed. I went on stage and just stood there, stretching my arms out left and right, tilting my head forward to the side and closing my eyes like this.' Phil rose from behind the desk in his Wardour Street office and demonstrated his Christ-on-the-cross pose. It was quite enough to silence anyone. 'Then, very softly but clearly, I told them that I'd known another night just like this. A very nervous little girl had come on to the stage and tried to please a critical audience but those people had played fair by her, oh yes.

'If they hadn't given her a chance that night, why, her little heart might have been broken and she'd never have dared to walk on to a stage again. And then, ladies and gentlemen, we would never have seen Vera Lynn become the great star she is today!'

Totally won over by this tale, the crowd allowed the singer to try again and gave her a huge ovation.

'And who was this girl, Phil?'

'Mmmm? Oh, nobody in particular. Just some third-rater.'

'But your Vera Lynn story, that was true?'

'Not one bloody word of it. But when a herd stampedes you've got two choices – fire a gun to turn them or do something a bit more clever.'

I told you that the incident in the Glasgow nightspot was my second-worst experience of a loose cannon. Well, my very worst experience only became the very worst in retrospect. It didn't give me the willies until a year later. But as a final illustration of how performers are exposed to the emotional decisions of any freak with the price of a ticket, come with me now to an evening in 1973 at the Shakespeare in Liverpool.

It was a massive old theatre, built like a stone battleship. As we drove up to the door for the first time, outside to greet us we saw the cabaret manager, compere, general dogsbody, resident singer and comedian. Their collective name was Pete Price, today the finest and best loved talk show host on radio in the north-west. Pete was up a ladder, putting my name on the marquee. When he spotted us he went into a state of ecstatic hysteria, one of his milder moods.

'Don't say a word till I get down there!' he screamed and fell off the ladder. After we'd helped him up and dusted him down, he gave us hugs of welcome and shooed us into the opulently decorated foyer, through the huge auditorium with its fabulous stained-glass roof and into a dressing room suitable for storing coal.

Pete assured me that throughout the week I'd enjoy wonderful audiences but warned that I had to be prepared for a very rowdy crowd on my last night. 'Anything can happen here on a Saturday!'

I must admit that the audience was boisterous that final evening and I had to work with even more energy and command than usual to control their enthusiasm. One fellow at a front table was especially excited, hooting and applauding after every gag.

In those days I always concluded the first sixty minutes of my act with those false tabs I mentioned earlier. On this occasion I'd have been wiser not to leave the stage at all because my new devotee took it as his cue to leave his table and clamber up on to the stage to seize the microphone and yell, 'Isn't he fuckin' great? He's the greatest ever! Come on, show our Bob how great 'e is!'

As I came back to accept the applause, my heated champion embraced me. He was in his mid-twenties, short and muscular with tufty sand-coloured hair, glowing with beer and exuberance, clasping me to his bosom and still shouting my praises in his fervour.

I calmed the audience down as best I could in spite of the fact that I was having to share the mike with my admirer, who wouldn't release it. Abruptly, he burst into tears and held up his free hand for silence.

'Bob, le' me tell yer,' he stammered through his sobs. 'I've come 'ere tonight with the sweetest fuckin' girl on earth and, no, listen to me, I want you to see this! Bob! Look 'ere!'

He let go of the mike to fumble in his jacket pocket, brought out a jeweller's box and opened it to display a flashy ring.

'Well, thank you,' I said. 'But I really can't accept it until I know what you're like in bed.'

He didn't join in the laughter because he had more to say.

'Bob! Bob, I want you to ask 'er to marry me, Bob! There she is, my Daisy, right there, lovely girl, I want to marry 'er, see, and I want you to ask 'er for me, Bob! Will yer do it?'

I appealed to the crowd for their approval and they gave it in full measure. From then on it was a matter of showmanship, persuading the reluctant Daisy to leave her seat and follow me up the steps at the side of the stage as the band busked the Wedding March. I milked the situation for all it was worth but eventually, with the proposal made and the ring on her finger, I dedicated a song to the happy couple, had the entire house singing, 'Daisy, Daisy, give me your answer do . . .' and made that my final bow. You really couldn't follow it.

We now depart from the Shakespeare in Liverpool and take up the story one year later at the Wakefield Theatre Club.

Business is booming for another packed week and I've been approached by the padre of Wakefield Prison to go along there one afternoon and put on a show in the prisoners' hall. All the musicians in Willy Hirst's band agree and we turn up at the prison gates at 2.30 p.m. to be met by the minister and the warden, who suggest a brief tour of the slammer before our performance. We walk through the minimum security areas where the prisoners greet us and I pause now and then for a chat.

Entering the maximum security area, the warden explains that this is where the institution keeps its worst offenders. It's at this point that I hear an oddly familiar voice shouting, 'Bob! 'Ow yer doin', Bob!'

And there he is, his sandy hair in a crew cut now, my ebullient fan from Liverpool. I indicate to the warden that I know this chap.

'Only a year ago I proposed to Daisy for you,' I remind him. 'What are you doing in here?'

'Well, it was that same night, Bob. After I'd taken 'er 'ome, me and a couple of mates robbed a ware'ouse and I 'it the night-watchman over the 'ead with a pipe but 'e wouldn't go down so I stabbed 'im like and killed 'im. Murder, Bob. Still, never mind about that, you was fuckin' great that night, I mean it, man.'

'I'm so sorry things went so wrong for you.'

His close-set blue eyes cloud over.

'I coulda done you, you know, Bob. One of me mates reckoned you groped my girl, put your 'and on her arse as you was walkin' 'er back to the table like. I asked 'er and she said she 'adn't noticed but after we'd dropped 'er off, my mate wound me up about it and we came back to the Shaky to find you but it was all closed up. Still, there you are, the luck of the fuckin' draw, eh, Warden? Forgive and forget, eh?'

He punches my arm with a matey grin and jerks his head towards the hall where I'm due to perform.

'You go out there and fuckin' kill 'em!'

He realises what he's said, blushes and adds, 'Your style like, not mine.'

### Friday, 29 July 1994

Today things keep happening that piss me off. We're off to Barbados again tomorrow so Jac's gone to have her hair done in Woburn Sands and I'm alone in the house. Five times the phone rings and I interrupt packing my cases to rush into Jackie's office where our answer machine is located and hover over it in case I recognise a friendly voice and decide to take the call. What do I get? Five hang-ups. Five anonymous dickheads who couldn't be bothered to leave a message. Sod them. Forget about them. Except I can't. I keep imagining who they might have been.

To take my mind off that, I load up my latest VCR, a very expensive machine with all the latest bells and whistles. It decides to chew up my videotape of a 1922 silent movie that only just arrived from Seattle last week so that's probably my first and last chance of seeing Mary Miles Minter in *Nurse Marjorie* for a while. My local TV engineer isn't answering his mobile so I go to make a note on my memo pad to call him again later and three felt-tip pens in succession run out of ink.

I start sweating with irritation so I take off my new suede leisure jacket but before I can hang it up, the phone rings again. In rushing back to Jac's office, the jacket's breast pocket snags and rips on a door handle. Meanwhile, whoever is calling hangs up.

I can now do one of three things: (1) scream and curse and test my blood pressure to destruction, (2) try to relax in a Radox bath listening to Stan Getz or (3) get matters into perspective by making a list of things that piss me off even more than what's already pissed me off today. So . . .

*Things that piss me off*
The French
Elvis Presley getting fat and dying at forty-two
M-way cones that close lanes with no men at work
Nearby car alarms that go off for no reason and get no attention
Supergluing my skin to whatever I'm trying to mend
'Put Stamp Here' instructions on envelopes. Where do they think I'm
   going to put the stamp, *inside*?
Woolly seat covers on toilet lids that make it impossible to prop them
   upright
The fact that everything delicious is bad for you and everything taste-
   less is good for you
The Channel Tunnel
Parents who take their kids to supermarkets to hit them
When the spare tyre is flat too
Running into an Australian soap whenever I change channels
Bone-rattling car stereos you can hear from the next town
Any more nude pictures of Madonna

Shirt labels that scratch the back of your neck

Getting up to answer a phone that's actually ringing on TV

People who end every phrase with 'right?'

Clingfilm wrapping in video cassettes that won't tear off. Supermarket cheese ditto. They ought to make condoms out of this stuff.

Spending an hour crawling in a M-way jam without finding out the reason for it when you get to the end

Running with anything that hooks itself on to door handles as I go past. (Yes, I know I've already mentioned that but it's still needling me.)

Finding out I've spent the evening smiling with spinach in my teeth

A speck on my milk that stays on my side of the glass no matter how much I turn it

The bright red cherry hotels put on half a grapefruit that leaves a stain

Renting a video movie that turns up on TV the next week

Rich film stars whining about how hard their work is

Being half awake and spraying my armpits with hair lacquer

Fast food that looks nothing like the pictures outside

Trailers that show you all the funniest gags and spoil the film

Pathetically unfunny and twee 'Love Is . . .' cartoons

Quiz show hosts saying, 'But you're not going away empty handed!'

White cat hairs all over my dark suits

Waiting for Sega and Nintendo games to get through their boring openings

Mirrors in hotels that face the window and make a silhouette out of you

Flipflops

Minicab drivers with body odour

Finding empty ice-cube trays in the fridge

Getting six more chances in a *Reader's Digest* draw that goes on for ever

Reading the wrong horoscope and finding it's just as applicable or inapplicable as your own

Roseanne Barr

Waiters/waitresses who instruct you to 'Enjoy your meal'

Receiving parcels smothered in ten miles of impenetrable Sellotape

Lap-strap instructions on planes. Anyone who can't understand seat belts shouldn't be allowed out. They should be in a home eating a banana with their feet.

Long, meant-to-be-funny telephone answering machine messages that waste my money

Ventriloquists whose lips move

That red vein in fried chicken legs. And that red clot in a boiled egg. And that one green potato crisp. Oh, yes, and the single chewy Malteser.

Discovering that I'm brushing my teeth with Preparation H

Having a cheque returned because I forgot to sign it

People who say 'No can do' and 'No way, José'

Taxi drivers who turn to look at me while they're driving

Sardine tins with no key

Hearing my wife say 'God, she's aged' every time an actress comes on TV

Instructions on shampoo bottles. One word: why?

Bowls for the dog that have FOR THE DOG written on them. Is that so visitors won't get down on all fours and lap it up?

JFK assassination theories

Finding a toenail clipping that's not mine on my hotel room carpet

The fact that more than half the *Carry On* films are dreadful

Drivers at red lights who 'vroom-vroom' their engines

Mental arithmetic. I can't do it. I'd figure out the sum on paper but all my pens have dried up again.

Not knowing what the show is on the colour TV in the coach I just passed on the M-way

Idiots who gabble their call-back numbers to your answering machine so that you can't possibly get them down

Cilla Black singing anything

Angry dogs repeating themselves over and over and over

Dentists who won't explain what they're doing to you

Potholing on TV

Tuning in Radio Three and it's always German *Lieder*

Cotton wool that won't come out of pill bottles

Opening a new cake of soap in a hotel and finding hairs already on it

Waving at someone you think you know and finding out you don't

Spray cans with more stuff inside but no gas left

Rich old people winning the Lottery

Checking your wrist for the time when you've left your watch off

People who return my pencil with teethmarks on it

Forgetting my PIN number

That smudgy, crinkly carbon you get back after you've signed the credit card receipt

People answering 'Definitely' instead of 'Yes'

Cutting my finger on a Band-Aid

Wine in a box

95

Huge, disgusting pictures of infinitesimal mites with the news that my
    mattress is infested with them
Easter eggs with nothing inside them
Picking up a magazine and having a dozen slippery ad inserts slide out
    on to the floor
There's only one piece of paper left on the toilet roll
Fishbones
A wasp flying in the bathroom window when I'm in the bath
Waxworks that look nothing like anyone who ever lived
The greasy lamb noisettes they serve at banquets
'This Window Closed'
The effluvium of porcine excrement
Being under the shower when someone flushes the toilet
Drunks at weddings
Humourless political correctness
Christmas
Hymns

And that's just for starters.

## Sunday, 4 September 1994

'I never would have admitted being nearer sixty than fifty, but no one
over ninety can resist boasting of it!'

Claudette Colbert gave that throaty chuckle so familiar to all her fans
and added brightly, 'And in two weeks, on September the 13th, I'll be
a hundred and one, won't I, Helen?'

'No, dear, not quite. You'll be ninety-one,' said her companion,
Helen Hagan.

'Oops!' Claudette chuckled again. 'Only ten years out! Oh, dear, I
thought I was more interesting than I really am, didn't I?'

That was the sole indication of any mental lapse during a delightful
four-hour lunch today at Claudette's charming villa on the outskirts of
Speightstown, Barbados.

A stroke had affected her right leg, hand and forearm but had left
unchanged the sweet face which had personified sophisticated gaiety in
this vulnerable yet feisty comedienne during her sixty years of stardom.

When Jac and I received her invitation we'd been cautioned,
'Claudette tires easily so please come at noon but be prepared for her to
withdraw after about an hour and a half.'

But I've adored the woman since I first saw her as Cigarette in *Under
Two Flags* in 1936 (I was only eight years old but I knew when I'd been

spellbound) and I also knew that no actress could resist a bit of honest-to-goodness worship mixed with genuinely intense interest in her views.

'The handsomest man in Hollywood? Oh, Gary Cooper, by far,' and she widened her eyes in recalled admiration, eyes made up rather more heavily than she probably intended. She had to depend now, not upon cosmetics experts at Paramount, but upon poorer eyesight and a less accurate left hand to apply her eye-shadow, blusher and lipstick. Yet the effect was as charming as it was spirited.

'The best actor? Well, Charles Boyer was great, Spencer Tracy was even better but for my money the best actor has to be Clark Gable.'

I expressed surprise. I thought that Gable succeeded on screen not because of his great acting but because he was effortlessly and sexually dynamic and one sensed behind his smile the promise of force.

'That's what made his smile knowing. But you're like so many who couldn't see past his powerful image. When a star shines as bright as Clark you get blinded and you just can't catch them acting. No, he was the best of them all.'

'Were you a little bit in love with him?'

'Every woman was but he was always madly in lust with someone special. His affair with Joan Crawford was long and fiercely passionate although all through those years Clark was married to older women who helped his career. It's funny really because Louis B. Mayer was so piously opposed to their big romance and yet he kept casting them together in movies because he made so much money out of it.

'Then Clark fell for Loretta Young – he was the secret father of her daughter, you know – but that affair collapsed after he met Carole Lombard who could be as tough and profane as him. Did you know he killed a woman in a drunk-driving accident? Metro got one of their executives to take the blame and go to jail. That's when Clark was loaned out to Columbia to make *It Happened One Night*, which he didn't want to do one little bit. Of course, none of us knew we were making a classic! My heavens, it won him the Oscar, the movie won Best Picture. Frank Capra won Best Director and Robert Riskin won Best Screenplay.'

'And who won Best Actress that year?'

She actually blushed and turned to Jac. 'Hasn't your husband got a lovely memory?'

As more drinks were served we were joined by a handsome young man who was introduced as John, marketing director for Christian Dior.

'How's the sinus, Claudette?'

'Wonderful, dear. It's never bad here. You see me in Los Angeles and New York and it's the pollen in one and the coal-dust or something in the other. Do you know,' she suddenly remembered, 'an admirer of mine, some professor out West, suggested that I try pushing cheese up my nose! I didn't do it, of course, this was in 1946 and we had to send all our spare cheese to starving people in Europe.'

A smiling staff served lunch, one young woman taking a seat on Claudette's right to cut up her food and feed it to her.

'I once had a scene in a movie where I had to eat two pancakes.'

I interrupted, 'That was *Imitation of Life*, 1934.'

She turned to Jac again, 'A truly lovely memory. Anyhow, the director . . .' Her bright eyes threw a challenging glance at me.

'John M. Stahl,' I responded.

'Still batting a hundred! Well, John was a stickler for perfection and he had the scene shot seventeen times.'

'I make that thirty-four pancakes in all,' said Jac.

'That's how many I ate that day, Jackie dear. I've never been able to look a pancake in the syrup ever since.'

As she left-handedly sipped from her glass of Sauvignon Blanc, Claudette listened to me expressing my admiration for her role in *Palm Beach Story*.

'I don't believe you were ever lovelier or more vivacious than when you blithely delivered that sophisticated dialogue.'

'Thank you, it's hard to go wrong with a Preston Sturges script and he was a hugely appreciative director too. Whenever I played one of his witty lines the way he'd envisaged it, he had to put his hand over his mouth so that he didn't screw up the take by laughing out loud. We made that movie in 1942, I think. By 1950 poor Preston's talent just vanished. It was weird. There he was, the wonderboy of the 40s, turning out those marvellous mixtures of urbane wit and slapstick farce, and then – zip! He lost it! The last time I saw him he was so miserable. He said, "I'm retiring to your native land, Claudette, I'm going to die in France." And he did, poor lamb. He just faded away and died when he was still young, about sixty-one, I believe. Some women can't go on living when their beauty leaves them. He couldn't bear to live without his talent.'

John asked her to tell her story of Gary Cooper's final farewell.

'Oh, that always makes me cry. I'll tell it to you if you don't mind me having a little weep.'

We all agreed that we could bear it if she could.

'This was in 1961. Coop was just sixty and very ill with cancer.

They'd taken him off chemotherapy, he was too far gone for that to be of any help. They drugged most of his pain away and let him have his booze so he knew the end was pretty close. He asked to see me and my husband, but Joel said, "It's you he loves, you go alone." So I sat by his bedside for a while till he woke up and we talked about people we'd known and cared for and the name of his old friend Ernest Hemingway came up and Coop said, "I ought to call him before I go." I said, "He's very, very ill, Coop, I don't think he's taking phone calls from anyone."

"'Let's try anyway." he said. "I can't leave without saying goodbye, it wouldn't be friendly."

'So I got the phone number out of Coop's book and placed the call. A nurse answered and when I told her who I was and why I was calling, she said she'd see how things were. The next thing Hemingway came on the line.

'I gave the phone to Coop and he chatted to Hemingway a little and then said, "I reckon we'll both be leaving this planet pretty soon, buddy."

'Then I could see that whatever Hemingway was saying was hitting Coop hard. He shook his head very sadly and said, "If you shoot yourself, old fella, they may try to keep you out of heaven. But leave that to me. I'm pretty good at explaining things to reasonable people and St Peter has to be a fair-minded sort of man. I'll make sure you get in."

'Then he gave a big sigh and a wry kind of chuckle and before he hung up the phone, he said . . .'

Claudette's eyes filled with tears and she raised her napkin to her eyes.

'He said, "So long then. I'll see you in the bar."'

### Monday, 3 October 1994

Ten years ago, on this autumnal morning in 1984, I first encountered the warm personality of the beloved Welsh entertainer, Max Boyce.

When Max arrived at the BBC's West Acton rehearsal room to discuss what he was going to do on 'The Bob Monkhouse Show', our production assistant, a tall young woman, greeted him with, 'Ooh, I thought you'd be big but you're little!'

Max answered in his best Lloyd-George manner, 'In Wales we measure people from the chin up. You evidently measure from the chin down.'

Max is famous for his oratorical style of storytelling and in my show he related a corker about Rorke's Drift and the making of the film *Zulu* that provoked a curious reaction.

Three weeks earlier I'd cracked a gag about my mother hating me when I was a child. I said, 'She used to dress me up as Hitler and send me on errands to Golders Green.' I got a very angry letter along the lines of 'How dare you, some of my best friends are Jewish' sort of thing.

In the next show I spoke of my unlucky uncle who died when the *Titanic* went down – 'He wasn't on the ship, he was on the iceberg trying to hitch a lift.' Once more I received an angry letter: 'You desecrate the memory of all who perished in that tragedy' and so forth.

As a result of my viewers' sensitivity, my opening monologue became about as innocuous as a comedian can get, all the gags vetted so as to avoid the slightest risk of offending anyone.

Max was equally irreproachable, ending his interview with a vivid description of the final scenes from the filming of *Zulu*.

With dramatic lighting and gestures, he conjured up the memory of the small band of red-coated soldiers surrounded by a vast army of bloodthirsty African warriors. As fear of death gripped some of the young Welshmen, Ivor Emmanuel's fine baritone voice was raised above the Zulu chanting and put new heart into the lads.

'Men of Harlech' rang out loud and clear as *swoosh* – a spear flew over the barricade and killed a private. As the song continued two more spears brought down a sergeant and a lieutenant. Ivor Emmanuel just sang out louder. A hail of spears followed, killing six more soldiers.

Michael Caine couldn't contain himself any longer.

'For God's sake, Ivor!' he cried. 'Sing something they know!'

The appreciative laughter was no palliative to Outraged of Swansea: 'Did our brave Welsh lads have to stain the African soil with their blood so that you could sneer at them with a cheap joke?' Max wasn't mentioned. I was the culprit. 'Serves you right for having your name in the title,' said my wife. Hard to argue with that.

## Tuesday, 18 October 1994

On my way through the reception area of the BBC TV Centre to keep a four o'clock appointment with Controller One, David Liddiment and the comedy executive John Plowman, Dudley Moore called my name and beckoned. Beside him was a nut-brown man in his seventies but radiating zest in his manner and expressions.

'Bob, I believe you were a guest of Sir George Solti's?' said Dudley.

'Whenever that may have been,' said the great conductor, 'I'm sure you honoured me with your presence.'

A charming way of putting it but not exactly true. In the summer of 1992 Jac and I had gone to spend a week nosing around Chicago, doing a spot of shopping and visiting the famous Second City revue. We always go to some trouble to arrange transport through the hotel of our choice but this time there was no limo awaiting us at O'Hare Airport and we had to take a taxi. The hotel management were most apologetic about the oversight and in compensation offered to upgrade the suite we'd booked.

Thus we found ourselves in the magnificent Solti apartments complete with grand piano and a breathtaking view of Lake Michigan reflecting a blood-red sunset with clouds swirling over it like steam over a bowl of bortsch.

I added that I watched it while listening to Tchaikovsky's Fifth Symphony on a compact disc I found in the CD player. Solti listened to this part of my explanation with apparent delight.

'By the Philadelphia Orchestra?'

'That's right, conducted by Eugene Ormandy, of course.'

'So that's where I left it, I thought it was lost! Rather good, isn't it?'

'It's very grand.'

'Yes, Gene was always fine with anything that doesn't require a sense of humour. Do you know how he got that job with the Philadelphia? Leopold Stokowski went on vacation and Arturo Toscanini was supposed to take over for a couple of weeks. But Arturo didn't like the way Arthur Judson, poor old Judson was the manager of the orchestra in the 30s, he didn't like the way Judson spoke to him on the phone. Not deferential enough. So, magically, Arturo had an attack of neuritis or bursitis or something in his arm. Couldn't appear. Judson went crazy trying to find another conductor but everyone was busy. So he calls Gene who was, I don't know, only about thirty years old at the time, and he offers him the job. He says, "Gene, I'm offering you what I hope is a two-week contract with me but, if you don't get it right, it's going to turn into a suicide pact!"

'So Gene steps into a two-week job with no prospects and, what do you know, in the audience is the agent for the Minneapolis Symphony who's in a terrible fix because his music director, Henri Verbrugghen, has fallen ill. So Gene gets that job too. I said to him once, I said, "Gene, you'll never have to buy shoes, just keep stepping into somebody's else's!"'

It was a typically down-to-earth view of an exalted profession but it seems that Sir George was always marvellously matter-of-fact.

Dudley told me that, after a particularly brisk performance, he'd commented on its extreme accelerando. 'Of course,' replied Sir George. 'It makes the music brighter, the crowd adores it, and I get home earlier.'

As for me, I'm now late for my appointment with the BBC bosses but, never mind, I have two amusing stories to tell them.

## Monday, 14 November – Sunday, 27 November 1994

I've just beavered through three hard-working weeks of speeches, shop openings, cabarets, radio and TV appearances and a few more unusual tasks including handing out *Slimming World*'s top ten awards to gorgeously slender women who once put their suntan oil on with a roller.

Now I'm starting a two-week recording session in Nottingham's Central TV studios, making twenty-six editions of the new 'Celebrity Squares' under the supervision of Alan Boyd, once known in TV circles as 'Mr Saturday Night' because of his successful light entertainment output for LWT, shows like 'Game for a Laugh' and 'Punchlines'. He's a hyperactive Scot who takes pride in being as busy as a bee. The way I see it, a bee is never as busy as it seems, it just can't buzz any slower.

Maybe I'm out of touch but I've never heard of half the 'celebrities' who've been booked to occupy the thirty-foot-high frame and I find myself pining for the first series I hosted in the 70s with real star names in the squares such as Peter Sellers, Douglas Fairbanks Jr., Dudley Moore, Joan Collins, Vincent Price, Kirk Douglas, Glynis Johns, Mel Brooks, Shirley Bassey and Peter O'Toole. My favourite clown used to set up home in the top left-hand square, fitting it with curtains and a flower-filled window-box and lowering a bucket on a rope for deliveries of food and drink. I'd asked if he could return for this new series but Alan Boyd wanted an entirely new look, which ruled out a comeback for Charlie Drake.

I've known Charlie since 1954 when he was half of the slapstick team called 'Mick & Montmorency'. On my TV series that year the plot of a spy sketch required Charlie to hide in a series of cupboards while I fired a revolver at each one in turn. We were on the air – live – when the plug flew out of the gun barrel, shot through the cupboard door and took Charlie's left ear half off. How he carried on in the sketch I'll never know but he did, keeping his left side away from the cameras and the audience so that no one could see the blood.

As soon as he got off stage (we were in the TV theatre in those days), Charlie fainted.

During the remaining twenty minutes of the live show some emergency stitches by the BBC's resident nurse repaired his half-severed ear and Charlie insisted on taking his bow in the final walkdown, wearing a borrowed beret at a rakish angle. He smiled and waved his acknowledgement of the applause he received, walked into the wings and fainted again.

Disaster was Charlie's trade. He told me he'd left school at fourteen to become an electrician's mate. 'On my first day he told me to unscrew a light switch. I stuck me screwdriver right through the wallpaper and caused an almighty fuse that blew up the whole circuit and burst the tank in the loft. Plaster and bits of pipe and about fifty gallons of water fell on me. I didn't think about danger or pain or injury, I was too busy thinking how funny that would look in a film or on a stage. Every job I did, I cocked it up and got the sack, moved on to another job and another accident, it was like I was hired to wreck places. I drove a tractor through a convent wall, toppled a crane into a canal, once I was put in charge of a steamroller. Have you ever seen a flat pram? Thank Gawd the baby was somewhere else!'

During his comedy career on TV and in films Charlie managed to break most of his bones in his arms and legs, a few ribs and a toe or two. His stunts remain unequalled in daring and hilarious effect, crashing through shop windows, falling from ladders into whitewash, swinging on a wrecking ball as it smashed into a chimney and, memorably on one of my shows, wedging himself inside a tympanum and rolling the big drum around the stage until it plunged into the orchestra pit. That one cost him a busted collarbone.

Despite his diminutive (five-foot-one) frame, his thinning frizz of ginger hair and his squeaky voice, Charlie was a great womaniser and successfully so. When he was starring at the London Palladium he demanded a separate dressing room for his amorous activities between shows. A bed was installed and some wag put a condom vending machine in the corner.

Charlie lost all the money he earned as a comedian through his addiction to gambling. By this date, he'd found a new career in drama and kicked the betting habit.

'Now I live a different life entirely. Very frugal, very quiet, a real attempt at self-improvement with no chasing skirts and no gambling. I couldn't afford it now if I wanted it, which I don't. I used to lose ten, twenty, even fifty thousand pounds on a single bet. When you've done that, a five quid flutter on the Greyhound Derby doesn't mean much.'

Told that the Greyhound Derby had been cancelled, he quipped, 'They can't find enough jockeys my size.'

**Tuesday, 13 December 1994**
Eric Sykes hated me for years. He took a dislike to me about 1950

without ever knowing me. During the next four decades my friends tried to change his mind but he would have none of it.

'But why don't you like Bob? He's a lovely man,' Hattie Jacques would plead. 'What did he do to make you despise him so?'

Answer came there none.

Then in late 1995 I wrote something complimentary about Sykes in the *Sunday Times*. Now here I am a few weeks later, walking into the makeup department of the Thames TV studios in Teddington to have my face made more presentable to Des O'Connor and his audience. Sykes is already there for the same purpose.

Just as I always had when encountering the man, I greet him courteously, expecting the usual grunt of begrudged acknowledgement. To my surprise, he half rises from his chair, giving one of those phoney coughs that seem to cover unexpected embarrassment. He extends his hand and I shake it as he says, 'Ah, very nice. The, ah, piece you did. Didn't know you were coming. Meant to write to you, you know, time, my memory . . .'

I tell him I hadn't expected any thanks, that I'd written in praise of his career in comedy with sincere respect and admiration.

'Very nice,' he repeats. 'Very kind.'

He falls silent. Then he picks up a discarded newspaper and I take my place in the next available chair. A few minutes later my makeup's been completed and I rise to go back to my dressing room where Jackie's waiting. But Eric lowers his newspaper and calls out to me.

'Bob, just a moment. Tell me something, I don't know, my memory's getting so bad. Can you remember – ah – why have I disliked you so much for all these years?'

'Eric, I have absolutely no idea.'

'No?' He smiles ruefully and shrugs. 'Oh, well, be bloody stupid to stop now.'

He goes back to his paper and I go back to my wife.

### Sunday, 25 December 1994

A family lunch at Flitwick Manor at which Jackie and I get a fantastic Christmas present from my daughter Abigail. She and her husband Mark tell us that she is pregnant. Our first grandchild is on the way. I tell them that this means more than the joy of grandparenthood to me – it means a whole new subject for comedy material. No one laughs.

### Monday, 26 December 1994

As Kathryn Edmonds is tucking up our goddaughter, Lucy Olivia

Veronica Edmonds (get those initials!) for a sleep, we slowly recover from demolishing the Christmas goose that Jac had cunningly cooked to perfection. Colin Edmonds and I relax with a glass of cheer as Boxing Day offers us a flamingo-tinted sunset through the framework of my garden's weeping ash and I find myself carrying on about one of my comedy heroes, a man who died on this day just twenty years ago. Col's kind enough to appear interested so I hope you'll do the same. I'll save my best story about him till last.

Had Jack Benny not entered vaudeville as a pit band violinist in Waukegan and, partnered by a pianist, graduated to the other side of the footlights with a low-price touring act, he might never have developed his natural gift for arousing laughter as a stand-up comedian. In fact, if Benny had found an early place in a stock or repertory company, he would surely have developed as the specialised comic actor that was always his essential performing disposition, never daring to stand alone in the spotlight. Great fame would surely have eluded him instead of embracing him as it did.

Most actors, no matter how assertively funny they can be in a play, dread the very idea of stepping outside their characters and situations to address the audience as themselves and try for laughs all alone on the stage. Jack Benny said to me, 'If I had ever gotten trapped behind that fourth wall, safe inside some library set or some make-believe bedroom, I could never have spoken directly to the folks out front, not "in one", not relying on only myself. I was real lucky that my training, my conditioning, was as an act. Once you can do an act, and do it well, you're free to do pretty much of anything else.'

He learned more about doing an act after enlisting in the US Navy during World War I. Returning to civilian life as a more assured performer, nightclub and resort hotel work demanded more from him than just his fiddle playing. He'd developed such a suave way of introducing his musical selections that managements had begun asking him to act as compere, to present the other acts and make announcements. Benny slipped in a few jokes here and there. Steadily, booking by booking, show by show, a polished comedian was finding himself and showbiz, ever alert to signs of that rare creature, was finding him. By 1926 he had reached Broadway in a revue called *Great Temptations* where he proved he could talk and get laughs.

That was interesting enough to New York agents and impresarios alike but to the bosses of the great new entertainment medium of radio it was a sensational discovery. They had swiftly got wise to a huge hunger across Depression-hit America in its honeymoon period with the wireless set – the listening audience wanted to laugh. Within a year Benny had become a very big star indeed and so he remained for the rest of his working life.

So is that it? Violin lessons as a kid, work in a vaudeville band, going after slightly better money by doing an act, being required to speak to the audience, using humour, getting better at it, headlining on the road, landing a New York break, being the sort of performer needed in radio, becoming a star and staying that way. No struggle? No setbacks? No scandal? In 1948 I was wondering if that really was all there was to it.

When I knew I was going to meet Jack Benny, I was very nervous. I had never spoken to such a famous and popular man before. In Britain we had been able to hear his very funny radio shows ever since the USA entered World War II, when both the BBC and the American Forces Network began to broadcast them for the benefit of US troops stationed first in the United Kingdom and then, after the war's end, in Europe. Over the next three decades Benny was to top the bill at the London Palladium and the Prince of Wales Theatre many times, touring our best provincial variety theatres and usually doing capacity business up until only five or six years before his death on Boxing Day, 1974.

A quarter of a century before that, I was a very raw comedian, just twenty years old and still in the RAF, awaiting my demob. My first few broadcasts had done well and my BBC superiors had been impressed with what they considered the 'American-style slickness' of my scripts.

It seemed logical to them that, meeting with a major US comedy star to discuss the best way to present him in person for the first time on British airwaves, they should include me in the working party as one of their bright young chaps. I was told, 'You might even find yourself writing his script!'

What I certainly couldn't find was the briefing I felt I needed for this meeting, the life story of the celebrity himself. All I could locate were the basic encyclopaedic facts: born Benjamin Kubelsky, 1894; began career as Benny K. Benny; films since 1928, radio since 1930; marr. 1927, Mary Livingstone (real name, Sadye Marks) – but no real biography. Why not? What had Mr Benny got to hide?

John Ellison, producer and presenter of radio's flagship interview programme 'In Town Tonight', led our stiffly formal welcoming committee of eight. We waited in some pink-and-green, Gilbert-and-Sullivan conference room at the Savoy Hotel, sitting awkwardly at one end of a bare table while the tea in silver pots upon a sideboard grew coldly undrunk for the lack of an enterprising pourer. Benny's nattily attired manager Irving Fein arrived and made a sufficiently long-winded

apology for whatever was delaying the star for Benny's arrival to interrupt it. Benny shook hands slowly and carefully with everyone as
though making a genuine attempt to memorise our names and faces, a
courteous endeavour doomed to be revealed as an instant failure. He
called John Ellison 'Ellis' throughout the meeting and addressed the
Head of Variety, Michael Standing, as 'Sir Guy' (the actual rank and
name of Standing's actor father in Hollywood). Me, he spoke to as
'kid'.

That he spoke to me at all was due to an audacious interruption on my
part when Ellison read out the description of Benny with which he proposed to introduce him to the listeners, something along the lines of,
'Those of you who only know his voice must picture a handsome man
with brown wavy hair and a very serious expression.'

'And blue eyes,' I murmured. Everyone turned and stared at me
blankly.

'How's that, kid?' said Benny.

'Sorry. It's just that on your show it's always funny when you mention that your eyes are blue.'

'Funny?'

'You know. Someone says, "They are blue, aren't they?" And you
say one of those wonderful vain lines like, "Bluer than the thumb of a
cross-eyed carpenter"' – there was uncertain laughter all round – 'Or
"bluer than the thumb of an Eskimo hitch-hiker!"'

There was a frozen pause and then Benny roared with laughter and
slapped his thigh. 'The kid's right, he's right! Say, you must be quite a
fan of the show, huh? That's a cute idea, Ellis, end on saying I have blue
eyes. Then make your first question to me like the kid said. "They are
blue, aren't they?" And my first line will be – er – write the line down,
kid, I'll never remember it.' And so my first experience in providing
material for a great comedian was giving him back his own gags.

Benny's timing put Greenwich Observatory to shame. In any comic
situation, delivering a monologue or playing in situation with others, he
was as sure-footed as a mountain goat. Johnny Carson drew upon the
reputation of a much-decorated marksman of World War I when he
said, 'Jack knows how to place a line like Sergeant York used to place
a bullet. No one in comedy has ever had better repose. When you stand
there doing nothing and it's funny, that's repose.'

Benny's earlier realisation that character and storyline were more
important on radio than jokes was the making of his career. It was a bold
step. Throughout the 20s in vaudeville he'd developed his easygoing
style of delivery but what he was delivering were jokes, big separate

jokes. Now he was prepared to abandon the kind of material he'd always depended upon in favour of what would later be called situation comedy.

While his gag-cracking contemporaries, headline comics like Frank Fay, Henny Youngman, Phil Baker, Eddie Cantor and Joe Penner, all relied upon a continuous supply of funny bullets, Benny had studied the huge popularity of carefully plotted radio shows.

Lum and Abner offered the smile-along domestic adventures of two smalltown hicks in a serial form. It had become essential listening for the masses. 'Amos 'n' Andy' was an even bigger hit and remained so for almost a quarter of a century, following the lives of three black nincompoops as played by two white actors, Freeman Gosden and Charles Correll. Benny didn't want his new opportunity to founder because it was based upon a supply of jokes that would inevitably run low while patter styles and tastes altered and more fashionable raconteurs and wisecrackers took the public's fancy. Enjoyment of comic characters in an appealing storyline could outlast such problems.

His sponsor was Jell-O and their advertising executives agreed with Benny: he needed enough money to hire the best scriptwriters available.

With such a budget he assembled a team of the highest calibre: John Tackaberry, George Balzer, Sam Perrin and Milt Josefsberg. Together they created and sustained Benny's wonderfully consistent, predictably funny character while around him they invented a wild bunch of comic associates.

Each would enter the plot of that week's show and score in an individual way. Eddie Anderson was Rochester, Benny's impudent valet; Phil Harris was the genially loud-mouthed and big-headed bandleader; Kenny Baker, later Dennis Day, the show's innocently dumb tenor; Don Wilson, the overweight announcer; Mary Livingstone, the sardonic lady friend; Frank Nelson played hugely sarcastic officials, head waiters and floor walkers wherever Benny went; and Mel Blanc was everybody else, from language-mangling Mr Kitzel to Benny's clapped-out Maxwell car.

With such a varied company of buffoons to aggravate him, the star hardly needed a joke. He didn't so much act as react. Few comedians have come anywhere near Benny's ability to multiply the length and volume of a laugh by simply staring at whoever had spoken the funny line. Then staring at us. Then back again. By which time we were laughing at what we imagined Benny was thinking far more than at the joke itself. A single instance:

As guest star on the Burns and Allen TV show, he sits on the couch as dizzy Gracie Allen prepares to pour him a cup of tea. She asks if he takes sugar and he tells her, 'Two spoons, please.' Gracie, being Gracie, doesn't find this at all strange, puts two spoons in his cup and hands it to him. Benny simply turns from her and stares into the camera. His blank expression seems to mean, 'Do you *believe* this?' When his unerring sense of timing tells him our laughter has been milked, he turns and puts a third spoon in his cup saying, 'It's not sweet enough.' Then he turns back to us again and gives us the same numb gaze as if to say, 'If you can't beat 'em, join 'em.'

It's been suggested that Benny used this impassive stare to ensure that whoever was working with him would have to wait, trusting his own instincts rather than risking a less intuitive performer stepping on a laugh. This would certainly have imposed a useful discipline on the likes of his chubby announcer, Don Wilson, whose capabilities didn't include fine judgement of audience behaviour. He told one journalist, 'It's understood that I never speak my next line until Jack's all through with staring at the audience and turns back to stare at me. The same goes for all of us. We follow Jack like musicians follow a great conductor.'

When his brash, conceited musical director Phil Harris says the line, 'Ya know, Jackson, I can't understand any studio wanting to make a picture of your life', it's Benny's slight pause in reaction that gets the laugh. Harris has insulted Benny, we imagine what Benny's thinking and it's funny.

'What do you mean?'

'I'm the guy. Colour, glamour, excitement! That's what they should make, "The Life of Phil Harris"!'

Jack explains, emphasising each word, 'Phil, the story of your life wouldn't pass the Hays Office. So don't be ridiculous . . . my life has been one adventure after another. It started when I ran away from home to face the world all by myself.'

'How old were you?'

Mary Livingstone chimes in, 'Thirty-two.'

Benny is quietly disgusted at her sarcasm, and that's funny too. He corrects her. 'I was twenty-seven. I remember because I didn't want to leave until I'd finished high school. After that – Broadway, vaudeville, musical comedy, radio! Why, when they make the picture of my life it will be as long as *Gone With The Wind*!'

Mary again: 'It should be, they both started in the same period.'

Benny's films throughout the 30s were simply commercial attempts to exploit his huge popularity on radio. None of them was particularly good, partly because of this purely commercial motive. The most overly mercenary had the slender charm of honesty about them with titles like *Transatlantic Merry-Go-Round*, *Broadway Melody of 1936*, *It's in the Air* and *The Big Broadcast of 1937*.

The poorer comedies, such as *Man About Town* and *The Horn Blows at Midnight*, showed Benny's difficulty in abandoning his unique comic attitude in order to act his scenes seriously. Aided by his superb radio scriptwriters he had created a lifelong character for his audiences, a lovably tightfisted ham in a toupee. Once he was required to put this character aside in order to handle plot exposition and sincere love scenes, his magic was dissipated. Despite all of this, Benny did make two remarkable films which remain showcases for his comic strengths.

*Charley's Aunt* (1941) had him wearing drag almost throughout. At the Academy Awards ceremony that year Bob Hope was the first emcee and announced a special award for Benny as 'the best cigar-smoking sweatergirl and the outstanding example of lavender and old lacing'. The trophy was an Oscar wearing a skirt and wig with a cigar in its mouth. Benny, genuinely unprepared, said, 'I'm caught with my gags down!'

He was less unready when he took over as emcee himself for the same occasion in 1944 and told the famous folk assembled in Grauman's Chinese Theatre, 'It seems to me that, to get a nomination, a picture must have no laughs. And they tell me I've come pretty close to that a few times already.' He could afford to be self-deprecating. In 1942 he had performed brilliantly in the Ernst Lubitsch classic *To Be Or Not To Be*, playing a conceited Polish Shakespearian actor caught in Warsaw by the Nazi invasion. It was a portrayal worthy of an Oscar nomination and everyone in the movie business knew it.

On one of his last visits to Britain, I asked Benny why he'd never written his autobiography. If I'd been hoping for some revelation, a secret part of his life as a cocaine smuggler or the confession of a jail sentence for farm animal molestation, I was out of luck.

We had just finished a lazy lunch at the White Elephant in Curzon Street. Two of our table companions, Leslie Linder and Stella Richman, had left us to go about their business but Benny showed no inclination to move and I was grateful for the chance to talk with him alone.

'Well, I've turned down so many publishers over the years that I sort of weakened a couple of years ago. I agreed to tell my story to a writer I admire. Then I thought . . . no, if you're gonna write your story down, you must write it yourself. I hate a book that says "My Life as told to So-and-so". You know the man didn't use his own words to tell his own story, some professional writer has come in between, you know? So I decided I was gonna write it myself. Yes, I spent two solid years on it. And I finished it last year.'

He picked up his napkin and polished his coffee spoon.

'And you're never gonna read it because I'm never gonna let it go out.'

Satisfied that the spoon was clean enough, he stirred his coffee and sipped it, watching me for my reaction. I managed a feeble, 'What a shame.'

'Now listen, Bob. Let me tell you exactly what happened. You know, it's tough for me to write an autobiography because I haven't got that much time. You know I'm doing nine million things. But I did take the time and I made notes first for about six months. Then I started to write my life story from the very start and I didn't read each chapter that I'd written as I went along, y'see, I decided I would wait until the whole book was finished. And I did. And I didn't like it.'

I laughed but he held up an admonishing finger.

'No, no, I wasn't happy about what I'd written. It didn't sound like me. So then I thought maybe it's because I know myself too well that I don't like it. Maybe I'm too close to me. So I let my longtime manager read it, you know Irving, Irving Fein, he's a wonderful fellow, very smart. I said, "Irving, read the book, tell me exactly what you think." He read it and he said to me, "Jack, I hate to tell you this but it is not good." So then I thought maybe the two of us are wrong! You know, maybe *he's* too close to me!'

The waiter refilled our cups but Benny didn't pause. He was warming to his story.

'So then I let my director, Freddie De Cordova, whom you know also, he's directed most of my television shows, I let him read the book. I said, "What do you think?" and he said, "It's bad, Jack, bad." So then I thought maybe the *three of us* are wrong!

'So I got my head writer, Hillard Marks, to read it. He hated it. So I said, "Listen, fellas, maybe you're *all* just too close to me!" So they all stepped back a little. I had to laugh, the way they did that.'

'Perhaps they wanted to lighten the mood.'

'Well, so did I. So finally I handed the book to my severest critic and you know who that is, my wife, Mary Livingstone. Not only is she my severest critic, she actually knows more about show business than I do when it comes to knowing what is good, why it's good, why it isn't, the reasons things don't work, she understands these things. So I said, "Now, Doll" – I always call her Doll, she calls me Doll – "Doll, I want you to read this very carefully, all of it."'

'Why hadn't you given it her first of all?'

'I thought she was too close to me. And she'd be too kind. Mary's such a lovely girl, she doesn't say terrible things or swear. So she read it all and, when she was through, she gave it back to me and looked at me and sighed. I thought she loved it. I said, "What do you think, Mary?" And she said, "It stinks!"

'Now for Mary to use words like "it stinks" is like a four-letter word coming out of the Pope. So when Mary said that and, oh, yes, my closest friend, George Burns read it and when I told him that Mary had said "it stinks", he said, "It isn't as good as that!"'

'What was wrong with it?'

'All right, let me explain to you what's so difficult about me writing my autobiography. I would rather have a biography by a great writer who knows me, who likes me, someone like Robert Sherwood, the playwright, he knew more about me than I did, he could've written a book about me. Or William Saroyan, maybe you wouldn't understand it but he could've written a book about me. You see, the nice, wonderful things that have happened in my life that I would like people to know about, I can't say those things about myself. You see? It sounds like you're bragging, it sounds like you're egotistical, and I want the people to know the wonderful things, the real great things, that have happened. I can't say it! If you were writing a book about me, you can say those things and I can't! And another thing . . .'

He signalled for more coffee and continued with rising passion.

'Another thing, I'll tell you another reason it's tough for me to write an autobiography. Mine would not be a Horatio Alger story. You know how people love to read books about a man who was so poor that when he was a kid he sold newspapers barefoot in the snow? Well, I was never barefoot in the snow. In fact, I was gonna call my book "I Always Had Shoes"!'

'But your father wasn't rich.'

'No, not rich, but he could afford to send me to school and pay for me to have violin lessons. There's no great story of a struggle from poverty to riches in my life. Now I'll tell you something else – I have never had any serious setbacks. I've been in show business over fifty-five years and it's been a smooth ride upwards from cheap vaudeville to big-time vaudeville, a headliner, movies, radio, then a star in radio, then television . . . there was never a time when anybody ever threw me out of a job! And what makes me glad that I'm as old as I am, it's too late to throw me out now!'

'You mean there's been no drama in your life?'

'Well, no, apart from a couple of my movies that weren't meant to be dramas. Now you take Frank Sinatra. He's had an exciting life, successes, failures, broken marriages, some scandal, till now he's the king of show business. But for a book to tell a great story it's got to have those ups and downs, troubles like that great comedian Joe E. Lewis had, cut up by gangsters. No gangster ever cut me up.'

'You sound disappointed.'

'Because nothing ever happened to me! I would love to have had that kind of an exciting life. All I've had is a great life, a happy life and, if I have to say it myself, a successful life in a business that I love, so what is there to read? I've been married to the same woman for almost forty-four years. Nobody wants to read that. They wanna read where I've had eight divorces. They wanna read that Mary is a guy in drag and I've got a crazy twin brother chained up in the cellar.'

Here's my favourite story about this extraordinary master of comedy. Elsewhere in these memoirs I comment on how scriptwriters love to use the truth about the comedian in such a way that he can't see it.

Galton and Simpson exaggerated Tony Hancock's pretentiousness and vanity in their scripts but he remained unaware of their inspiration. David Renwick has used some of Richard Wilson's real-life characteristics to flesh out his irascible Victor Meldrew in 'One Foot in the Grave'. So it was with Benny. Oh, he was conscious of the accuracy of his writers' references to his toupee, his unwillingness to admit his age and his unquenchable thirst for public acclaim. But he didn't believe that he was really stingy. He thought he was very generous with money although he was as tight-fisted over minor money matters as Bob Hope and that's as tight-fisted as you can get.

One day my late writing partner Denis Goodwin and I visited Benny in his suite at the Dorchester Hotel in Park Lane. He was due to open at the London Palladium the next Monday and he was keen to see some special material we'd written for him.

After reading our stuff he selected four jokes that he liked and asked his manager to pay us for them. We were given a cheque for £40, £10 a joke. Then Benny said, 'Boys, you want to earn another £10? Write me a joke about this hotel. I wanna say something that's funny about the Dorchester but kinda nice too, y'see?'

We saw.

On the following Tuesday evening we presented ourselves at the Palladium stage door before the first of Benny's twice-nightly performances and Milt Josefsberg ushered us into the number one dressing room. Meeting Milt was a great thrill for us. He was a veteran writer with one glass eye from an old bow-and-arrow accident. He told me he could wink but could not blink.

Benny came out of the toilet in his blue silk dressing gown and Sulka slippers. He sat on the banquette and leaned back, tilting his bifocals forward to read the two pages of Dorchester jokes we'd written. His unerring comic judgement spotted the best gag immediately. It went like this:

> *While I'm in London I'm living in a place that overlooks the beautiful Dorchester Hotel. Which is better than paying Dorchester prices and overlooking the dump I'm living in.*

He loved the gag, all £10 worth of it!

'Gee, that's a great line! Milt, I'm putting this great joke in tonight!'

'No, not tonight, Jack. You know how you are, you need to memorise new lines and sleep on them.'

'Oh, don't fuss! I'm just lucky their press guy wasn't sitting out front last night. This has to go in the act tonight and there's no more to be said.'

Benny retired to the inner section of the dressing room to dress, closing the door and leaving us talking to Milt.

'You did a nice job, guys. Now Jack can get his rate.'

'His what?'

'From the Dorchester. Why do you guys think he wants to mention the hotel in his act?'

Denis and I gaped at one another. Milt laughed at our innocence.

'Sure! Jack plugs the hotel every performance in exchange for a reduction in the rate for his suite. He's done it for years but none of the American hotel jokes would go over here. He figures the hotel's publicist may come in to see him work this evening so . . .'

We stayed chatting with Milt while half listening to the sound of the supporting acts coming over the Tannoy speaker on the wall. At the first house interval an immaculate Benny emerged from the inner chamber.

'Lookit, Milt. I'm putting that Dorchester joke in right after the Dickins & Jones line. That's a change to Phil's cue so tell him not to come on too early, I wanna milk the laugh. Have Phil come on after I say, "Y'see?"'

Milt vanished to speak to Phil Harris, and Benny smiled at us warmly. 'We don't keep a chequebook here in the theatre but I'll see you get paid tomorrow. Ten pounds a joke, huh? That's pretty good money. Putting the strong arm on us Yanks, eh? That's OK.'

The second half of the stage show began, Milt returned and we heard the orchestra strike up 'Love In Bloom', the signature tune of the star's radio programme.

The three of us listened attentively to Benny and the huge laughs he was getting. Soon he reached his piece about being in London.

'My wife Mary's been shopping. I can't tell you what she's spent in one store but Dickins phoned up to congratulate Jones!'

The audience knew the famous Regent Street shop and roared.

'While I'm here in London I'm living in a place that overlooks the beautiful Dorchester Hotel,' continued Benny – and promptly forgot the rest of the joke. Milt shrugged and shook his head at us regretfully.

But while Benny was silently struggling to remember the rest of the gag the famous effect of his deadpan repose allowed the audience to perceive humour in what he'd just told them. Here he was, boasting about living in a place that merely overlooked somewhere better!

During his absent-minded pause the audience laughed lengthily. So long was the laugh that it enabled Benny's memory to recover.

'Which is better than paying Dorchester prices,' he went on, 'and overlooking the dump I'm living in.'

An explosion of laughter greeted this, mingled with the applause almost always given to a 'topper', a gag that builds on its predecessor.

We all gave a sigh of relief.

But then something curious began to happen. Benny's timing sounded slightly off. He interrupted Phil Harris too soon and rushed another piece so that the audience had no time to react.

Milt started chuckling.

Benny reached another part of his act and was clearly hurrying through it. Tears were coming from Milt's good eye.

'Listen to him! Just listen to him!' he spluttered.

'What's happening?' we asked.

'Don't you get it?' gasped Milt. 'He can't wait to get off and tell you guys that's still only one joke!'

## Saturday, 7 January 1995

Larry Grayson, blessed with just enough ill health to satisfy his demanding hypochondria, was a frequent guest on both 'The Golden Shot' and the first, very successful series of 'Celebrity Squares' in 1975–80.

His desperate concern about his health took the form of some very funny remarks. At a fundraising concert in Bristol he told a dressing room full of admirers, 'In my will I've specified that I have to be buried in the no-smoking section of the cemetery.'

I've never met anyone who didn't love the man and many tears were shed when he died today.

I remember walking with him along the King's Road in Chelsea when we passed a church that was frequented by hippies, druggies, anti-government campaigners and religious nuts.

One scruffy fellow stood outside distributing leaflets about some church event with one hand while holding a sign on a pole in the other that proclaimed JESUS IS COMING.

Larry looked at the sign, then looked at the man holding it. He had a tea cosy on his head, a filthy blue anorak buttoned to the neck, trousers that had once been yellow, and army boots.

Shaking his head in disapproval, Larry sniffed and commented, 'Jesus is coming and you're wearing *that*?'

Larry had once undertaken some training as a male nurse but was too squeamish about injuries to continue.

'But it came in handy once when I was rehearsing a pantomime in Hull. The comic playing Idle Jack got up on a rickety chair, pretending he was riding the panto horse. The chair gave way and he fell badly, breaking his collarbone and slamming his face on a carpenter's bench so hard it started gushing blood from his nose and a gash in his cheek. It was ghastly!'

Larry gave a shudder at the memory.

'But thanks to my training as a nurse I knew exactly what to do, thank God.'

'And what was that?'

'I sat down and put my head between my knees, otherwise I'd have fainted for sure.'

## Sunday, 8 January 1995

After a busy start to the New Year doing nightly cabaret at the Lakeside Country Club, I slept away the four-hour trip by Concorde to Barbados. We always feel very safe here. The island is generally peaceful and law-abiding although there was a year when crime briefly flourished before being firmly suppressed by the Barbados Royal Police.

We'd rented a beautiful house on the West Coast with the curious name of Baggywrinkle. With the house came a maid, cook, butler and night guard. Having satisfied herself that she could get along with the domestic staff, Jackie asked me to check out the reliability of the night guard, a grizzled old chap with only one visible tooth. 'My wife's a bit nervous about after-dark intruders,' I told him. 'Are you a good night-watchman?'

'Oh, jus' fine, master,' he assured me. He sucked the tooth thoughtfully and added, 'The slightest noise wakes me up.'

No matter how accustomed you think you've become to Bajan logic, it will still catch you unprepared. At Sunset Crest, Holetown, there's a large supermarket where we buy all our basic provisions. Teenage lads in yellow and red uniforms are busy at the checkouts, packing the customers' purchases into plastic bags and carting them out to the car park. Not everyone tips the boys who do this but we do and consequently one tall fellow always makes a beeline for us, showing a special enthusiasm as he energetically tucks the goods away, chatting and smiling. All very well, but time and again we found he'd put the eggs at the very bottom of the groceries, causing several of them to be broken by the time we'd got them home. 'We must remember to tell him not to do that,' said Jackie.

The next time we shopped and pushed our trolley to the cash desk, up popped our lanky assistant and I saw him grab the eggs and start to push them into the bottom of a fresh bag.

'Hold it,' I called out. 'The eggs ought to go on top.'

He shook his head at my foolishness and rolled his eyes.

'Eggs got to go on the bottom, man! Then when they break they won't run all over the rest of your stuff.'

Sometimes you might suppose that English was a second language in Barbados, so quaint is its use. Staying at another rented house in Merlin Bay, we discovered a problem with the lavatory. Esther, our cook, said she had a cousin who was a good plumber and she phoned him for advice. Apparently he asked her what the problem was. She explained as only a Barbadian could. 'It can't swallow,' she said.

## Wednesday, 11 January 1995

Sitting on the sundeck of our beachfront home, I am contentedly browsing through my scrapbook and remembering a little man I met for the first time twenty years ago today when I walked into a recording studio in St John's Wood unannounced and invited Kenny Everett, the most mischievous and original funnyman, to be the unseen voice-over that described the prizes of 'Celebrity Squares'.

He accepted the idea warily but when the ATV series began on Saturday nights his zany descriptions were an important part of the show's terrific success. The first run of twenty-six shows was immediately extended to forty-four and we were in for a five-year run.

The producer/director was the enthusiastic and talented Paul Stewart Laing. He insisted that Kenny make his first ever TV appearance, even if he only ran across the set.

Reluctantly, shy Kenny agreed.

On the night, he appeared totally naked except for his shoes and socks, running wildly and screaming, 'Moths! Moths!'

In the bar after the recording, Paul shook his head reproachfully at Kenny and told him, 'You've been cut.'

Kenny replied, 'Oh, you noticed.'

## Wednesday, 25 January 1995

We're dining this evening at one of the West Coast's finest restaurants, named the Cliff because it's perched upon one, looking out through its flaming torches at the myriad undulations of the Caribbean, etched with the soft light of a crescent moon so lazy that it's rolled over on its back. Our guests are Val and Brian Cooke, he being the creator of numerous TV sitcoms including 'Man About the House', 'Robin's Nest' and 'George and Mildred'. When I announce that, although Benny Hill died in 1992, this is the seventieth anniversary of his birth, we raise a toast to the man *Variety* called 'Global TV's Top Banana'.

Brian says, 'I must confess, I never quite understood his success.'

I remember chatting with the legendary film-maker Hal Roach, who gave the world 'Our Gang', Laurel & Hardy and Harold Lloyd. Hal was then ninety-eight years old and widely regarded as the Solomon of screen comedy. I asked him if in his judgement any present-day comedian ranked with giants like Chaplin and Keaton. His response was immediate. 'Oh, that would have to be Benny Hill. He's right up there with the best.' He thought for a moment longer and added, 'I just wish he'd clean up his act.'

When I first knew Benny in the late 40s we were both bloody hungry and looking for the next meal. There was no rivalry between comic novices as there often is today. Peter Sellers, Peter Waring, Michael Bentine, George Martin, Terry Scott, Benny and I all pooled information about agents and dates but it was with me that Benny always shared most generously. I think he felt sorry for me and he knew more than anyone else where the best bookings were, what money they'd pay, the best time to go on and how many spots you were expected to do in an evening.

One evening I was in the Nuffield Centre doing free shows for the troops when Benny overheard me moaning to the *Bumper Funbook* comedian, Robert Moreton, about the shortage of cabaret work in London.

'Are you working anywhere next week?'

'Oh, hello, Benny. No, I just finished two weeks at the Ninety-Six, Piccadilly, that paid fourteen quid, but I've nothing ahead of me.'

Benny had his datebook out already and, having torn out a blank page, started scribbling.

'Try the Ridgeway, Hammersmith, but ask to do Sundays when they don't get so pissed and noisy. Have you done the Mildmay? Well, phone Syd Jerome, he books it. He'll pay a fiver plus bus fare. And call this number at the Liberal and Radical Club, Tottenham, ask for Mr Simms and say you can do three spots for a pound and, if he doesn't hang up, say "each".'

'What sort of act do they want, Benny?'

'A bit bluer than you'd do in a variety theatre but keep it simple, play up how young you are and don't give yourself airs,' he advised. 'And look up this bloke. Here's his name and address. He'll pay you half a crown for every new gag you sell him.'

Half a crown is 12½p today. The name was Max Bygraves.

Benny was the next to go on stage in the little theatre, part of a stage-door canteen near Trafalgar Square. It was sponsored by Viscount Nuffield, the philanthropist who had made his millions from Morris and Austin cars and, though it was intended for the benefit of the forces, it also provided us young entertainers with a marvellous nursery.

Most of Benny's act was considered pretty racy in those grey days of post-war austerity. Not that there was much around to laugh at. Britain was short of food, clothing and fuel. Most families were still mourning loved ones lost in the conflict, the blitz had decimated housing and the bitterest winter for fifty years had made 1947 a grim time for everyone, in particular the entertainment business.

Here's Benny being saucy that evening at the Nuffield: 'I'm from Southampton where my family ships cattle. We shipped 9,000 bulls last year. We're the biggest bull-shippers in the business! Nine thousand young bulls! I bet you think that's a load of bullocks!'

'Much too rude for broadcasting, dear boy,' a BBC radio producer told him. 'You need to clean up your act.'

Benny couldn't get on to the wireless no matter how he tried. Radio was the only gateway to national fame in those days and the life of an unknown funnyman was not easy.

Benny once had to pawn his army greatcoat and spend his last few coins getting from his room in Cricklewood to an obscure club in south London where he'd been promised a chance to entertain for a fee of fifteen shillings (75p).

Shivering in his thin, second-hand dress suit, but smartly turned out and carrying his guitar with optimism, he hiked to the Embankment and handed over his pawnshop pennies for the bus fare to Kennington.

119

Halfway there, the bus broke down.

When he reached the club at last, he was turned away because he was too late to perform.

Penniless, he began the ten-mile walk home without an overcoat in the numbing cold. As he crossed Waterloo Bridge a storm broke. Icy rain flattened his carefully combed hair, drenched his clothes and began to disintegrate the cardboard soles of his cheap shoes. His guitar case wasn't waterproof and the contents sloshed.

With his empty stomach rumbling louder than the thunder that doubled the downpour, he staggered along the deserted Strand and up Charing Cross Road.

His tears of despair mingled with the rainwater on his cheeks, his sneezes warned of the flu to come and his entire body began to rebel against the long march that still lay ahead of him. He ached, he had no money, no food, no prospects of any kind. He came to a standstill in the middle of Soho and shuddered with misery. There was a momentary lull in the deluge.

'It was the lowest point in my life,' Benny told me many years later. 'And at that very moment, a tart stepped out of a doorway, chucked me under the chin and said, "Hello, cheeky!"'

By 1954 we were both regularly employed by BBC TV which, while boasting few viewers back then, was creating stars overnight due to the enormous press attention. Publicity was clearly the key to attracting audiences up and down the country and so making money. We put our heads together and decided to set up a running gag. We had a mock feud in public modelled on the success of the apparent enmity between the great American radio comedians, Jack Benny and Fred Allen.

I would make rude remarks about him in my TV and radio appearances, calling him Benny Hell, Belly Hill, the son of Fanny Hill, and generally disparage him with gags like, 'Last night Benny Hill got a laugh and it threw his timing' and 'He always wears a tie, he just never ties it tight enough.'

Benny responded on his shows with names like Boob or Blob Monkhouse and such insults as, 'Bob should go to the doctor and have his brain lanced. Of course, he'll have to pay a search fee.'

The waspish kidding got us easy laughs and free publicity but, although it was working awfully well for us, Benny suddenly stopped doing it. I recognised the signs. Benny had started to happen. He was reaching the viewers in a way that was unique, communicating through the camera at a level of intimacy unequalled by any other new personality. Furthermore, his image was coming through to the public as a cheeky but lovable young man. Insults weren't his line. His BBC TV producer Kenneth Carter was assuring him that he was on his way to becoming a big, big star and instinctively Benny was beginning to separate himself from the rest of show business. I'm sure he was saying to himself, 'Every time I plug Bob I'm putting myself at his level. But I'm going up to a higher level now.' I believe that's why he dropped it, and I dropped it too because he was right. I sensed the same feeling: that Benny was destined to achieve something phenomenal.

As Benny's star ascended, he relished the public's adulation with as much modesty as appeared seemly to him. The television studio was a very comfortable milieu for him where he was popular and in charge. Formal social occasions were a different matter. His discomfort was obvious. His uncertainty about etiquette embarrassed him. He only came once to my home on Loudoun Road, St John's Wood. It was a dinner party with a wide assortment of chatty people but he just couldn't seem to relax. The conversation was largely about theatre and books and Benny made awkward jokes about his ignorance of such things. His laughter rang false and, although he normally drank very little, he must have decided that a cocktail would help him to appear more sophisticated. After two vodka martinis, he got the giggles.

Jackie remembers, 'I was Bob's secretary in those days and Benny began to chat me up. In almost no time at all, during the first course at dinner, he proposed to me quite ardently. He said I was just the sort of wife he'd been searching for. Then between courses he went out into the garden for a breath of fresh air and never came back. Just vanished into the night. The next day he sent me an enormous bouquet of flowers with a contrite note. I spoke to Elizabeth, then Bob's wife, and she said Benny had phoned to apologise and asked her advice as to how he could make amends for his bad behaviour. Later he invited me out one evening and we had a simply marvellous time together. He was charming, attentive and very proper. But the subject of marriage never cropped up again.'

Everyone seemed to be whispering that Benny was homosexual, seemingly based upon his fondness for appearing in drag. The truth is that Benny knew he could get laughs dressed as a woman and that was his sole reason for doing it so often. But the prurient public of the non-permissive 50s and 60s wasn't satisfied with that explanation. They figured that any man who cross-dressed was more than a bit queer.

In truth, anyone more devoted to the pursuit of women I have seldom

known. When he said, 'I'm buying a circular bed so I can sleep around',
he was only partly joking.

His attitude towards women depended on them. If they were classy
ladies, like my Jac, he was courteous and genteel. To girls of a more
accessible kind, he was benevolently predatory.

A very close friend of Benny's told me that his technique for picking
up willing girls was to go and wave his face in the downstairs bar at the
Empire Ballroom, Tottenham Court Road, or the Hammersmith Palais.

He'd nurse an orange juice for as long as it took for him to get recognised. Soon the word would go round: 'Look, there's Benny Hill!' As
soon as he'd got a group of admiring girls around him, he'd sort out the
one he fancied and whisk her off to his flat in Maida Vale. The girls said
that if you owned three pairs of differently coloured knickers – red,
green and black – plus three similar shades in see-through nighties and
one bottle of Max Factor's Primitif perfume, you'd been with Benny
seven times!

One day in the early 80s I taxed Benny with the tale.

'Oh, that's such a long time ago, Bob. I was a bit of a saucy boy in
those days. Weren't we all? But I used to get lots of free stuff from
doing celebrity shop openings. I had a huge stock of lingerie from some
factory I went round and I think all the perfume was discontinued stock
from somewhere or other. But I never got any girl pregnant, I only ever
wanted a little, ah, lip service.'

In a decade when the sexual preferences of Gillian Taylforth and Bill
Clinton have been so explicitly proclaimed, Benny's choice of phrase
seems almost delicate.

The fact is that Benny's sexual relationships were always with
younger females, never older and more demanding women who might
expect more from him than he was willing to give. He was quite frank
about his preferences.

'I like free-and-easy girls who come from working-class back-
grounds like myself. Factory girls, shopgirls and typists. I get a kick out
of taking ordinary girls to places they wouldn't normally visit. I suppose
I want to be a bit of a hero to them, a White Knight. Is that a bad thing?'

No bad thing for his career. Benny's real-life attitude to sex is what
informed his on-screen interpretations.

The men in his shows, most of them absurdly lascivious but frustrated refugees from a Donald McGill seaside postcard, would rather
peep through a keyhole to watch a pretty girl undress than be in the
room with her. Skimpily clothed dancers pranced desirably but unob-
tainably; ugly matrons bullied decrepit husbands; innocently sexy

nurses in tight uniforms and stocking tops tended to randy but impotent old codgers; playful Benny's polka-dotted beach ball became confused with the bottom of a girl wearing a polka-dotted bikini and he got slapped; it was all naughty goings-on of the behind-the-bike-shed kind, fantasies in gymslips without the ugliness of real life intruding to spoil the schoolboy fun.

Benny's intensely personal view of what was funny awoke a sleeping giant of international appreciation.

A total loner, he had a great instinct for what his fans wanted without realising how many millions of them there would be. His songs and lyrics were credited solely to him and, while most of his best ideas were recycled jokes with a long history, his version of them, an expertly paced revue complete with the vital ingredients of smut, innuendo and the occasional fart, were just the fare that so many millions in so many countries craved but couldn't get from more fastidious comedians.

No scriptwriter I know has ever admired Benny's writing. They found it irritatingly unoriginal and repetitive in theme. What they had to admit however was that Benny alone had the gift of taking silent film comedy, mucky music hall jokes, corny puns, old-fashioned sketches and riddles and rhymes and somehow transforming them into a crowd-pleasing formula that defied his critics. Weary anecdotes became energetically played scenes with funny stereotypes recognisable the world over. Novelty songs and doggerel of the kind considered too dated for use were rejuvenated. Slapstick videos whizzed by at treble speed to eccentric music and viewers from Timbuktu to Tennessee could see the joke.

Every show was guaranteed to contain the required quota of vulgarity delivered with Benny's truly inimitable (see Freddie Starr) style, his extravagant makeups and costumes, his mastery of accents and, above all, that grin. Never has a comedian's grin conveyed so much complicity. It tells us that he knows that we know what he knows.

Great comedians aren't normal. Their genius distorts their sanity a little: not enough to make them insane but unsane. Benny called himself 'just a very ordinary, boring normal guy' but his assiduous lifelong dedication to his on-screen persona combined with his passionate attachment to personal solitude set him apart as an endearingly obsessive eccentric.

Benny died as he spent so many of his reclusive years, comfortably slumped on his old flowered sofa in front of his two TV sets and twin video recorders. In spite of his estimated £14 million fortune his rented flat was sparsely furnished, his kitchen empty but for a few sandwiches and bottles of inexpensive wine. His world was a fantasy one, needing no actual trappings of wealth. In his mind, troupes of gorgeous girls were still unable to keep their hands off him and if they didn't really show up, well, that left his imaginings intact and unspoiled by reality.

The newspapers called him lonely. That's the wrong word, carrying overtones of sadness and friendlessness. He just liked his own company. He was isolated by choice.

In 1989 Benny's TV series was dropped by Thames, the company for which he had generated a massive fortune. If Benny was hurt he was also silently resigned to changing circumstances. He knew Thames was right.

Over twenty-one years they'd assembled a tremendous stock of his programmes that could continue in distribution for years. New shows meant new money would have to be invested and Benny's shows were costing more than any comparable product. And lastly, British TV was facing a very uncertain future with deregulation about to test the company's manoeuvrability to the utmost. Benny told Thames not to worry, he'd be just fine, thank you.

The press preferred a different version of events: Benny had been cruelly axed, the old clown had a broken heart behind the painted smile, and even he didn't seem to grasp the awful truth: that his reason for living had vanished overnight. Articles pointed out that Benny had always feared and detested personal appearances, eschewed cabaret and stage work, and was no longer excited by his solo jaunts to Marseilles and Bangkok. His spiritual home was at the Thames TV studios and he'd been locked out. Benny was a rejected hermit, they said. You can occasionally see such comments printed even today.

The fact is, news of the split from Thames had Benny fending off a feeding frenzy of offers from Australia, Holland, France and the USA. He appeared to overwhelming acclaim at the International Emmy Awards ceremony in New York and was fêted by companies anxious to finance his future shows. When he came back to Thames's Teddington studios to make his US-backed productions, the doors were open wide. Only one cloud had appeared in his blue sky. He was being criticised by the very people he'd always admired and tried to help – comedians.

A handful of newly popular comics, dubbed 'alternative', dismissed his comedy as chauvinistic and racist. One tiro in particular told the public that he could find nothing funny in Benny's little old men chasing girls round the park when the incidence of rape was up 45 per cent. Placid Benny was stirred into defending himself despite finding the criticism hard to understand.

'First of all, my comedy doesn't demean woman, if anything it glorifies lovely girls in a way that's time-honoured from Ziegfeld to the *Folies Bergère*. If I chased pretty girls that wouldn't make me a dirty old man, just a silly old man. In actual fact, I never chase girls round the park. I try to flirt but I make a mess of it. The entire premise is that my male characters fail in their pursuit. I don't downgrade women; just the opposite, they downgrade me. On my shows it's always the men who suffer, never the girls. The girls score off us every time. We're always the losers. And it's me who gets chased by a vengeful mob at the end of each show. As for racism, my Frenchman and Japanese and other foreigners are always superior to their English counterparts. If I'm racist it's at the expense of the British.'

The last time I saw Benny was at the Teddington studios about six months before his death. We stood in the foyer and reminisced for ten minutes or so.

'Funny, isn't it?' he said. 'When you and I started in this game, you couldn't make jokes about politics and the church. Now we can't make jokes about women and race. All these politically correct geezers have done is change the taboos!'

'They'll learn, Benny. We did.'

'I suppose.'

We shook hands and parted, me on my way to tape a Des O'Connor show, he returning to his riverside flat. At the doorway he turned and showed me that twinkling grin. 'New is easy,' he called out. 'Funny is hard!'

## Monday, 6 February 1995
Kathryn and Colin Edmonds, Jac and I explore Bridgetown and stop at Fisherman's Wharf to grab a touristy lunch and raise a glass to Jimmy Tarbuck, fifty-five years old today.

Jimmy Tarbuck's crowd-pleasing technique begins with his ability to exude goodwill and mockery simultaneously. At the banquet held to honour Bruce Forsyth's fiftieth year as an entertainer, Tarbuck rose to his feet with an expansive gesture as if to encompass all in friendship. He started off slowly and emphatically to give import to his words:

'We're here tonight . . . to honour one of the great men of show business, a man of principle, a man of love for his fellow man, a man of dignity and human decency – but enough about Harry Secombe. Tonight let's talk about this long-chinned prat over here, right!

'Possibly one of the greatest entertainers of our generation. Now that's not only my opinion, that's Bruce's. And in celebration of his fifty

125

years he's doing a week on Broadway . . . and he's very big in Hammersmith and I wish him the best of luck.

'Bruce, you started off your career as the Mighty Atom and look at you now – the Nackered Neutron!

'What can you say about Bruce? The first thing to go's usually your eyes, with Bruce it was the hair. But it hasn't all gone. Some of it's still in a drawer at Wentworth and I think he lent the rest of it to Roy.'

Roy Castle, regrowing his hair since losing it during chemotherapy, joined in the laughter as Tarbuck suckered the crowd again by resuming the semblance of genuine admiration.

'Bruce is a generous man. We were out in the West End, me and Lynchie and Bruce, many, many years ago and Bruce was so generous . . . but cautious, a cautious man. We passed a club, a spiv came out, he went, "'Ere we are, chaps, Kipper, Tarby, Brucie, in you come!" he said. "A bird for the night, a pie and a pint for a fiver!" Well, me and Lynchie were right down the stairs. Bruce said, "Hang on, lads, hang on, hang on, there's a catch here. Whose pies are they?" Now anyway I'll tell ya . . .

'He was born at home in north London. His mother saw him. And *she* moved to the hospital. But let's go back to his early days. Bernard Delfont discovered him in an all-nude revue . . . and then put him in the stage musical *Little Me*.

'People ask me on many occasions, "What's he like to play golf with?" Well, I'll tell you from the heart. He is the most miserable, moaning bastard God has ever put life into on the golf course!'

Now Tarby does his impression of Bruce's famous dithering sound, the one that every impressionist gives thanks for – a kind of 'va-va-va-va-va-va'. The audience loves it, so he repeats it.

'You go to his house, he's got a bloody dog going va-va-va-va-va-va! But, Bruce, you are fun at times. I have to go back thirty years ago when a very nervous young man was going on at the Palladium. Bruce, you were in charge that night when I came on that show and you'll always be in charge.'

Once again Tarby had shone brighter than his material. The old crowd-pleaser had pleased everyone. We wish him Happy Birthday and many more years of laughter.

## Wednesday, 8 February 1995

Not many people get to meet their heroes; even fewer get the chance to interview them. I was lucky because it was his birthday and he was in an expansive mood despite an injury that had his leg in plaster. We sat in the Polo Lounge of the Beverly Hills Hotel on this day in 1975. He was just fifty but pointed out that that was only ten Celsius.

There are only three men who have been nominated eight times or more for Best Actor and/or Best Supporting Actor by the Motion Picture Academy. Two are Laurence Olivier and Spencer Tracy. The third is Jack Lemmon.

He was voted Best Supporting Actor in 1955 for his role as Ensign Pulver in *Mister Roberts* and a week later the thirty-one-year-old actor was observed driving down Sunset Boulevard in a red Thunderbird with the Oscar on the front seat beside him. He quipped, 'Maybe if I win another one some day I'll get my ears pierced.'

He was nominated Best Actor for his performance in two Billy Wilder films, *Some Like It Hot* in 1959 and *The Apartment* in 1960, and again in 1962 for *Days of Wine and Roses*. Emceeing the Academy Awards in 1963, he reflected his own emotions during previous ceremonies when he announced the Best Actor category by saying, 'We're in the adrenalin section.'

Firmly established at these ceremonies by now, Lemmon's recognition as a great comedian was further endorsed by his selection to present special awards to a speechless Charles Chaplin in 1971 and a tearful Groucho Marx in 1973, the year of Lemmon's Best Actor Oscar for his portrayal of a menopausal garment-factory owner in *Save the Tiger*.

Nominated again for Best Actor in 1979's *The China Syndrome*, he racked up his eighth nomination for *Missing* in 1982.

A more complete list of Lemmon's films would underline the wide range of his work, encompassing the lightest of light comedy to the darkest of dramas. Does he decide this is his year for funny and next year he's going to make us cry?

'No, Bob, I have no preference. It's just a part that either grabs you or it doesn't. If, say, Paul Newman and I read the same script he might say, "Oh, man, I love that part" while I'm saying, "I dunno, it just doesn't grab me."

'See, it might be that I've already played aspects of it or the character's too much like someone I've played before, whereas for Paul it's new and different. That's what both of us are always looking for – something different. Then again I might go ape shit over a part that he'd turn down. So I don't care whether it's funny or serious; either way, what it has to be is a part that appeals to me.'

Most performers who are able to play both comedy and drama extremely well usually say that comedy is harder. Lemmon says he only knows certain aspects of why this is so.

'There's a certain embarrassment that occurs when you do comedy for an audience. Live in front of a theatre audience, you depend on the feedback. Occasionally you set up a joke, do it and nothing happens, they don't react. And there you are, you and the audience, both a little bit embarrassed. You've misfired somehow and they know it. You haven't dropped an egg, you've dropped an omelette and it's just lying there. You signalled to them that you expected them to laugh and they're aware that they didn't. There's a loss of mutual confidence. It can take you five minutes to get them back. But it's different with a dramatic scene when it goes adrift. You can hear them moving around a little bit, that tight wire between you and the audience may have a little slack in it, but what you're doing still holds a little interest so it works. That fact alone makes doing drama less complicated.'

That's plainly so in the theatre, where actors are tuned to the moods of the audience and can time their lines to accommodate laughter or its absence. But Lemmon has made his worldwide reputation on celluloid. How does he anticipate the behaviour of cinema audiences as they watch a performance which he had to create for the camera without the guidance of their reactions?

'Early on I learned from a few films that were not cut well, poorly edited, that you cannot count on a laugh and you cannot time a laugh on film unless, like Billy Wilder, you are smart enough to fill the moments with something very legitimate. So that, if the laugh is not there, the scene still carries, it still has energy, and you are still behaving believably during the space left for the interruption of laughter.'

His flow was interrupted as a waiter brought fresh drinks.

Lemmon came to comedy without seeking it. Fresh out of his late wartime service on an aircraft carrier as a communications officer, his mercurial, almost neurotic, acting style seemed to make him suitable for tortured, lost and angry characterisations in his early theatrical career. Then in 1949 he was cast in a TV series called 'That Wonderful Guy' as an ambitious but frustrated actor who becomes the clumsy valet of a snooty drama critic. He was more popular than the show and from 1950 he spent the greater part of six years in equally forgettable TV sitcoms playing opposite his first wife, Cynthia Stone.

Clips from 'Heaven for Betsy' and 'The Couple Next Door' display all Lemmon's key mannerisms, the fast-talking, double-taking, stuttering swings from self-assurance to panic, the explosive indignation and rat-a-tat delivery that have filled his comic output ever since.

Theatrical work enlarged his power to control, contain and exploit the moods of live audiences and taught him to modify and refine his great reserves of energy. By the time Columbia signed him for movies, he had all his assets well in hand and could easily relax into allowing his good nature to warm his first big screen roles and charm public and critics alike.

Lemmon's likeable charisma gave him the star presence to match Judy Holliday's comic strengths both in *It Should Happen To You*, all about a daffy/wise girl who fulfils a crazy ambition to see her name on a giant advertising hoarding, and *Phffft*, a farce about divorce.

Some of his films were bad but everyone liked Lemmon. Meanwhile he learned more and more about his art and ability alongside such stars as Kim Novak and Ernie Kovacs, helping them to raise the quality of such plain stuff as *You Can't Run Away From It, Operation Mad Ball* and *The Notorious Landlady*. What he needed was a 24-carat film role worthy of his comic power.

The first of his Oscars came as a result of striking just such gold in the part of the hilariously unstable Ensign Pulver in *Mister Roberts*.

'Oh, once I had seen the stage production I was dying to play that part, literally more than any part I've ever wanted at any time in my entire professional career. John Ford was directing a picture at Columbia called *The Long Gray Line* starring Tyrone Power. In this movie a guy at West Point, a janitor or something, aged from his twenties to eighty. I was shooting my first film with Judy Holliday at the time and the studio made me test for the eighty-year-old man. Made me do it, a waste of time. While I finished off my picture with Judy, the kid who was running the daily rushes for Ford tacked my test on the end. So here's Ford sitting in the rushes apparently, first he's looking at Ty Power's scenes, then all of a sudden comes my test and now he's looking at me aged twenty-seven trying to play this old guy!'

The memory sets him shaking with laughter.

'Well, I was told it was absolutely terrible, Ford couldn't believe what he was looking at. The lights came up and he says, "What the hell was that? Who was that?"'

'And Jerry Wald was there, one of the top men at Columbia, and he says, "I don't know why they put that on there, it's a mistake. It's a kid who just made a film here with Judy Holliday, his name's Jack Lemmon and we just tested him to check his range."'

'God's truth, Ford said, "Well, I'll tell you something! He's a God-awful old man but he might make a very good Pulver!" How did he know? He'd never seen me before. But he saw something there, underneath a ton of makeup and white hair, that he liked and I owe my first great part to that mistake in rushes.'

I mention that Ford, one of the greatest of American film directors, was not known for comedy.

'Well, that brings me back to the problem of comedy timing on film even with the best of producers and directors who've done everything else except comedy. Remember the soapsuds scene?'

No one who's ever seen *Mister Roberts* could forget the soapsuds scene. The frantically unreliable Pulver, destined eventually to toss the hated captain's equally hated potted palm into the ocean, blows up the ship's laundry with fulminate of mercury.

As naval officers William Powell and Henry Fonda stand helpless, a tremendous explosion rocks the hold and Pulver totters out of the laundry, smothered from head to toe in soap bubbles. He has a speech of only a few lines but each line has been shown to score a big laugh in the theatrical production of the play.

'Oh, each line is a gem! He's just caused a catastrophe and his first words are *"THAT STUFF'S TERRIFIC!"* And the audience screams. It's so funny because this idiot should be anything but enthusiastic. But he goes on raving about the explosion with lines like *"It was a winter wonderland! Oh, God, you should have seen it!"* It's a comic aria and we shoot it and it's fine. Now they see it and they say, "Oh, boy, we've really got something funny here, but they're going to miss a lot of the lines because they'll be laughing."

'So they make us shoot it again at half-speed, like you could take a funny record and slow it down. They said, "Take time in between the lines." Well, I was getting a stomach ache trying to do this, it was illegitimate. It was bad acting. I'd do a laugh line, then I'd try to shake the bubbles off, do the next line, then fill in the gap with catching my breath and making hand gestures, do the next line and so forth. We shot it that way, horrible, and then a third way *even slower*, OK?

'They previewed it using the slowest way. Zero. The audience laughed once and then it just took an interminable length of time.

'Second preview – and I did not see these previews, thank God – they used the second-slowest one, so the people could still hear all the words. Still not good, not funny because not real. Finally they gave in and used the first version, the fast-paced version where, if you miss a line, it doesn't matter because it's all happening and it's funny.

'From then on I'd learned something. This was only my third or fourth movie and I hadn't felt I could argue with very experienced men. But now I knew a big secret – that if the audience loses lines because they're laughing, there's nothing better than that, you should suffer from such a disease the rest of your life!'

Lemmon's fascination with technique may have begun with his orderly early life, formal education and naturally enquiring mind.

His was a comfortable upper middle-class background in the Boston area. He attended Phillips Andover Academy and Harvard. With this background, the need to stand up and perform may have been an involuntary act of gentle rebellion against comfortable conformity.

'It started when I was about seven or eight years old. I can remember, vividly, the day. A boy called Billy was a pal, a kid up the street, we still communicate as a matter of fact, and he was playing a part in a little one-act play they were going to put on at our school lunchtime, the Rivers Country Day School it was. That morning Billy is sick so when I get to school the teacher says, "You'll have to take Billy's place."

'He has one speech, about eight or ten lines. It isn't quite up to the soapsuds scene but . . . I learn it. Then I have to put on Bill's black Western hat and Billy's a big kid so the hat comes down to the ears. I'm in trouble already. The cape that came down below his knees, it's Marie Antoinette's train on me!

'I walked out, can hardly see with the hat coming down to my nose, the cape trailing behind me, and the first thing I hear is a laugh. It's great. I try to say my lines, some Edgar A. Guest poem or other –

*Somebody said that it couldn't be done . . .*

– then I went up, "dried" you call it, so I walked up to the wings to get a prompt, got it, walked back to centre stage -

*But he with a chuckle replied . . .*

Boom! They go! So now I fake forgetting my next line, do the walk, get my prompt, walk back. Well, they're in hysterics, the kids and the parents and everyone. So I kept it up for four lines and they're screaming and I guess one of two things would have had to have happened there that day. Either I would never go back on a stage again, never, never . . . or, thank God, a little bulb switched on in my head and something told me, *"Do it! Do it again!!"*

'I blew every stinking line of that recitation and the laugh kept going and going – well, I was a hero! I started telling jokes in between classes, I was making up things, I found I could imitate Mae West, W.C. Fields, I would do bits, they would all start coming to me now.

'I had found a way so that I could be accepted by all the other kids. Up till that day I was really very, very shy.'

131

Once more we have found the socially timid child who discovers a knack with manipulation that leads to approval. It's a pattern that repeats itself throughout my lifelong exploration of the comic mind.

Young Lemmon borrowed 300 dollars from his father to go to New York City in the hope of making it on the stage. The stake lasted a long time.

As recently as 1992, while in New York to film *Glengarry Glen Ross*, he began his first day of shooting at the China Bowl on 44th Street.

He looked across the street at an unfamiliar building and clearly recalled the structure that had once stood there, the very first place he had lived when he'd come from Boston 'to save the New York theatre', the Hotel Lennox, just up from the Hudson.

'It was seventy-five cents or a buck a night. So my dad's money went a long way. I ate cheaply and it must have been eighteen months before I started to make any real money. That was in radio soap opera. Then television got bigger in New York, that was a big break. I got fired a lot in radio, then I got a lead. I got passed over in theatre auditions, then I got another lead. Same thing with television: no one wanted me and then I got a lead part on Kraft Playhouse.'

It was a ripoff from *Charley's Aunt* called *The Arrival of Kitty* and was the only time Lemmon worked in a dress until Wilder's *Some Like It Hot*. Since he didn't enjoy the TV experience greatly, what persuaded Lemmon to accept a part that required him to play in drag for most of a major film?

'If it had not been Billy Wilder, well I would have had the courtesy to at least read the script but done so with misgivings. But with Billy, I didn't hesitate, I immediately said yes. Months later, sixty to seventy pages came. I was reading it lying on my couch and I started to laugh so hard I actually fell off on to the floor. That script has got to be *the* model for young writers in comedy to read and dissect. Not just because of its funny lines but because of its construction, the development of the characters, the way Billy and Izzy Diamond make the lines serve the storyline and the different actors so perfectly.

'With such writers and others I've been lucky enough to work with, like Neil Simon and Larry Gelbart, there's one trait that sets them apart. It's not just what they write, it's what they don't write. It's down to the bone.

'You might as well start ad-libbing Shakespeare as alter one syllable of those economical lines. I've done seven films with Billy and he doesn't let you change lines or fool around. You don't want to, you don't have to. And if by mistake I've happened to blow my line a little bit, to add a word or leave one out, it hasn't worked, the rhythm's gone.'

Lemmon speaks with respect of the comedic ability of Marilyn Monroe.

'She could use what talent she had as fully as any actor I've ever known. We never get to use all our talents in one go. If we get to use 80 per cent we're lucky. And in flashes, sometimes "bang", in that one take, that one night in the theatre when it all comes together and you're electric! But you can't do it each time. And Marilyn had an uncanny ability to use whatever it was that made Marilyn Monroe live to this day. She's still the star she created – and she did create it, somebody didn't do it for her. And I think she did have a good sense of how to do comedy. A nice feel for exaggeration. Natural rhythms.'

Back on to the subject of timing, Lemmon checks his watch.

'The secret of comedy, right? Always leave 'em wanting more.'

Of course I want more. But there's another secret of comedy: know when to get off.

## Saturday, 25 February 1995

This evening I get heckled. I'm in the middle of my seventy-five-minute cabaret at the Willows, Salford, and the place is packed. Cannon and Ball have a table and they are generously applauding and laughing, the crowd is equally responsive and all's going well. I come to a gag that needs a pause in the middle to make it effective. That's when the heckler strikes:

*''OW MUCH LONGER?'*

It's one of four women at a side table. I've heard them talking but not so loud that it was worth my stopping to deal with it.

*'Sorry, madam, what was your question?'*
*'I SAID "'OW MUCH LONGER?"'*
*'About another inch since I turned fourteen.'*

Over the laughter, she shouts again.

*'WE WANT TO TALK! FINISH UP AND GO!'*

The people around her are shushing her and a bouncer is on his way from the back, but I'm enjoying myself.

133

> *'Madam, do you make this much noise when you're*
> *making love?'*
> *'NO!'*
> *'Then will someone please start screwing her?'*

I cue the musicians and they play a loud introduction for my version of 'Tie a Yellow Ribbon Round the Old Oak Tree'. This covers the distraction of the bouncer escorting the heckler outside.

Hoary-handed old club comedians like me often have to use the strength of mucky gags to quash the disruption of a really hostile heckler, although there are a dozen ways to handle a dozen different kinds of interruption.

Sometimes it's fun to ask the person to repeat what they've said and pretend that it's brilliant, asking the audience if they'd like to hear him say it again. It's never wise to hit a drunk with harsh insults because everyone quite likes a drunk. It's necessary to tickle him along amiably until he starts to annoy the other customers. Then you can bring out your squelchers:

> *You could be a stand-up comedian if you were funny and if you*
> *could stand up!*
> *Tell me, have you ever considered freezing yourself until they*
> *find a cure?*
> *Keep shouting so the bouncers will know where to find you.*

Sometimes the hecklers win.

I attended a business seminar once. I listened to the speakers during the day so that I could refer to the points they made during my own speech after dinner that evening.

During one boring and monotonous lecture, a young man at a front table rose and slowly walked out. The speaker paused and scowled. A voice called out, 'Don't mind Harry, he often walks in his sleep!'

## Saturday, 4 March 1995

My sort of comedy relies largely on picking the right targets. First and foremost comes oneself; the more you knock yourself, the more you gain the right to have a pop at others. Next come the newsworthy names of the day, being careful not to affront your audience's sympathies. The less popular the figure, the bigger the reaction. With this in mind, Colin Edmonds has written a fine sketch for me to do on 'Noel's House Party' today. I appear as Robert Maxwell complete with bushy eyebrows, a vast waistline and a pension-funded takeover bid for Noel Edmonds's country mansion in Crinkly Bottom. I want to put in a couple of cracks at Maxwell's sons but Colin's concerned that this might amount to slander.

If co-writers agree on everything, one of you is redundant. It's only through reasoned argument that the material you are producing improves to your eventual, mutual satisfaction. That doesn't mean shouting matches. You have to respect your colleague's opinion or else find a new partner. Of course, when you're both sure that your view is the right one, it can become an interlocking dictatorship. But there's always a solution to each dispute. Here we are, in disagreement about a comedy routine. Time did not allow for a standoff; the show was due to go on the air live in an hour or so. He had a point but then I had a point. The answer was a compromise – because that's the shortest distance between two points.

So I only did one crack about the Maxwell brothers ('They're trying to float a loan, which is more than I can do') and the five-minute routine with Noel was a riot.

Three days later the BBC's Head of Light Entertainment circulated a memo forbidding any more comedy references to the Maxwell family. Ah, well, there's another target pulled out of range. Next time I'll come on the show as Saddam Hussein.

## Friday, 10 March 1995

I'm in a cinema in a north London suburb burbling all I know about eight Oscar-winning films to a camera. These four-minute introductions will be used to showcase an octet of features that copped an Academy Award for Best Film of the Year due to be screened by UK Gold. The satellite station and I like each other. They like me because they are attracting good ratings by re-running my six years of doing 'Bob's Full House' and I like them because they're paying me lots of money for doing bugger all.

Come to think of it though, a huge amount of work went into creating that bingo-based quiz show that became a cornerstone of BBC 1's Saturday night viewing figures from 1984 to 1990. All we had to go on was a sheet of foolscap with a sketchy set of rules that needed a total overhaul and some pretty drawings of bingo cards in primary colours. We had to build a format from the ground up, and it wasn't easy.

We almost took up residence in the BBC's Acton rehearsal rooms, spending all day long exploring ways to make the game work in a manageable number of rounds of increasing suspense.

After four months of such experimentation I was starting to forget what variations we'd tried and which we had yet to attempt and reject. Jim Moir spent a weekend thinking it over and came into the BBC's Acton rehearsal rooms with a beaming smile on Monday morning.

'Good morning, guv'nor! Here's the plan!' he announced and sat on a bentwood chair that creaked under his rotundity. 'Six contestants have a choice of bingo card with either 60 or 30 numbers on each, leaving either 30 or 60 blank spaces. You offer a choice of 15 questions and they have to get two answers right to qualify for the card of their choice, the 60 or the 30. If they go for the 30 they're penalised by missing every other question because with only half the 60 they have a 50 per cent higher chance of scoring the first four numbers in the corners, right? And if they choose the 60 then they have to get every four answers right in a row or else they get penalised by not being allowed to answer another question until all the other five contestants have answered a question but not necessarily correctly. That's your first round sorted.'

I said, 'Right. Um – could you explain that last part again, Jim?'

'Which part do you mean?'

'The part that came after "Good morning, guv'nor, here's the plan."'

## Saturday, 11 March 1995

Two days ago I had a charming letter asking me what I knew about the first Doctor Who. Today I wrote this reply:

Dear Jessica Carney,

Congratulations on finding a publisher! If the following is of any use to you, please feel free to use it.

My first knowledge of William Hartnell is that of a mere picture-goer, spellbound in the darkness of my local Odeon or Gaumont, watching his gritty portrayals of small-time crooks and hard-as-nails sergeants throughout the 30s and 40s. After seeing *The Way Ahead*, and later *Brighton Rock*, I was a fan.

By 1957 I'd been a professional performer myself for ten years and, at the age of twenty-nine, was one of TV's new comedy stars. The British film industry, while hating television, was not averse to recruiting its latest attractions to boost flagging cinema attendances.

Producer Peter Rogers sent me the script of *Carry On Sergeant* and invited me to play the juvenile lead, £1,500 for five weeks' work. Wonderful – and, of course, I'd get top billing? Ah, no, you see, that's been guaranteed to the actor playing the eponymous hero, William Hartnell.

Well, I argued and reasoned and blustered to get my name above the much more experienced and recognisable player but to no good effect.

To some bad effect, however. Bill Hartnell had been informed about my demand and didn't like my uppishness one little bit.

From the first day of filming he made it quite clear that he had it in for me. During the rehearsal of scenes together he would pause after I spoke my lines, shake his head a little in mild disbelief, sigh, and look at director Gerald Thomas with a bleak air of expectation. Gerry would feel obliged to ask me to do something else with the words, to add more reality or speak faster or slower. I don't think Gerry knew what Bill was finding wrong with my efforts but he just had to respond somehow to the implicit disapproval from such a seasoned actor.

Of course, my reaction to Bill's coldness was typical of me. I tried everything I could think of to get into his good books, fetching him cups of tea (often refused and, if accepted, with poor grace), telling him anecdotes (they got the fish eye), plaguing him with questions about his film roles (he couldn't remember, it was too long ago, it was a rotten part, it was a lousy picture, he didn't want to talk about it, OK?)

I earned Bill's further contempt by being unable to carry out some of the exercises required during scenes of basic training on the army camp, shot in the paddock behind Pinewood Studios. Notably, my arms didn't support my weight when I had to swing over a mudhole on a rope. The only thing I did that made him laugh was to fall into the mud three times in a row, only to be hosed down and told to try again. I never could do it and was the only one of the troop absent from that scene.

After four weeks I'd given up trying to make friends with Bill. Then I asked the producer for a day off due to a bereavement. They continued shooting scenes that didn't involve me and I returned the following day.

Between shots I walked away from the set, not wanting to talk to anyone. I must have looked very mournful as I sat alone at a table in the corner of the bar at lunchtime, staring into a whisky. I had just downed it when a hand placed another glass of Scotch beside me. I looked up at Bill.

'Do you mind if I join you? I hear you lost your dad. Were you very close to him? No? What went wrong then?'

I found myself pouring out the story of my estrangement from my parents when I'd married eight years earlier. Bill encouraged me to tell him everything, how my mother had disowned me and how she influenced my father into doing the same.

My misery over never having achieved a reconciliation before my father's heart failure obviously affected Bill. Twice he put his hand on my arm as a comforting gesture. By the time he'd finished getting the whole story out of me, there was no time to eat lunch.

'I'm so sorry, Bill, I couldn't eat anyway but I've made you miss your meal.'

'No one makes me do anything, son. Listen to me for a moment. Your mum and dad were sadly mistaken when they cut you out of their lives. As a result, they've missed a lot of joy and pride in what you've achieved. Right now you're feeling sorry for yourself but you shouldn't. The sorrow you should be feeling is for your dad and what he lost, what he had to do without for the past eight years. Think fondly of him, poor chap, because he got it wrong. But think of this too – I'll bet that man's quietly followed every step of your career and silently cheered you on. Now . . .'

He stood up and finished his drink.

'. . . let's see if this bloody film is good enough to make your mum so thrilled with you she'll come round at last.'

I thanked him.

'No, don't do that, I don't want thanks. I don't do anything to be thanked. Tell you what I want. A letter from you one day, telling me you've made it up with your mum. I'd like that.'

In 1968 I wrote that letter to Bill. I still think of him with gratitude. But I was careful not to thank him.

Yours very sincerely,

Bob Monkhouse

## Wednesday, 22 March – Sunday, 26 March 1995

We go to Las Vegas with our closest friends, Dodie and Dave Ismay. We have adjoining suites at the Mirage overlooking the man-made volcano which erupts spectacularly every twenty minutes. The food on the plane has me doing the same. Indigestion sends me to sleep.

I'm recovered on Thursday and we do a round of the other hotels, deciding that ours and Caesar's Palace are the best of the bunch. We have a ghastly Chinese dinner at the MGM Grand before seeing Rita

Rudner and Dennis Miller on stage. As you probably know, I avoid using four-letter words in my act. Miller, on the other hand, must have used the f-word thirty fucking times.

Next day we roam around the MGM Grand Adventures, a sort of mini-Disneyland operation with rides and shops and fast food outlets. Jac funks a helicopter trip over Grand Canyon but encourages the rest of us to go and we love it, gazing down into the red-brown fissures and steep gorges cut by the Colorado river into the high plateau of north Arizona, marvelling at the broad, intricately sculptured chasm that contains between its outer walls a multitude of imposing peaks and buttes, of canyons within canyons and complex ramifying gulches and ravines.

We enjoy a wonderful if expensive lobster dinner at Rosebank, the best food in town, before seeing the Cirque de Soleil's stunning show *Mystère* at Treasure Island Hotel.

Saturday takes us to the Rio Hotel for a fishy lunch with too much garlic in it. Thence to the jet-black, pyramid-shaped Luxor where we watch a special-effects-packed, sci-fi movie about some supernatural crystal on a screen as big as a vertical football pitch. It's so incomprehensible I wish I had indigestion again.

In the evening we see Michael Crawford in *EFX*, a lavishly mounted stage musical about magic with giant fire-breathing dragons, a 3-D movie of time travel and fantastic theatrical trickery with Michael leaping, flying and scaling a cliff face. We see him afterwards and ask him how long he can keep up this incredibly strenuous role.

'Oh, you know me. Pushing the envelope's a habit. And you know what habit's like, it starts out as a thread.' He shrugs and grins helplessly. 'As new threads are added it becomes a rope you can't break.'

Alas, there will be no rope to save Michael in a few month's time when he falls and suffers extensive injuries.

We have a fine lunch at Koko Mo in our hotel, look at the famous white tigers on show in a huge, comfortable lair behind plate glass and then see them again in the spectacular magic show presented by Siegfried and Roy, or 'Seek and Destroy' as Dave prefers to call them.

As our wives wisely retire, he and I end our Las Vegas visit on a low note, taking in a late-night and poorly attended performance at the Comedy Store. The comedians are lacklustre and boring. 'Their careers are so far off course,' comments Dave, 'they don't need an agent, they want a St Bernard.'

## Monday, 27 March – Thursday, 30 March 1995
Leaving Las Vegas it seemed as if all the flying routines about frightful

airlines that Dave and I have done over the years had all come true at once. Why had they told us to check in at the gate half an hour before departure time? For our own good, we reckoned – the sooner you check in, the sooner you know about the delay.

We had an hour's wait without explanation or apology. I think they were waiting for the glue to dry on the wings.

The food was served by an air hostess who could have sold her leg hair to wigmakers. We had a tough piece of cold chicken but Dave had asked for the vegetarian meal. He was given, and I'm not kidding you, a plastic bag of carrots, unpeeled and apparently unwashed. He nearly led a passenger insurrection. The airline was Continental, by the way.

We checked into New York's Parker Meridien Hotel where a French receptionist, indifferent to the point of hostility, was unable to find our reservations in her computer. After a long delay in the foyer, an equally haughty colleague located our booking and we were shown to rooms instead of the suite we had requested. We sat watching the Oscars ceremony on TV feeling as if we deserved an award too.

Tuesday had us all going our separate ways, Dave and Dodie having their own shopping agenda, Jac seeking Easter eggs, tapers and napkin rings (don't ask!) and me on my usual Manhattan expedition round the bookstores, video shops and those identical New York electronic boutiques with desperate sales clerks who would sell you the pacemaker out of their grandmother's ribcage.

After an early dinner at our favourite Italian restaurant, Il Tinetto (you can find a pearl in your oyster and still only break even), Judy from Andrew Lloyd-Webber's Really Useful Group provided four tickets to splendid seats at the Minskoff to see Glenn Close in *Sunset Boulevard*, a production superior to London's due in great part to the star's use of comedy to relieve the Gothic gloom.

Rain misted the air next day and the warm winds that had gusted through the canyons of the skyscrapers yesterday turned Wednesday into great weather for microbes.

We continued our buy-till-you-die policy until a wonderful and wildly expensive Chinese dinner at Tse Yang, 34, East 51st Street. We remembered Rita Rudner's gag on my BBC 2 chat show in the 80s: 'They don't even have prices on the menu, just pictures of faces with different expressions of horror.'

Dave and I left our wives at the hotel and looked in on Rodney Dangerfield's club but the comedians we saw were deeply unfunny and we felt pretty good about that.

The Stage Delicatessen provided us with one of the great lunches next day and I asked a waiter about another restaurant I once visited on Broadway but now couldn't find called the Parker Suite.

'Sure, my brother worked there for a while. It's long gone.'

So's the man I had a meal with there over thirty years ago. Shame.

I got to know Sammy Davis Jnr when he did cabaret at the Pigalle, a favourite 50s nightspot that flourished in Piccadilly for a decade or so. Our mutual enthusiasm for everything to do with motion pictures led to our lifelong competition to outwit each other with obscure Hollywood facts and quotes. Sammy would throw me a line of dialogue like, 'Stop smoking in here!'

I might have been stymied but for the fact that Sammy couldn't resist doing the lines in a perfect imitation of the original speaker. His Bud Abbott was spot on. Thus clued up, I'd do my Lou Costello, 'Who's smoking?'

'You are.'

'What makes you think that?'

'You have a cigar in your mouth.'

'I've got shoes on but I'm not walking!'

Then I'd have to supply the origin, easy in this instance: '1948, *Abbot and Costello Meet Frankenstein*.'

Sammy wasn't so lucky with my questions due to my lack of ability as an impressionist but he could safely rely upon his phenomenal knowledge of movie dialogue.

Over the ensuing years, whenever we met we would greet one another with a movie quote. Two or three times Sammy phoned my London home from America and the first thing I'd hear would be Bob Hope's voice saying, 'What has Casanova got that if I had I probably couldn't handle anyway?' or Ginger Rogers's husky mutter, 'Must have been tough on your mother not having any children.' (Quotes from *Casanova's Big Night*, 1954, and *42nd Street*, 1933.)

In 1964 I was in New York acquiring some rights to silent comedy films for my TV series 'Mad Movies' and I happened to pass this restaurant on Broadway called the Parker Suite. Sitting at a table by a first-floor window I could see Sammy.

I ran up the stairs and crossed to his table with no thought in my mind except the movie quote with which I intended to stump him. I'd just watched a 1952 comedy on TV called *Abbott and Costello Meet Captain Kidd*. In it, an innkeeper says, 'Are you stupid? A nincompoop? Moronic? Idiotic? Imbecilic? What are you laughing at?' and Costello replies, 'You went right by me and didn't know it!'

Sammy looked up from his plate and was confronted with me,

141

breathless with exertion and obviously excited. 'Are you stupid?' I began. 'A nincompoop? Moronic? Idiotic? Imbec—?'

I got no further.

A massive hand on my shoulder spun me round and I was raised off the floor and propelled forward through the restaurant, my feet flailing uselessly, taken to the top of the staircase and lifted higher in preparation for being pitched down it.

Thank God Sammy was a very nimble man, otherwise he might not have reached my assailant before my suitability as a stuntman was put to the test. I heard him shouting, 'No, Cal! No, don't do it! I know this guy! He's OK!'

The mountainous man who had hauled me across the room without effort now released me and used his gigantic hands to fuss with my rumpled clothing, smoothing it down apologetically, as Sammy gasped through his laughter, 'Bob, I'm sorry but I've had death threats from the Klan. I only hired Cal yesterday. He thought you were an assassin!'

'Sidney Poitier, *The Defiant Ones*, 1958?' I asked hopefully.

As we sat and ate our food Sammy laughed on and off for the next hour. When he laughed he shook with uncontrollable joy as if he'd just swallowed a pneumatic drill and enjoyed the taste. It's a vivid memory and I treasure it.

## Friday, 31 March – Saturday, 22 April 1995

We departed JFK Airport at 9.30 a.m. and arrived at Grantley Adams Airport, Bridgetown on time at 3.05 p.m. I love the name Bridgetown, it is so very typical of Barbados. You have a town with a bridge in it so you call it Bridgetown. You have a town with a hole in it so you call it Holetown. Everything is called exactly what it is.

When we used to stay at Sandy Lane Hotel year after year in the 70s we became interested in the local birdlife because it swarmed all over our balcony and challenged us for our breakfast.

The three main raiders were a large, ungainly starling-like bird with jet-black feathers and manic yellow eyes, an aggressive sparrow type and a small, needle-beaked sugar thief whose yellow vest and long black coat made it look like a dandy.

When one of the older room service waiters was setting up our breakfast, I asked him, 'What do you call the black birds we see every morning?'

He took a moment to think and then said, 'We calls them black birds.'

'And the brown birds?'

'We calls them brown birds.'

'And the small birds with the yellow breasts and sharp beaks?'

'We calls them small birds.'

'But surely the birds have names?'

He regarded me as if I were an idiot.

'Well, sir, you can give dem names if you want but I don't believe dey'll answer to dem.'

Then his face broke into a broad grin, he clapped his hands, winked and went.

## Sunday, 23 April 1995

Home in our Bedfordshire hideaway I'm making a note to take more video cassettes with us next time we go to Barbados.

My multi-standard VCR does fine with either the British PAL format or the American NTSC system which is used in Barbados but there's a snag with the local software.

Although one can hire the most up-to-date movies from shops in Sunset Crest, Holetown, many of them are umpteenth-generation copies of original recordings made in some Miami hotel room from the in-house service. Others are derived from the promotional copies that video companies distribute to wholesalers and the press hoping to attract bulk orders and favourable newspaper reviews. Apart from being barely watchable, every few minutes a dire warning of prosecution scrolls across the picture: 'IF YOU HAVE HIRED OR PURCHASED THIS MOVIE YOU HAVE BEEN INVOLVED IN A CRIME. CALL FREEPHONE "0800 NO-COPIES" AND REPORT DETAILS.' It's a bit off-putting to say the least, trying to care about the brutal treatment of convict Kevin Bacon by the Alcatraz warden Gary Oldman in *Murder in the First* when you keep being reminded that you could be in jail yourself.

Last week we ran out of cassettes from the UK and were reduced to looking at some old audition tapes from my discovery series on BBC 1, 'Bob Says Opportunity Knocks'.

Mind you, some of them were pitiably funny. I thought I had a gift for star spotting. There's a pigeon outside the TV Centre that spots more stars than I ever did.

One of the worst acts we saw was in a church hall in Exeter; a singing conjurer who fumbled coin production and dropped playing cards while warbling 'It's Magic' off-key.

At the end of the song the man paused before continuing with his next trick. Our heavyweight producer Stewart Morris spoke into the microphone on his table, 'You're wanted outside.'

'Oh?' said the surprised magician. 'By whom?'

'Everybody in here,' answered Stewart.

## Wednesday, 26 April 1995

One of the questions I'm most often asked is, 'What?' Well, I am inclined to mumble.

Another question I get is, 'How have you developed your memory?' I can't remember how many times I've been asked that.

Today in Manchester we start taping a series of eight half-hours for BBC 1 called 'Monkhouse Memory Masters'. Stephen Leahy's Action Time is the production company and John Junkin is writing the script. Each of the shows will feature three members of the public who have volunteered to have their normally poor memories trained.

Throughout the series they'll demonstrate their newly acquired and quite astonishing skills of retention, recall and retrieval employing a mnemonic system called 'pegging' in which new facts are mentally 'pegged' to an easily remembered sequence of familiar objects, such as parts of one's body from head to toe, places along some habitual route or items around an often-used room. The method seems daunting at first but becomes easier the more it's used.

I used to employ a similar technique, known to professional magicians as Corinda's Amazing Memory System, but only as a party trick. It requires the initial memorising of some childish doggerel: 'One is a gun, two is a shoe, three is a tree, four is a door . . .' and so forth. Once you have this simple list of numbers committed to memory, it's quite simple to 'peg' the thing you want to remember to a number just by using your imagination. The more obscene the mental picture the easier its recollection.

Say you are given a shopping list of twenty items to remember. Perhaps the tenth is a household electric massager. In your memorised nursery rhyme, ten is a hen. All you have to do is put the two images together. The imaginary picture of a hen laying an electric massager, its violent vibrations shaking every feather of the shrieking bird as it slowly emerges into view, is not one that will quickly be forgotten.

Up to several hours later, when asked which item was the tenth or at which number the massager was listed, the absurd fancy you conjured up will provide you with the answer.

It's true that I am naturally blessed or cursed with a very good memory but I attribute its efficiency firstly to my deliberate storing of people, events and related words, secondly to a retrieval method which involves intense concentration supported by my conviction that the information which I want exists and so must be available.

Sometimes this memory search lasts thirty minutes or more. I have to focus my thoughts on the target and tunnel towards it.

For long-forgotten incidents, my almost trance-like state resembles a home-grown version of self-hypnosis. Two conditions determine my success before I embark upon this process: I have to be very sure that I won't be interrupted and I need to replenish my supply of confidence in the belief that nothing is ever really forgotten.

This latter effect is achieved by considering the evidence of my previous mental exercises, occasions on which an obscure recollection has opened up to me like the time-lapse blooming of a flower, replete with detail. I've rediscovered entire scenes from my past in this way. It's like knowing that facts are concealed somewhere in a computer if only you could find the pathway to them.

Having exhumed these long-buried events, I do all I can to check them against the contemporary evidence to be sure that I'm not kidding myself. Simple historical research then reveals enough about the period in question, who was where and what was when and which was currently how, to back up the accuracy of my reminiscence. At the same time, I'm aware of the unlikely nature of total recall.

One of the most emotive topics to surface in the 1980s was Recovered Memory. Quite suddenly it seemed as if everyone was busy awakening hitherto repressed memories of sexual abuse in childhood. Aha, I thought, so that's why that faded photograph of Uncle Stephen has always given me an erection.

But it was mostly women, thousands of them, who claimed these revelations. Assisted by hypnosis, they unearthed horror stories from the newly freed subconscious that appeared to reveal them as victims of parental atrocities. In America, a Mrs Eileen Franklin Lipsker announced that she now remembered watching her father rape and murder one of her childhood chums. Very largely as a result of her testimony, George Franklin was tried and convicted without corroborating evidence. Then in 1995 his conviction was overturned, the legal conclusion being that recovered memories are unreliable.

As families were torn apart by accusations of Satanic blood drinking and ghastly sex acts so came the inevitable backlash from parents who denied it all. 'False memory' societies were founded both here and in the USA. Therapists faced lawsuits for instilling fallacious memories of childhood damage in their subjects' minds. They had no verification of this ill-treatment to offer other than what the self-proclaimed victims were insisting and seemed so sure about.

The proof of child abuse is often difficult enough to establish at the time of its occurrence. Twenty or more years after such alleged offences, neither the accusers nor the accused can with absolute certainty prove the recollections to be either real or unreal. Leaving aside the more essential question of what really lies behind this psychic epidemic and what it can tell us about human needs, it doesn't inspire much faith in the infallibility of memory, does it?

## Thursday, 4 May 1995

I witnessed a crime today and it took me back to my own criminal past. I'd just finished an 11 a.m. rehearsal at Claridge's Hotel for the afternoon's presentation of Emap Images' Video Games Awards and was standing in the hall outside the banqueting suite admiring a tabletop display of the competing software. There must have been forty video game cartridges on show.

As I stood gazing, a boy of about thirteen or fourteen passed me from somewhere within the hotel, walking towards the street doors. He moved close to the table, his hand shot out to seize one of the games and he strolled on, slipping the stolen cartridge into his pocket. I was just about to call out to him to bring it back when the boy stopped at the door and looked back at me with a dazzling grin and a conspiratorial wink. Then he was gone. And I was left with my jaw swinging and a sudden recollection of my own naughty boyhood in the long-forgotten scene of my crimes.

I stole salami sausages, when I was about thirteen or fourteen. There was a cornchandler-cum-grocer's shop in Beckenham High Street that had these salamis hanging up near the back, about eight feet up a roof support post. The rear of the store was dark except for the dusty sunbeams poking through the cracks in the wall planks and striping their golden bands of light across sacks of grain and dog biscuits.

When the owner wasn't in the shop his pretty daughter was in charge but she'd usually be daydreaming behind the counter or reading some romantic novel.

All I had to do was walk past her just as quietly as the youth who had glided by me in Claridge's. Then came the challenging part: to run and jump so very softly, unhooking a salami whilst in mid-air and thrusting it down the front of my trousers, landing with bent knees so as to make no sound. Keeping the stolen sausage in place by distending my belly muscles, it was now child's play to stroll around as if browsing and thence reach the safety of the pavement.

I thought it very unlikely that the grocer's daughter would stop me and say, 'Young man, is that a salami in your trousers?'

And should such a remote possibility occur, I was ready with my answer: 'Well, miss, why don't you put your hand down there and check?'

The way I had it figured out, even if she had then called my bluff and I'd been caught in that way, well, at the age of fourteen it would've been worth it to have her put her hand down there. That never happened.

Of course, I savoured the risk of discovery, hearing the grocer's harsh voice at the doorway. But then, if he'd ever stopped me and demanded, 'Is that a salami in your trousers?', all I'd have to say was, 'Well, thank you very much, sir, I'm not exactly ashamed of it myself. And I'm only fourteen! Imagine my future.'

**Monday, 8 May 1995**
Jackie, Peter Prichard and I checked into first class today at 4 p.m. for Air New Zealand flight 001 to Los Angeles. We took off at 5.30, landed in LA at 8.30 p.m. and were in the Bel Age Hotel de Grande Classe, 1020, San Vincent Boulevard, West Hollywood by 9.30, all on time, a happy augury for the job we've come to do. Michael Hurll is the producer and the show, due to be taped in the CBS studios in five days' time is 'The ITV Movie Awards of 1995'.

Hurll welcomed us with splendid news. He'd already arranged personal appearances from Dennis Hopper, the cast of 'NYPD Blue', the leading ladies of *Star Trek: The Next Generation* and, to my utter delight, one of my American comedy heroes. I recall my last meeting with him just ten years ago.

I was five minutes late. He was standing alone in the large rehearsal studio. As I approached, my palms extended in apology, he regarded me calmly with the gentle smile of a priest.

'I'm so sorry I wasn't here to greet you. I'm Bob Monkhouse, the host of the show. We've met before, about thirty years ago I think, when you did six shows for BBC TV. You've hardly changed.'

He rocked his head in mild disagreement. 'Believe me, the man I used to be wouldn't have been standing here quietly waiting for you. That Sid Caesar, he would have smashed every piece of furniture in this room by now. And when all the chairs and tables were smashed, he'd have gone into the men's room and ripped all the wash-basins out of the wall and used them to smash the lavatory bowls.' His smile suddenly broadened and his blue eyes twinkled with charm. 'Could I have a drink of water, please?'

\*

IN 50s America, Sid Caesar was to television what Chaplin had been to film. He presided over a group of comic geniuses who dominated the screen and stage today – Woody Allen, Mel Brooks, Neil Simon, Carl Reiner, Larry Gelbart and others who fought for a place on what was the most highly regarded team in the business.

With the help of this extraordinary clique, Caesar developed original live comedy that rocketed him to stardom in 'Your Show of Shows' and 'Caesar's Hour'. But when rising costs and bad executive decisions killed his hit shows in 1958, his personal nightmare began.

The combination of crushing insecurity and the driving need for weekly success led first to his dependence on alcohol and pills and then to helpless addiction. The explosions of violence were worsened by Sid's enormous strength. A horse once threw his wife Florence while they were out riding and Sid KO-ed the horse with one punch between the eyes. Mel Brooks told me he was present at that scene and used it many years later in his film *Blazing Saddles*.

The next twenty years still remain a blur to the great comedian. He remembers working whenever he could pull himself together but the details are not in his memory. When films he made during this period appear on TV, they come as a complete surprise to him. 'All that mattered,' he told me, 'was that I could get it over quickly, no matter how inane it was, and go home to my friend the bottle.'

Because of his remaining name value, he could always go on the road or get cameo roles in the plays and films written by his old gang. Neil Simon entrusted him with a tour of his Broadway hit *The Last of the Red Hot Lovers* and Mel Brooks cast him as the bewildered studio executive in his film *Silent Movie*. Sid had to play his entire role sitting down. He had broken the bones in his foot when a blend of whiskey and drugs had affected his judgement during a joy ride in a wheelchair which met a wall.

Sid's condition was exacerbated by irrational envy of his old employees. Simon's plays and movies kept coming out at a rate of roughly two a year; Brooks was inventing box-office smashes; Carl Reiner was writing and directing successes for Steve Martin; Lucille Kallen, the only woman in the group, was turning out popular novels; Mel Tolkin, his senior writer, had found a TV triumph with 'All in the Family'; Larry Gelbart had not only developed 'M.A.S.H.', the long-running TV classic, but also created *Oh, God!* for George Burns and gone on to big Broadway musicals with *A Funny Thing Happened on the Way to the Forum*; and we all know about Woody. Whatever happened to the self-destructive Sid?

The repair of the mind. 'Some junkies and drunks do it through organisations like Alcoholics Anonymous. Some use therapy to kick chemical dependency. A few manage to white-knuckle it by themselves. *I* went to Paris.'

A minor part in a poor film took Sid to France where he embarked upon an unlikely cure for his sickness. Alone in his room at the little Hotel Victor Hugo on the rue Copernic, he pulled out his cassette recorder and began.

His idea was born out of utter desperation. He had hit rock bottom, estranged his friends and family, all but wrecked his talent. Now he had only himself to turn to. And that's exactly what he did.

On the morning of 22 September 1979, he began a long series of conversations with himself. Overcoming self-consciousness, he persisted in his mission to find out who he really was and what he really thought. Gradually, unaware that he was applying techniques which had entered his mind subliminally during his lengthy sessions with psychiatrists throughout the years, Sid split himself into two personalities.

Soon he was having fascinating discussions with the wayward personality he thought of as Sidney. He'd plead with him, argue, even have terrible fights with his *alter ego*. In the tapes he made can be heard raging accusations and humble confessions. The subject of booze had Sid lecturing Sidney like a passionately concerned father. As for his anger and his guilt, Sid explored his psyche relentlessly, demanding answers, rooting out the hidden reasons behind the excuses. But there was praise there too, praise for his honesty, his newly sustained sobriety, for his courage in facing his devils. Sid was finally coming to terms with his real self and learning to like the man.

In two years' time from today's date another milestone will be reached. Sid, aged seventy-four, fit and freed from the clutches of addiction and the emotional rollercoaster it fuelled, will walk in front of an audience to be reunited with his cluster of super gagsters. I have the benefit of hindsight, adding these words to my memoirs in 1998. The precious occasion was filmed for 'Arena' and it's strangely moving to see the elderly men whose youthful portrayals are enacted nightly somewhere in the world in Simon's play, *Laughter on the Twenty Third Floor* which concerns the Sid Caesar fun factory of the 50s, as did the old boys' get-together.

The reminiscences were rich: Brooks frenetic, Gelbart softly witty, Sheldon Keller clever, Carl Reiner stimulated into hilarious recollections of those wonderfully hellish years of live TV comedy.

But the best part of their class reunion was the warmth of remembered camaraderie in the cause of serving Caesar. He's a man who inspired such love that he couldn't destroy it. And, as Sid himself says, 'All I did was face reality. It's really not that hard if you really want it.'

## Tuesday, 9 May – Sunday, 14 May 1995

It will be a few more weeks before I figure out that irritable red welts that are periodically forming in itchy ridges all over my back, chest and armpits are caused by my allergic reaction to cayenne pepper, an ingredient in the health food I'm using. I'm coming to the conclusion that it's called health food because, to survive this food, you have to be in perfect health.

As for regular food, Tuesday we all ate in Mirabelle on Sunset – just terrific.

The next day we dined in the fashionable restaurant, Le Dome – not at all terrific. I had no idea you could get cuisine of this standard at under 35,000 feet.

It annoys me when US comedians sneer at British cooking. When they come to our country they eat in McDonald's anyway. And then they rave about the overpriced eateries in New York and LA where your napkin comes à la carte and, if you ask for Mussels Marinara, the owner shows up.

The next day John Bishop, Head of Entertainment for Carlton Television, takes Jac and me to a renowned Chinese tavern named Joss. This is high-class Pekinese. Bish beams at us shinily over a fine meal although I find it strange to have duck pancakes served along with the other entrée. But what do I know? For years I thought 'dim sum' meant 'I am stupid' in Latin.

Thursday we get down to a little bit of work and rehearse. It seems that many of the stars whose agents guaranteed their appearance will now be no-shows. Sandra Bullock's award will now be accepted by Dennis Leary on video. Likewise, John Cleese will appear on tape from Pinewood Studios presenting an award to Jamie Lee Curtis with the words, 'Please accept this charmingly heavy but surprisingly inexpensive trinket.'

Tom Arnold, Roseanne's ex-hubby, will also collect his prize on video saying, 'This is the first time I've ever won in my life – apart from a $50 million divorce settlement.'

And so the toast to absent friends continues to be raised, with Wet Wet Wet in Rotterdam, Hugh Grant in Devon and Keanu Reeves in Minnesota. It seems it's going to be one of those nights when all the stars are out.

On Saturday, the day of the recording, we have a packed house in the CBS Studios. The chairs are filled with many expatriate Brits including my dear friends Isobel and Josephine, fans of mine since the 50s and still loyal despite the seductive luxuries of Hollywood or, as Hugh Grant knows it, Tonsil Town.

My opening monologue ('Welcome to the ITV Movie Awards or, as they're known in Los Angeles, the *what*?') wins knowing laughter and Mariella Frostrup and I have fun interviewing Dennis Hopper, Theo from 'The Cosby Show', Gates McFadden and Marina Sirtis from *Star Trek: The Next Generation*, Dennis Franz from 'NYPD Blue' and Sid Caesar. The big shock for me is Bob Hope. It's heart-breaking and that's no exaggeration; I care deeply for the man, having had an association going back more than forty years.

When I first met him in 1953, Hope was at the peak of his powers. I was amazed how big he was, over six feet, and so full of vitality. I'd deliberately stayed away from his last two appearances in Britain because I didn't want to destroy my memory of him.

When I eventually see him, ninety-two years old, slumped in a wheelchair in the wings, he looks so tiny. That familiar face is slightly longer, but not puckered or wrinkled, amazingly smooth; his eyes are dead, unfocused in what appears to be senile oblivion.

I greet him and he hums a high musical note. He does this every twenty seconds or so, 'Hmmm-mm-mmm!'

His companion Grant speaks my name into Hope's ear several times very clearly until eventually he waves his hand abstractedly and mumbles, 'That's OK, he knows me.'

As the time for him to give and accept his two awards grows nearer, I become increasingly anxious. He seems to be asleep. Grant has wandered off somewhere and I'm standing beside his wheelchair wondering what to do. Suddenly he hums his musical note again and speaks quite faintly.

'What am I getting?'

'The readers of the *TV Times* have voted you a Lifetime Achievement award, Bob. I'm presenting you with that. And you're presenting the award for the Best Film of the Year, *Four Weddings and a Funeral*.'

'Four funerals and a what?'

'No, it's *Four Weddings and a Funeral*.'

'Whose funeral?'

'No one's funeral. You just say that the winner of Best Film of the Year is *Four Weddings and a Funeral*.'

'It's not one of my movies.'

'No, it's the Best Film of 1995.'

'It's too long.'

'The film is too long? You've seen it?'

'No, the title. The title is too long. Needs a shorter title.'

'Too late to change it now. Can you remember it OK?'

'No, I haven't.'

'You haven't what?'

'Seen it. I never heard of it.'

'Would you rather I announced the winner? Then you can give the award. Would that be a better arrangement?'

'Hmmm-mm-mmm!'

Now I'm really worried. I can't see how the old chap can hobble as far as the lectern, let alone announce the winning film and then make an acceptance speech. Then the recorded orchestra strikes up 'Thanks for the Memory' and I witness a minor miracle.

Hope rises to his feet, his eyes brighten into a beady twinkle, his wide mouth twists into that famously sardonic grin, the chin juts, the backbone straightens and, albeit with my arm in support, he makes his entrance to a standing ovation.

Reaching the lectern, he grips it with both hands and I remove my arm. He surveys the cheering throng as they resume their seats.

'I know why you stood up. You just wanted to straighten your pants,' he tells them. Then with a burst of gusto, 'The winning film is *Four Weddings and a Funeral*, hey! Sounds like Zsa Zsa's life story!'

Where did that come from?

It later occurs to me that the single note he's been humming all evening is the opening note of his signature tune, 'Thanks for the Memory', in his key. He was getting ready to work.

## Wednesday, 31 May 1995

This evening I've been booked to give an after-dinner speech at the Ramada Hotel, Heathrow, for the InterCyber Computer Company with this brief: 'At least 40 of the 150 guests are from our branches overseas and have at best a slight grasp of our language. Please make it simple for them.' Oh, sure, sixty minutes of comedy in pidgin English.

I go to the seven o'clock reception to gauge the level of comprehension. It's not as bad as it might have been. All but a couple of the foreign visitors have a formal knowledge of our grammar and vocabulary. The correct use of the words properly assembled into sentences will make sense to them. I am strongly reminded that, for foreigners arriving in Britain, the most difficult thing for them to understand is not what we say but how we say it. The language is not so difficult, they can learn that in their schools. It's the way we *use* the language. Even if they've learned our entire mother tongue, how can anyone who didn't grow up in Britain be expected to understand the ridiculous things we say?

'By and large', 'Just as well', 'Be that as it may', 'Neither here nor there', 'Notwithstanding', 'In one fell swoop', 'Sorted!', 'I'll go to the foot of our stairs', 'You're driving me up the wall you are,' 'Some mothers do 'ave 'em!' And a pet hate of mine: *'Now then!'* Which is it? Is it now or is it then? It can't be both.

But then again (and by the way, what does *that* mean, 'then again'? Then *again* suggests then twice, which would be 'then then'), sorry, where was I? Back to square one. Then again, why do we say ridiculous things? Who knows? Aha, there's a ridiculous thing right there – 'who knows'. It's not a real question, I'm not really asking you anything, am I? I'm not saying, 'Why do we say ridiculous things? OK, who knows? Come on, who knows? Put your hand up, who knows?'

And look how, when people are upset, they use insane expressions like 'For crying out loud!' Where did that come from? Some wife turns on her husband and shouts, 'Do stop saying ridiculous things, for crying out loud!' What's a foreigner going to make of that? 'For "Crying Out Loud"' should be an award you give to a little kid in nursery school. 'And here's the award for Crying Out Loud and our winner is Cryin' Bobby Ryan, let's hear it for him! Bobby wins the award for crying over spilt milk! Little Bobby'll cry at the drop of a hat! Look at him, he's crying his eyes out!' Boing, boing!

Where did these idiotic expressions come from? Who knows? Now then! Then again . . . be that as it may . . . here's another one: 'needless to say'. If it's needless to say, then don't say it.

'Well, it goes without saying . . .' Does it? Then shut up.

And here's another one: how many times do we hear people preface a sentence with, 'I know this is going to sound crazy but . . .'? What's a foreigner going to expect? 'I know this is going to sound crazy but yabba-gabba-oogle-poogle-smurtle-poo-pah! I told you it was going to sound crazy!'

And how about people who say 'just kidding'? These are two words that simply mean the opposite of what they say. Whenever someone says to you, 'Hey, just kidding' – they're not. If I tell you that knowing that you bought this book of mine makes me love you, I mean it.

But if I say that knowing you borrowed it to read it for nothing makes me hate you, hey – just kidding. Then again, be that as it may, by and large, who knows?

If I seem peevish about our verbal oddities, just don't say to me, 'Hey, Bob, you're not yourself today.' That drives me purple. In fact, the next time somebody says that you – 'You're not yourself today' – ask them, 'Then why are you telling *me*?'

## Thursday, 1 June 1995

Another birthday, this time it's the sixty-seventh.

Last Saturday Mystic Meg told me I'd live to ninety-nine. She didn't say whether she meant my age or the year.

I'm feeling my age anyway, recovering from yesterday. The daytime was spent in the London photographic studio of the very amusing David Bailey, posing for a portrait for Jameson's Irish Whiskey and their 'Old Smoothie' campaign. I was treated to a tumbler or three of their finest. The stuff really does improve with age: the older I get the more I like it.

Last evening found me at Heathrow's Ramada Hotel dining with and speaking to the 300 senior managers of EDS Computers. Their hospitality rivalled Jameson's although it was a bottle of twenty-six-year-old Glenfarclas they put on the table before me, distilled in 1969, deep amber with bronze and ruby highlights. I asked how they knew my tipple. It seems their booker Jilly Bushell had asked my agent and Peter had told her, 'Bob's of Scottish descent and he likes to keep permanently in touch with the spirit of his ancestors.'

I seem to remember the malt whisky experts John Lamond and Robin Tucek describing this marvellously rich hooch as having 'an individual nuttiness'. I've suffered from the same condition for sixty-seven years now.

## Thursday, 8 June 1995

My scrapbook lists this day in 1983 as not only the fiftieth birthday of my favourite funny lady but also her British television début in BBC 2's 'The Bob Monkhouse Show'.

I'd known Joan Rivers since 1978 when we appeared together on a slapstick series called 'Bonkers', taped in England for US consumption. The show wasn't good but she was hilariously funny, mostly during rehearsals when she'd ad-lib lines like, 'Never let a panty line show around your ankles.'

Required to haul a huge potted plant around the set for obscure plot reasons, Joan lamented, 'I have bad luck with plants. I bought a philodendron and I put it in the kitchen. It drank my soup.'

Elton, Ben and me. Standing between the two great men, my smile denotes my foolish hope that talent is catching. It isn't.

Major and Monkhouse formed a comedy double-act at the Police Bravery Awards. After they'd heard our jokes, they gave awards to both of us.

HRH is asking, 'And what do you do for a living?' I wouldn't have minded but I'd just hosted the 1997 Royal Variety Performance.

The Three Baritones in rare juxtaposition – Lionel Ritchie, Tom Jones and I, on stage at the Dominion for a charity bash.

A beachbum's paradise where I wrote the book you're holding.

Jackie's at the smart Lone Star Brasserie with Lou Manzi, our Barbados neighbour, and Des O'Connor, a favourite entertainer of yesteryear.

Our sandcastle on the Barbados beach. Come see, come sigh.

Pete Price and I hope this paparazzi snap will lead to rumours of a gay romance. Then we can sue the papers and make a fortune.

Mac and I spend many hours like this, standing guard over our fake Picasso.

On *Have I Got News For You* you can see how effortlessly I'm keeping the resident trio in fits of hysteria.

Wet Wet Wet and Rowan Atkinson join me on the National Lottery. I love this show. It's all over in 15 minutes and it's live so I can't watch it.

In David Renwick's *Jonathan Creek* with Alan Davies and Caroline Quentin, I played a nasty old man. Quite a stretch for me but, hey, I'm a pro.

Me and Jac and dear friend Jeremy Beadle realising we've been filmed.

My birthday cake was a huge surprise. At 70, either one could be fatal.

In 1979 Jackie and I went to see her act in Las Vegas where she was triumphantly funny but not the show's main attraction, an honour which went to 'The Polish Prince' of pop stars, Bobby Vinton. Joan's self-penned material dealt so frankly with subjects like sexual ignorance, female problems and childbirth that the audience was divided into the horrified and the hysterical, the latter joyfully in the majority.

'The gynaecologist says "relax, relax, I can't get my hand out, relax."'

'I wonder why I'm not relaxed. My feet are in stirrups, my knees are in my face, and the door is open facing me . . . can we talk here?'

'Men don't understand. For a woman to lie in those stirrups, is that the worst? And my gynaecologist does jokes!'

'Dr Schwartz at your cervix!', 'I'm dilated to meet you!', 'Say aahhh!'

'There's no way you can get back at that son of a bitch unless you learn to throw your voice.'

Afterwards, in her hotel room with her husband Edgar Rosenberg, she was a mass of uncertainties. 'Was I talking too fast for the crowd? I always talk too fast. Did I move around too much?'

The mask of the powerfully confident comedienne who had just commanded the auditorium was off and Joan's frailties were exposed. 'Did I work too dirty? Sometimes I wonder who I am when I'm out there.'

Within another twelve months Joan became a white hot star, mostly as a result of her dazzling routines when deputising for Johnny Carson as the permanent guest host of the legendary 'Tonight Show'. She was acclaimed at Carnegie Hall and returned to larger venues in Las Vegas, this time as the sole headliner.

As a result of her sensational appearance on my 1983 show, Joan returned for a BBC special called 'Bob Monkhouse Meets Joan Rivers' which in turn led to her hosting a late-night BBC series which used her catchphrase as its title, 'Can We Talk?'

As the 80s continued, she had everything she and Edgar had strived for. No one could have foreseen that she was destined to lose it all, that a career, already marked by years of struggle, insecurity, self-doubt and now this great fulfilment, could be demolished.

She's always been so proud of being accepted by the British public and boasted of her 'English husband'. In fact, the South-African born Edgar was a tough intellectual who, after surviving a clinical death from heart failure and the resulting personality change, guided her career so badly in the years that followed the BBC series that, physically ill and emotionally devastated, he killed himself with a lethal cocktail of

Valium, Librium and alcohol from the courtesy bar alone in a Philadelphia hotel room in 1987.

In her grief, Joan became bulimic. Although anger with Edgar for deserting her came to her rescue and fired her with purpose, aiding her in coping with the terrible peripeteia in her life, her situation was still dire.

Her late-night TV show on the Fox network had unsuccessfully competed with Johnny Carson's and had been axed. Other employers were unwilling to take the risk of hiring a comedy star whose image had been so tragically damaged. She became *persona non grata* in Hollywood.

Slowly, painfully, the wretchedness of her situation worked itself out and the shockwaves of her loss became less frequent and severe. Joan, having hit rock bottom, began the long climb back to reclaim her career and the public favour she had previously enjoyed, using hard work as a therapy to heal her wounds.

On the evening of 28 June 1990, in New York's Marriott Hotel, three years after her world had been shattered by Edgar's death, she won the Emmy Award for Best Talk Show Host in competition with Oprah Winfrey, Phil Donahue, Sally Jesse Raphael and the Frugal Gourmet.

She described the moment as 'entire, immaculate joy, nothing mingled in it, no fear, no guilt. If I had fallen and broken both legs, I would still have gotten on to that stage.'

She told the audience, 'Two years ago I couldn't get a job in this business. My income dropped to one sixteenth of what it was before I was fired. My husband had a breakdown. It's so sad that he's not here because he always said you can turn things around. And, except for one terrible moment in a hotel room in Philadelphia, when he forgot that, this is really for him, because he was with me from the very beginning.'

Tearfully but in a rush of triumph, she thrust the Emmy above her head like a Lilliputian Statue of Liberty. She had regained the peak and she knew that whatever fate threw at her, she could do it again and again if she had to.

Joan has learned that you can face anything if you are true to yourself.

As Neil Simon wrote of her, 'The deeper the personal pain, the richer the vein of humour – she not only wears her heart on her sleeve, she passes it out to the audience for personal inspection.'

## Friday, 9 June 1995

A *Daily Mirror* reporter rang me this morning to get my reaction to a statement made by some Oxford Professor of Sociology to the effect that the comedian does more for society than the politician, the lawyer or the scientists. Dangerous talk, I say. A comedian's got to know his place. You can get an exaggerated idea of your importance if you're not careful. No one on his deathbed has ever said, 'I think the end is near, send for a comedian.'

No airline pilot has ever told his passengers, 'Ladies and gentlemen, I'm sorry to tell you that both engines are out, fuel is low and landfall is over two hours away – but thank God we have a comedian on board!'

For that matter, you'll never hear a government minister on 'Question Time' saying, 'The Middle East crisis can be tolerated no longer – send in the clowns!'

## Wednesday, 14 June 1995

I'll say one thing about showbiz: there's no danger of getting bored by the same old thing day in and day out.

Yesterday: a speech for the Annual Investment Property Forum dinner at the Royal Lancaster Hotel where I was seriously instructed to keep it clean.

Tomorrow: a concert performance on the stage of Cheltenham Town Hall where I've been asked to observe the proprieties.

Tonight: a charity stag show in Enfield where I share the backstage facilities with six very bare young ladies. One of these exotic dancers wears an illuminated G-string. Now that's my kind of strip lighting.

Was I embarrassed by the proximity of so much flesh? Come, come, I'm a man of vast experience of nudity as entertainment, and I mean from way back when.

By the time I had served my three years in the RAF in 1949 I had become pretty well established as a radio comedian and scriptwriter.

That meant I was of some value to those whose increasingly desperate responsibility it was to lure audiences into Britain's 300 variety theatres.

Two world wars had given them booming business but now they struggled in the stark decade of 50s austerity. Consequently, the proprietors were prepared to present attractions they would have disdained in their more imperious days: horror shows, sexploitation plays, cine-variety, amateur nights and women who came on and danced, in Ted Ray's descriptive phrase, 'wearing only a dozen beads, eleven of which were perspiration'.

So as a newcomer to the variety stage I found myself engaged at £25 a week to act as compere with two twelve-minute front cloth spots at the first theatre of a seven-week tour, the Camberwell Palace, in support of

Phyllis Dixey, the 'outrageous' stripteaser whose ladylike presentation was closely modelled on the American, Gypsy Rose Lee, right down to the climactic conclusion when, after stimulating the men in their audiences with the constant promise of bare breasts, the temptress exposed a chest flatter than the Netherlands.

Also on the bill that week was a very fat young percussionist named Peter Sellers who sat centre stage behind his kit doing violence to five drums, two cymbals and a temple block. After five minutes of this din the young man walked to the microphone and propped up a placard which read, MR SELLERS IS QUITE DEAF. IF YOU CARE TO APPLAUD, PLEASE DO SO LOUDLY.

He wore a suit obviously too big even for his rotund frame.

'I had it made in Leeds,' he explained to the audience. 'I'm a bigger man there than I am here.'

Then, to my surprise, he delivered wonderfully exact impressions of Groucho Marx, George Sanders, Peter Lorre and the best-known characters from the 'ITMA' radio series.

The voices were very funny but the material was weak. By the middle of the week I was writing jokes for Peter and he was putting them into his turn with increasing success. This lengthened his performance and he received a warning note from the theatre manager telling him to stick to his allotted time or risk being fined.

By the Friday evening I'd persuaded Peter to drop his dreadful drumming altogether and rely on his act as an impressionist. Together we'd devised a funny routine in which he played a ukulele, sang as George Formby and then had all his other characters joining in with parodied lyrics.

It was such a success that a talent scout named Alf Brandon who had been sent to judge my suitability for a booking at the Windmill decided that Peter was a much better proposition and booked him for six weeks at London's famous bare-skin revue, a launching pad for numerous new comedy stars.

The big attraction at Vivian Van Damm's famous showpiece was the parade of lovely girls who stood around the stage not so much naked as nude. I know naked and nude mean the same thing but somehow naked sounds like a surprise and nude is on purpose.

Looking back, it wasn't all that exciting. Law required the young women to pose onstage without any movement whatsoever but these tableaux vivants were enough to fill the theatre with yearning men who had little interest in the interruptions of blackout sketches and musical interludes.

The comedian had to work hard to get noticed at all.

Still, Peter's £36 a week made my variety wages look a bit sad. That is, until one figured out that the Windmill was putting on six shows a day. That meant Peter was getting £1 per performance while I was doing twice-nightly at £2 10d. per performance.

'Yes,' smiled Peter, 'but you only get to see Phyllis Dixey's bee-stings twelve times a week while I, my friend, am living in titty city!'

## Sunday, 25 June 1995

First of all, Marianne is a fabulous cook. Secondly, her food is all veg-etarian and great for your bodily functions. Thirdly, she gives the best lunch and dinner parties anywhere in the south-west Midlands and lastly, her husband is Dave Lee Travis, not only a fondly regarded broadcaster but also a man with a knack for coining sage wisecracks. At a previous Travis party fellow radio presenter Mike Read phoned on his mobile to explain that he'd run out of petrol and would be late for lunch. Dave mused, 'To a woman driver the "E" on the fuel gauge means "empty". To a man it means "enough".'

'I wish I'd said that,' murmured Paul Gambaccini.

'You will, Oscar, you will,' quoted Dave.

I remember an amply wined dinner party after which Dave added to his unique collection of video portraits by having each guest speak to his handicam. Better than asking us to sign a guest book he reasoned, and one by one we all contributed a short speech, a poem or a joke to his series of taped souvenirs. My wife Jac told him, 'I can't think of any-thing funny to say.' Dave replied, 'Runs in the family, eh?'

One guest had arrived in a bad mood that got worse. Eventually he quarrelled with his wife and left alone.

'He snores too,' she told us.

Someone said, 'Use an extra pillow.'

'I've tried that and it doesn't help.'

Dave chimed in. 'Try pressing down more firmly, dear.'

Today we enjoy a wonderfully sunny day inside and out of their exquisitely decorated farmhouse, sharing it with a gang of friends and some very well-mannered dogs, ducks, chickens and Vietnamese pigs.

DLT likes to invite fellow disc jockeys to the feast and, although many such are not regarded as the intelligentsia of the arts, the Travis choice of guests always turns out to be company quite as literate and sophisticated as our host. There are exceptions, of course.

Ed Stewart is a nice man but I've always found him to be a couple of discs short of a full Top Twenty. He has a way of paying compliments that makes them turn out like unintentional insults. It's pretty well known that Dave is a very gifted and creative photographer. The way I heard it, Ed once looked through a book of his best work and commented in a patronising tone, 'Not too bad at all – you must have a good camera.'

'Thank you,' said Dave softly. 'Your radio shows aren't too bad either – you must have a good microphone.'

## Thursday, 13 July – Wednesday, 23 August 1995

Over these weeks BBC 1 takes a chance on my ability to hold its Saturday night audiences after the 9 p.m. watershed with thirty minutes of adult stand-up comedy. Alan Nixon produces, Colin Edmonds is as always my comedy consultant and we call the series 'Bob Monkhouse On The Spot', taping midweek with me responding to my audience's questions but adding topical gags on Saturday in an empty studio with a virtual reality studio audience.

Alan, a neatly made Scot with zero dress sense who will later become Channel 5's light entertainment chief, says, 'This is your own world of comedy, Bob; others may enter to enjoy sharing it with you but they mustn't influence it.'

It's a flattering conceit and for a moment I believe it. But in my heart I know that I'm not really in the class of those comic giants who truly fashioned an individual and separate world of comedy, an eccentric realm of madness into which their audiences are not forced but enticed.

In what insane universe could Stan Laurel pull down the *shadow* of the window-blind? Only in the marvellous wonderland of *Blockheads*.

Why did we go along with the lunatic pretence that a clumsy, guffawing giant in a fez, with fingers like bananas, could perform delicate sleight-of-hand conjuring tricks for us 'just like that – not like that, like that'?

How could Abbott and Costello base their most memorable routine on the impossible premise that baseball players had such names as Who, What, I Don't Know, Because, Today, Tomorrow and I Don't Give A Damn?

As with the Goons and Monty Python, explanations are not on offer. Either you accept the rules (or the lack of them) in each cuckoo cosmos or you won't be allowed to play.

Such an *outré* milieu was occupied by certain of our great variety comedians for the duration of their stage performances. They walked on stage as the zany inhabitants of an otherwise unknown comic dimension and they didn't appear too bothered whether you joined them there or not. If the most genuinely deranged of these was the astonishing Frank Randle and most unreliably glorious was Max Wall, there's little question that the most universally loved was Jimmy James.

Eric Morecambe said, 'He must have been one of the most creative, one of the funniest comics that this country's ever seen. He had that thing that broke all barriers with an audience. He was loved by the pros and loved by the audience; he had this fantastic gift that he was liked and loved, and this is an important word, loved by both. One of the few comedians that all the comics used to stand on the side and watch. One of the greats.'

Tommy Trinder agreed. 'One of the greatest people, a real human person, was Jimmy James. He was a great artist on the stage with a wonderful sense of humour. There was one thing we had in common: we were both teetotallers. And this was a great gag because, whenever we got on the bill together, Jim'd say, "Hello, Tom" . . . "Hello, Jim" . . . "Let's get a quarter of a pound of wine gums and get stinking!"'

Arthur Askey added, 'He was a comic genius. A god in my eyes. Such a funny, funny man, the comedian's comedian.'

For Christmas 1993, radio producer-writer and comedy guru Mike Craig assembled well over 500 James aficionados at the City Varieties in Leeds to celebrate the centenary of the man's birth in Stockton-on-Tees. He reminded us of the Drunk Sketch, James's rough-hewn face quite at odds with his silk hat and tails as he slumped on the steps of a shop doorway, keeping at bay a policeman eager to get his hands on his bottle of whisky.

> *'There's a nip in the air, sir!'*
> *'There's a nip in this bottle but you're not having it.'*

And the Chipster Routine where two new complaints entered the medical dictionary: the Chipper's Wink and the Batterer's Elbow.

In attendance was Jimmy James's son James Casey, once Craig's mentor at the BBC in Manchester. His first memories of his dad's turn were still fresh and clear.

'The first time I saw him, I was about four and he was doing what he used to call an Italian act. He had a large hat and a velour coat and a big moustache which he wiggled about and he used to talk in a phoney stage Italian accent: "Whatsa matter for you, uh? You come inna my shop, six o'clock inna da morning, you stoppa till eight o'clock atta night, you buya nuttin, how'm I gonna live?

"'If ita wasn't fora you British cana box justa like that, I blow your nose!" And he used to end on a song, he had two or three that he wrote:

*"Come onna get up, come onna get up,*
*Itsa seven o'clocka, get up.*
*Sleepa no more, sleepa no more,*
*You wake-a da kids when you make-a da snore.*
*You wan' me to fetch your breakfass in bed?*
*You suffer too much with a swella da head,*
*You sleepa as much as you want when you're dead,*
*Itsa seven o'clocka, get up!"'*

As a boy James had picked up a few dance steps to augment his strong singing voice and regularly entered the inexpensive talent competitions with which Teesside theatre managements strove to fill their seats in the lean times.

A boyhood mate was Dave Morris, later a variety comic of almost equal fame in the north of England. Morris told Casey, 'If I knew your dad was entering the competition I reckoned I stood a good chance of coming second. When your dad was about twelve years old – and this just tells you how he was a natural for show business – he'd been entering this contest all week and he'd reached the finals on Friday all right but it looked as if he was going to lose to this angelic boy soprano in a beautiful velvet suit. The audience was mostly women, working-class mums, and they were besotted with this saintly kid with the golden curls and buckle shoes. Your dad had different ideas. First he said to the bloke in charge, "I'm going to sing a different song", a real sob story of a ballad about being an orphan. And second, he came on in his bare feet and with newspapers under his arm, getting the man to introduce him as the boy who sold newspapers round the corner and had no shoes! Jim'd won it before he opened his mouth.'

This boy bamboozler next joined one of the many kids' troupes that were touring the variety circuit, an outfit called the Singing Jockeys, befriending one of the more talented lads, named Jimmy Howells. Before long the two of them had broken away to form a double act described as 'The Dancing Boys in Black & White, THE TWO Js.'

The name of the act seemed fine until they were booked to play the Panechticon Theatre, Glasgow, said to be worse than the dreaded Glasgow Empire because it had wire netting over the orchestra. The quirky theatre manager had an idiosyncrasy about minor performers' names. With a famous lavatory disinfectant of the day in mind, he billed the boys as 'THE TWO JEYES – THE FLUID COMEDIANS'.

Soon James was working solo, offering a wide range of songs with whistling bird impressions and lightning cartoons thrown in for good measure. He even joined a mind-reading act to keep working, his natural humour finding its free-wheeling expression more securely with every passing year. One advantage to playing twice-nightly variety was the side-effect of boring repetition, a playful sense of irresponsibility that came from doing your act over and over to houses often no more than a quarter full. James experimented with capricious monologues, often invented on the spur of the moment. His reputation as an original and whimsical comedian spread.

When the impresario George Black gave him a part in a West End show, a play with music called *Jenny Jones*, he had his first encounter with the strict discipline of a script. Its American author was a tough woman who wouldn't allow him to change a word in rehearsal. Then the show opened, the critics panned it, the author went straight home and Black told him, 'Jim, do anything you like with it.'

That night the play began its second public performance. Playing the part of a reporter in search of the heroine, an unsuspecting actress entered and approached James where he sat on a village bench. Speaking her lines as written, she asked, 'Excuse me but do you know where I can find a girl named Jenny Jones?'

The script called for James, playing Jenny's father, to say only, 'At the top of the hill' and walk off. To this day Casey proudly remembers his dad's reply: 'Are you an actress by any chance?'

Flustered, she answered, 'Er . . . I'm a reporter.'

He said, 'Oh, it was just the red on your lips. I know actresses wear that. Mind, I was an actor meself, you know. You might've seen me. The play ran for three nights. It would've gone four only the vicar wanted the hall for the Harvest Festival.

'It was called "The Lighthouse Keeper's Daughter". It opened with me lying there on the couch with the lighthouse keeper's daughter and we're just about to when suddenly . . . suddenly we hear her father, the lighthouse keeper. He'd been up there at the top trimming the wick.

'And he had a wooden leg. Bitten off by a shark or something. So we could hear him coming, you see. Because it was like a clonk and a soft one. And that'd give me time to get down the other end of the couch and she could get on with her knitting.

'Anyway, he called out to me, "Row ashore for a pint of paraffin oil for the lamp!" So I said no, 'cause I'd been ashore twice that day, once for the milk and once for the papers, and it's a four-mile row each way. I was adamant, I said no. At that he used to lose his temper and he'd leap from the top of the lighthouse, down the steps, and land on his wooden leg. Always got a round of applause. One night it went so well, he had to do it five times.

'Then I'd whip his leg from underneath him and we'd go into the struggle scene. I wrote some special music for that. "Tara, chadda-da, chadda-da, chadda-da, chaa-aa!" Noel Coward came in four times just to hear the music. And he knocked it off. He knocked it off! You've heard that "I'll see you again, whenever -"? It's the same thing only slower.

'Anyway, then we went into the struggle and when we were on the floor, he started wrapping the wick around me neck. Well, if you know how tall a lighthouse is, you've got a fair idea how long the wicks are!'

Casey says his dad never did that speech again anywhere but he never forgot a word of it. Neither did the wretched actress, I should imagine.

It may be that this incident gave James the idea that he could work with a stooge who simply stood beside him and listened. To address an audience directly with such bizarre vagaries might risk rejection but retailing nonsense to a companion created a situation which the audience could enjoy at another level, observing the silent partner's absurd credulity. He must have decided that such an idiot needed a reason to accost him onstage.

To that end he engaged the services of his brother Andy and invented one of the truly enduring catchphrases of the variety age: 'Are you putting it about that I'm barmy?'

Those weeks when Andy couldn't make it, his floor-length topcoat was passed on to a third brother, John. Another long-serving ally was James's brother-in-law Jack Derby although he wasn't allowed to use that name for long. James liked to give everybody names he felt suited them better. The team was driving through Yorkshire one day when he saw a village signpost.

'Now look at that, there's a lovely stage name for you, Jack! You're Hutton Conyers from now on.' And so he was.

Andy rejoined the act renamed Bretton Woods after the political conference. Dick Carlton, another childhood chum, was enrolled along with the longest-running stooge of all, James's stammering nephew whose real name was Jack Casey. He was rechristened Eli Woods. Finally the family adopted Roy Castle and the legendary brood of gentle maniacs was complete.

In 1956 Castle had already been playing the minor theatres in revues for quite a while, hearing folk tales about such major stars as James as they drifted down from the big circuits of Moss Empires and Stoll Theatres. Then he got his solo break from 'Uncle' Peter Webster, the benevolent entertainment boss of Blackpool's Central Pier. 'Mr Webster told me I'd be feeding Jimmy Clitheroe as well. He still didn't grow.'

Castle had his own spot at the start of the show, singing and dancing and impersonating Jerry Lewis,

*'Never smile at a crocodile . . .'*

followed by Ken Dodd and James. 'Gosh, they couldn't have paid us now,' he reflected and added, remembering, 'They didn't then.'

James was working the six-month season with Eli as the Singing Skunk Trapper, six foot three, eight stone wringing wet, in a Davy Crockett hat. He'd ask him, 'Have you caught any today?' Told no, he'd sniff the air twice and say, 'It's you then.'

When Woods fell ill, Castle could easily take his place in the sketches. He'd watched them every night and knew them by heart. Woods returned in time for the winter tour and James gladly hired Castle as the nutcase in the full-length duster coat for the famous Box Sketch.

Once he'd taken you into his ménage, you were his kin for life. His loyalty was absolute. When sharing the bill at the Bristol Hippodrome with the great British trumpeter Kenny Baker, Woods recalls getting to the theatre on Monday afternoon to find a disconsolate Castle. The show's promoter, Dave Forrester, had cut his act. When James heard the news he told Woods to go and fetch Forrester to his dressing room. 'Ah, there you are, Dave. I believe you've cut out Roy's act.'

'Yes, well, we're overruning, Jim, and Kenny Baker's a big star, he doesn't want some lad playing trumpet before him.'

'Roy doesn't have to play the trumpet. He sings, he dances, he does everything. It's important for him, his first time playing a great theatre like this, Dave.'

'There just isn't time for his act, I'm afraid, and that's that.'

'Tell you what, then. How long have you got me down for?'

'Well, your first spot is fourteen minutes. And your second spot's sixteen.'

'Well, Dave, you've got no problem! You're going to run half an hour early!'

'You can't do that!'

'You know I will, Dave, and you'll have a doctor's certificate first thing tomorrow morning to justify my absence. So make your mind up. Is Roy's act in or out?'

Roy's act was in.

Castle never did get to play his trumpet that week but he used to practise in a dressing room at the top of the theatre. He said that James sent a message asking him to stop practising because 'Kenny Baker's afraid people might think it's him.'

In smaller theatres the team shared the number one dressing room and, as a newcomer, Castle had to adjust to a long-established status quo. James had gradually developed his own language over the years. They'd say one thing and mean another, particularly in the presence of intruders. Whenever a visitor to their bedroom became boring or dropped in to borrow something, James would say to his fourth brother, 'I'm just going to check the hamper, Peter' and that meant 'Get him out!'

Another phrase was, 'This chap's tall enough to be a policeman' which meant, 'He's a total bloody idiot.'

Many an arrogant young comic got that judgement together with a regular James shaft, 'Don't worry about what they're all saying, I think you'll go down all right here. Besides, what does the stage-door keeper know?'

Jimmy's brother Peter had lost a leg in childhood and moved about with the aid of a single crutch. He was deaf as well and kept coming into the conversation three conversations back. What with Peter being out of sync with the rest of the room all the time and Eli Woods's lifelong impediment of stuttering, a chat between the two of them was what Castle called 'A long job. They sounded as if they were both tall enough to be a policeman. But Jimmy told me something fantastic about Pete. He had the one leg and he found another chap in Northampton who had the other leg. And they had the same size feet so they used to buy a pair of shoes between them!'

Second house, Friday night, at the Glasgow Empire was the comic's abattoir. English comedians walked out on stage like secret documents going to a shredder. Part of the reason was booze.

In those years the last drink a Glasgow audience could buy was during the interval of the second house. By the time the final curtain came down, all the pubs were shut so the crowd really supped some stuff in a jig time while they had the chance. Four or five pints each followed by a whisky was the average intake in fifteen minutes. They'd return to their seats for the second half of the show too stunned with cirrhosis juice to understand human speech. Castle again:

'They could see that the juggler was a juggler because they could make out there was juggling going on. "Jings, 'a's a'reet, yon's a juggler!" And if anybody sang, they could vaguely join in, they could still understand what music was. But God help you if you were a talking act. You just made them angry if you talked to them.'

Top of the bill was the yodelling American country singer who played his guitar left-handed, cross-eyed cowboy Slim Whitman. His record of 'Rose Marie' was at number one and he was a great attraction.

The James gang went on and did their first-half spots and the crowd tolerated them.

'They didn't shout anything nasty. They just sat and watched it. Waiting for us to juggle maybe. But then came the interval and they got well tanked up. After which we had to go out and do this eighteen-minute spot. Jimmy went on first to introduce our Eli which always took eight minutes, then I'd go on to do the last ten. They'd barely begun when the hissing started. Then the slow handclap. Then the two combined, the whole place! Well, Jimmy gave me my cue after only one minute, "The lodger got more meat than your father got!" out of nowhere and that was my cue to come on.

'So out I went and the audience was quiet for a moment because they'd noticed a bit of movement, you see, they thought we might start juggling soon. But as soon as we began talking it started again – 'ss-ss-ss-ss-ss' and the slow clapping. Well, we went through the whole eighteen minute act, never missed out one word, and we did it in four minutes!

'We came off walking in a straight line – Jimmy in front, still starting his first cigarette of the act instead of finishing his third, then me in a long coat carrying the box, then Eli, seventy-five inches of malnutrition – and as we're marching along in crocodile, we pass Slim Whitman's dressing room.

'Slim's standing in the doorway in only his shirt. With two bits of white ribbon hanging down which were his legs. He sees our little parade tramping past and he says to Jimmy, "Hey, what's going on here?" And Jimmy says, "You are."'

Many star comedians, especially in their later years, do not suffer fools gladly. It's apparent from James's euphemistic backstage messages to his colleagues to curtail visits from nuisances that he preferred not to be openly rude to anyone. His forbearance was such that he often appeared to suffer fools very gladly indeed. They prompted his mildly sarcastic Muse.

At the rehearsal of one of his too few television appearances he was approached on the studio floor by a bustling floor manager who should have known better than to reveal his ignorance. 'Mr James? Sorry I haven't had time to speak to you before but, er, what exactly do you do?'

James regarded him soberly. 'Well, I'm glad you asked me that because Eli's been worried about it. I've told him it'll be all right because, I said, these fellows, they work it all out. But I'll tell you what's bothering him. When we open the act on the trapeze and it's swinging backwards and forwards and we're dressed in the Chinese costumes singing "By a Blue Lagoon She's Waiting" in three-part harmony, that'll be fine because the camera can move with us, can't it? It's the finish that's got him anxious.

'When we hang upside down with the strings of bowls of goldfish on the ends, we spin 'em, you see, and they go right out sideways, what you call centrifugal. It's our proud boast, twenty years, never spilt a drop. But you'll have to move your orchestra or else Eli will be through that harp like a sliced egg.'

Mike Craig, a dedicated archivist of classic comedy, has a rare recording of a sketch mostly written by Casey in which James and Woods play themselves as no one else ever could.

With the gormless ectomorph in tow, James approaches the animal keeper in a zoo and explains, 'Last Monday our Eli bit a fella's ear off. So the magistrate said he'd have to see a cyclist and get himself examined.'

The keeper corrects him. 'You mean a psychiatrist. Have him analysed and see what he's made of.'

James nods, turns to Eli and shouts, 'The man wants to know what you're made of!' to which Eli responds like a child reciting, 'Sugar and spice and all things nice, that's what little girls are made of.'

During the laughter that follows this inanity, James rolls his cigarette from one corner of his extraordinarily wide mouth to the other and back again, belching clouds of smoke, then confides to the animal keeper, 'We've never told him any different, you see.'

The audience is utterly happy. They know that the zookeeper represents dull sanity and that James and his moronic charge are about to drive him to despair. James continues to regard Eli fondly. 'Such innocence! You wouldn't think he bit a fella's ear off last Monday, would you? No, we've been to the psychiatrist, you see, and he told us to see you because he only deals in human beings.'

The keeper says that Eli strikes him as a bit of a phenomenon. James is shocked. 'Oh, no, oh, no, I'm not having that! Fair's fair! He's always been a good lad to my mother.'

'I'm not talking about your mother.'

'You'd better not either. Up to now you've got two ears!'

Nothing James did was more mysteriously wonderful than his Box Sketch. Certain lines occur in this routine that are quoted by lovers of comedy like shibboleths to test mutual acceptability.

Apart from the basic structure of the mad story, the sort of bit that American knockabouts such as Reese and Davis did in burlesque, I feel fairly sure that the scene was never scripted, that it grew its jokes like fruit on a tree. If one perfectly placed phrase, one punctuation of comic business, appeared spontaneously one night, it stayed in the next. Eventually it was complete and as perfect a piece of stage nonsense as ever was.

Picture James in a natty suit and trilby as he concludes eight minutes of insanity with Woods. From the wings comes a stranger in a horrible hat and a coat that covers him from neck to ankle, carrying a box under his arm. Henceforth, the weird stranger SPEAKS IN CAPITAL LETTERS, while Jimmy James speaks in lower case and [*Eli's lines are written in this style.*]

'HEY! ARE YOU PUTTING IT AROUND THAT I'M BARMY?'
'No, no, it's not me.'
'WELL, SOMEONE'S PUTTING IT AROUND THAT I'M BARMY. IS IT HIM?'
'I'll ask him. (TO ELI:) Is it you that's putting around that he's barmy?'
*'I don't want any.'*
'He doesn't want any.'
*'How much are they?'*
'How much are – no – never mind, it's not him.'
'WELL, SOMEBODY'S PUTTING IT AROUND THAT I'M BARMY.'
'Did you want to keep it a secret? Listen, your face is very familiar – where have I seen you before?'
'OH, I'M OUT OF THERE NOW!'

'Oh, that's where I saw you, in there. I didn't know *I'd* been in. I know I won't be long with you two. No, I've seen you making a political speech somewhere.'

'OH, YEAH. I'M THE MEMBER OF PARLIAMENT FOR (THE LOCAL TOWN)'

'What are you, Conservative, Labour or Democrat?'

'YES.'

'Well, it's nice to know we've got one. (TO ELI:) We've got one.'

*'Have we?'*

'When I look at you, I think we've got two.'

'I'VE BEEN AWAY, Y'KNOW.'

'It doesn't show, no one'd guess, no.'

'I'VE BEEN TO SOUTH AFRICA. I WAS VERY POPULAR IN SOUTH AFRICA AS WELL. JUST BEFORE I CAME HOME THEY GAVE ME A LOVELY PRESENT.'

'What did they give you?'

'TWO MAN-EATING LIONS.'

'Real lions? Did you fetch 'em home? Where do you keep 'em?'

'IN THIS BOX.'

(TO ELI:) 'Go and get two coffees, one with strychnine in.'

'ARE YOU TELLING HIM ABOUT THE LIONS?'

'Oh, yes, you've got two lions in that box. Are they in there now?'

'YES.'

'I thought I heard a rustling. (TO ELI:) He's got two lions in that box.'

*'How much are they?'*

'He doesn't want to sell them.'

'I'VE BEEN TO NYASALAND AS WELL.'

'Ah, they're nice people, the Nyassas. I bet they gave you a present.'

'THEY DID. THEY GAVE ME A GIRAFFE.'

'Did you bring the giraffe home?'

'YES.'

'I don't like to ask him. Where do you keep the giraffe?'

'IN THIS BOX.'

(TO ELI:) 'Get on the phone! Nine nine nine, I'll keep him here.'

'ARE YOU TELLING HIM ABOUT THE GIRAFFE?'

'He's got a giraffe in that box.'

*'Is it black or white?'*

'Our Eli wants to know what colour the giraffe is.'

*'The coffee I mean.'*

'You have the one with the strychnine in it.'

'HERE, DID I EVER TELL YOU I'D BEEN TO INDIA AS WELL.'

'Oh, hell, he's been all over! I bet they gave you a present.'
'YES.'
'What did they give you?'
'AN ELEPHANT.'
'Male or female?'
'NO, AN ELEPHANT.'
'I don't suppose it makes any difference to you whether it's male or female.'
*'It wouldn't make any d-d-difference to anyone, only another elephant.'*
'I'll stop you going to those youth clubs.'
**'Hey, ask him where he keeps the elephant. Go on.'**
'Our Eli wants to know where you keep the elephant. In the box?'
'OH, DON'T BE SILLY. YOU COULDN'T GET AN ELEPHANT IN THERE.'
(TO ELI:) 'Why don't you mind your own damn business? You couldn't get an elephant in there. There's no room!'
*'He could ask the g-g-giraffe to move over a bit.'*
'HE'S CRACKERS!'
'I think it'd be a photo finish between the two of you.'
'I KEEP THE ELEPHANT IN A CAGE.'
'In a cage, of course. Where do you keep the cage?'
*(SPEAKING TOGETHER:) 'IN THE BOX!'*

One of Jimmy Casey's fondest memories of his father encapsulates the man's humour, that mixture of the surreal and the wry. Together they passed a gang of workmen hard at work in the sun, sweating and gasping with effort. James stopped and drew his son's attention to the exhausted labourers. 'Look at those lazy buggers. Too idle to learn a song and a routine of patter.' The great original died on 4 August 1965, but he's remembered whenever someone warns, 'I'll stop you going to those youth clubs!'

And it's during this six-week period that my gag files, something Jimmy James never seemed to need, were stolen. I'd left them inside an attaché case in the locked production office above Studio Eight at the BBC Television Centre.

After recording 'On The Spot' on 20 July, my amanuensis Robert Purdie had packed all my gear into his Merc and we'd travelled home to Bedfordshire quite unaware that my precious files were missing. In fact I'd no idea until the following Sunday when I went to Windsor

Great Park to deliver an after-lunch, pre-polo-match speech for Michael Smith, the Group Chief Executive of API (they seem to lead the market in everything to do with office products and computer communications and other stuff that makes my brain hurt). His gorgeous wife Merilyn was curious about 'Monkhouse Memory Masters', the series I'd done for BBC 1 last spring, and asked, 'Tell me, Bob, do you use a mnemonic system to remember all your jokes?'

'Partly, but I have a naturally retentive memory for comedy of all kinds. And every time I get an idea I put it into my loose-leaf files, two thick Twinlock books that travel everywhere with me.'

'I'd love to see them.'

'Certainly, they're in the car boot. I'll fetch them and show you how they work.'

I went to the nearby car, Robert opened the boot, I opened the strangely weightless case and there they were, gone. Picture my dismay.

As soon as my duties had been discharged and the polo was under way, Robert and I made for the TV Centre, me hoping against hope that when Security let me into the production office I'd see my books tidied away on a shelf perhaps or lying on a desk. No such luck.

The next day I met with investigators from the BBC's own safety and security department and the local CID but made little headway. They suggested I offer a reward for the return of the files and I did, spending most of Tuesday on the phone to newspapers and radio stations and in my garden talking to TV news cameras with my promise of £10,000 for any information that led to the recovery of my work.

It was a slow news week so the press was glad to spread the story of my missing 'joke books'. Cartoons appeared in several papers, all good-naturedly pulling my leg about old jokes and offering £10,000 to the thief to keep them. I tried to smile along with the joshing.

On Sunday, 6 August my mind was taken off the loss when a gloriously sunny day blessed our garden party. Jac had arranged for the proprietor/chef of Paris House, Peter Chandler to cater for eighty friends in a marquee at the top of our large garden and what was meant to wind down around 5.30 p.m. kept going till midnight.

During the late afternoon an impromptu concert was staged on our terrace with Laurie Holloway at the piano and his wife Marion Montgomery singing duets with Cleo Laine. John Dankworth felt like joining in so he drove all the way to his home in Wavendon and back again to play his sax. Meanwhile comedian Ted Robbins had taken over the task of emceeing the improvised programme. He got his super sister Kate Robbins to parade her stunning impressions, Pete Price belted out some great songs and Des O'Connor's glorious girlfriend Jodie was persuaded to show off her beautiful singing voice. Then Des himself promised to sing a song for us, but he let everyone down. He sang five.

By the weekend of 18–20 August I'd given up all hope of seeing my gag files again. I figured they'd either been thought of as rubbish by the cleaners and were now on a tip somewhere or their value had been correctly assessed and a thief was planning to sell them to a comedy professional somewhere abroad. To hide my despair at the loss of so much hard work I joked about it, but the joking was hollow. The two books represented the investment of twenty-five years of invention in the form of plots, routines, lyrics, stories, cartoons, visual and verbal gags, sketches and monologues. Still, I told my audiences, 'I'm just waiting to see if Jim Bowen suddenly becomes funny, then I'll pounce!'

# PART II: MY DIARIES

*4 September 1995 – 1 June 1998*

## Monday, 4 September 1995

I have a sinking feeling that today I'm attending the long, slow funeral of my beloved SOS.

The Executive Meeting is at 11 a.m. and the General at 1.30. The charity, originally named the Stars Organisation for Spastics, was founded in 1955 by a handful of celebrities including David Jacobs, Wilfred Pickles and Vera Lynn.

Cerebral palsy was not clearly understood at the time and the idea was to bring it to public attention and raise funds to aid those already afflicted by this form of brain damage and to pay for research into ways of reducing its occurrence.

Lady Nell Arran was its patron when she seduced me into joining. For many years I had resisted the urge to become a member lest anyone suppose that I was seeking special treatment for my oldest child, Gary.

He was born in 1951 when my first wife was only six months pregnant and he had suffered injury during the birth struggle and in the early weeks of his life in an oxygen tent.

As soon as Gary was an adult, settled into what was to be the regular pattern of his life until his premature death in 1992, I felt free to help my colleagues in their work.

Now, after serving eight years as vice-chairman and chairman, I was vainly supporting our little charity's campaign to become independent of its overbearing parent, the Spastics Society, later to be renamed Scope. Freddie Forsyth had benevolently agreed to take my place in the chair and was presiding over the battle for our freedom from the bureaucracy of the larger organisation but it was becoming clearer at each meeting that our little SOS was destined to become a mere department of the Society.

Under Freddie's leadership and with the inspirational guidance of our tirelessly enthusiastic director, Carol Myer, we would eventually form a new kind of SOS called the Society of Stars. But I didn't imagine that could happen on this day as I looked around the General Committee at the faces I knew so well and regarded as valued friends: Pierre Picton, Sarah Greene, John Goldcrown, Roger Kitter, Martyn Lewis, Michael Grade, George Layton and twenty more. What I saw was the beginning of the end of a hundred such gatherings, all fired with comradeship and good humour.

Of course, when you assemble showbiz people round a conference table you know that keeping matters on course won't be easy. They'll gossip and gas and set ego against ego but also inject a level of levity that's always fun.

When Leslie Crowther outlined his proposal for a fundraising dinner for city businessmen to be hosted by Roger Moore, he told us the fee would be fixed at £250 per guest and invited suggestions for an attractive slogan to head the invitations.

Up went Dickie Henderson's hand. 'How about ALL YOU CAN EAT FOR TWO HUNDRED AND FIFTY QUID?'

## Thursday, 7 September – Tuesday, 19 September 1995

We're staying at Washington's Madison Hotel which is OK but our suite is rather old-fashioned. We wish we'd stayed at the Four Seasons but it's too much trouble to move now we're unpacked. The general manager's welcoming gift is one apple, one pear, six grapes and half a bottle of Evian.

Our first day is spent at the Chevy Chase Mall, shopping for a gold handbag and pumps and stuff for Christmas in Barbados. We've always enjoyed shopping malls in the USA but they're becoming very samey, as we discover on subsequent days trudging round the Pentagon Mall and the Georgetown Park Mall. There's a customer-free Ann Taylor clothing store everywhere we go. Who is Ann Taylor and how does she stay in business? We figure she must be sleeping with Sam Goody: his ubiquitous record shops are doing fine.

We eat at some very elegant joints, among them the strangely un-Chinese Chinese Mister K, the inestimable J. Paul in Georgetown, Galileo with its incredibly flavourful dishes, sunny Sequoia for the ideal open-air lunch, splendidly Italian Tiberio, Mortons with its massively tender steaks and, in Old Alexandria, the Fish Market where the soft-shelled crabs slip down sideways.

The Smithsonian Air and Space display is totally fascinating, displaying the historic and claustrophobic space modules right alongside *The Spirit of St Louis* and other antique kinds of frail aircraft that look as if they couldn't have survived a collision with a humming-bird.

There are no British tourists about so we feel pretty anonymous as we take a cruise on the Potomac aboard the *Odyssey*, a huge ship that resembles a glass-covered football field, built so wide and low in order to pass under the river's rigid bridges. My cover's blown when I'm recognised by half the staff: Irish students on working vacations.

On Thursday we're driven to Wilmington where we lunch at the beautiful Dupont Inn. The restaurant manager is a friendly face from the Savoy in London. We drive on to New York and do a lot of touristy stuff like visiting South Street and Fulton's Pier 17 and sailing around the Statue of Liberty. The lunch is tolerable at even the worst of these sightseers' traps because competition for custom is so strong.

We're tipped off by the Ritz-Carlton concierge to dine at René Pujol, 321, West 51st, and the tip deserves and gets a tip. It's top class and sets us up for *Showboat*. We hadn't booked for this great production so we phone a scalper on 581 4900 and get wonderful seats for six times the regular price. Hey, we're on holiday!

On Sunday we lunch at the Tavern on the Green in Central Park which is fun though a bit haphazard. Afterwards, we tour SoHo on foot and I buy some weird stuff for no reason including penis bones and a giant cockroach in a glass box. Jac thinks it's high time we went home.

As we fly back on Concorde one memory of Washington remains outstanding. We only ever saw one policeman. After asking him for directions, I said, 'Washington is the murder capital of the East, right?'

'That's what they call it, sir.'

'Then how come it's so peaceful and we see so few cops?'

'Well, sir, this part of the city is real secure. If you want to get murdered you'll have to go to Anascostia or Williamsburg.'

'How do we get there?'

'You can go by bus or train, sir. But if you're in a real hurry to get killed, I'd recommend you rent a Mercedes and drive there. Someone should shoot you and take the car within minutes of your arrival.'

'Thank you, officer.'

'No problem, sir. Have a nice funeral.'

**Tuesday, 3 October 1995**
In the sports section of today's *Sun* newspaper they've carried out a survey which says most men would rather watch a football match on TV than have sex. Why do we have to choose? That's what half-time is for.

**Wednesday, 4 October 1995**
Our twenty-second wedding anniversary and I'm in trouble at home. She's only talking to me through the cat.

Sometimes the rows are my fault. I speak my mind before I think. Like yesterday when she called out, 'I'm off to the beauty parlour' and before I could stop myself I called back, 'Don't take no for an answer.'

But then I think honesty is everything in marriage. I have no secrets from Jackie. Well, none that she knows about anyway.

OK, enough of the jokes. I'll leave the rest of my marriage routine until this evening when I pound around the cabaret floor at Gleneagles Hotel in Scotland, downloading my stuff for the delegates of a computer conference. As I leave to catch the 3 p.m. shuttle to Edinburgh, Jac says

'Hope you don't get tired of the animal' and I know just what she means.

Most long-married couples have verbal shortcuts. As I described in my autobiography, *Crying With Laughter*, when one of us is pursuing an obviously fruitless conversation, explaining something complex to a fool or trying to get information out of a person with none to give, the other will offer the simple warning, 'Scrap the Caddie, Clyde.' Familiar? Only if you've heard Clint Eastwood say it to an orang-utan.

The phrase was his instruction to wreck the Cadillac of a debtor in his *Any Which Way* movies and we appropriated it as a handy way of signalling 'drop it'.

As for Jac's parting phrase to me this afternoon, well, back in the 30s an American vaudevillian named James T. James used to perform a monologue about seeing a cat trapped at the top of a tree. He told how he climbed up to rescue the creature only to find that it was a wildcat. His doleful account of all his subsequent efforts was contained in the single phrase, 'I never got so tired of one animal in all my life.'

When I come home after encountering an audience ill-disposed towards my prolonged attempts to entertain them and Jackie asks how my performance went over, she knows exactly when I reply, 'I never got so tired of one animal . . .'

Had they known the saying, such an audience might well have used it about me.

### Saturday, 7 October 1995

Today I flew to Amsterdam to do my cabaret for the Mergat 200 Club. Mergat makes and sells machine tools and this year's reward for their top 200 sales people is a long weekend in Holland. Having settled in my hotel room, phoned Jac to tell her I'm safely installed, I check the sound and lighting in the ballroom where I'm due to perform and then spend a couple of hours looking around the city.

Racial bigotry is a crime against humanity, against society, democracy and every religious tenet. It is morally and spiritually and socially criminal to deprive, deny or discriminate on the grounds of colour, creed, faith or race. So I ask you why is there still prejudice against black people, Jewish people, gay people, Hispanic, Asian, Arab, Muslim, Tamil, Christian and Kurd when we all know full well that the people responsible for every problem on this planet are the Dutch. Oh, those evil Dutch with their tulips and their windmills and their loathsome wooden shoes.

Our cobblers starve while the disgusting Dutch clatter around exchanging their greasy cheese for our precious diamonds, trying to get us to use their caps and sticking their fingers in dikes.

Do you know that marijuana is legal in Amsterdam? Pot, hash, hallucinatory drugs of all kinds – legal! Prostitution – legal! Live sex shows – legal! That's why I hate Holland, it's as if an entire country's going, 'Bob, come here, Bob!'

## Monday, 9 October – Wednesday, 29 November 1995

I didn't know a sixty-seven-year-old comedian could work quite so energetically for so long. These are seven and a half weeks of non-stop gigging plus a spot of telly to fill in any spaces. From the first of these evenings, a Philip Talbot production of the Glass & Glazing Awards at the Grosvenor House Hotel, Park Lane, to the last one, the final recordings of a BBC 1 comedy panel show called 'Gagtag', I never seem to have time to relax. The only rest I get is when I faint now and then.

What do I learn during this marathon? Only that, in my hoarse-throated opinion, the ballroom of the Dorchester has one of the worst sound systems in London, I think the Crown Hotel in Harrogate has become very tatty (this being written in 1995 and both hotels may have since addressed these deficiencies), that Highclere Castle isn't the very best place in the world to make a lunchtime speech if you expect to get laughs, that the Ritz Bingo in Croydon attracts people who couldn't spell Oxo backwards, that Brian Conley's *Jolson* is a portrayal of phenomenal power (yes, all right, one night off!), that the Willows in Salford is still the best comedy pub in the North, that Gary Wilmot is a terrific guy to work with when you have to sing a tricky duet that needs a lot of rehearsal (it was on BBC 1, a series called 'Showstoppers'), that doing a Chris Evans phone-in is like juggling with flour while walking the tightrope over a snakepit, that GMTV interviews always make you look as if you're wearing so much makeup you ought to be talking through a straw, that Gleneagles Hotel in Scotland has towels so thick and fluffy you can hardly close your suitcase, that the Moat House in Stratford-upon-Avon is a great place to leave unless the road takes you to the Moat House in Stoke-on-Trent, that if you can't locate Birmingham's Hyatt Hotel you'll find it situated just outside your income, and that entertaining at Jeremy Beadle's Paul Gorman Charity Ball is the most enjoyable way of doing a bit of good anyone ever invented.

Jeremy invites me to a punning contest. He is having fun digging double meanings out of adverbs, the wordplay known to Americans as 'Tom Swifties'.

During the 20s Victor Appleton penned a popular series of boys' novels about a hero named Tom Swift who discovered lost cities, circumnavigated the globe and performed other feats of derring-do. One of the author's most infuriating habits was never to have Tom say anything without a word to describe how he said it. Every time he spoke it was eagerly, shrewdly, honestly, peremptorily or in some other manner. Before long some advertising executives began to play with the practice to produce punnish results:

'I have mumps,' said Tom infectiously.

'I've sprained my ankle,' said Tom lamely.

'This is my impression of the Venus de Milo,' said Tom disarmingly.

Jeremy offers: 'I'll have another Martini,' said Tom drily.

I counter with: 'There's no Angostura,' said Tom bitterly.

Jeremy dreams up a hat trick: 'I'm seeking a gift for my husband,' said the wife presently. 'How about a shaggy sweater?' asked the sales assistant doggedly. 'He's just your size,' she answered fittingly.

OK, Jeremy, if it's a fight you want . . .

'They've cut off my electricity,' she cried delightedly.

'Here's my offer,' said the builder tenderly.

'I can only give you an afternoon appointment,' explained the receptionist mournfully.

'I have entertained a few sailors,' confessed the Portsmouth slut fleetingly.

'Try planting these,' said the head gardener proceedingly.

'About your good fortune,' began the gypsy reluctantly.

'I'm overflowing with close harmony songs,' she trilled gleefully.

'I've discovered a real professional!' declared the manager profoundly.

'I like it under canvas,' she whispered inattentively.

'You're overdrawn,' read the bank manager's note incredibly.

'Is it eczema?' pondered the dermatologist rashly. 'No, I hope it's only a Caribbean insect bite!' he continued indistinguishably.

'I'll do some feline impersonations,' she purred musingly.

'I'll become a dictator!' he stated deliberately.

'I am the substitute's wife,' the woman announced approximately.

'I've found a fossil,' gasped the professor indignantly.

'A puppy's urine goes piss-sss-sss!' the lecturer observed onomatopoeiacally.

'I'm knitting something for the teapot,' she murmured cosily.

'Life of our species began in this small side-street,' he proposed originally.

'I write the music for Brecht,' spat the German both curtly and vilely.

'I've been chucked out of Equity,' despaired the thespian exactingly.

'I was fated to be the laird,' explained MacTavish clandestinely.

'We need donations for psychiatric research,' he begged fundamentally.

And last but not least.

'Is that your anus?' enquired her lover indifferently.

## Saturday, 2 December 1995

This evening two hours of live ITV were given over to the Comedy Awards, craftily hosted by Jonathan Ross. Jac and I attended because we'd been tipped off that I was to receive some sort of trophy. In the event, Max Bygraves presented me with a Lifetime Achievement Award in Comedy. I don't deserve it, of course. But then I've got vitiligo and I don't deserve that either.

Asked by a journalist if I could point with pride at any particular attainment in my career, I could only think of the three years I spent hosting 'Bob Says Opportunity Knocks', a title still on everyone's lips surely.

We didn't discover many performers who have since risen to great heights although we found some young comedians who have done pretty well; Boothby Graffoe, Mike Doyle, Darren Day and Lee Evans all came through our auditions.

Working with fledgling comedians to prepare them for their TV débuts, advising them on joke construction and placement, editing their best ideas into sequences and suggesting where pauses and recapitulation would improve delivery, I realised a truth: that to teach is to learn twice.

I hope to do more teaching and directing. It's a calling I've respected ever since my schooldays were enriched by the best teacher at Dulwich College, a man known to everyone as 'Horsey' Grange.

A very large, untidy figure with an uncombed grey thatch, his old tweedy suit hung off him with sagging pockets as if it had once been used to smuggle turnips. This eccentric, shambling fellow instructed us in German, History and English Literature. In addition, he taught us how to open and close a door quietly; how to massage our lips daily to expel any accumulation of fatty tissue; most importantly, how to sit on the cold steps waiting for him to unlock the classroom with our books between our bottoms and the stone so as to postpone the advent of haemorrhoids.

I once responded to one of Horsey's snap exams by writing a note explaining that, rather than attempt to fake it, I preferred to admit that I had not done the necessary prep. When the paper was returned, he had not just given me an F minus but drawn above it a very neat halo.

During one of our history lessons, Horsey taught us something about ourselves. The air raid siren sounded as it often had before but, instead of dismissing us to proceed in orderly fashion to the shelters, Horsey held up a finger and cocked his head. 'Who can hear a doodlebug coming?'

We all raised our hands. The ugly buzz was only faintly audible but clearly approaching. These unmanned flying bombs had just enough fuel to reach London. You would hear the engine due and then wait for the silence of its descent to end with the muffled whump so horribly familiar to us all.

'Who hopes it will pass overhead and go on its way?'

Again all hands were raised.

We sat puzzled and quiet as what was once called Hitler's secret weapons came nearer and nearer. Slowly, its engine wavering in tone, it moved through the sky above our school and onwards towards Brixton. There was a general sigh of relief. 'And finally,' said Horsey. 'And finally, who now feels a sense of guilt for having wished the bloody thing on someone else?'

Once more every hand was raised.

My work has been essentially ephemeral. There's nothing in any of the thousands of radio and TV shows I've had a hand in that's more than mere nostalgia; yesterday's dusty topical jokes, game shows that once showed off their gaudy sparkle and now haunt satellite telly like tired old tarts, stale cabaret routines replayed on brittle tape that smells like your great-grandma's house. But here's my comfort.

Every time I perform, *every* time, I know I'm reflecting the ways and means of comedy practitioners I've admired: this little backwards check-step, that's Arthur Askey; that trick of emphasis and repetition, that's Max Miller; these gestures, they're like Max Wall's. Not conscious imitations, no, I'm no impersonator. If you're an apt pupil, you can't help but absorb technique by osmosis. Those grand old comics have, in a small way, lived on through me. I'd rather like to do the same. It's not a lot to leave behind when you go but the mere idea of my being the cause of future laughter makes me feel less selfish.

## Sunday, 3 December 1995

At my cabaret this evening for Sainsbury's Christmas bash in the

Empire Suite of the Café Royal, Regent Street, the chap who's booked me is full of last night's live Comedy Awards.

'Did you know you were going to get the Lifetime Achievement Award?'

'Well, there'd been some broad hints that I wouldn't go away empty-handed.'

'And Bruce Forsyth, did he know he was getting a Lifetime Award too?'

'Bruce acted very surprised but since he'd been there rehearsing a duet with Liza Minnelli all afternoon, I imagine he was putting on a bit of a show.'

Due to overrunning, the Bruce and Liza song had been cut at the very last moment and you could tell that Brucie wasn't best pleased, Award or not.

Born with the gift of a jutting chin that meets studio problems like a plough, the master entertainer doesn't suffer fools or production faults gladly.

Everyone who works on his TV shows seems to agree that Bruce's overwhelming talent is matched by his enviable self-confidence. It's said that when Bruce returned from abroad to start taping a new series of 'The Generation Game', his plane was delayed. Camera rehearsals went ahead at the BBC TV Centre in preparation for the evening's recording while the producer awaited word from Heathrow that the flight had touched down. When, to his relief, confirmation came through, the following announcement was made to the delight of every-one in the studio:

'Ladies and gentlemen,' boomed the loudspeakers, 'the ego has landed! The ego has landed!'

No personality as powerful as Bruce's can remain at the top of light entertainment in all its forms for over forty years without generating stories like that one, some true, some apocryphal. You can't achieve legendary status without legends. Yet such fame as his is never unas-sailable. Bruce's face has been on our screens since the 50s but that doesn't stop London taxi drivers from getting his name wrong.

One story has it that a cab delivered Bruce at Paddington where he was already late for his train. As he paid the fare with a fiver and awaited his change, the cabbie did a double-take.

'Don't tell me, I know who you are! You're that bloke on the telly, aren't you? No, don't tell me, let me remember for myself. You're Jimmy . . . no, no, not Jimmy . . . you're Tommy . . . no, hold on . . . you do that thing on Saturdays with the wossname . . . Joe, is it? No! No, it's

Harry Somebody, isn't it? Oh, let me think, I'll get it in a minute . . . Brian. No, not Brian, no.'

Running out of patience, his passenger said, 'Try Bruce.'

The cabbie considered this, then said, 'Bruce, no, no. Not Bruce. Hold on though – I'll think of it in a moment.'

The next time the star clambered into a taxi with a golfing pal, he wasted no time on the driver's guesswork. As soon as he heard the man behind the wheel say, 'I know that voice. Who are you?' he answered, 'I'm Bruce Forsyth.'

The driver chuckled. 'Yeah? If you're Bruce Forsyth, I'm James Bond.'

'You can't be James Bond, because I am,' said the voice of Bruce's companion, Sean Connery.

Tap-dancing his way through life while bestowing his prodigious gifts upon us all, Bruce has had the companionship of exquisite women, three of them his wives. Penny Calvert was the sexiest of Windmill Theatre's ecdysiasts, Anthea Redfern was foxy enough to make loins combust, and the current and last Mrs Forsyth, Wilnelia, has a beauty that refreshes tired eyes. Bruce's daughters are lovely, his ratings have always been high and his handicap low. His genes have allowed him to become a skilled pianist, tuneful singer, convincing actor and magnificent TV host; it would have been going too far to make him an intellectual too.

In the late 70s the *Daily Mail* ran a feature on quizzing the quizmasters. Without preparation six or seven TV game-show hosts were asked twenty general knowledge questions along the lines of, 'What disease is prevented by the Sabin vaccine?', 'What's the meaning of troglodytic?' and 'Which Greek dramatist wrote *Seven Against Thebes* and *Prometheus Bound*?' (The answers being poliomyelitis, resembling a caveman and Aeschylus.) I made a fair fist of it by correctly answering fifteen, Nicholas Parsons did better with eighteen and the other quizmasters had varied and moderate success.

Only Bruce's answers were funny. Each question was followed by his exact response: 'You what?', 'Strewth!', 'Cor blimey!', 'Oh, Gawd!', 'Oh, come on!' and 'Do me a favour!'

A scriptwriter I know well worked quite recently on a show for Bruce and was amazed at his ability to read typewritten scripts and scribbled handwriting without glasses or contact lenses.

'Yes, I've got marvellous eyesight for my age,' agreed Bruce. 'And do you know what I put it down to? Not reading much.'

## Wednesday, 6 December 1995

Early in life I learned the lesson that, in comedy, less can be more. Aged about eight, I was taken to see the great Bertram Mills Circus at London's Olympia. The star was Emmett Kelly, the tramp clown whose painted facial mask never changed from its expression of gentle melancholy. In addition to his principal routine in the ring, Kelly spent the entire show moving from one position to another amongst the audience. He would find a vantage point on the aisle steps or leaning on the front railing, fix his gaze upon one customer and simply stare. For up to ten minutes, unmoving and seemingly unblinking, he'd maintain his steadfast watch upon the selected individual. Sometimes the subject of his hypnotised attention remained unaware of it for the first few minutes. Then the giggling of those seated around him or the nudges of his family or friends would awaken the chosen mark to the situation and he'd become conscious of Kelly's concentrated regard. Thereafter, the fun for everyone in that section of the audience was rooted in the comedy of embarrassment.

Kelly had polished his technique during his years in America with Ringling Brothers and Barnum & Bailey's circuses. He chose his suckers with as cunning a skill as a stage hypnotist or magician. I remember seeing how each victim reacted with blushes, chagrin, confusion and a discomfort that simply had to surrender to laughter. Kelly was doing nothing, but it was an outrageously anti-social nothing, behaviour that no one would tolerate in normal life except from an imbecile. Somehow this cartoon vagrant, white lipped and tomato nosed in stylised rags and battered hat, made his harmless though unrelenting contemplation into a quite hilarious sideshow. Accustomed to the frantic capering of the eager circus clowns I'd seen thus far, I thought the quiet composure of Kelly must indicate some kind of genius.

The absence of expression allied with a monotony of speech underpinned the screen comedy of many Hollywood comic actors in the 30s. Highly employable comedians like Elizabeth Patterson, she of the blank countenance and gurgling disapproval; Zasu Pitts, a silent screen favourite who brought a fixed big-eyed helplessness and see-saw vocal style to talkies; and most notably Ned Sparks.

With a frozen face that made him look as if he had been 'weaned on a pickle' and a much-imitated, toneless, nasal delivery, Sparks became an essential supporting player in a hundred wisecracking roles.

As audiences grew accustomed to the energetic assault on their senses mounted by most entertainers, so a small number of comedians were

187

discovering that they could achieve their best effects by reducing apparent effort and adopting a more laid-back, even offhand manner. Light comedians like Jack Buchanan and Jack Hulbert brought an attractively diffident air to their stage shows from the 20s onwards.

Radio comedians too were discovering the effectiveness through the microphone of an intimate delivery. In Britain Gillie Potter employed a patrician monotone while in the USA Jack Benny was mastering the throwaway asides and unhurried demeanour that were to become his trademark.

Benny told me, 'I loved the straight-faced reserve of some British comedy actors. The less they tried to be funny, the funnier they were. My favourites in the 30s were Claude Allister and Arthur Treacher and, considering he was an American, I thought Charles Butterworth had a real languid, sort of stupefied way with him. But in Charley's case, the booze had him pretty near paralysed anyhow.'

During the 40s this subtlety found its expression in the almost apologetic murmurings of Eric Barker, wartime star of the BBC's 'Mediterranean Merry-Go-Round' and later his much-loved radio shows 'Waterlogged Spa' and 'Just Fancy'. Barker was a keen observer of successful comedy. Though no fan of US gagsters, he'd seen how Jack Benny had kept still and let a regular gang of realistic funny characters rush around him. In British radio Tommy Handley had suited national tastes by sustaining his fairly normal central figure in a maelstrom of freaks, all quite unreal. Barker cleverly chose the middle ground and surrounded himself with believable but exaggerated zanies, most memorably the *nouveau riche* Lord Waterlogged, blithe Flying Officer Kite played by Humphrey Lestocq and powerful Jon Pertwee, both as a burbling postman with an inexplicable catchphrase ('What does it matter what you do as long as you tear 'em up?') and a deranged Scandinavian repeating his mysterious and untranslatable apothegm, 'Neggiddy-cromp-de-bombitt!' Barker let them get on with it. After all, he'd written the script.

He told me, 'I'm not comfortable on the stage alone. It obliges me to do too much. Once I can be seen striving for results, all the refinement is lost. What I do is much better for me. I put myself beside some absurd, overstated performance, d'you see? Let some other fellow shout and spit. Then the audience can laugh at my reactions to all his frenzied nonsense; small reactions, the smaller the better. Let them work out what's in my mind. It'll be funnier than anything obvious from me.'

Twenty-five years earlier a few silent film comedians had exploited the same device. Buster Keaton's enigmatic visage as he watches the house he has assembled wrecked by a train; Harry Langdon's vacuous façade while sweeping the streets of Chinatown in the middle of a tong war; these void exteriors require us to use our imaginations and so make ourselves laugh at our own comical assumptions about their state of mind.

Soon talking comedy teams covered elsewhere in these pages put this formula to work, bringing to their audiences a ready-made relationship between the personalities on display that was all the more laughable because of the numbed reaction of one to the other. Jimmy James's rock-faced appraisal of his mad stooges, George Burns with his ruminative humouring of Gracie Allen's daffiness, Dean Martin's poker-faced double-takes at Jerry Lewis, Oliver Hardy's dumbfounded despair, each drew upon our suppositions about their thoughts as the craziness of their situations sank in. It appeared to be easier to do less if someone else was doing more.

But if underplaying works best when seen in contrast to extreme performances, how can the stand-up comedian, alone on the stage, offer a similar appeal? All those named above were acting by reacting. There was plenty of excitement going on around them to keep the audiences amused. A solitary figure without the assistance of such diversions seemed unlikely to succeed, yet the trick of holding our attention all by oneself while expending minimum energy began to fascinate some of the more experimental funnymen and women.

In British wartime variety, Suzette Tarri presented herself as a worn-out charwoman with a wobbly, downbeat recitation of her problems. The character caught on and Tarri was stuck with it for the rest of her life.

George Williams, inspired by Tarri's low-pressure success, gave up his rather ineffective career as a drag artiste and took to the stage with his face painted deathly white and a tremulous account of his ill health interspersed by the catchphrase 'I'm not well.' As with Tarri, audience sympathy allowed him a soft, subdued way of performing.

Williams was contemporary with both Roy Barbour and Reg 'Confidentially' Dixon who jointly shared a catchphrase which each claimed to have originated, 'I'm poorly, *proper* poorly!' Dixon, a lovable stage Northerner, secured the resident top spot on post-war radio's hugely popular 'Variety Bandbox' and Barbour was forgotten. Dixon's huge frame, swathed in brightly checked suits, made his slow-paced narratives about his frail condition all the funnier and he enjoyed top-of-the-bill fame that took him from pier shows and provincial panto to West End stardom in the musical *Zip Goes a Million*, replacing George

Formby. Until his death in 1984, Dixon never raised his voice or gesticulated or mugged on stage. He was a model of comic minimalism.

In America, Jackie Vernon had developed an equally unlucky but far more dejected character. His dumpy body immobile, his eyes vacant, he intoned his catalogue of personal disasters in the voice of a resigned loser:

> *Hello again, fun seekers.*
> *So help me, if I fell into a barrelful of bosoms,*
> *I'd come out sucking my thumb.*

> *I started my career at the bottom . . . and stayed there.*

> *Unlucky? If I went into the funeral business, folk'd stop dying.*

He told me, 'When I started out I was a trumpeter in a nutty band called the Loony Lunatics. I got laughs doing silly stuff, quick impressions, prop gags and a big Al Jolson finish. It went well enough for me to quit the band and go solo but I knew I hadn't got it right. I was dying from trying, y'know? It was real discouraging, going out every night to some cheap joint and getting nowhere with a bunch of dumb jokes. My wife used to call me the Willy Loman of Comedy. The more I pushed to make 'em laugh, the more they'd clam up on me. I'm not naturally like that, pushy or wiseguyish.'

Vernon was getting low-paid work and flopping more often than not. Then he stumbled on the style that was to lead him to fame by accident.

'It was this one night I went on to a real tough crowd and I guess I was tired so I just did my regular material the way I'd tell it to a stenographer. No expression in my voice, the way I'm talking to you now. And it scored. Not huge but good enough. So I figured I'd expand on that, cut down the shtick and the trumpet bits and do some sick lines. This would be around 1960, '61, and sick was big. Lenny Bruce was happening, man. He was a pal of mine and he told me two things.

'He told me to stick with my attitude, you know, to thine own self be true? He said, "Jackie, you're not funny as some smiling dude, you're funny as a sad, sorrowful slob." And he said I should do more weird stuff, lines like I wrote with Danny Davis that were pretty much off the wall except Danny called it "off-the-wall-they-ain't-built-yet."'

> *Recently I looked up my family tree – found it was a weeping*
> *willow.*

*Now on with the fun . . .*
*Recitation:*
*When I wake in the morning, when I go to sleep at night,*
*I think of you.*
*When I hear music, when I see beauty or when I breathe in the*
*sunlight,*
*I think of you.*
*You're the sister I never had, the mother I've almost forgotten,*
*The wife I have always dreamed of.*
*There is no relationship that exists between a man and a woman*
*that I wouldn't say, 'Let it be you, let it be you.'*
*Mussolini, 1936*

There was nothing very new about appearing on stage as a wretch. Victor Moore had once cornered the Broadway market in hopeless innocents, his querulous bleat and infantile gestures injecting laughter into numerous revues and musicals added to his bumbling air of defeat his squat body and a balding dome. In the 40s he brought this portrayal of an inadequate dope to Hollywood and made a late life success in such movies as *Louisiana Purchase* and *The Seven-Year Itch*.

On US television in the 50s, mild Wally Cox was briefly but intensely famous as the nerdish Mr Peepers, an exemplar of meekness at bay. Likewise, 'Lonesome George' Gobel's wistful sad sack won him enormous popularity and a 1954 Emmy Award. He was henpecked by 'Spooky Old Alice', bewildered by life and seemed to be unable to think straight:

> *If it wasn't for electricity you'd all be watching this show by*
> *candlelight.*

In Britain from the 30s to the 50s, Horace Kenney's portrayal of a walking disaster delighted variety and radio audiences. With a quavering voice and a shuffling gait, he always made the crowd feel happily superior to him as he played in self-written sketches as a theatre fireman getting the sack or as a useless 'trial turn'.

> *I was nearly in a film once with Rin Tin Tin, sir.*
> *But they said I wasn't strong enough to play the lead.*

But like their low-key predecessors, Moore and Kenney, and to a significant extent Cox and Gobel, required situations and supporting actors

to display their comic incompetence, whereas Jackie Vernon was working directly to the audience every night, steadily dropping jokes that
didn't suit his newly adopted air of defeat, fitting in bizarre new gags
and letting the people detect his haplessness for themselves.

It started to take off in 1962. Television producers, always hungry for
novelty, recognised it in Vernon's newfound despondent air and surreal
patter:

> *I walked by a funeral parlour the other day.*
> *They had a sign in the window that read:*
> *'Closed because of a birth in the family.'*
> *Someone sent me a weird gift for my birthday – a bowling ball*
> *with a thumb in it.*
> *I read an item in the newspaper that was rather confusing – the*
> *State is appropriating five thousand dollars for a new electric*
> *chair – the old one is unsafe.*

All of his unusually angled monologues were spoken in Vernon's
melancholy tenor with the shrugging acceptance of an inexplicable
world from a man reconciled to his low position on life's totem pole:

> *Just this afternoon I saw a cross-eyed woman*
> *telling a bow-legged man to go straight home.*
> *If you are shy, timid, meek, you shouldn't feel too bad about it*
> *because the meek shall inherit the earth – they won't have the*
> *nerve to refuse it.*

Vernon became a fashionable guest on more and more important television shows. Johnny Carson often invited him on 'The Tonight Show'
and dubbed him 'Mister Excitement' and his billing appeared high outside every major Las Vegas hotel. Patter like this convulsed audiences
attuned to Vernon's TV presentation:

> *To look at me now you'd never believe that I used to be a dull guy.*
> *At parties, I'd stay in the room with the coats.*
> *Memorise labels.*
> *No one liked me – the Reverend Billy Graham once punched me*
> *in the mouth.*
> *In desperation I even joined a club called 'Nondescripts*
> *Anonymous' – a special club for rejected people – it was founded*
> *by Whistler's father.*

*For excitement, we'd go to department stores, try on gloves.*
*We'd hang around bus stations, pretend we were leaving.*
*Sometimes we'd take black-and-white pictures of rainbows.*
*For real excitement we'd go down to the Old Soldiers' Home*
*and blow the cavalry charge.*
*You're probably wondering what changed me from the prosaic*
*deadbeat I was . . . to the effervescent gay blade I am today. Let*
*me explain.*
*I think it was Albert Einstein who said,*
*'Scratch a man who looks like a turnip – and you'll find a man*
*who looks like a scratched turnip.' How true.*
*For years I was walking around with this guilt complex – I'd go*
*to the beach, kick sand in my own face.*
*I went to an analyst, he told me I did not have a guilt complex – I*
*was guilty.*

Who knows how much further this one-note act could have taken the trumpet player from the Bronx, born Ralph Verrone in 1928? Had he mastered the next necessary stage of his career and consolidated his appeal by enlarging his 'dull man' character, landed himself a sitcom to suit his style while it was still in vogue, pushed to get into movies and worked harder on fresh, higher-quality material, Vernon might have parlayed his creation into a long-term stay at the top. But, as he told me, he was never cut out to be 'pushy or wiseguyish'.

'My trouble is I'm kinda like the schmo I play onstage. I'm quiet, I guess, shy too. Being ambitious embarrasses me. I get very depressed and I give up easy. When that holiday crowd in Atlantic City and Vegas stopped laughing at the clever lines, I had to do blue stuff to crack 'em up. I sort of came full circle, back to doing obvious, commercial jokes.'

When Vernon died in 1988 aged fifty-nine the tradition of quirky, understated solo comedy had already lost its foremost pioneer and practitioner in his surrender to coarser tastes. All that remains are the jokes, many of them lines of such quaint and literate originality that they still have the power to evoke Vernon's distinctive presence, almost the American counterpart to Les Dawson with his deliberately mundane way of narrating loquacious, nonsensical anecdotes:

*The greatest positive thinker of all time was General Custer.*
*Hopelessly outnumbered by thousands of Indians, he turned to*
*his sergeant and said:*
*'Don't take any prisoners.'*

*My grandfather was an old Indian fighter. My grandmother was
an old Indian.
Sadly, my grandfather had to leave his home on the range.
They made him leave because he broke the Code of the West –
one day he said a discouraging word.
But he once told me the Legend of the Lake. Many moons ago,
before the White Man came to inflict his logic on the Red Man, a
young Indian brave heard the love call of a young Indian maiden
from far across the lake. Every night he returned the love call
across the watery vastness until he became so enamoured of his
distant beloved that he leapt into the icy waters to swim across
them to the arms of his unseen sweetheart. He swam about ten
feet out, froze and drowned. And to this very day the legend lives
on . . . because the lake still bears the name of that Indian brave
– Lake Stupid.
What an amazing audience – you have fantastic self-control.
As I call your names, please pick up your belongings and get on
the truck.*

In 1970 Granada TV's 'The Comedians' attracted great public attention to a bunch of gagcrackers previously unseen by most of us. They
were loud and cheerful, lapel-grabbers and barnstormers almost to a
man. Squeezy-eyed Bernard Manning spat out hard-as-nails racist
jokes sweetened by his Humpty-Dumpty geniality; Frank Carson
couldn't withhold self-congratulation as he brimmed over with tales
of Irish idiocy; Charlie Williams, brown as overdone Yorkshire pud,
had a laugh just as warm and irresistible; chuckling Duggie Brown,
wry Jim Bowen, shrewd Tom O'Connor, plus Colin Crompton, Mike
Reid, George Roper, Dave Butler, Eddie Flanagan, Mike Burton, Josh
White, all were instantly impressive professionals who had honed
their bang-bang delivery in the hustle-bustle of cabaret in the 60s,
first in the working men's clubs, then the snazzy nightspots that
sprang up around gambling tables in the sidestreets of almost every
north England town. They had learned to use energy, confidence and
attack.

Only two of these new blokes on the block chose to take the quiet
path: Ken Goodwin and Roy Walker.

Twinkly-eyed Goodwin grinned and gangled and acted like a shy kid
telling children's jokes at a party. After reciting some simple-minded
riddle, he'd shake with suppressed glee and ask, 'Do you get it?' When
the audience applauded he'd forget that this was the approval he was

supposed to be seeking and admonish them, 'Not too loud, I've got a 'eadache.'

A well-dressed gent with thick greying hair and a polite air, Walker's soft Ulster voice, his lack of aggression, the composed expression barely hiding a gentle smile, his amazing pauses which defied interruption, somehow overawing and silencing hecklers, all gave an uplifting quality to quite ordinary one-liners and multiplied their laughter value to an almost incredible degree:

> *Five hundred New Age Travellers have been evicted from*
> *Stonehenge.*
> *They thought it was a Barratt's show house.*
> *My brother Shuey's naïve. Thinks a peach is a suede apple.*

Such workable but unexceptional jokes could be (and have been) rattled off by a score of holiday camp comics to win indulgent chuckles from their well-disposed crowds. Delivered by Walker in his slyly adopted pose of worldly innocence with undertones of hidden meaning, the same jokes evoke explosions of long-sustained mirth. The longer he stands silently regarding them, the longer the people delight in the situation, stimulated to further laughter by released impulses that have less to do with the absurdity of the jokes themselves than with the immediate absurdity of the moment. Once again it's an example of the art of the best comedians, elevating the material by the implication of an unspoken understanding between themselves and the audience.

Walker's comic epiphany occurred at one of the toughest working men's clubs in the North-East and, as in so many instances, it was inspired by fear. Earning a small but comfortable living on Tyneside as a singer who told jokes, and coming from a Northern Irish tradition that 'a comedian is a man dressed as a woman', Walker's ambition to be accepted as a nattily attired stand-up in the American tradition of Burns and Benny looked like a non-starter. Imitative of his contemporaries, he 'was attacking the punters and getting nowhere'.

'Then one Friday night in 1974 I was booked into Pennywell WMC, lads' night out, industrial-strength boozing going on. It was no fit place for a good comedian, or me either for that matter. I stood there on the stage in a state of terror. Then I heard myself saying, "My mother's doing well." Just like that, ever so soft and gentle. And another part of my mind is saying to me, "Why did I start this joke?" but I was still talking on automatic pilot, "She went to the doctors . . ." while at the back of my brain I'm thinking, "Get out of this joke somehow!" But my scared little voice is carrying on, my face is set like stone but for a puzzled look and, wonder of wonders, the lads have started to listen. They're going, "What's he saying? Sssh, I can't hear him." And I finish the joke and there's a laugh, a real solid laugh.

'That night I came off to the most satisfying applause I'd ever had. And I knew that my attitude until then had been completely wrong. That night was the making of me. Call it deportment, outlook, whatever it was, I knew I had a new attitude and that would be my style from then on.'

Within three years this technique had won Walker effusive praise from the panel of judges on ATV's 'New Faces' and a place among Granada's 'The Comedians'. Slightly misunderstood by the producer, Walker's contributions to the Manchester-based series suffered from the use of only his most lugubrious gags. Had he remained restricted by such editorial control his TV career would surely have suffered, viewers unaware of the subtlety of his conspiratorial glances and the almost private amusement that hovered behind them. Fortunately, others saw his potential more clearly and encouraged him to continue developing and deepening his stage presence as the hypnotic funnyman who never raises his voice. The resulting character of Walker's comedy has much of the whimsicality of Chic Murray but with the extra dimension of an emotional undercurrent not unconnected with the darkness and light we associate with Ulster itself.

This discovery of a personal style at the very brink of a public humiliation has happened more than once among those comedians capable of surviving the crisis with an intuitive grasp of reality and a sudden perception of the essential nature of their comedy. Walker's revelatory performance is echoed in Les Dawson's despairing adoption of contempt as a defence against just such a difficult WMC audience and his self-realisation of what was to become his lifelong approach.

If Walker was driven by fear to his deceptive mildness and Dawson to his deceptive pugnacity, the ultimate in funny minimalism was achieved by the paralysing dread experienced by the extraordinary American comedian, Steven Wright.

It's 10 a.m., Friday morning, 13 May 1983, in the BBC's Acton rehearsal block. I'm in a huge room on the fifth floor, sitting at a trestle table with the producer and writers on 'The Bob Monkhouse Show' for BBC 2.

Each week, following animated cartoon credits that show a high-speed montage of familiar comedy figures – Askey turning into Jack

Benny, Flanagan & Allen becoming the Two Ronnies and so on until finally Buster Keaton changes into me – I do my opening eight-minute stand-up spot.

After that I introduce my guests, usually a young American first, like Rita Rudner, Jim Carrey, Larry Miller or Emo Phillips. Then an established British star such as Norman Wisdom, Victoria Wood, Ronnie Barker or Max Bygraves. Some weeks we vary this: when a major US comedian becomes available and we open with a rising British act, Duncan Norvelle perhaps or Hale & Pace, and devote the second half of the show to names like Sid Caesar or Bob Hope.

This week our young American doesn't look like much of a catch.

He shambles into the room, gazes around blankly and waits. Producer John Fisher and I rise to greet him. He looks anxious as if he expects to be attacked. We guide him to the table and ask him what sort of material he'd like to do. He pulls a dog-eared school notebook out of his army surplus jacket and consults it silently.

As he turns the pages, all crowded with random jottings, we are looking at this twenty-eight-year-old and wondering what he uses for a personality. His frizzy hair is fast becoming history, his face is one you'd barely recognise again and his air of abstraction could be a borderline coma.

Then he starts to read from his notebook. He speaks in a low, flat manner without expression and we all have to lean towards him and pay close attention. He says,

> *It's a small world. But I wouldn't want to paint it.*

It's so strange and funny that we break into loud laughter, then stifle it to hear more. He says,

> *One time I went fishing with Salvador Dali. He was using a*
> *dotted line.*
> *He caught every other fish.*

We have never heard jokes like these. They're weird and wonderful and perfect, like haiku, those Japanese poems that have an exact number of syllables that must not be increased or decreased. He says,

> *Whenever I pick up someone hitch-hiking I always wait a few*
> *minutes.*
> *Then I say, 'So how far do you think you're going?*

*Put your seat belt on, I want to try something.*
*I saw it in a cartoon but I'm pretty sure I can do it.'*

For forty-five minutes this droning fellow has us laughing till we're
hoarse and sore and he hasn't raised his eyes or his voice. By this time
though I can detect his rhythms, the subtlety of his pacing and the very
slight drag he places on key words to give them an almost secretive
emphasis. His apparent absence of technique is a technique in itself.

Economy is essential to his humour, each joke pared to its irreducible
minimum. Word selection too is a finely tuned process for him. One
joke concerns meeting a girl on a bus who tells him she is a nymphomaniac but that she's only turned on by Jewish cowboys. She tells him
her name. He introduces himself as 'Bucky Goldberg'. We suggest that,
for a British audience, the gag would be more immediately accessible if
he changed 'Bucky' to 'Hopalong'. He regards us sadly, as if we've
come to tell him of a death in the family. He gives a tiny sigh and
promises, 'I'll try' – but on the night of the show the name is 'Bucky'
and the laugh is terrific.

'He's marvellous for us,' says comedy writer Dennis Berson. 'But if
we get an unimaginative studio audience, things could get very quiet.'

'I'll make sure there's a large ticket allocation to students,' says Fisher.

We've decided to divide his spot into two: a seated interview, in
which I'll lead him to the jokes we believe will be easiest for our audiences to grasp, followed by a stand-up spot of indeterminate length, per-
mitting judicious post-production editing to cut jokes that misfire.

I drive him back to his hotel in South Kensington and talk to him over
a light meal in the coffee shop.

'What got you hooked on comedy?' is my first question. I know I'm
not going to hear a familiar answer.

'Well, I have an older brother who was in charge of the TV so I pretty
much had to watch whatever he wanted to watch. And he was a Johnny
Carson freak. After a while I got attached to 'The Tonight Show' too. I
loved watching Johnny come out there and do the monologue – and
Richard Pryor and George Carlin and David Brenner and Robert Klein
and stuff. And I just thought, "That would be amazing to go on that
show and do that for a living."

'From then on the fantasy never left me. I was always watching
stand-ups, any show, every show. I watched all kinds of funny movies
too and I was listening to all the good albums, some on the late-night
radio and others that I bought, especially Woody Allen, I'd play him
over and over. And I liked Carlin for his sense of observing everything

differently. I was so into comedy of every kind that I look back now and I realise that I was studying it without knowing that I was. I was immersed, fixated a little, so I was learning but I wasn't aware of it.'

'Were you writing down ideas of your own?'

'No, no, I didn't start collecting material or anything, I was just looking at it all. I'd memorise Bill Cosby and then perform it for the guys in school, that was all. And Jackie Vernon, I just loved that resignation of his when he'd say stuff like, "My father died. We buried him because he would've wanted it that way."'

'All this concentration on comedy, didn't your family worry? Didn't it interfere with your education?'

'Well, *I* worried about it. So I went to Emerson College in case this fantasy of mine didn't come true. A lot of me thought, "I'm never going to pull this off, I'm living in a dream world, and I'd better have some kind of education for when this doesn't happen." But after I was done with college, after I'd graduated, then I had to deal with my fantasy.'

'Right away?'

'No, not right away. The first thing I did, I went to Aspen and got a job shovelling snow off the roads. Then I was parking cars in Las Vegas. I still had the dream in my head but I didn't know how to go about it. I was living up in a cloud like a dreamer. I didn't think, "Come on, I've got to go to LA, New York, go where the clubs are and do it!" Then I had to come back to Boston because my brother was getting married and that's when I heard about this new comedy club right there in town. And I thought, "This is too close to be true, this is amazing, I don't have to move to LA or New York, I can go down to this place in Boston and confront the fantasy. See if this thing I've had in my head for nine years can really be done.'

There were two clubs in Wright's corner of Massachusetts, in 1979: The Comedy Connection and a restaurant known locally as 'The Chinese Place'.

Wright's informant thought that his better choice would be the Open Mike Auditions at the Connection. He took two weeks to prepare what he was going to do, filled with understandable anxiety.

'It was my big thing. Because I didn't want to end up being, oh, I don't know, some insurance man in Wyoming who'd always be wondering what would have happened if only he'd had the nerve to try.'

'How about encouragement from your friends and family?'

'None, because I kept it inside my head for so many years and, in all that time, I only ever told one other person about it. I never told my family because they'd say I was crazy, like I wanted to be an astronaut.'

'Tell me about your first time on stage.'

'It was too much. I didn't know what happened till it was over. I only had two minutes. That's all I'd prepared, a two-minute scenario thing, and the first joke was about going into a bookstore and "I saw a very French-looking girl . . . she was a bilingual illiterate . . . she couldn't read in two different languages." And that got a laugh. So I went on with the rest of the story and finished and came off and, oh, I was so down. I was so disappointed because they had only laughed at about half my stuff. I thought that was really bad. I had nothing to judge it by.'

'You felt you'd failed because every line hadn't registered?'

'Right, but then one of the comics who was working there took me aside and said, "What's your problem? Just rewrite it. Take out the stuff that didn't work, put other stuff in and come back and do it again." And I'm walking home that night, so amazed by it all, so confused, because nine years of this daydreaming just ended, and suddenly it hit me. They did laugh at half of it. They laughed at something I made up. It had come true after so many years. I just focused on that positive fact. I had stood there, I had made stuff up, I said it to them and they laughed. Incredible.'

Later, at the BBC Television Theatre, Shepherd's Bush, Wright arrives for a run-through. I remind him of my feedlines and he has no need of any other *aide-mémoire*. When it's showtime, I follow 'Squire' Ronnie Hayward's gently witty warm-up with my own. I tell the theatre audience that we have an American guest who's wowed them on 'The Tonight Show' and make some slight crack about having to sit up lest his jokes go over their heads.

The show begins, my opening routine goes well and I go into the interviews with my first two guests, then: 'Ladies and gentlemen, he's been called cerebral, bizarre and the Wizard of Odd, Steven Wright!'

He all but shuffles on, no bright smile, no here I am, folks. He seems dazed. He blinks and rubs his eye.

'Good evening, Steven. Are the lights bothering you?'

He says

*I wear eye glasses during the day.*
*Yesterday, I was walking on the street, wearing my eye glasses,*
*and all of a sudden the prescription ran out.*

The audience takes a moment, then gives out a burst of laughter. From that point on, every single gag does the business. For his stand-up spot, he paces to and fro, his gaze vaguely unfixed, like Hamlet on the battlements of Elsinore. The jokes become even more eccentric but the laughs only get bigger.

> *Babies don't need a vacation but I still see 'em at the beach.*
> *One time I was hitch-hiking and a hearse stopped.*
> *I said, 'No, thanks, I'm not going that far.'*

The applause is ecstatic. I come off the stage and say to writer Neil Shand, 'A new American star for Britain.'

Shand says, 'He's splendid, Bob. Original, very delightful. But I don't believe he's a performer that people are going to want to see too often. Minimalism has its charms but generosity isn't one of them. People are accustomed to warmth as well as wit. I think Mr Wright is at the furthest extreme of non-performance permissible. His jokes are glorious but he could almost have mailed them in.'

Wright calls into my dressing room to say thank you and goodnight. He agrees to sit and sip a soft drink. I have a few more questions about the way in which this extraordinary droll became funny for money.

'That first time you made your dream come true, did you work as you did tonight?'

'No, I talked much faster then because of nervousness. I paced to and fro for the same reason. Then, as I got more relaxed, I started talking slower till it was like I really speak. Though it's never stopped, the pacing slowed down too.'

'How about your impassiveness?'

'That was nerves too. Being such an introvert, it was scary out there. And when I'm scared, I have a blank face like someone has a gun on me from off stage. I just haven't changed that because it would be artificial. The insane things I'm saying, they made me laugh when I first thought of them, but I can't pretend that I still find them funny. I have a serious face because I'm doing a serious job of making people laugh. While I'm on, I'm thinking of six or seven things at the same time. I'm thinking of how the last gag went, what I'm saying now, the rhythm of the words and the reaction I'm getting, what I'll do next, and it's almost like it's not even funny any more. I don't hide the fact that I've got to say it all in the exact right way or it won't work. And I've got to remember eighty other jokes. And I think the fact that I don't try to conceal all that has sort of become my trademark.'

'You're not enjoying the fulfilment of your dream?'

'It's not that I'm not enjoying myself, it's just that it's hard work and I'm not covering that up. I do enjoy it when the laughs are coming in.

201

When I see someone just dying with laughter, I can take a brief moment of pleasure before I go on.'

'That joke you did tonight about the electricity in your house going off. You got around using a flash camera. You had to take sixty pictures of the kitchen just to make a sandwich. The neighbours thought there was lightning in your house. That's three big laughs. Where does a triple score like that come from?'

'It's to do with seeing everything through the eyes of a child. We might think, "The lights don't work, I'll get a flashlight, some candles", that's because we're older and our minds have narrowed down to familiar options. But to a little kid, light is light. Try flash bulbs. It's surreal but it's what children do every day and we laugh. Like the sign on the store says OPEN 24 HOURS and the manager's locking up. I say, "But the sign says you're open 24 hours" and he says, "Not in a row." Now, you see, adults know that 24 hours means one day but a child isn't brainwashed yet, he hasn't been taught that assumption, so to him it could mean 24 hours a month.'

Wright is still filled with wonder at things generally taken for granted: ordering a Coke five miles up in the air, satellite TV, tunnels, batteries . . .

'A kid might wonder what batteries run on. If a kid hears the line is busy, he might wonder what it's doing. When the sign in the restaurant says BREAKFAST AT ANY TIME, I order French toast during the Renaissance. It's just avoiding normal assumptions.'

'Playing with language, taking things literally, finding connections between ideas that no one else has found, that's your comic writing, your mind at work. Is performing it over and over ever going to pall?'

'I'm not sure. I still get a rush doing a stand-up, like tonight when it could have all gone so horribly wrong and it all worked. That's still a great feeling. But there's so much more to comedy. Stand-up is verbal pictures. I like to tell them pictures but I'd like to show them pictures too.'

Four years after this conversation took place, Steven Wright wrote and starred in *The Appointments of Dennis Jennings*, a Home Box Office Special which won him a 1988 Academy Award for Best Live Action Short Subject. It was subtle, offbeat and got its best effects through the smallest amount of effort.

Most comedians who play 'themselves' in extrovert style, broad in gesture and brash in speech, reach their peak aged from thirty to mid-forties. Their appeal is based on foolishness and it's less attractive in older people. Those who have espoused underplaying, luring us into their traps with soft voices and composed features, are no less susceptible to changes in public taste, slackening of invention or the danger of monotony. They have one sure advantage though: by conserving energy in performance, they won't be seen to lose it with the passage of time. Unlike dancers and athletes and the louder comics who, depending upon fire and force, may find themselves running out of steam, the less demonstrative jokers can take some satisfaction from that. At least the day is never likely to come when we will say of Roy Walker, Jack Dee or Steven Wright, 'He doesn't laugh as much as he used to, does he?'

(In case you're wondering what inspired these pages under the date 6 December, well, forty years ago today Steven Wright was born.)

## Sunday, 10 December 1995

After a hectic dash from doing last night's late cabaret at Rovers' Social Club in Solihull to reach Heathrow in time for a 9.40 a.m. take-off, a philosophic state of mind was required to endure sitting on the runway for two and a half hours because of fog. At least Barbados doesn't go in for fog. What it does go in for in a big way is wrong numbers.

Considering that the island has the world's most sophisticated telephone exchange (a million or more transatlantic calls are routed through it every day and all calls within the island are free), it strikes me as curious that, whenever any of the 261,000 inhabitants want to speak to each other on the phone, they dial our number by mistake.

I try to adopt a positive attitude towards them. Wrong numbers used to annoy me a lot. Not any more. I enjoy them. Some woman calls up and asks if she can speak to Kenny, don't tell her she's got a wrong number – where's the fun in that? Let her think she's got a right number. 'Kenny isn't here right now, madam, can I help you? I'm Detective Sergeant Cartwright of the Serious Crimes Squad, who are you? You're Kenny's mother, well, yes, we are hoping to talk to him at about 6 p.m., that's our time here, I don't know what time it'll be in Rio de Janeiro. Please keep your voice down, madam, I don't know what he's to be charged with – all we've done is raid the premises, defuse the bomb, release the hostages and recover the bullion. Oh and by the way, honey, you've got a wrong number.'

## Saturday, 16 December 1995

Fifty years ago, on this day in 1945, I left Dulwich College to take up my first job prior to being conscripted into the RAF the following June.

So for five months I worked as a cartoon film animator for J. Arthur

Rank's Gaumont-British Company situated at Moor Hall, Cookham, near Maidenhead. The old house had a very creepy atmosphere and, since many of us living there were teenagers, there was the inevitable adolescent gossip of ghosts. Even so, none of us was prepared for the two strange incidents that took place.

First it was the grand piano in the great wood-panelled hall. Stains on its keys had led to a rumour of some previous owner blowing his brains out while seated at the keyboard.

Perhaps the suppressed nervous hysteria this produced affected events. At 3 a.m. on the first of May, the grandfather clock on the main staircase struck the hour and immediately the sound of the piano being played was audible throughout the mansion. Each one of us woke at the same time and each one of us lay quite still and calm for about three or four minutes hearing the notes clearly wherever we were sleeping. As the last notes sounded, panic set in and we all rose from our beds and crept out to see what was happening, taking courage from each other's company.

We gathered on the stairs and around the hall in our night attire and stared at the piano which sat silently in a shaft of moonlight. We whispered about our shared experience and many surmised that a prankster had been at play. But no one could explain our simultaneous wakening and those minutes of calm repose before becoming alarmed.

Seven nights later every one of us woke at 3 a.m. and heard the grandfather clock strike – and then begin to rock.

It was a very big, very old clock that towered at the top of the first wide stairs that led up from the entrance hall. The stairs were then divided into two flights that rose to the gallery. Some of our bedrooms were off this gallery, others were further away down various corridors. In later discussion we agreed that each of us heard the sound of the great clock rocking as clearly as we had heard the piano.

We all lay as before, quite at ease, listening to what we knew beyond doubt was the steady rocking forward and backward of the clock, slight at first, then growing louder and slower as the motion increased. The chimes clanged in response to the rocking movement, the back of the clock's top began to strike the panelled wall behind it on each backward tilt and finally the clock leaned so far forward that its balance was lost and it toppled, crashing down with slightly more than half its length extending over the downward stairs. Glass shattered, wood splintered, as the clock's heavy face and head caused it to tip downwards, upending and sliding down the steps to smash into the floor of the hall.

Just as in the case of the piano, the end of the sounds seemed to signal our release from composure and we rose as before to gather in the gallery and look at what we expected to see, the huge clock in smithereens upon the hall floor. Instead we saw the clock where it had always been, ticking serenely on its wide landing, quite undamaged.

Many of us surmised that we had experienced the sort of sensory deception that is often ascribed to the activity of a poltergeist, those antic spirits that often seen attracted to the presence of adolescents.

Me, I went to Padgate, put on a uniform and stamped the demons out of the parade ground for ten weeks of hell where the only evil spirit was our drill sergeant.

## Monday, 25 December 1995

I think Christmas should be a day for prayer . . . for religious meditation . . . a time to thank God. I can sit quietly at the table, surrounded by all of my relatives, and think, 'Thank God it'll be another 365 days before I see these greedy bastards again.'

I'm mighty glad we're in Barbados again this holiday and dining this evening with twenty new friends at the beautiful beachfront villa called Sara Moon, courtesy of Alan and Ray, two hugely generous hosts from the Midlands. Bang goes any further attempt to diet in what remains of '95.

That's the real problem with Christmas Day: all the food we feel obliged to cram down our necks. Everyone's under some sort of traditional compulsion to overdose on turkey and pudding. I don't care whose house you go into, it's the same situation. Swollen survivors from a stomach distending contest, 'Woof! No thanks, no more for me, oof, I couldn't eat another thing! Ooh, I shouldn't have had that last roast potato, thirteen's an unlucky number.'

In every home back in Britain no one can move. If Red China ever decided to attack us, this is the day they should do it. 'Dad, the Chinese army is parachuting down all over Britain!' . . . 'Sorry, can't help!'

The entire population paralysed by calorie consumption from 2 p.m. till 6 – you could tell President Clinton they were giving away free women, he'd go, 'Too full.'

My father used to sit there, scratching wherever it itched, belching whenever the bubble was ready for expulsion, scratching inside his ear with his car keys – looked like he was trying to start his head. He might've been too, he kept backfiring.

After a meal my father would push his chair back a few inches and unzip the top of his trousers the same amount. In fact, how far he unzipped was in direct proportion to how much he'd enjoyed the food.

Once in a restaurant he unzipped the entire zip. Other fathers were going, 'I'll have whatever he just had!'

Mind you, my mother wasn't the greatest cook. Some women, they cook a turkey and it tastes even better the day after. Hers tasted better the day before.

She'd go, 'Who wants stuffing?' and we'd be too polite to tell her.

Whoever came up with that idea, stuffing a turkey? It must have been a long, long time ago. Some people in a kitchen somewhere, the turkey's plucked, all ready to go into the oven, and suddenly one of them says, 'Wait just a minute! Hold it! Let's thrust something up that turkey's rear end! Let's shove some wet bread up that baby's fundament!'

What a weird sort of an anti-ornithological, anally fixated necrophiliac freak this person must have been.

'Come on, let's push everything edible up that big bird's back passage! What's in the pantry? Onions, celery, grapes, walnuts, sausage meat – what's that, a box of baking soda? Shove it all up there! Bung in some popcorn so when the turkey blows its arse off, we'll know it's done!'

## Sunday, 31 December 1995

Here I am, back from three weeks in the Bajan sun and doing my New Year's Eve routine on the familiar stage of Bob Potter's Lakeside Country and Cabaret Club. And, kidding aside, what a peculiar year it's been.

Blackburn Rovers won the European Premiership, a seventy-four-year-old pensioner named Bob Maund had his pals pull his tooth out with pliers in the pub ('It was agony for a moment but my mouth felt perfect after they gave me a pint of mild'), we were told that peace had come to Bosnia, our royal family strove to keep their adultery off the front pages of the tabloids, Russia goosestepped backwards toward the October Revolution, the police dug up Fred West's cellar (his loyal daughter Mae said, 'He was a brilliant dad really . . . you'd never think he was a murderer'), and Tony Blair cautioned us, 'If people think that, by going back to where we were twelve years ago, we are going to win power, then they require not leadership but therapy.'

Tory Party Chairman Brian Mawhinney had paint lobbed over him by protesters and was overcome with emulsion. When Paula Yates said her book had taken just six days to pen, Ian Hislop asked, 'Did you have writer's block?' Richard Parker Bowles remarked of his sister-in-law, 'If Camilla had been a child on the beach she'd have knocked other children's sandcastles down. She's a wrecker at heart.'

Oh, there were some Monkhouse-style jokes to be made too. On a lighter note, during a flight to Saudi Arabia, BA managed to lose a coffin. It's bad enough waiting at the carousel when your suitcase doesn't come round.

Dame Vera Lynn slammed industries in Britain for not donating money to her VJ Day celebration but they all still refused . . . Nissan, Sony, Toyota, Mitsubishi, Samsung . . .

Liz Hurley announced her plans to star in an 007 James Bond spoof and there was a part for Hugh Grant, a sort of cross between Blofeld and Oddjob. He's called Oddfeld, that's right.

And finally, my hero, J. Howard Marshall died at the age of ninety. He was the multi-billionaire who was, for the last eighteen months of his life, married to the amply curved Anna Nicole Smith. The only man to die and *leave* heaven.

They said he was in bed with Anna Nicole when he died of a massive stroke . . . what a way to go!

## Saturday, 13 January 1996

Off on Concorde to Barbados again, this time with our dear friend and my co-writer of topical funnies, Colin Edmonds. Col's wife Kathryn felt that he needed a holiday so she entrusted him to us. He was so excited about his first experience of supersonic flight that Jac and I felt a tinge gutted on his behalf when we had to stop to refuel in Antigua.

During the flight's interruption, Col browsed round the airport gift shop and, resisting tax-free watches and cameras and exotic perfumes, bought himself a fly-swatter, saying, 'I mean to earn my keep.'

It took me back thirty-four years to a story that's silly but true.

For no obvious reason, while Barbados has no shortage of flies during the humid season, the same could not be said of fly-swatters; at least not in 1962 when my first wife and I stayed at Sam Lord's Castle on the east coast. Our virtually free accommodation there had been arranged by a good friend then living on the island, novelist and playwright Wolf Mankowitz (author of *Expresso Bongo* and *A Kid for Two Farthings*).

He phoned us before our departure from London to say, 'As a friendly gesture to the family that owns Sam Lord's, could you bring out enough fly-swatters for all the rooms?' It seemed the least I could do in exchange for our lodging.

I went to a hardware store called Mence Smith in St John's Wood and asked for fly-swatters. The assistant fetched me one and told me the price. 'No,' I said. 'I'm going abroad, Barbados. They have a lot of flies at this time of the year. I'll need all you've got.'

He came back with twenty-eight.

'This is our entire stock, sir.' He laid them on the counter and scratched his head, hesitating to speak. Then he regarded me with serious concern for my innocence and said, 'You *do* know that you can use these more than once?'

### Friday, 19 January 1996
Barbados will soon have a magnificent new golf course. I drove up to the site of the Royal Westmoreland to reconnoitre and remembered why I don't play golf. A day has enough frustrations in it without adding another eighteen.

### Monday, 29 January – Thursday, 7 March 1996
These Barbados sojourns are turning out to be more sociable than ever.

Apart from Colin Edmonds and Pete Price as our house guests at Sandcastle, we find ourselves dining out with Joy and Ronnie Barker (staying at the Sandpiper Hotel as usual), Sue and Jeremy Beadle, Gloria Hunniford, Fliss and Alan Nixon (she's a fine actress, he's the newly appointed Head of Comedy for Channel 5), Hazel and Jasper Carrott, Amanda and Les Dennis, Marion and Lou Manzi (he owns the stunningly successful Southend club called TOTS) and Lionel Bart.

Other friends encountered here include John Cleese, Shakira and Michael Caine, Carol and Julian Sacher (he's the island's most knowledgeable importer of wines), Des O'Connor with his scrumptious little daughter Kristina, Tricia and Russ Abbot, Bonnie and Nigel Lythgoe (she's a theatrical producer and choreographer, he's Head of Entertainment at LWT), Katie Boyle, Moya and George Layton (writer, actor/singer, he played Fagin in *Oliver* at the London Palladium), Dulcie Gray and Michael Denison, Anna Walker and Ross King (she's the most gorgeous TV weathergirl, he's a popular actor/singer/TV presenter) . . . well, the list of famous faces grows longer and browner by the day.

Our adopted West Indies home attracts show people of all kinds, from Kevin Kline and Joan Collins to Sir Harry Secombe, Cilla Black, Luciano Pavarotti, Jimmy Tarbuck and Freddie Starr.

The first celebrity I ever saw here was also the first time I ever came here just thirty-four years ago during a break from Neil Simon's long-running play *Come Blow Your Horn* at the Prince of Wales Theatre.

My first wife and I stayed at the then privately owned Sam Lord's

Castle as I've already mentioned. One evening we crossed to the west coast resort hotel, Coral Reef, and ran into the man I've just been asked to talk about upon my return to England. It's to be a tribute to his memory and his legacy of laughter. I'll be as generous about him as I can but I hope some honest recollection won't go amiss.

Dick Emery's show was the BBC's official entry for the 1973 Montreux Festival. At his peak on television, he was voted BBC TV Personality of the Year. His most popular comic characters were the sanctimonious vicar; Hettie, the sex-starved spinster; doddering Lampwick with his endless memories of World War I; the sly and sinister solicitor, Partridge; gay Clarence ('Hallo, Honky Tonks!'); the delinquent bovver boy; College the tramp; the nasty neighbour; the pompous traffic warden; the dodgy sporting gent; the ton-up boy in black leather; and, favourite of most of his fans but not liked by him, the busty and flirtatious Mandy who dislocated male shoulders with the punch that always accompanied her punchline, 'Ooh, you are awful – but I like you!'

Like Tony Hancock, Emery suffered terribly from fear of failure, so much so that he very often vomited before a performance out of stage fright. He sometimes escaped into sleep. I once arrived rather early for a Royal Variety Performance at the London Palladium and went to hang my clothes in the dressing room which was to be shared by six comedians. Dick was already there, fast asleep on the banquette. I moved as quietly as I could but, as I slid the cupboard door shut, a hanger fell off the rail and clattered to the bottom. Dick woke up with a start, glared at me and screamed, 'You stupid shit! I've got to sleep! Why did you wake me up, you bastard?'

'It was an accident.'

'Why don't you have an accident under a bus, you prick? Oh my God, look at the time! Another four hours to go before I'm called for rehearsal! I'll never get back to sleep now! Jesus, I could kill you for this!'

'Calm down, Dick, for heaven's sake. How long were you expecting to sleep anyway? There'll be four other blokes in here before long.'

'Yeah, I suppose so,' he said bitterly. 'All five of you yammering away without a bloody care in the world. I don't know why I said I'd do this sodding royal show. Look at my chest.'

His shirt collar already opened, he unbuttoned further and pulled his shirt open to show the scarlet patches of a vivid rash on his otherwise white skin.

'That's what nerves do to you, mate. That's what you've woken me up to. Unbearable bloody tension. Never mind.'

Suddenly more annoyed with himself than me, he tugged his shirt closed and turned away. He muttered something.

'What? I couldn't hear you.'

'I said you can keep that to yourself. It's nobody's business. I don't want to be talked about. Just forget it, all right?'

Dick had no need to fear my discussing his terrible stress, even though I kept quiet as he asked. His phobias were well known throughout the business. He spent long hours in analysis, submitted to hypnotic sessions, tried all kinds of sedatives and other drugs even though he was just as terrified of the pills and potions as he was of the horrors they were meant to ease.

He feared agents, producers, directors and, most of all, audiences. He was haunted by the spectre of rejection, never free of the dread possibility of being a flop even in his most successful and reassuring years.

He told his friend and comrade-in-arms Roy Kinnear, 'I don't just envy the confidence that other comics seem to have, I resent it. I hate them for it, just like my dad did. If there's such a thing as a chip off the old block, it's on my shoulder.'

In 1979 Dick's once hugely successful show for BBC 1 was axed after twelve years. Eager for alternative exposure, he accepted a booking for two tapings of the popular ATV game show 'Celebrity Squares'. We used to record one show at four o'clock in the afternoon and the second at 7.30 in the evening, leaving time to change over those personalities who were doing only one show that day and provide them all with supper. Since Dick was in both shows and had no appetite due to his usual nervous tension, I joined him for a stroll around the small town of Borehamwood. He was in an unusually communicative mood and I asked him how he'd got started as a comic.

'I was quite literally born into the business,' he told me, explaining that the truculent father he remembered with mixed emotions was a fitfully employed variety entertainer whose best material was an amalgam of patter and songs appropriated from such diverse comedians as W. C. Fields, John Tilley and Billy Bennett.

'He blew his money on the gee-gees and booze and then shoved off when I was eight. Yes, a real charmer my dad was,' he said with a sudden scornful laugh.

His mother was a singer with a sweet but small voice who had been glad to give up her performing life when Dick was born in 1917 in Bloomsbury. Dick said he'd had a lot of starvation in his childhood.

'One time my mum and I were down to a little tin of baked beans and half a loaf of bread with no prospects of where the next meal was coming from. I had to quit school at fifteen and take any odd job I could get, one on a newspaper as an office boy, another mucking out and such on a farm. The best job I had was as a driving instructor. If I hadn't been able to get into the entertainment business, I'd probably have found my career working with cars. I like cars. They're easier to handle than people.'

He'd inherited a fine singing voice from his parents and, when his work had earned enough to put food on the table, he used his meagre earnings to pay for singing lessons with the Italian Chekko Mattania.

'At the age of nineteen I had cards printed,' he said and, pulling out his pen and his wallet, he found a scrap of paper and sat on a low wall to show me how they had looked:

### Richard Emery
Tenor vocalist – Juvenile Character Parts
Drive *ANY* make of car.
Sports: football, cricket. Knowledge of guitar. Good torso.

'Pompous little bugger, wasn't I?'

We continued our steady stroll and Dick picked up his story. In 1937 he'd landed a job as assistant stage manager and general dogsbody in a summer concert party at Minehead. Such small seaside companies functioned as a nursery for fledgling performers throughout the first half of the century and Dick found himself on stage for the first time, joining in the opening and closing songs, supporting the six leading players in comic sketches and understudying both the red-nosed comedian and the romantic baritone.

He remembered developing an act of his own in which he portrayed two characters in conversation, an idiotic yokel and an old gardener.

'It was a lot easier to go on as someone else. I didn't much like having to go on as myself to announce things. I preferred a disguise and a funny voice.'

Conscripted for war service in the RAF, Emery's talent and experience won him a place in 'The Gang Show', an entertainment section led by the energetic singing star and Boy Scouts' organiser, Ralph Reader.

'There was more than one company travelling around so we didn't see much of Reader – though he did see some of my character work and said I ought to do more of it. Well, we had a lot of old sketches, rubbish mainly, but I adapted them so that I could play different parts – a very old geezer with a funny walk, a nervous spinster, a drunken Scotsman –

and that was how I got my laughs. And I had this cheeky grin. I could get laughs with that too.'

Our circular path had brought us back to the ATV studios and we took a table in the corner of the big canteen. By the time I'd fetched over two cups of tea, Dick had turned oddly morose.

'God, those days were bloody easy if I'd only known it. Wartime audiences in uniform were easy to amuse, I suppose. It was a lot tougher afterwards in peacetime. I'd got this vicar act and sometimes it just died, not a titter. That's when I got this bad habit of drying, you know, forgetting my words. Bloody nerves. They paid me off in Brighton. I thought, "Bugger this, I'll just sing" but they paid more for comics. So I auditioned for Vivian Van Damm at the Windmill in London and he paid me thirty-six quid a week to do thirty-six shows. One pound a show! Slave wages. Funnily enough, I stuck it for thirty-six weeks.'

I remembered seeing Emery in some of those shows, taking the afternoon off from school to take the train from Dulwich to Victoria station and a bus to Great Windmill Street to stare at the stationary nudes in the non-stop *Revuedeville*. Rows of stony-faced men filled the front stalls. As soon as one got up to go, there was a scramble for his vacant seat by those who had perched behind him. The girls posed in various tableaux, discovered, as the curtain rose, naked but for strategically placed feathers and a Greek vase or two. The feeling in the auditorium was one of prurient apprehension. It was no place for a neurotic funster.

Just a few comedians could offer six acceptable shows a day to this ever-changing, ever-similar male crew, all impatient for the next display of female flesh. Arthur English was one, blithely regardless of whether or not he was getting laughs, just pouring out his breathless and breathtaking cascade of nonsense in a ceaseless onslaught, half chuckling throughout as though his own amusement was all that concerned him, all the while windmilling his arms like a market trader, adjusting his wide-brimmed trilby over his merry face with its thin spiv moustache, sliding his lanky frame around under the oversized shoulder pads and flapping a vivid kipper tie at us as he checked the wings for eavesdroppers before confiding the next unlikely part of his tale.

Others whom I saw doing sterling service in the cause of justifying the title 'revue', so evading the accusation of staging nothing but a peep-show and the consequent possibility of closure, were George Martin, accurately billed as 'The Casual Comedian' in view of his unshakeable composure (and later to create the best-loved TV routines of Basil Brush); Michael Bentine at his most frenetically inventive with a giant inner tube and a broken chair-back; Bruce Forsyth, bringing his challengingly conversational approach to bear on the impassive mob and forcing them to respond; Terry Scott, irresistibly mockable, declaiming garbled Shakespeare in tights and skimpy tunic; the Alberts, two of the most whimsically insane acrobatic comics in living memory; Robert Moreton, big and bashful and plummy, giving schoolboyish readings from his *Bumper Fun Book* and 'accidentally' switching the punchlines from one joke to another.

'And you, Dick,' I recalled, 'working as a cockney, hammering out your jokes like a soap-box orator, all garlanded with different accents, gurgling, winking, and sudden flights of comic song.'

'That good, was I? Getting nowhere, though.'

One gateway to national fame for such hopefuls was the Peter Brough-Archie Andrews radio success, 'Educating Archie'. Each series featured young comedians with the individuality of voice and strength of personality to play the role of the season's new tutor for Brough's wooden dummy. The popular show was a finishing school for those unknowns ready for fame and, perhaps, a catchphrase or two: Max Bygraves ('A good idea . . . *son*', 'I've arrived and to prove it, I'm here'), Hattie Jacques, Tony Hancock ('Flippin' kids!'), Benny Hill, Beryl Reid, Robert Moreton ('Oh, get in there, Moreton', 'Crisp, very crisp!') and – Dick Emery, recruited to provide voices for a dozen ancillary characters.

'It was money for old rope really. Not much money though. Twelve guineas a show. I hate the fucking BBC.'

His facility with regional inflections and the range of his diction immediately brought him work on other radio programmes, 'The Goon Show' among them. When ITV began operation in 1955, Emery's face became familiar to viewers on 'Two's Company' with Libby Morris. Appearances for BBC TV on Bentine's 'It's a Square World' led to his own series, 'Emery At Large'. And so to his years of huge popularity with 'The Dick Emery Show' in the 60s and 70s, a dozen years of riding high in the BBC TV ratings as he switched wigs and costumes and prosthetic teeth to give us Lampwick, Mandy and Co.

'Yeah, lovely, then the ratings aren't good enough for them and I'm thrown out like a piece of shit.'

Few funnymen have relished fame and fortune more than this stocky, wide-mouthed lady-killer. He reckoned his success had been too long arriving and was losing no time in exploiting it to the full. For years he owned and piloted his own plane, drove his high-performance cars and motorbikes in the fast lane and pushed himself to his physical limits in a portable gym.

He married five times, each one a showgirl, and deserted the fifth to live with yet another showgirl, a pretty woman named Fay who was thirty years his junior.

The setting sun spotlit Dick's wide face and snow-white cap of hair as he sat at the canteen table, beginning to grumble about the stupidity of women now. A callboy appeared at his shoulder. 'Makeup'll be ready for you in ten minutes, Mr Emery.'

'Mmm? Oh, yeah, better let the girl give me a touch-up.'

He stood, sat again, then looked at me quizzically and added, 'I don't normally talk about myself like this. You're a rum bugger, Monkhouse.'

Then followed our last few remarks, a conversation I remember so clearly we might have exchanged it only yesterday. I said offhandedly, 'Well, I'm glad you agreed to do this show. Have you seen it much?'

'No, I don't watch comedy shows. There isn't a comedian living that I'd cross the road to see. The great ones are all dead, although I never thought Chaplin was funny. He could only ever do that one character really, the tramp. Peter Sellers used to be good, over-praised of course and he's lost it lately. What these people don't realise, and I'm not excluding you from this, they think being funny is a lark. Sellers goes on the set, there's a hundred million dollars involved, and he gets the giggles. Can't work for giggling. Amateurs. I'm not saying you don't take it seriously, Bob, you do all your writing and that, but you and Tommy Cooper and Ernie and Eric and Des, you're all more concerned with larking about than knuckling down to it. I realised early on that comedy, if you do it properly, is the hardest work in the world. Comedy is bloody grim. It's a killer.'

'I saw you in cabaret once, Dick. You worked very hard.'

'Yes, I remember that. At La Dolce Vita in Birmingham. You brought your son. I found out that you were out front and refused to go on till you left, have you forgotten that?'

'No, I've got a good memory.'

'Yes, well, I didn't want you having a good memory for my jokes. I told the manager, Len Green, I said, "I'm not going out there till Monkhouse has gone."'

'He told me. Then I asked your partner, Peter Elliott, if I could have a word with you in your dressing room.'

'Peter wasn't my partner. He was a straight man on stage and a roadie off it. Well, I agreed to see you and I made you promise not to nick any of my stuff, didn't I?'

'Honestly, Dick, did you really think you were doing material that I'd want to steal?'

'Hmm? Well, I don't know. I was under a lot of pressure. I hate cabaret, it's terrifying enough without some pro sitting out there in judgement. I was doing six costumes and makeup changes in that act, for God's sake. And while I was offstage trying to make a quick change, Elliott was pattering away, letting the act go to hell. Look, let's forgive and forget. I'm sorry if I embarrassed you in front of your lad and all that. But you see, that's just what I mean.'

He stood up to emphasise his point.

'I starved when I was a kid. Left school at fifteen. Could've wound up a car mechanic, a chauffeur or something, taking the easy way. But I wouldn't let comedy beat me. It's been the cruellest master a man ever had. A monster, a bugbear. Fear and trembling, sickness, year in, year out, never getting any easier. Hard labour. I've worked hard and played hard and I've no time for pampered jessies from Cambridge Footlights and Monty Python crap and Tarbuck fucking about because he can't be bothered.'

He sat down again briefly and sighed.

'Comedy. Jesus! It's never made me laugh.'

I watched his odd, swaggering walk as he left me and, apart from seeing him in his 'square' on the show that evening, never laid eyes on him again.

He died four years later in 1983 at the age of sixty-five, having spent all his money and his strength.

## Monday, 18 March 1996

Rosemary Clooney is still one of the world's best popular singers. We're the same age, both born under the sign of Gemini in 1928, and I first worked with Rosie back in the early 50s when I hosted radio's popular 'Showband Show'.

She was married to the Hollywood actor José Ferrer in those days and they seemed to be in love for ever. So when she sang with me on 'The Bob Monkhouse Show' on this day in 1984, I asked her why she thought her marriage hadn't lasted.

Rosie said, 'Bob, marriage is like a bank account. You put it in, you take it out, you lost interest.'

## Saturday, 27 April 1996

Today's my first time presenting 'The National Lottery Live' on BBC 1. The guest star is Tony Bennett, a man I like with a voice I love. But my chief concern is my topical monologue at the start of the show. I'm following Anthea Turner into this job with none of her feminine attractions so my gags had better be funny.

Comedy writers have varied specialities. Some are best at sitcom plots, some are dialogue wizards; others like me find it most comfortable inventing stand-up routines and topical one-liners. Give me a subject and I'll worry at it, exploring its facets, its related words, and the mental pictures it suggests, until the first comic possibilities have emerged and are ready to be expressed in the effective phrases. I've never met any two writers with quite the same means for arriving at a funny idea.

Ted Kavanagh had a unique view of this creative process. He was the prolific wordsmith who pioneered a style of radio fun for the nimble tongue of Tommy Handley in the 1940s. Writing alone, he churned out hundreds of scripts for 'ITMA', lunatic comedy that's dated badly today but was greeted with national joy during World War II. I was a twenty-year-old comedian on a Midlands series called 'Radio Ruffles' when I asked Ted his secret for overcoming writer's block.

'Hang a birdcage somewhere in your imagination,' said Ted, sucking his old pipe and settling his tweedy plumpness into a hotel armchair. He had a chubby, rather bland face with a permanent expression of lurking doubt; at least, he did while he was in my company.

I was sent to fetch two beers from the bar and, after he'd taken a good suck out of one, he told me how he'd once bet a pal of his that, if the man were given a birdcage to hang up in his house, he would have to buy a bird.

'He said I was wrong and took the bet. So I bought him a birdcage on a stand, beautiful gilt thing, antique, French I think. The only condition I'd made was as to its location in the house. I wanted visitors to see it. So I got him to put it in his sitting room. Well, you can imagine what happened. People would walk in and say, "Clarence, when did your bird die?" and he'd say, "I never had a bird."

'"Then why have you got a birdcage?"

'Bob, that man got so sick and tired of explaining why he'd got an empty birdcage in such a prominent spot in his home that he gave in. He said it was simpler to put a so-and-so bird in the cage than to go on explaining our barmy bet to everyone who passed through his house. So he bought a cockatiel and grew to love it too, I believe.'

Ted finished his pint and roses to go up to bed. 'Ideas are like birds, fluttering through your head. Try hanging empty birdcages in your mind. Next time you look, you'll find something in them.'

## Saturday, 4 May 1996

Today I made k.d.lang laugh. I've been a fan of the Canadian singer ever since I saw her on American TV and, during a break in rehearsals for The National Lottery Live, I told her so. She seemed a little tense and suddenly said, 'You're a comedian, right? You're not going to make jokes about my sexuality I hope?'

I said, 'No, but I am worried. You see, I fancy you. Does that mean I'm gay?'

She hooted with delight and gave me a hug. I felt terrific.

I lay no claim to understanding female psychology but just occasionally I've got it right. My first wife enjoyed shopping and took her time about it. Once she kept looking through everything for sale in a boutique for over an hour. I smoked heavily in those days and, since the shop didn't permit it, I had to wait outside. It was a cold day and I was weary of staring in the window, hoping to inspire pity. A very attractive young woman was walking by and I approached her politely.

'Excuse me. Would you mind talking to me a few moments?'

She half recognised me and smiled uncertainly. 'Well, I'm not really sure. Why would you want me to do that?'

'My wife has been in this shop for ages now. I just need to have her see us chatting.'

'What shall we talk about?'

'No need at all, she's coming out now. Thank you.'

It's wonderful what a bit of simple strategy will do.

## Monday, 6 May 1996

My passion for old black-and-white movies is fairly well known. I feel the same about old TV and cinema adverts. Tonight on ITV I present a Bank Holiday special called 'Bob's Fab Ads', my personal selection of the funniest commercials ever made. There isn't one for a certain confectionery product because I can't watch a Mars Bar commercial without feeling a slight sense of nausea.

It's got nothing to do with the quality of the ad or the product but everything with my first experience as a celebrity advertiser.

Way back in the 50s I presented some commercials for Mars Bars. When I arrived at the film studio in Shepherd's Bush I was shown into a small dressing room, a makeup man did his job on me, I put on my best silk-and-mohair suit and reported for duty on the set.

Mars Bars were laid out on a sweetshop counter by the hundred. The plot was pretty simple. In each of the three commercials we were shooting, I had to tell a pretty singer named Petra Davies that I was here after

217

her goodies, tear the wrapper of a Mars Bar, bite into it, chew and say, 'Mmmm! Mars are mm-mm-mmarvellous!'

In rehearsal I had nowhere to throw the wrapper. The director told me to drop it on the floor. I was brought up by a tidy mother and dropping litter is against my nature. At that moment a prop man came up to me with a bucket. I thanked him and used the bucket as a waste-paper basket for each wrapper.

The three ads lasted 60, 120 and 180 seconds respectively. They took a lot longer to film, running to as many as twelve takes for each scene. By the time the director was satisfied, I'd eaten twenty-four Mars Bars. Sweetly agreeable though they may be, two dozen of them is really too much of a good thing. I feel sick and twitchy with sugar shock.

On the way out of the Goldhawk Studios I met Tommy Trinder coming in. Tom was a major comedy star in the 40s and 50s and he was there to do a voice-over for the Mars Bar commercial which he'd shot the previous week.

'How many bars did you get through?' I asked.

'Gawd knows, Bob, I wasn't counting. About twenty or so.'

'I've eaten twenty-four. I feel ill.'

'You don't mean you actually swallowed them, do you?'

'Didn't you?'

Tommy laughed at me incredulously.

''Course I never! I just bit into them and chewed for a moment. The prop man should've given you a bucket to spit 'em out!'

### Friday, 31 May 1996

Back from an after-dinner speech last night for Shroder Ventures at Castle Ashby, I had a few malt whiskies before bed. I hate performing in castles. Comedy timing takes a holiday in these acoustically unsympathetic settings and I wasn't happy with the way I'd gone over. Peter Ustinov once told me, 'If you can be boring in a new and original way, people will find you amusing.' This time they didn't.

This morning I felt mildly hung-over but knew I'd be fine for this evening's presentation for The Guild of Chefs Awards at the Four Seasons Hotel, Park Lane. I've done this one before and I expect to enjoy it. My optimistic view of the day was shattered by an emergency phone call. A well-known comedian, scheduled to address an after-lunch audience of metal brokers, had been taken suddenly drunk. Could I fill in at two hours notice? Yes, I could and I did and scored very well with approximately the same speech that had bombed 16 hours earlier.

Many comedians have been inveterate boozers but Jimmy Wheeler brought it to an artform. He was a great bear of a man concealing a small black moustache under a prow of a nose above which his blinking eyes nestled closely. As the orchestra in the pit played his signature tune he would hurtle onstage in loose-fitting pale grey suit, waving his fiddle and bow, shouting at the bandleader in strangulated cockney, 'All right, we've 'eard it, we've 'eard it!'

A wonderfully insane stream of unrelated gags followed, punctuated by Jimmy's nimble but limited fiddling, and he'd conclude his act with the inevitable catchphrase, 'Aye, aye – that's yer lot!'

His performances were seemingly unaffected by his persistent and sometimes phenomenal inebriation. Other comedians, especially Ted Ray and Tommy Trinder, would repeat the legends about Jimmy's drunken excesses, often in his presence. Jimmy never denied them. If it was untrue that he once took a plane to Turkey under the impression that he was fulfilling an engagement in Torquay, he went along with it.

One of the stories about Jimmy I know to be true was the incident at the Turk's Head Hotel in Newcastle-on-Tyne about 1958. Seven or so years later I checked the tale with an elderly porter who assured me of its truth. Jimmy had returned from his evening performance at the Grand Theatre about ten forty-five and retired to his room with a bottle. An hour later he appeared at the reception desk and began thumping the bell. The porter appeared and was greeted with a glassy stare.

'I want a different room,' said Jimmy.

'You're in one of our best rooms now, sir.'

'I don't give a monkey's. I want a different room and I want it right away.'

The porter fetched the duty manager.

Observing that Jimmy was red-faced and swaying beyond all reasonable argument, the management told the porter to move their fuddled guest out of his present room and into an empty one elsewhere.

Then, seeing that this appeared to satisfy him, the manager asked, 'Would you mind telling me, sir, what it was about your previous accommodation that you disliked?'

Jimmy belched and said, 'Well, for one thing, the fucking room's on fire.'

## Monday, 10 June 1996

This morning marks three years since the death of Les Dawson. In 1970 I took top billing in summer season at the Floral Hall, Scarborough, but it was Les who was the hit of the show. We spent long hours talking about comedy and I discovered that Les was a true word lover.

'I relish them, Bob. Not big words just for the sake of using them like so many people do. The English language is full of such funny words. Like in an old Frank Randle film on TV the other day where he came out of the NAAFI and said, "By gum, I'm full of gas!" Now "gas" is a funny word to the British. "Placard" is funny, funnier than "poster".

'One of the lines that always got me from Robb Wilton was when he was on holiday with his wife in the Cotswolds and they went to a remote tea-room near Stroud, tiny, back of beyond. Robb asked for "two cream teas, please" and the old fella that served them was snuffling, in tears. He said, "I'm sorry, sir, lady, but I'm a mite upset as I've just lost me uncle, a grand man, ever so good to me, left me all 'is clothes, and just last week he were buried here in our village churchyard. Did you hear about it?" And Robb said, "No, we don't get out a lot." Now, do you see? It's the use of words, the understatement, the brevity.

'Dave Morris was another example, wasn't he? Great comic. He said his bride "came down the aisle in freshly whitened pumps", a lovely line. The equivalent in written humour to me is P. G. Wodehouse. He has Bertie Wooster "toying idly with his vol-au-vent" when he sees out the window his bank manager approaching, drifting "like a bank of fog". In that phrase you see this huge, billowy man. Phrase-making can be funnier than the actual jokes.'

Les's love affair with words has sometimes produced odd results, when he has actually misused a word but made it do the job he wants done. What would normally be an inappropriate choice of word has less to do with Les's lack of much formal education than with what he feels the word ought to mean.

'There's glory for you!' said Humpty Dumpty.

'I don't know what you mean by "glory",' Alice said . . .

'I meant, "there's a nice knockdown argument for you!"'

'But "glory" doesn't mean "a nice knockdown argument,"' Alice objected.

'When *I* use a word,' Humpty Dumpty said in a rather scornful tone, 'it means just what I choose it to mean – neither more or less . . . The question is which is to be the master – that's all.' Les would have been well cast in the role of Humpty.

'I get a lot of words from old novels, Bob. I'm reading *Anthony Adverse* and there the "miscreant" is discovered "behind the rattan screen". The hero says, pulling a horse-pistol, "I shall blow a hole in you via the application of this fire-arm." Beautiful stuff, it's heavy but funny.'

Does it matter whether Les was quoting Hervey Allen's historical novel correctly? He wasn't giving a lecture to a Literary Society, he was explaining where he found inspiration for his florid flights of comic language. His purpose was not to educate, only to make us laugh. And to do it in a manner different from any other living British comedian, although echoing the fanciful loquacity of W. C. Fields and Gillie Potter.

'I love to read Sherlock Holmes because Conan Doyle hated the character and put things in there so ridiculous . . . well, one of them is where Watson says, "Who do you think the murderer is?" Holmes says, "It's quite apparent it's the lady pianist." Watson is aghast: "Good God, Holmes, you can't suspect her, she's a musician." Holmes says, "My dear Watson, as a criterion of instance, Moriarty was a positive virtuoso upon the bassoon."'

Don't ask whether those are the exact words used by the great detective. Who cares? Sherlock wasn't out to get laughs.

We sat together on a bench in Scarborough's Peasholme Park, watching the passing parade of silent holidaymakers trudge along, so intent upon their own numbed limbs that they never noticed the two comedians wrapped up thoroughly against the bitter winds from the North Sea and the threatening fret which mists the North Yorkshire coast as even the warmest summer's day dies.

I listened as Les told me how he'd entered show business in the north-west of England as a bar pianist, playing in pubs for ten shillings per three-hour session. Sometimes, if he sang as well, he could earn twelve shillings. A promise of an £8 fee, largesse unheard of, took him to Hulme Hippodrome to audition for a Manchester show called *Top Town Stars*. The sleazy promoter booked him and Les's parents came to watch.

They saw him playing the piano wearing a ginger wig and imitating Quasimodo. Nobody laughed.

The promoter tried to abscond with the takings but Les and the other performers caught him halfway through a dressing-room window, took what money he had and spent it in a pub.

Les had no idea that he had been anything less than successful. He remembered the shock he felt when he got home that night and his mother pulled him in through the front door, hissing, 'Get in before any bugger sees you, you were bloody awful!'

We rose from our park bench and strolled towards the town. Now passers-by recognised us and I noticed that they gave Les an especially friendly greeting. That wonderfully mournful comic pose of his never really concealed the warm, sentimental man behind it. The public wasn't fooled for a moment by all that grumpy nonsense. What we could sense was the gritty reality of a slum kid who had battled the hard way, the squaddie, the boxer ('I was knocked down so often I had a cauliflower bum'), the insurance agent, door-to-door salesman, even a pianist in a French brothel.

He'd come out of the army, 'a war hero who'd fought valiantly against NAAFI prices', and made his way to Paris to become a writer. He admitted it was a bit naïve but he'd thought that was the place to create deathless prose. 'If I'd known then what I know now,' he told me, 'I'd have written a book in Barnsley.'

Living from hand to mouth on the Left Bank, he became a bit emaciated, if you can picture that. Needing money to feed himself, he got a job playing piano from midnight till 3 a.m. in a dingy club called Al Romance. 'Gone now,' he'd sigh. 'I think they pulled it down to make way for a sewer.'

After a week of playing 'Limelight' over and over again in a bar empty but for him, a dozing steward and Eva, the owner of the joint, 'the sou finally dropped' – he was merely a front for the naughties upstairs. The clients were coming in the back door and using cubicles on the first floor to frolic with five ladies of the evening while Les was only banging out tunes.

One night business must have been bad because one of the girls came into the bar and said in broken English, 'You can sleep wiz me for 5,000 francs', which was then about £5 in English currency. Les answered, 'Well, I'm not very tired but I could do with the money.'

Back in England at the age of twenty-three, Les was now existing on £7 a week plus commission earned by selling and servicing Hoover vacuum cleaners and washing machines in the slumland of Moss Side, Manchester.

'I took jobs playing the piano in some of the roughest dumps. Just thumping out singalong crap. A few drunken pals'd show up to lead some applause for me. Then we'd get pissed together.'

He didn't mention telling any gags on these occasions, yet we can be fairly sure that Les's wonderfully cynical lines would already have been spicing his conversation and convulsing those disreputable friends of his. Surely they would have been creeping into his musical introductions, night by night, club by club?

As always Les ducked the issue, allowing only, 'These working men's clubs were the start for all of us, and anyone who refutes that is an idiot. Sources for trying out new material. Start your act, try it out, find out you can do it.'

Yes, that's the way it works, especially for as different and original an act as Les was developing.

But as we settled in one of Scarborough's many saloon bars with our drinks and I pressed him again about his earliest attempts at comedy and the big decision to become a full-time professional comic, Les was true to form, taking refuge in his skill at spinning frivolous apologues.

'What happened was, I had a little business called Garden Fantasia, we used to make shopfired clay gnomes and pigeons and polystyrene deer. I had six dwarves who worked for me and they were militant, well, I know for a fact they deliberately sanitised the feet on my puffins which I sold to Iran. Even to this day there are some Lakeland cats at Liverpool Docks that should have gone to an orphanage in Uganda and they never arrived. Besides, I'd just got married and I needed an excuse to get away from home, only a small place – bedroom, toilet and dustbin. And I was having this hideous recurrent nightmare that I was a piece of loose machinery. And the wife was chasing me with a spanner saying, "Come 'ere while I tighten your nuts!"'

Such whimsy wouldn't have gone down a storm in the working men's clubs of the day; in fact, apart from the final gag, it's just the kind of wordy absurdity that would have died a death. It was obvious to me by this time that Les had chosen to forget his earliest comic efforts, preferring to remember only that his was a strictly musical act. I suspected that he was denying the pain of failure, evenings of humiliating rejection, until one extraordinary evening in Hull. About that, he waxed fulsome.

'It was my night of comic self-realisation. I'd played there all week to a scattering of local oafs and on the Friday night the din was dire. I lost my temper. I stopped playing, swivelled my piano stool to face them, seized the microphone and proceeded to lambast these dunderheads and their doxies. But instead of resenting my tirade, they laughed. A revelation! A star was born that night.'

Well, maybe, but it really doesn't happen that way. What seems to me to be a less exciting but truer version of Les's experience in Hull is that his act had cut no ice with the sparse weeknight audiences in a concert room without much atmosphere for comedy. Then, with a packed house on Friday, Les attacked the crowd with more aggression than before and found himself getting consistent laughs. Just as Paul Merton and Jack Dee would discover many years later, Les found that a scowl could be more effective than a smile.

Despite his entertaining account of the birth of his comic style, beyond doubt he was already using comedy in his presentation, interspersing such numbers as 'Hey There' from *The Pyjama Game* and the 1929 chorus song 'Mama Don't Allow' with the kind of wry patter I heard him using four years later in Blackpool.

I'd finished my two shows at the Blackpool Winter Gardens and gone through heavy rain in search of a light meal. I chanced upon a large restaurant with walls of fishing nets and trellis strewn with plastic ivy and its tables filled with glum, gently steaming holidaymakers. The proprietors offered late cabaret and, after two hirsute brunettes had demolished a couple of songs to thin applause, Les Dawson trudged on to the small stage.

The audience stared at him glumly and he gave as good as he got.

'I love Blackpool . . . it's a sort of Bournemouth with chips. You can eat rock, candyfloss, fish and mushy peas on the Golden Mile . . . then throw up in Fleetwood.

'I'm not saying my room is small but it's the first time I've had bed, breakfast and cramp pills.

'My bed creaks like a Darby and Joan Formation Dance Team.

'It's only rained three times since I got here – morning, noon and night.

'This next joke will kill you. I hope it does, we'll have an early night.'

Not a titter. Those early years were as tough on Les and his offbeat gloomy delivery as on any of the forgotten club comics who had to give up in despair.

After Les's death in 1993, I talked with a club booker of the 60s named Harry Barrel. He'd seen the act that Les was so anxious to forget.

'He just couldn't seem to click. His cronies in Manchester would come along and laugh it up but what's one table of laughers against 200 people giving the act the cold shoulder? And his mates couldn't travel with him to Wigan or Blackburn or Rawtenstall. It was in them places that I saw young Les struggle for a bit of approval till my skin crawled. I thought to myself, "Is this courage or blind obstinacy?" I booked him because he was a stoic and I admired that. More than once I advised him to pack it in. I'd seen him sobbing his heart out after a show.'

But Les continued to suffer the disfavour of silent audiences or, far worse, the drunken boos and jeers that had him weeping in his cheap digs afterwards. But surrender was never even a consideration. Harry was right: Les was a stoic.

Supported by his first wife Meg and his own indomitable spirit, Les's determination eventually paid off as his deadpan manner steadily gained strength and began to garner laughter.

He broke through on TV thanks to the talent show 'Opportunity

Knocks' and there was no looking back except, perhaps, to that romanticised benchmark of an evening in Hull that served to blot out the unhappy memories of all the misfired jokes that went before.

His successes as a clown on YTV's 'Sez Les' and 'The Dawson Watch' on BBC 1, his brutal wit as the host of 'Blankety Blank', the glorious winter months of his panto dame on the great provincial stages – these are part of the reason that British laughter can never sound quite the same without him.

After that first encounter with his cabaret act in Blackpool, I thought a word of encouragement might be acceptable, especially coming from the star of the town's most successful show.

I sought him out in the restaurant's kitchen and told him I thought he was going to be a great comedian. That lumpy, unsmiling gaze sized me up and he muttered, 'I can remember your name perfectly but I just can't think of your face.'

### Saturday, 15 June 1996

John Willan is a horticultural lecturer who was offered the job of National Lottery drawmaster by an old friend within Camelot and accepted it as he seems to accept most things in life – without expressing much emotion. He's not a man to lavish his charm upon anyone, least of all the television team who make 'The National Lottery Live' happen every Saturday at 7.50 p.m. on BBC 1.

Preferring to maintain a sober mien, John's supply of smiles is meagre. Whereas a more exploitative man might have seized upon nationwide exposure to a vast audience as a way of becoming a popular celebrity, he has ignored that temptation in favour of a more private and formal mode of behaviour. He is a paradigm of probity.

After observing his contribution to the shows for the past eight weeks, I asked one of the producers, 'Apart from loading the balls, what exactly does John Willan do?'

'He gives us our spirit of unity,' he explained. 'We'd all like to strangle him.'

### Monday, 1 July 1996

Alfred Marks died today aged seventy-five and when I heard the news I decided to sit quietly and sadly for a while to remember him and recall all our times together. Two minutes later I was smiling; then I giggled. I couldn't help it, Alfie was one of the most naturally funny men I've ever known and all my memories of him are filled with his wicked drollery. The only person who could match his casual wit was his wife

Paddie O'Neill, but then she had the advantage of being a lion-tamer's daughter.

He was born in Holborn and in a way never left it. The son of Russian refugees, Alfie's tough London upbringing informed his approach to life. One of his earliest jobs was as an auctioneer in Petticoat Lane and he loved the gritty opportunism of the traders who worked on the crowds looking for bargains.

'There was one leathery old blighter who sold tuppenny bags of cough candy from his stall and he'd kid the customers that there was a shilling in every seventh bag. You didn't have to be a mathematician to see that was an impossible way to do business – six bags would only fetch ten-pence plus the twopence for the seventh bag, making a shilling in all. How could he afford to give away the entire amount he'd sold the seven bags for? Ah, but he had the patter and he didn't give 'em time to think. And he had five sons to help him fool the people. I'll tell you how.'

We were chatting between takes on the set of our 1962 movie comedy *She'll Have To Go* in which we played penniless aristocrats who planned murder for profit; a film of which Alfie said, 'If we make only one person miserable we've done our job.'

We strolled out of the studio while the next scene was being lit and stand-ins took our places on the set. I smoked a cigarette in the sunshine while Alfie explained the con.

'On Saturdays the throng was constantly in motion. You had to collect a mob round your stall by sheer strength of personality and a great line of sales talk, flog your stock to them quickly and then let them move off while you got ready to deal with the next bunch of suckers.

'Once old Max had hooked his audience he'd go into his pitch about a once-in-a-lifetime chance to get a lucky seven. For only two pennies you'd get a paper bag of these broken cough candy pieces which he insisted was incredible value enough. But he guaranteed a silver shilling was hidden inside a candy lump in every seventh bag.

'As he'd approach the climax of his spiel, one of his own lads would stick his hand up and be the first to buy a bag. Then, as Max turned his attention back to the crowd, the lad would shout, "I gog a thilling! I gog a thilling!" and step up on to the wheel of the stall so everyone could see him. Then the boy would make a big show of bringing a shiny coin out of his mouth and holding it high for all to see.

'Well, after that Max would sell bags of candy hand over fist with his wife's help for about ten minutes. As soon as sales began to thin out he'd pretend that his stock was exhausted and let the customers drift away. Of course, there were no shillings inside the sweets but no group of people was going to stand around sucking every piece in every bag to find that out.

'Twenty minutes or so later he'd start again and another of his sons would do the play-acting. Old Max could've kept up that scam for ever if he hadn't been so mean to his sons. He was horrible to them. Paid them slave wages. That's what backfired on the old devil and put paid to his candy racket.'

We were called on to the set to shoot the next scene two or three times. I was eager to get the acting over so I could hear how Max got his come-uppance. The lunch break was announced and the two of us made our way towards the canteen of the MGM Studios, Borehamwood. As we sat at a corner table and polished off some cod and chips, Alfie continued his story.

'The boys chose the right moment for their revenge. As soon as Saturday football was over, the Lane filled up with blokes who'd roam about the stalls waiting for the pubs to open. There were some rough types about and Max was always a bit nervous of those louts. Nevertheless, he'd done his usual cocksure act about ten or eleven times that day and the takings had been good.

'He might have found it odd that, while all five of the boys had taken it in turns to find a shilling throughout the day, now they were all banded together and watching from the passing mass.

'The mostly masculine pack that was attracted by his oratory listened to his well-polished hooey about the hidden shillings but when he reached the cue for one of his lads to buy the first bag, all five pushed forward offering up their money. Confused by this, Max couldn't very well turn them down and five bags were quickly sold. Max resumed his harangue, awaiting the customary interruption.

'Then, according to the regular plan, one boy choked and yelled out that he'd got a shilling. Then the second boy did the same, then the third, fourth and fifth. All five boys hoisted themselves up on to the stall above the spectators, yelling that they each had "gog a thilling". And as Max watched them in mounting horror, each boy slowly removed from his mouth twelve old pennies.

'As each large copper coin was produced from each young mouth, Max's sons turned to let everyone see, holding the pennies up in mock triumph. They'd got to about the sixth one when, as you might say, the penny dropped.

'The crowd didn't know exactly what was happening but they knew how to smell a rat. A low rumbling of anger began to rise in volume and someone shouted, "Swindler!"'

'The lads sensed that they'd done enough and simultaneously dropped out of sight and dispersed, ushering their mother with them. Max was dazed. If he had thought of any placatory words to shout they'd have been drowned out by the mounting fury of the mob.

'Men at the front had seized the sides of his wooden stall and started to rock it back and forth. Max clung on to it as if on a boat in a storm. It was a sturdy construction but it wasn't built to withstand a riot. Within seconds its struts were splintering apart and the excitement of it stimulated a rampage.

'Five minutes later the stall was no more, shattered into kindling. The stock of cough candy and paper bags had vanished, the busted till was empty and Max was running the gauntlet, legging it through the hostile rabble with tattered clothes and a bloody nose, lucky to escape with his life.'

Alfie ate his last chip, unbuttoned his waistcoat and leaned back at the satisfaction of a tale well told.

'And the moral of that story is this. When you're making it, share the wealth with your loved ones. Take care of the bill, will you, Bob?'

After five wartime years in the Royal Air Force Alfie had been demobilised and, like so many ex-servicemen who sought a career in the theatre, worked at the famous Windmill, the nudie revue theatre just off Shaftesbury Avenue. Unlike the others, however, not as a comedian. He was a scene shifter.

Being also a man well trained by observation of Petticoat Lane's shrewd traders, Alfie always had his eye on the main chance and, after watching a succession of young comics who used the Windmill as a jumping-off ground to get into show business, he organised his best anecdotes into a fourteen-minute act and, on his début at the Kilburn Empire in 1946, also revealed a splendid bass baritone voice with which to conclude his turn. Modestly, he told the audience, 'I'm one of the few singers who've performed at the Wailing Wall and nobody noticed.'

My favourite example of the man's quirky humour arose from his friendship with the Canadian actor and comedian Lou Jacobi. Paddie and Alfie had befriended Lou when he was struggling to find work in London.

One Tuesday Lou's agent phones him in a panic.

'How soon can you get to New York? Be there Friday and you've got the part of the uncle in *The Diary of Anne Frank*.'

For the next frantic hours Lou makes his flight booking and puts those few belongings he can't take with him into storage. With no time to lose, he takes one last look around the furnished flat that has been his north London home for five years. That's when he spots the stack of a dozen books tied with string on a shelf that's been hidden behind the front door. Hastily he scoops them up and hurries to the waiting taxi.

Bouncing along towards Heathrow with the awkward bundle on his lap, Lou realises that the cab is about to pass the end of the road where Paddie and Alfie live. He's running very late but it's the only solution.

Dissolve to the next scene: the kitchen in the Marks home. Paddie is cooking breakfast, Alfie is in his pyjamas, dressing gown and bedroom slippers, sitting at the table sipping tea and reading the newspaper. Through the back door hurtles Lou. He dumps the heap he's been carrying on to the table, gasps 'Look after my books!' and runs straight outside to leap into the taxi and speed away.

Paddie looks at Alfie, Alfie looks at Paddie, they both say, 'Who was that?' and then burst out laughing.

Dissolve to three months later: Paddie and Alfie find they have a week or more free. *The Diary of Anne Frank* has opened on Broadway and is a big hit. After the Saturday night performance, Lou Jacobi is standing outside the stage door on the sidewalk signing autographs.

As he hands back the last autographed programme, out of the darkness walks Alfred Marks.

He's wearing pyjamas and dressing gown and bedroom slippers and he's carrying the pile of books still tied with string. He shoves them into the arms of his amazed friend and says, 'Look after your own fucking books.'

Then – and this is the classy part – *he walks away*.

### Monday, 8 July 1996
Capital punishment should be reserved for poisoners, serial killers and people who talk to each other in the cinema during the film.

I arrived in Stevenage today to proclaim its new Cineworld Complex well and truly open. In this agreeable duty I was assisted by Mystic Meg, an endearing and humorous lady who predicted a great future for the multi-screen cinema. If this forecast proves as accurate as her prognostications on 'The National Lottery Live', the joint should burn down tonight.

### Friday, 26 July 1996
For these past six weeks I've been repeating the satisfying success of last year's BBC 1 Saturday night series, 'Bob Monkhouse On The

Spot'. It's attracted some rather good reviews. Dammit, why am I being so coy? It's got the best reviews of my life.

You'll have gathered from accounts elsewhere in these memoirs that I've had my share of flops and I'm happy to share my embarrassments with you. I make no secret of my failures or the intense dislike I inspire in some people. Unluckily for me, many of these people are journalists. It's not that I'm impervious to being found detestable, I'm saddened and depressed by it, but I take comfort in the fact that I'm not alone. Politicians get it worse than comedians who polarise their public.

Throughout my fifty years in showbiz my press has generally been much more vituperative than approving, so much so that many journalists who have come to interview me have been shocked in their researches by the amount of bilious abuse I've attracted. I've been sneered at by the best. It was John Osborne who wrote of me, 'his greasy ingratiation made me cringe' and Jean 'The First Lady of Fleet Street' Rook who told her readers, 'I have to wipe the slime off my TV screen after he's been on.' (When some months later Jean was a guest on one of my TV shows, I said, 'That was a rather hurtful piece you wrote about me.' She answered, 'Oh, Bob dear, don't be so bloody sensitive, it's only copy. Besides, I'm supposed to be fierce.' It didn't help much.)

One *Mirror* correspondent wrote a 400-word piece about me in which he used the word 'smarmy' eight times. I sent him a copy of Roget's Thesaurus.

At any rate, I hope you'll agree that my suffering from all this distaste in the past helps to excuse my unabashed wallowing in the compensation of unexpected and almost universal favour.

I'm not really good at blowing my own trumpet but for once others have blown it for me.

'Unmissable . . . the man is simply the best' wrote Margaret Forwood in the *Daily Express*, a lady who hasn't hesitated to trounce me when she thought I had it coming.

In the *Independent* Thomas Sutcliffe referred to me as a 'respected craftsman of comedy . . . a storming performance', while Stuart Collier expressed his approval in the *Observer* with such phrases as, 'There can be no doubt Bob is one of the ultimate professionals . . . genuinely funny'.

Never have I had such good notices in the broadsheets, quite the contrary in fact. When I see my name in *The Times*, I wince in anticipation of the critic's contempt. Not this time.

'Like many, I am still reeling from the impact . . . he is out to claim the comic high ground, albeit with the help of some distinctly lowbrow, adult material . . . hugely impressive,' said the seldom impressed Matthew Bond.

Likewise Stuart Jeffries, writing in the *Guardian*, used such gratifying expressions as, 'very funny . . . it is a delight to see Monkhouse at full comic stretch . . . expert comedic presence.'

You can imagine my delight at opening the *Daily Telegraph* to read 'breathtaking . . . a bravura performance' (Henry Dimbleby) and if I was expecting a good review from my friend Garry Bushell, it still came as a very pleasant surprise. Garry has ripped into me in the past if he's felt I've deserved it, but this time his column in the *Sun* said, 'a revelation . . . he gets through more strong gags than a bondage club. He is our sharpest stand-up comedian.'

Of all these astonishing critiques, it was the *Evening Standard* that hit me hardest. Victor Lewis-Smith is notorious in TV circles for his merciless and wittily scornful opinions. When he's deigned to acknowledge me in past years it's been to discharge bile. Now I can hardly believe the evidence of my eyes:

'The sharpest, fastest and most hilarious stand-up routine of the year . . . Facing his helpless audience with a slightly dazed expression and indiscriminately strafing them with gags like a comedic Michael Ryan at Hungerford . . . displaying the speed and agility that few performers half his age possess, offering what is virtually a masterclass in technique and timing, and giving all the arrogant young whippersnappers of the stand-up circuit a damn good whopping!' going on to conclude:

'A good deal of pure smut . . . unfailingly brilliant . . . How *dare* he now be so effortlessly and spectacularly funny?'

How much more of this extraordinary welter of enthusiasm can I expect you to endure? To tell you the truth, it's beginning to discomfort me. OK, I'll indulge in just one more quote:

'Steam-hammer irony, double bluff, layers upon layers; we should treasure him.' (Eric Bailey, the *Daily Telegraph*).

What would be your reaction to such an apparent volte-face? Having hardened yourself to dismissive and spite-filled press criticism could you trust such sudden approbation? And why would anyone court either reaction? What drives moderately intelligent persons to put themselves up for acceptance or disparagement? In short, what sort of individual wants to be a comedian? When we hear the very word, what does the label suggest?

Other professions, callings and occupations attract separate and distinct types of practitioner. Some stereotypes are so familiar as to be cheaply laughable examples from the world of travesty, among them absent-minded professors, innocent vicars, coke-head musicians, venal lawyers, golden-hearted tarts, gloomy detectives, drunken matelots, promiscuous milkmen, irascible film directors, vacuous débutantes, sceptical bank managers and cynical reporters. But what corny characteristics do we attribute to comedians?

Are they all the traditionally glum Hamlet aspirants?

To a man or woman, are they generally parsimonious, vulgar, shallow, arrogant, introspective, hysterically insecure, smug, autocratic, alcoholic, amoral, superhuman, selfish and sorrowful saps?

Read their superficial stories in the tabloids and so they would appear. Rather than look at the complete image, perhaps we need to explore the initial motives behind a choice of career.

Consider first those who prefer a sort of anonymity in life to a public role, the one who'd rather wear a uniform. The psychological makeup of individuals who actively seek to resign their individuality is apparent among those who enter religious orders to become humble monks and nuns or surrender to the discipline of a military life.

The emotional and intellectual course taken by those who are drawn to incognoscibility is easily observed but not easily deflected. They want to be told what to do and then be required to do it over and over again in the safety of a routine, often behind the disguises of a number of livery. If their egos ache with the need for recognition and praise, it's a pain that must be contained, frustrated or satisfied within the rut they occupy. The mere idea of standing up in front of an audience and demanding attention is abhorrent. I've never met a monk who moonlights as a clown.

Nor will we find our comics among the doormats and dormice, the meek who, if they ever inherit the earth, will most likely get a lump of it in the face. There's precious little comedy in the lives of quiet hobbyists, bashful scholars, hermits, anchorites and recluses, the discreet and the modest, ones who deliberately select a position of obscurity and seclusion.

Abiding quietly in this stratum of society, somewhere well below public attention level, there is humour, yes, since humour can endure in the least favourable circumstances, persisting like lichen in Antarctica. And jokes. Many lesser-known comedy writers compose their material in the secret corners of an unassuming existence. I know of two, both content to be minor figures in the civil service, who send in topical jokes to radio and TV shows on condition that their real names are not revealed.

In both cases I've noticed that their comic invention, though clever, is based upon wordplay, puns and similar equivoques, never an aggressive comic observation of life. Just as there may be a certain sterility in the self-effacement of a humble life, so it seems feasible that the selection process of what's funny is emasculated before it even commences. If you have no ginger and snap in your daily round, with little familiarity with strong emotions, it seems likely that your sense of fun will be limited by timidity to a simple juggling with language.

Great comedians, insisted Eric Morecambe, aren't great until they're forty, 'when they know a thing or two about life'. Perhaps the invention of powerful comedy needs personal experience and ego too.

If the comedian's genesis is unlikely to be founded in social submission, it's also improbable among the top echelons of our civilisation.

Backsides that sit upon thrones are not kicked in the cause of commercial mirth. Those born to privilege rarely run away to join a circus and he who is august does not become Auguste.

Among the heterogeneity of comedians that occupy this book, none is the son of a millionaire or daughter of a duke. Once again, *humour* can be found among the majestic. Nobles and royals, statesmen and lawmakers, have their wits. Jokes and jokers circulate at the loftiest level of every advanced nation but being high-born seems to carry no compulsion to make the hoi polloi laugh. Some of our rulers do make us laugh but that's not what they're paid to do. And, so with the constricted comedy of those who live a constricted life, that which amuses them may lack the common touch.

Having eliminated the parts of society unlikely to breed funnymen, it's to the middle ranks of humanity, beneath the exalted and above the invisible, that we must look to see where the comics come from and why.

And are they, like nurses and nuns, called to their vocation? As the mountain calls to the mountaineer and the pentameter to the poet, does the need of the mirthless masses summon forth the funster, ready to administer relief as his sole *raison d'etre*? We've often heard it said that someone's a 'born comedian' but will it do for all of them, or even most of them?

Perhaps we like to think of our greatest jesters as we do our greatest painters and composers, preferring to believe that their gifts are inescapably driven to expression. But in our exploration of the comedy mind, hopefully finding some such, we are sure to find some quite otherwise.

It's possible that two of the only three things that all successful comedians have in common have already been offered to the reader; they don't arise from the obedient and they don't descend from the

233

mighty. And the third is that they make us laugh and that's it. There is no other commonable property. Otherwise, they are as diverse as fingerprints.

When I first took the stage to deliver my untested notions of levity, I was a bit of a novelty. There were almost no educated, middle-class, solo comedians around. The few exceptions were actors who specialised in comic roles in plays and films, making rare excursions into solitary stand up, mostly on the wireless or in West End revues. The great majority of funsters was working class. Leon Cortez, a cockney comic, once button-holed me in the street.

'What are you up to, slummin'? Young feller like you, good schooling, money in the family and that, you shouldn't be pushin' yerself in where you've got no business, taking jobs away from them as need the work. It's all wrong, posh people comin' out of the army and thinkin' they're pros just 'cause they've done a couple of camp concerts and made the lads laugh in the middle of some bleedin' jungle. Variety's for the working class, on the stage as well as in the seats. Do yerself a favour and fuck off out of it.'

But I already sensed the truth. That, although the tradition of working class origins was strong in comedy performers, poverty didn't teach timing. Having holes in your shoes as a kid wasn't what made you quickwitted and no one ever learned how to do a perfect double-take by starving. Comedians are singular and so was I.

In July 1961 *The Times* published a sombre but significant article, 'Evening Shadows in the Music Hall' with this comment upon the development of the life of a solo purveyor of fun:

> *His is the lonely road of self-education, copying from this one here and that one there, until he finds his own strength and the particular medium fitting the gift which nature bestowed upon him. How difficult those groping years are, only the seeker would know and only the honest would tell.*

The need to hear laughter and know that you are the cause of it, that's a delight to almost every child. The desire to repeat that experience *ad infinitum* is the driving force behind the comedian's ambition, notwithstanding the risks of rejection and failure.

As John Fisher wrote in his masterly analysis of the appeal of British music hall comedy, *Funny Way To Be a Hero*: 'All members of the Variety profession have their sights set on the same immediate target, the demands imposed upon them by the live, flesh and blood audience with which they are always at their greatest ease, an audience which they will coax and coddle to be cooed at and caressed in return.' But he reminds us that, heart-liftingly essential to his spirit though that process may be to the clown who conjures it up, the breaking of that bond can be fatal. So many music hall comedians who fell from popularity ended their lives in tragedy. Tony Hancock's suicide brought back memories of the ebullient comic star who made famous the song 'I Do Like To Be Beside The Seaside', Mark Sheridan, who shot himself after a hostile reaction in Glasgow. Peter Waring, whose coolly stylish wit won him his own radio and TV series in the early 50s, had his contract cancelled and hanged himself in jail. Robert Moreton, the *Bumper Fun Book* comedian who played the plummy tutor of the 50s radio success 'Educating Archie', killed himself after the BBC dropped him. The pressures of fame and the demands of their public led to the premature deaths of two music hall legends, Marie Lloyd at fifty-two and Dan Leno at forty-four. The greatest of French film comedians, Max Linder committed suicide at only forty-two. The list of comics who have died prematurely or violently is out of all proportion to any other peaceful calling.

Life is painful at birth and too often in death. If it gets a bit poisonous in between the two then laughter is the antidote. Life is a cabaret, old chum, so send in the clowns.

Every age and every society produces what it needs in terms of leaders, doctors, clergy, teachers, artists, composers, musicians, writers, architects, inventors, and so forth. We also need the laughter-makers. We need them to risk our scorn. We need the equivalent of Shakespeare's Jacques to mock us gently in all the 'seven ages' of our existence as members of the same foolish species.

And those who live by the tickling-stick must be prepared to die by it. Clowns cry. So does everyone. Lighten up, Punchinello! You got a good press today!

## Saturday, 10 August 1996

So much for my wife's much vaunted claim to be the flesh-and-blood embodiment of Miss Marple! I planned today without her even suspecting what I was up to.

All she knew was she had to be ready for a sixtieth birthday surprise so she arose early as usual and made herself look pretty snazzy, no mean achievement after last night's dinner party at the imposing Barbados seaside mansion of Iris and David Button. She's a sweet, dark-eyed lady all in white with sexy legs and he's a multimillionaire with a barking laugh who's outlived his hair. As a keen golfer David claims the unique distinction of getting a hole-in-nothing; he missed the ball and sank the divot.

As soon as Jac and I are in the car with our house guests, Dodie and Dave Ismay, she susses we're heading for the airport. The first surprise is in the departure lounge. There sit four of our closest friends in Barbados – the Hudsons and the Sachers. The second surprise is waiting on the tarmac – an eight-seater private-hire Learjet complete with air stewardess and breakfast. Julian Sacher's brought iced champagne to enhance the meal. A smooth flight of an hour or so gets us to St Maarten where a stretch limousine takes us to do some shopping in the French half of the island. For lunch we board a tiny plane that I haven't seen since it chased Cary Grant through a cane-field.

This bravely putt-putts its fifteen-minute journey to St Barts. Halfway there I turn on the reading light and the plane slows down.

The runway at St Barts was designed by Airfix. The plane has to crest a hill, avoiding a road full of passing cars along its rim, then tilt dramatically downwards towards this concrete tennis court which ends on the beach. Topless sunbathers scatter attractively as our propeller churns up sand.

We have a long, late lunch at the exquisite Carl Gustav and I present Jac with a pair of diamond earrings I've had flown to Bridgetown from New York two days ago. Dodie, Carol Sacher and Veronica Hudson look at me like a hero. Dave, Nick Hudson and Julian Sacher look at me like a traitor.

More champagne is consumed on the two return flights and we get back to Sandcastle about 8.15 p.m.

'Can we do it again next year?' asks Jac.

Never satisfied, some women.

## Wednesday, 4 September 1996

Ever seen your own vocal cords? I was really glad to see them on the ear, nose and throat specialist's TV set, even with a fibreglass tube running up one nostril and down the back of my throat. There's nothing wrong with my voice box, I'm just manufacturing too much goo and that's what has been causing my trouble, an inability to talk without sounding hoarse and dropping out syllables.

I phone Peter Estall, heroic producer of 'The National Lottery Live', to tell him that I'm fine and I'll be back presenting next Saturday's show with the beautiful guest singer Belinda Carlisle. It comes out more like, 'I'm fi . . ., Peter, I'll be ba . . . . . . senting next Sat . . . ay's show with the beaut . . . . . . linda Carl . . .' plus a fit of coughing that sounds like a lung trying to escape. Mind you, I've had it worse.

When the 1969 summer season in Bournemouth began I was still a heavy smoker. Having to use a lot of voice projection in the farce I was doing and suffering from a throat infection aggravated by cigarettes, I woke up one morning to find my voice had become a froggy croak.

The doctor advised abstinence, no smoking and a policy of complete silence during the day. After a week or so of this regime I was getting depressed. Nothing seemed to make me smile.

Then, as happened so often, my dear old dresser Harry Butterworth was unintentionally hilarious. The tiny Blackpudlian was precious in both the senses of being cherished by me and in his effeminate prudishness.

I had scribbled a note to the effect that I wanted my stage suit dry-cleaned and pressed and returned in time for the next evening's performance. Harry couldn't make out my scrawl at all. He peered at the words and muttered helplessly. Rather impatiently I grabbed back the note and wrote in big capital letters: GET SUIT CLEANED! Harry looked at it and pursed his lips in reproof.

'Now, now,' he said. 'There's no need to shout.'

My burst of laughter must have blown the soot out of my larynx because I was almost back to normal overnight.

## Tuesday, 24 September 1996

I've had this throat problem for about three weeks now and it's turned into a bad cold. My nose is so sore I feel like an Eskimo nymphomaniac.

I've had more congestion on my chest but I'm a private patient so my doctor came round last week and gave me some medicine that made me cough up £50.

Jac's caught this infection too. She's just sitting up in bed going through my press clippings. I wish she'd use tissues.

Anyway, I have to dose myself with symptom suppressants and get my sad old body down to the Hammersmith Palais this afternoon to rehearse for tonight's Home Entertainment Awards.

Computer games are great but buying them for kids' birthdays really sucks. As soon as you've bought them a console and a set of games, the company upgrades the product.

Nintendo, Sega, Atari, they all bring out new models and, of course, the kids want them. That means you also have to fork out for yet another new set of games.

The companies say each new product is superior to the former because it has more pixels. What does that mean?

'Well, it makes the sky bluer, the clouds whiter and the grass greener.'

I think we had that when I was a boy.

It was called *playing outside*.

(I loved the slogan Nintendo used when they introduced their Game Boy: FUN IN THE PALM OF YOUR HAND!

We had that when I was a boy too.)

## Sunday, 6 October – Friday, 11 October 1996

I never imagined that I'd be squeezing Boston between Lottery guests Luther Vandross and Frank Bruno but that's what I'm doing this week.

With 'The National Lottery Live' requiring my presence in the BBC TV Centre at 7.50 p.m. every Saturday evening, we could only fit in a five-day break and Jac and I have chosen the capital city of Massachusetts.

During a great flight lasting six hours and forty minutes, we were pleased to find that 4 E & F and 5 E & F are the only two seats together in the middle of the plane. The food turned out to be good too except for the cheese. Who chose Brie to be served in a confined space? This is food that smells so strongly that when I opened it the oxygen masks popped down. Then the man in the seat across the aisle woke up and told me to put my shoes back on.

We were up at 8 a.m. and the view from our suite at the Ritz-Carlton delighted us, all beautiful trees stirring in the warm sunlight. Autumn was coming and from leaf to leaf the news was being whispered. We walked in the park among parading ducks and countless squirrels milling around fearlessly demanding food. After a rather dull bit of shopping in the Copley Place Mall, we settled for dinner in the hotel, which was a mistake. It was the sort of cuisine that makes starvation an agreeable option.

Tuesday found us walking the red line in the sidewalks that's called the Freedom Trail. We lunched at Durgin Park in Quincy Market where they leave the hooves on the steak. The restaurant is famous for its belligerent waitresses and we could hardly wait to be insulted by the burly woman who came scowling to take our order.

She took one look at me and said in a broad Cork accent, 'Sure, you're my mother's favourite, so y'are! What are ye doin' so far from home?'

Despite the heaped helpings our appetites returned after three more hours of walking and sightseeing. We dined in very French style at L'Espalier, an elegant town house, and returned to our suite to watch a video of Michael Keaton in *Multiplicity* which we abandoned after twenty tiresome minutes.

Next day the concierge arranged a limo to take us to Rockport on Cape Anne and advised us to take our own wine. It's a dry town where many years ago the strong-minded wives of fishermen lost patience with their hard-drinking husbands and imposed permanent prohibition. Our bottle of Trefethen Chardonnay was still cold enough to complement the lunchtime lobster. Shopping along the quaint cottages by the sea was fun and some impressive local arts and crafts occupied our afternoon. We weren't very hungry but the dinner in Boston's Ristorante Toscano was so terrific we managed to cope with it.

On Thursday fellow travellers in the north-east US arrived at our hotel, my manager Peter Prichard and his wife Joan. We took a chance on the Ritz-Carlton food again and compounded our previous error. I've never seen such small portions. As we were leaving, the head waiter said, 'You must have lunch with us again soon.'

Jac said, 'Great. How about now?'

Our flight departed at 8.50 p.m. and we slept all the way back home, getting through our front door at 9.45 a.m. feeling very satisfied.

I took the day pretty quietly since, after the hundredth 'National Lottery Live' tomorrow with Frank Bruno, Anthea Turner and Vanessa Mae, I've got to do cabaret at 11.15 at the Starlight, Enfield. It's a great club and I've enjoyed working there about twice a year since the mid-70s. I'm glad they've changed the signs on the toilet doors back to 'Gentlemen' and 'Ladies'. For a while they had them marked 'Kings' and 'Queens' but then one night they had this big party of male hairdressers.

**Thursday, 7 November 1996**
Today at the BBC Television Centre I keep my appointment to record a half-hour in close-up for 'Face to Face' with, according to my contract, someone called Jeremy Isaac's. All right, perhaps the programme was once listed as 'Jeremy Isaacs's Face to Face' and the apostrophe got juggled around during a title change. For Sir Jeremy it's probably a matter of indifference whether his surname appears on my contract spelt Isaac, which is wrong, or Isaacs, which is right, but it jars on me.

I do my very best to use correct punctuation. If it's obviously awful it can irritate. I sigh with peevish pedantry at London place names spelt without possessive apostrophes: St Johns Wood, Kings Cross, Grays

Inn Road. I find it equally annoying when apostrophes abound improperly. When the comedy magician Jack Rogers quit the poorly paid Masonic circuit and, together with his soprano wife Phyllis, emigrated to Hong Kong, the gregarious pair opened an English pub in the financial district and named it 'The Bull and Bear'.

Jackie and I lunched there regularly during our months in the one-time British colony and only one thing about our meals there was less than perfect. Outside the entrance a painted sign announced, RIB'S, STEAK'S, LOBSTER'S. The incorrect use of apostrophes nettled me but I held my tongue. Jack and Phyllis were such jolly old friends from my earliest days of concert and cabaret that I couldn't bear to point out the error and see them embarrassed.

Then one day Jack had an extra sign put up: 'PRIVATE PARTIE'S ACCOMMODATED INCLUDING FREE WAITER'S, PLATE'S & GLASS'S . . . The Proprietors.'

Jack saw me staring at it with a despairing expression.

'What's up, my old darling?'

'The apostrophe, Jack. It should be possessive.'

He regarded the sign seriously for a few moments, then slapped his thigh. 'Oh, my God, how did that slip by me?'

Next time we called at the pub the sign had been altered to: 'PRIVATE PARTIE'S ACCOMMODATED INCLUDING FREE WAITER'S, PLATE'S & GLASS'S . . . The Proprietor's.'

## Friday, 8 November 1996

Trying to save face for someone else can be very dodgy. About twenty-three years after the surfeit of apostrophes in Hong Kong and twenty-four hours after yesterday's encounter with Jeremy Isaacs, I ran into an abundance of blandiloquence in Mayfair. The woman sitting next to me at a charity luncheon declared herself to be my greatest fan. She told me she never missed any of my shows on TV and wished I would sing more as I had such a lovely light baritone voice. She added that her children were just as devoted to me as herself and crowned all this welcome praise with the statement, 'I can't imagine what my youngsters will say when I tell them I've actually been sitting next to Des O'Connor.'

I hesitated to correct her. It would make her entire outpouring of flattery seem so ridiculous and humiliate her unnecessarily. As her expressions of adulation continued, I wrestled with indecision. What if she mentioned Des to someone else at the function and was then told of her gaffe?

Well, I decided, that was none of my affair. I'd be a coward and play out my appointed role as Des. By the time she found out her error, if she ever did, well, she might feel absurd but still not quite remember whether or not she had mentioned to me the name of the person she thought I was. The hope that she had not might sustain her. Yes, I was definitely doing the right thing by playing along.

As the meal concluded with coffee and brandy, my resolve wavered. I saw it as she drew it out of her handbag – a dreaded autograph book. 'I don't suppose you'd be so kind as to sign your name in my daughter's book? She made me bring it along in case there were celebrities here but we neither of us dreamed that I'd even meet you, let alone sit next to you all through lunch. Could you write it "with love to Jeannie"?'

Here was a real dilemma. Was I to keep up my enforced masquerade to the point of forgery? My mind raced for a means of saving this poor woman's dignity. For a moment I toyed with writing a message to Jeannie – 'your mother thinks I'm Des O'Connor and I've never been so flattered, love, Bob Monkhouse' – but that would simply delay her mother's mortification.

Inspiration struck.

'Madame,' I addressed her with sudden coolness. 'I have something in common with Harrison Ford and Sir Clement Freud. I never *ever* give autographs.'

She stared at me briefly and then clicked her handbag on the replaced book.

'Well, how very mean,' she said. 'You're a very mean man. If this is how you treat your public, I'm surprised you've lasted as long as you have. I'm leaving now but before I go I'll tell you something, Mr O'Connor – I shall never watch you on television again. Good afternoon.'

And with that, she was gone. And Bob Monkhouse's reputation was unharmed. Sorry, Des.

## Thursday, 14 November 1996

Today the National Lottery is celebrating its second birthday. After two years of moans, groans and scandals it's become one of Britain's best-loved and most reviled institutions. I tell the studio audience, 'Twelve million people are watching us. Why? What are they getting? Fifteen minutes of fragile hope in anticipation of a joyous but unlikely climax, only to have it end in the usual, seemingly inevitable disappointment. Good Lord, I've had that at home every Saturday night for twenty-five years!'

It was launched as the answer to a debtor's prayers and the white hope of many worthy causes on hard times. While anti-gambling factions fulminated, the public flocked to the shops to romance with the idea of paying a pound coin to become a multimillionaire.

My lugubrious newsagent told me, 'You know, Mr Monkhouse, I have as much chance of being struck by lightning as you have of winning the Lottery.' I replied, 'Mr Patel, you have your dream and I have mine.'

Despite the grumbles, in its first two years the Lottery sold 6,956 million tickets, raising £2.493 billion for sports, the arts, charities and millennium causes.

Each week it enticed about 30 million people to fork out an average contribution of £2.50. So far the winners total 127,149,448. Curious winning patterns have emerged. The luckiest place to live is in the Wolverhampton area. Then, when you win, you can move as far away as possible.

## Monday, 18 November 1996

Today my babies came home. Tomorrow, my favourite headline will proclaim, BOB HAS THE LAST LAUGH AS HIS STOLEN GAG BOOKS ARE RETURNED.

I feel as ecstatic as I did on my wedding day twenty-three years ago. I'd written the books off, despite the fact that they contained a quarter of a century's industry. After advertising a £10,000 reward with no questions asked (and being threatened with prosecution by the police for doing so!), and making appeals through all the media to no avail, I gave up. I had poured myself a large eighteen-year-old Macallan malt whisky, the second greatest invention known to man (the greatest being the fast-forward button on your VCR) and toasted my books's disappearance, 'Bye bye, babies!'

They went missing from a metal briefcase in a locked BBC production office (see p.171) to which very few people had access and I was distressed not only by the loss but also because a couple of my friends were under suspicion.

One of them, the fluent and inventive Irish comedian Adrian Walsh, had been a valuable contributor to the series we were taping. Because he was around on the day the two files vanished he felt the burden of mistrust most painfully, concerned that he might be thought guilty of taking them. When Adrian returned to England from starring in cabaret on the *QE2*, my staunchest friend Dave Ismay even went so far as to drive all the way from his Midlands home to Southampton to meet the ship and face Adrian with that conjecture, and it's indicative of their maturity that no resentment has resulted. Recently I had further evidence of Adrian's utter integrity.

Only two weeks ago, fourteen months after the theft, he requested that I meet him in London for the sole purpose of assuring me that, far from carrying off the books, he would never have asked me if he could even look at them. He said he was more respectful of my privacy than that.

'I don't care what anybody else may think, Bob. The only thing that matters to me is that you believe me innocent.'

I wanted to make a joke about it to lighten the moment but I could see how severely Adrian had been affected by the rumours. A bitchy allegation like this gets round our business very quickly. I spent some time and effort convincing Adrian that I was quite certain of his guiltlessness.

There were others in our business who thought the whole thing was a publicity stunt but kinder friends sensed the truth and were genuinely sympathetic, like Maureen Lipman and her writer husband Jack Rosenthal who sent me a wonderfully supportive card and Dillie Keane of Fascinating Aida who wrote a warmly understanding piece in her newspaper column that asked, 'Why do people make fun of someone losing his work?'

Of course, that's what they did. There wasn't much news to fill the papers for about two weeks after the story broke so cartoonists and columnists poked fun at me, a corny old comic who'd lost his crappy collection of chestnuts. The *Daily Mail* ran a Bob's Lost Jokes Appeal and devoted two full pages to the antique wheezes that poured in. They were awful.

Apart from the negative nature of this publicity and the trauma of losing all the work I'd prepared for future programmes, I attempted to treat the affair as a blessing. With my comfort blanket gone I had to knuckle down and produce a prodigious amount of new material, create sequences of gags based on a fresh premises and make greater use of topical input. I told myself it was doing me no harm at all in that respect.

In the *Daily Telegraph*, Eric Bailey wrote, 'It hasn't helped that the files have been characterised in chortling press stories as "joke books". No: you buy joke books at any bookshop.

'And at 67 Bob knows enough jokes to see him out. This is *material*: the warp and weft of scenarios, occurrences, experiences, rarely funny in themselves but which just might be capable of being woven into an instinctive comedic pattern.

'Each file is stuffed with 200 loose-leaf sheets, one filled and one with five or six sheets left; he took them everywhere with him, wrote dialogue, sketches, parts of plays, even segments of one serious novel and an outline of another.'

He picks out one gag of mine. 'Many people would like to die in a blaze of glory, doing something heroic. Not me. I'd like to die like my old dad. Peacefully, in his sleep. Not screaming like his passengers.'

Like so many of my jokes, it's based on a news item, a terrible incident when a coach went over a cliff in Yugoslavia and the passengers all went down the mountainside with their eyes open, falling for over a minute. The story was so horrific it made me feel giddy and ill and I had nightmares about it. So I made up the joke in order to come to terms with it and that's how weird gagwriters can be. But Bailey understood that. There was something he wasn't so sure about.

'But why is he so upset about the files?' he concluded. 'He can work, after all, and his burden is a mind that won't stop extruding material. But, like all of us, he's going over a cliff with his eyes open. Maybe what he's *really* lost, snapped tightly into maroon binders and unrepeatable in the time it takes to hit the bottom, is his own evidence of depth and dimension. Proof to himself that he was there all the time.'

Maybe.

Now the *Daily Express* reported, 'The last laugh was on the BBC when a mother and son employed by them were arrested on suspicion of stealing Bob Monkhouse's prized ledgers.

'The arrested pair were a BBC buildings manager with access to every room at BBC TV Centre, and her son who also works there. They were arrested in full view of their shocked colleagues and taken to Hammersmith Police Station. A management consultant of Bayswater, London, has been charged with handling stolen goods.

'When the books, which held up to 400 pages of gags, ideas for films and plays together with plot outlines and cartoons, were stolen, Monkhouse put up a £10,000 reward which he later raised to £20,000.'

Of course, that offer had been withdrawn as soon as it became clear to me that the books were not merely lost but stolen.

The *Daily Star* explained, 'Bob's agent Peter Prichard was recently contacted by a man wanting cash for the books. He met the fixer but tipped off the police who had undercover cops standing by to grab the 47-year-old man as the ransom money was handed over.'

I don't know the whole story and I don't suppose I ever will. Why the books were taken in the first place I have no clue. They're of little use to anyone else but me. Perhaps they were removed out of idle curiosity; in which case one might guess that they weren't returned as soon as their loss was reported because of the hue and cry itself, frightening the culprits into inaction.

But why, well over a year later, any respectable person should authorise a management consultant to approach my agent and demand money I've no clear idea. The charges were subsequently dropped. The puzzles remain. Still, what care I? My babies are back!

## Saturday, 30 November 1996

Today I presented Luciano Pavarotti and Elton John on 'The National Lottery Live'. The director of the show was Geoff Miles who made such a great job of directing 'The Bob Monkhouse Show' on BBC 2 in the 80s and he'd worked out a brilliantly complex shooting plan for the Pavarotti–John duet. As soon as he began explaining it to the singers he was cut short by the size-sensitive Pavarotti.

'No, no, no, you do not show me full length, you do not show me from the sides, you do not show me below my nipples!'

He and Elton began rehearsing their song together, an unmemorable tune yoked to an incomprehensible lyric entitled 'Live Like Horses'.

After the second run-through I asked Elton, 'What's this song about?'

'Fuck knows. It's the worst fucking song in history. I hate the fucking song. I never want to have to sing it again in my entire fucking life. Still . . .' and he beamed at me brightly from behind his outsize spectacles. 'Still, what can I do? Luciano likes it.'

During a break Pavarotti asked me if I liked opera. I said, 'I love a lot of the music but I hate the plots and some things about opera give me the creeps. Like the castrati.'

'Ah, yes.' He shook his head in sorrow. 'You mean what they used to do to get male singers with high voices. They used to cut off their . . . ah . . . you know how in tennis they have ballboys? These were *no*-ballboys.' His huge frame began to heave with laughter. 'Yes, they'd been awarded the No-ball Prize!'

Then he became earnest. 'But for the castrati this *was* a prize, a reward, because they only picked the boys with the best voices.'

I said, 'Hey, that's one audition I'd make sure I screwed up!'

'Oh, yes, like so . . .' and Pavarotti began to sing in a high treble voice, then broke a top note into a basso profundo growl. 'Then the teachers they say "Oh, no, young signore, you sing sharp" and the young signore, he say, "Not as bloody sharp as that knife you've got behind your back! I'm not walking around with an empty jockstrap just to sound like the Bee Gees!"'

He slapped his thigh, laughed at length and then sighed.

'We should tell these jokes on the show instead of singing this fucking song. But what can I do? Elton likes it.'

## Wednesday, 25 December 1996

We love Christmas here in Barbados. There's something strangely hedonistic about eating Christmas pudding while reclining in your plunge pool in ninety degrees under a sky that's bluer than the buttocks of a frozen Smurf.

Among my presents is a copy of a play, John Osborne's *The Entertainer*. I've been invited to take the leading role of Archie Rice by Laurie Mansfield, a terrific agent and the entrepreneur behind the successful stage musical *Buddy*, so I've spent a couple of hours reading it and it's even worse than I remembered.

Archie's meant to be a faded front-cloth patter comic steadily decaying in his own tatty seaside show, yet only one line of his material rings true – 'Don't applaud, this is a very old building' – and that was appropriated from a 1953 gagbook by the American joke writer Robert Orben. The rest of what are intended to be the stale jokes of a has-been are more like those of a never-was. It's a bad pastiche and the entire façade of unrealistic realism fatally undermines the main storyline.

I saw Laurence Olivier play Archie on stage and in the 1960 film and I thought his performance very clever but utterly unconvincing, unlike the great man's personal charm in real life.

Billie Whitelaw was playing Desdemona at the National Theatre and advised my first wife and me to attend both the matinée and evening performances. 'Otherwise you'll go away thinking that it's all Frank Finlay's show. Seeing it the second time will give you a different perspective.'

She was quite right.

Finlay's stunning theatricality as Iago appeared to overwhelm Laurence Olivier's soul-searching Moor.

Between the performances, my wife and I went backstage to express our delight at Billie's wonderfully vulnerable portrayal.

As we talked in her dressing room, Olivier appeared barefoot in the doorway wearing only the briefest briefs. Always most gracious to nervous strangers, he introduced himself by saying, 'How do you do? I'm Larry Olivier.'

It seemed in no way affectation. From head to foot he was as black as Cherry Blossom boot polish. Had I not just seen his matinée performance I might not have known who this surprisingly short and shiny fellow was.

I remembered that he and Vivien Leigh had attended a charity concert the previous year in which I and the Beverley Sisters appeared in blackface to sing and dance an old-time minstrel medley of Al Jolson numbers. I told him that I'd used the traditional burnt coke to darken my complexion.

'Nasty stuff that.' He wagged a black finger, exposing a pale brown palm. 'I prefer this Leichner Negro paint. It doesn't come off on the props.'

'No shower between shows?' asked my bluntly spoken wife.

He laughed. 'This black skin takes forty-five minutes to acquire, my dear. I like to get my money's worth out of every application.'

He gave me a sly wink and tilted his head to indicate a private word. We stepped into the empty corridor for a moment, leaving the young women to talk.

He tucked his lower lip behind his front teeth with the grin of a naughty child and whispered, 'I can't play a black chap if my privates are white, can I?' After a quick glance up and down to make sure we were alone, he coyly peeled back his pants at the hip to show that his body makeup was total. 'See? I'll bet you never blacked up your bollocks to sing "Mammy"!'

Watching the play for the second time in one day it was possible to appreciate the great subtlety and depth of Olivier's work. In the flashier role of Iago, Finlay was superb but it became easier to discount some of his more obvious effects and see how intricately massive was Othello's shift from powerful assurance to fearful jealousy.

His extraordinary talent aside, I also observed a memorable example of Olivier's quick-witted charm that night. As we left the stage door of the National Theatre the usual group of admirers gathered round him. One tiny, elderly woman was jostled aside but he made a special effort to bring her forward.

She held out a pocket diary, opened at the blank page of that day's date.

'Please, Mr Olivier, your autograph for a very, very old lady.'

'Why, most certainly!' Olivier replied with great courtesy. 'But where is she?'

## Wednesday, 26 February 1997

Last night on BBC 2 I was interviewed by Sir Jeremy Isaacs on 'Face to Face' during which he asked me about the life and death of my disabled son, Gary. I never duck the issue because I've found that frankly discussing the problems of cerebral palsy in public can be of real value to others who have to deal with it in their families.

This morning one newspaper critic, in commenting kindly on the programme, praised my 'lack of self-pity'. While always grateful for a favourable review, I winced a bit.

Lack of self-pity isn't praiseworthy any more than a lack of self-mutilation. Self-pity is merely an indulgence to be detested and so avoided.

As a prescription-free drug, feeling sorry for yourself is as habit-forming, corrosive to the spirit, perversely gratifying and delusory as any narcotic. If its temporary satisfactions ever lure you, use all of your will to shun it as you would a poison.

Concentrate on its absurdity and mock it out of your mind.

## Monday, 3 March 1997

During one fortnight in 1948 I went to see the show at the London Palladium six times. Danny Kaye was the reason.

Britain's love affair with the attractive thirty-five-year-old comedian was phenomenal and remains unique. The royal family came to see him, eschewing the royal box to take their places in the front row of the stalls where they roared approval. I know because it was one of the nights I was there.

Subsequently I learned that they accepted an invitation to a small party backstage where the King drank Danny's rare Scotch with obvious enjoyment and asked, 'Where did you manage to get this? It's unobtainable.' Kaye's answer was, 'Your Majesty, you just don't know the right people.'

Kaye's personal magic lay in his effortless, almost diffident, charm. Such a nice young man, you thought, with his shy smile animating a sensitive hero's face under a boyish mane of fair hair. It was almost enough. In those austere post-war years it seemed an act of kindness that he'd come to see us at all, travelling all the way from the glamour of his Technicolored Hollywood paradise to visit us in our smoggy, rationed, rubble-strewn Britain. And what was this printed in the programme after 'Interval: 15 minutes'? Just the words 'Danny Kaye', that's all.

We had come to expect the headline stars of any variety bill to give us a bit more of their time than the supporting acts that preceded them but no one had ever offered to fill the entire second half of the show alone.

But sure enough, for fifty minutes twice nightly he became our court jester, spinning marvellous stories full of gesticulation and grimaces,

248

twisting his dextrous tongue through impossibly complicated lyrics, softly crooning instructions for 'Balling the Jack', dancing on feet that flew until, exhausted, he perched on the side of the stage and drank a cup of tea while he chatted to us – well, it was so magnanimous that we could only exchange it for our grateful devotion.

Perhaps the best critique he ever had was reported by an American newspaper correspondent. Danny had completed his triumphant run and the British press announced his return to the USA with the headline, OUR DANNY'S GONE AWAY. Two commuters sat on opposite sides of the carriage on the London Underground, strangers to each other. One of them sighed sadly as he consulted his newspaper. The other shook his head from across the aisle and called out, 'It's a lot different with him gone, isn't it?' The first man nodded back ruefully, 'Aye, it is.' Both sighed together and fell silent.

When Danny returned in 1952, Val Parnell, proprietor of the London Palladium, had arranged for him to tour Britain's major variety theatres. I was engaged to advise the star on local colour, place names and dialects. By this time Danny had been so fêted by the upper crust that he was confidently socialising with every sort of British nob from HRH Princess Margaret to the Oliviers. When we met in his hotel suite he was less interested in customising his act for the provinces than he was in getting transport to Cliveden for a weekend bash at the high life.

'It's so tough to get a limousine in this country, let alone the gas to put in it,' he complained.

The impresario Henry Sherek had a suggestion. Why didn't Danny borrow his vintage Rolls-Royce?

'She's been in dry dock since the war began, Daniel dear boy. She's just been done by the people at Owen's, she's big and beautiful and she's got a full tank of petrol. Just take bloody good care of her, won't you?'

A week later I met with Danny backstage and I asked if he'd driven up in the Sherek Roller. This is the story he told me.

'I was about halfway to Cliveden when the car stalled. I stopped a lady driver and asked her to give me a push. I told her it was a big engine and she'd have to get up to around thirty-five miles an hour to get me really rolling. How was I to know I was talking to a maniac? I climbed back behind the wheel and waited for her car to start nudging me forward. She seemed kind of slow in getting on with it so I peeked my head out the window and looked out for her. There she was, bearing down on me at thirty-five miles an hour!'

He said that the damage to Sherek's Rolls-Royce was extensive and cost Danny almost £1,000. 'A costly ride,' I said.

'Yes but a cheap piece of material,' said Danny. 'It goes into my act this week.' A few embellishments and what Danny swore was a true tale became an excellent crowd-pleaser.

When his immense popularity on both sides of the Atlantic began to wane in the late 50s, Danny devoted more and more time to travelling the world on behalf of UNICEF, entertaining children with extemporised clowning that heeded no language barrier.

His film appearances grew fewer and in the mid-60s he turned first to TV with a four-year run that won him an Emmy and a Peabody Award, then to Broadway for his 1970 musical *Two by Two*.

He died at seventy-four of hepatitis and internal haemorrhaging, the consequence of a transfusion of contaminated blood during quadruple bypass heart surgery. It was on this day in 1987. I can't think of a better epitaph than that phrase spoken by one stranger to another on the London Underground so long ago.

'It's a lot different with him gone, isn't it?'

## Friday, 11 April 1997

Clive James has invited me to be a guest on his show again tonight. I'm doing the comedy spot where the news of the week is reviewed.

Luckily for me, after a dull six days, some of this morning's headlines offer a toehold for comedy:

'Wonderful news for all you women. Scientists say they may be able to develop a pill to stimulate the female orgasm. They're also trying to develop another pill that'll call you the next day.'

The younger females in the audience love that one.

'Now Russian scientists are saying apples cause cancer. Apples! What's left? You can't have sex because that'll kill you. Now you can't even have an apple *instead* of sex!

'I think God's angry with us. Apples and sex. Weren't they the two things He told us to leave alone in the Garden of Eden? *AHA!*'

The spot is off to a good start. After a few more short gags, I have two strong pieces to end on.

'Clive, did you read where a Baptist Church survey in the USA asked 10,000 of their regular congregations what causes the most misery and the most joy in the world? The most common answers were "sex" and "money". Sex and money. The two things my wife and I argue about most – I am convinced she's charging me too much.

'And my friends tell me I'm right.

'Money can bring joy if you've got it and misery if you haven't. Me,

I've got enough money to last me the rest of my life. Unless I want to buy something, then I'm in trouble.

'Everyone's short of money these days. Our Government's in worse trouble than they're admitting. Only this week I got a tax rebate from the Inland Revenue – £75 – with a note saying would I hold it till Monday.

'We all need money if only to eat – look at food prices today! I'll tell you how bad it is – I went into the supermarket with a trolley full of money, I came out with a walletful of food.

'You know my biggest ever expense? Educating my son. Because I opted for a private education and that's expensive. My son's education cost me £38,000. He owns £38,000 worth of information. Know what he does for a living? He plays drums in a holiday camp. I could have let him stay stupid and bought a Lamborghini.

'And finally, Clive, a feature in the *Daily Mail* asks whether animals are happy in zoos. I don't know, do you? Some zoos – San Diego for example – are superb for animals and people too, but others tend to pay lip service to popular concern about the animals' comfort. I saw a sign at Regent's Park zoo: EVERY EFFORT IS MADE TO RECREATE EACH ANIMAL'S NATURAL ENVIRONMENT. Well, obviously. That's why they give the gorilla that big rubber tyre off a lorry, the jungle's full of tyres.

'As for the polar bear, he's got a cement island painted blue. Oh yes, that'll fool him he's back in the Arctic. That's like driving around in the winter with a picture of a heater in your car.'

Clive is a generous straight man for comedians and he leads the laughter as always. After the recording he thanks me and adds, 'Truth is funnier than fiction, isn't it?'

I'm thinking about that when a very tall, broadly built man approaches me.

'Bob, got a minute? Something happened last week and I thought you might be able to use it on TV. I work in the ambulance service. A land-lady called us out in an emergency. One of her boarders, a married woman, was screaming for help. We had to break open the door and, Bob, you wouldn't believe what we saw.'

'What had happened?'

'This couple must've decided to spice up their sex life. She'd stripped naked and he'd tied her to the bed. Then he'd put on a Batman costume and climbed up on the table to jump on top of her. When he jumped, he hit his head on the ceiling and knocked himself out. With him uncon-scious and bleeding on the floor, the wife could only yell for help. Her screams eventually woke the landlady and she called us.'

'Rather embarrassing for the wife, tied to the bed and naked and seeing you blokes bursting in. How many of you were there?'

'Two ambulance service and the three guys with us.'

'What three guys?'

'Cameraman, sound and lighting. They were a TV crew following us around, making a documentary. They can't use the recording they made but I can get you a copy if you like.'

'Thanks but it's not the sort of thing I could show either. Try the Playboy Channel.'

You can't make up stuff like that.

It's funnier than anything I've said all evening.

## Saturday, 19 April 1997

There's one thing I dread above all during a live TV broadcast. It's worse than a nosebleed or an attack of Tourette Syndrome and it happened this weekend on 'The National Lottery Live'.

At seventeen minutes, it's a very tight show and must end on time to preserve the rest of BBC 1's Saturday night schedule. This means that the presenters, from Anthea Turner to Terry Wogan, must stick pretty closely to the script which is rolling up before their eyes as they gaze into their main camera.

My opening monologue consists of about a dozen precisely worded topical gags which must be delivered hard and fast without allowing audience response to spread the allotted two minutes into three or four.

The rest of the job depends upon reading the tightly phrased continuity off the same autocue on the same camera with enough energy and accuracy to keep the programme running to time.

In short, the host is dependent upon the autocue, that blessed device whereby a reflection of the printed script is scrolled over the camera lens, invisible to the viewers. I walked out on stage at the start of last week's show, greeted the audience and found myself staring at a blank square of glass. The crib was gone.

In the theatre the actor who dries can call 'Prompt!' in the desperate hope that the assistant stage manager is actually in the wings with his finger on the right line and not reading the *Sun* in the loo.

On the cabaret floor or the speaker's podium, a forgotten script requires only an emergency paraphrase, a jovial ad lib, even a gracious confession.

None of that will do when you're on live TV and mustn't overrun. What made it worse was that no one on the studio floor or in the gallery knew that my autocue was up the spout. The fault was in the single unit on the camera that I was addressing. I alone knew that I was smiling at

15 million viewers with nothing to say to them.

Saying nothing but still talking is a trick well known to politicians, insurance salesmen and motormouths like me. I chattered my way through that ordeal using every device previously employed over ten years of taking arms against the slings and arrows of outrageous 'Golden Shots'.

When we came off the air, the producer came over and asked me if I agreed that the show had a more excitingly dangerous air about it than was usual. I couldn't have put it better myself.

Comedians are supposed to be able to think on their feet, it comes with the job. I'm more impressed when dramatic actors are able to depart from the text of a play to accommodate some hitch in the proceedings.

In 1964 I toured in a stage comedy by Sidney Sheldon called *Roman Candle*. My character was a frustrated scientist dealing with the supernatural powers of a witch played by the beautiful Canadian actress Toby Robbins. Alone on the stage during one scene in *Roman Candle* I was supposed to light a cigar and puff on it furiously while enumerating aloud to myself the faults of the heroine.

Since the stage manager had forgotten to put a box of matches where it was supposed to be, I had to make do with an unlit cigar and delivered my speech while sucking on it noisily. As I concluded with the words that cued Toby Robbins's entrance, she walked on and, rephrasing her usual reference to the smoky air, said, 'Phew, what a horrid smell of . . . wet tobacco!'

During the run of another play, *The Gulls*, Basil Ashmore's translation of Le Sage's *Turcaret*, the crowds swarmed into the Jeanetta Cochrane Theatre like bees. The trouble was they *were* bees.

They began to arrive in the middle of the second act, at first just five or six of them humming around the stage, their wings caught in the stage lighting like fireflies. Steadily their numbers increased until the air was thick with them and the leading lady, Frances Day, rose from her couch in a panic and fled to her dressing room leaving me and an actor named Lloyd Lamble to play the rest of the scene without her. 'Forgive my lady,' I extemporised. 'She has much on her mind.'

Lloyd replied, 'More likely she's got a bee in her bonnet.'

It was the only laugh in the play and, sadly, not repeatable on subsequent nights.

The second act was abandoned, the audience refunded, and pest control people brought in to smoke out the insects over the next forty-eight hours. Meanwhile I sent a telegram to my agent who was holidaying in

Switzerland saying, SHOW STOPPED BY MASON BEES. He wired back, EXTEND THEIR BOOKING.

### Saturday, 26 April 1997

I can't do any political gags on 'The National Lottery Live' tonight because we've got a general election and I think the big problem, of course . . . is someone will win.

It doesn't matter who because each elected Government only stays in office for four years – they don't have time to make any big differences. The country's really in the hands of the ranking civil servants and you need Jonathan Woss to say that correctly. Senior civil servants stay for ever, year after year, in Whitehall – where their office hours are twelve till one with an hour off for lunch.

As for all the sleazy ministers – Mellor, Yeo, Mates, Hughes and the like – they pledge us their integrity to get voted in, don't they? But as soon as they're elected, they go mad with power. Suddenly there's no time for anything but sex romps with secretaries and researchers and rent boys and satsumas! Look what we've endured over the past couple of years: vote-rigging, adultery, insider trading, a Chancellor who couldn't even manage an Access card, an engraved watch for a bail-jumping tycoon, a Minister caught lying about planting questions to block the Disabled Bill, and as if that weren't bad enough, Lord Archer! Look up the word 'politics' in the dictionary. It's actually a combination of two words: 'poli' which means many . . . and 'tics' which means bloodsucking vermin.

The band on tonight's show is No Mercy. Very apt.

### Friday, 16 May 1997

The packed house at Lakeside Country Club near Camberley is such a treat tonight, quick-witted and quick to laugh too. I'm glad because three of my friends are in to see my show: Helene Olley, who researched my autobiography and the book you're holding, together with my most loyal fans, Joe and Margaret. They travel countless miles to see me perform all over England and I feel that, if I ever did forget a favourite gag, they could easily prompt me.

I don't think I'd appreciate a truly responsive audience as much if I hadn't worked in front of a few real stinkers.

There was once an excellently run nightclub near Manchester called the Talk of the North. An Eccles entrepreneur named Joe Pullen owned it and kept it very efficient and profitable. Over a span of twenty years I'd appeared on its stage over 250 times and always successfully.

Then Joe sold the place and subsequent owners loosened the managerial grip bit by bit. The last time I agreed to appear at the joint for a one-night engagement, I'd been wary of its tumbling standards but my doubts were overcome by my starry cockiness. 'Hey,' I thought to myself, 'you've always been a hit at this venue so, whatever the problems, how could you fail?' I'll tell you how.

First, get yourself in a foul mood. That's easy. After driving for four hours through torrential rain, then having to park three streets away from the nightclub and run through the downpour, you reach the stage door after negotiating the muddy puddles in the unlit alley beside the nightspot. Not all of them, just the puddles you can barely make out in the wet darkness of the unlit alley. The rest you splash through, decorating your trouser legs with wet clay.

The stage door is firmly locked and no one answers as you beat on the door with your umbrella handle, busting it clean off in your hand. Nothing for it but to go squelching back down the alley carrying your case, suitbag, shirtbag and broken brolly, and make your way round to the front of house. You don't want your public to see you looking as if you've been sleeping in a ditch but there are plenty of them in the foyer who do.

You can't make things worse by pushing through the cabaret room and letting all the customers see you like this so you explain the situation to a scarred, shaven-headed bouncer, a Schwarzenegger lookalike who looks tough enough to see the lions of Longleat on a bicycle.

He tells you to go back to the stage door, he'll open it. Back you go into the northern monsoon, round the building, up the alley, and wait. And wait. No fewer than ten minutes later the bruiser opens the door without apology or explanation. All he says is, 'You're on in five minutes.'

You clatter down the dirty staircase to your dirtier dressing room which is underneath the stage. Above your head you can hear tinny music and the shuffling feet of patrons and waiters as powdery dirt drifts down on you. You can't see anywhere clean enough to put down your overnight case. There's enough dust on the dressing table to write your name in it or, if you had time, *War and Peace*.

The mirror's clouded and cracked and the bare light bulb is flickering ominously. If it goes out, you've had it. It goes out.

You change into your stage clothes by the light of the torch which bitter experience has taught you to carry in your case.

You climb back up the stairs with your sheet music in your hand and stand in the wings, waiting for someone to come and greet you, the musicians perhaps. Suddenly the loudspeakers in the cabaret room fall silent and you realise there are no musicians employed here any more, just a record player. You hear a disembodied voice announcing, 'It's cabaret time! Please put your 'ands together for a local favourite, Bob Monk'ouse!' You drop your music on the floor and walk out to indifferent applause from eighteen people. The place can hold three hundred but there are only eighteen and they look like the cast of a zombie film.

Directly in front of you is a table of six women ugly enough to walk through a wood and find truffles. They were talking loudly before you came on and they're not about to stop. You pause and ask them, 'Am I ruining your evening?' and the ugliest one shouts, 'No, you're not that good!'

That exchange turns out to be the highlight of the night. You decide to make a joke about the absent bouncer.

'Please, no trouble, folks! Don't make me send for that musclebound moron they've got on the door here! Have you seen it?'

''E's fuckin' gorgeous!' yells a harpie. 'Shurrup!'

'Think about it, ladies! His shoulders are sixty-eight inches, his chest is fifty-seven, his waist is thirty-six . . . what does that indicate?'

There's a gormless silence.

'That's right! It means he get smaller as he goes down.'

As you complete this witticism, Schwarzenegger suddenly emerges from behind some curtains over an exit door. He folds his arms and glares at you like your worst enemy. For the first time the audience sits up and pays attention.

'Are you gonna take that from 'im, Terry?' screams another hellcat.

You try to continue, going into your most reliable material, but the small mob is still waiting for what Terry might do now that his manhood has been belittled in what passes for public. They're not listening to you so what are you going to do now, you king of comedy? Fake a nosebleed? Clutch your chest as if in cardiac arrest? Vomit and run?

No, old trouper that you are, you fulfil your contractual obligation and soldier on. The table of viragos, losing interest in the possibility of seeing you castrated with a bare fist, resume their jabbering. The rest of the dull-eyed bunch sit apathetically as you move around the stage with the microphone in your hand, spewing out the very same patter that has convulsed happy admirers in the past but which this evening has the effect of a sedative. Only one person remains gloweringly alert. Terry, stock-still and menacing, is giving you the evil eye from his doorway.

Time's up and you can finally quit the stage. Pick up your music from the floor and plunge down the wooden stairs into the blackness below. No time to change your clothes by torchlight, just pull on your damp overcoat, grab your stuff and get out of this Gehenna. You reach the bottom of the stairs but the light shining from the top is obscured by a giant figure standing there with arms still folded. You move up the staircase slowly. Your escape route through the stage door is beyond Terry's threatening bulk. You take two more steps up and you're face to midriff with the man. Are you about to descend again from the force of a blow?

You hear your own nervous cough and you try a feeble smile as you say, 'Well, I'll be off then!'

Terry unfolds his arms and reaches out a right arm as thick as a thigh towards you.

He takes your case.

He speaks at last, pushing a scrap of paper into your top pocket with his free hand.

'This place'll close down soon. That's my name and address. If you ever need a minder, I can drive and that. Come on, I'll walk you to your car. There's some nasty boys about this time o' night.'

It's stopped raining. As the two of you move along the alley by moonlight Terry adds an afterthought.

'Tossers and tarts, them lot. I thought you was quite good meself.'

## Thursday, 22 May 1997
In writing my life story up to the age of sixty-five in 1993, I confessed to some of my love affairs and, as you might reasonably expect, I have nothing to report subsequent to that date. Events jog the memory however and today I came across a packet of stills from a commercial shoot in Italy in 1964 that brought back a forgotten image of a beautiful film star dressed only in a thin housecoat and bra, disappearing up one of the Seven Hills of Rome on the back of a policeman's motor scooter as a pale sunrise lit her bobbing silvery-golden tresses with all the newborn innocence of dawn.

The story really begins five years earlier at the Hillcrest Golf Club in Los Angeles where I was the guest of the legendary comedian Milton Berle. I'd been befriended by Berle in the mid-50s when he visited London. At that time the most famous TV comic in America, he'd been a little dispirited to find himself virtually unknown in Britain and, when I was taken over to his table in The Stork Club by its proprietor Al Burnett, he found my awestruck admiration very soothing to his bruised ego. I'd followed his work on radio from the 40s and knew all about his unique lifetime contract with NBC, the result of his live comedy hour regularly emptying theatres and restaurants as every American with a TV set stayed home to watch 'Uncle Miltie'.

By the time Berle invited me and my then agent Sid Grace to join him for an early supper at the starry Hillcrest, I'd also learned that every man in the American entertainment industry thought him the luckiest guy in the world, not because of his phenomenal success but because he was rumoured to have the largest penis in the business.

A featured film actor named Forrest Tucker was also believed to have been blessed with a prodigious appendage and excitement ran high because both these champions were in the club that night, the first time such a clash of the giants seemed possible.

Our table had been expanded to include George Burns, his manager Irving Fein, the comedian-actor Jack Carter, singer Mel Torme and the bandleader for Martin and Lewis, Dick Stabile.

Dick said, 'You know Forrest Tucker is in the bar? There's a lot of smart money says he's got the biggest schlong in Hollywood.'

There was some coarse laughter and everybody looked at Berle who grinned his trademark toothy simper, rolled his eyes and shrugged modestly.

Moments later a group of men moved from the bar towards our table, the most massively built being Tucker. He appeared to be sheepishly embarrassed but resigned. One of his companions spoke first.

'We have a proposition for you guys.'

George Burns rose and waved his cigar for attention.

'Now hold it, you guys. I'm on the committee of this fine establishment, remember. We-we-we don't want any vulgarity here. I've known Milton Berle all his adult life and I think as-as-as gentlemen we should accept his word that Berle is hung like King Kong's grand-daddy.'

'No, George,' said a voice I vaguely recognised and from behind Tucker stepped the small, dapper figure of Audie Murphy, America's most decorated war hero turned Western star. 'This is a matter of honour. Mr Tucker is the bearer of God's greatest gift to man.'

'Or woman,' said Torme.

'And I've placed a five hundred dollar bet on Mr Tucker's great reputation,' Murphy announced. 'And I say this as the cowboy with the fastest dick in the West.'

Voices were raised both for and against and, though there was a lot of laughter, some serious wagers were on offer. Burns topped them all.

'Okay, okay, if you men must have such a juvenile contest, here's the closing deal. Five thousand bucks on Milton!'

While the good-natured Tucker stood by helplessly, Berle rose and held up his arms for quiet. 'Gentlemen, please! Let's not disgrace ourselves. I understand the odds are in my favour . . .'

Our table cheered.

'. . . I have no wish to humiliate Forry in any way. George, I'm deeply touched that you're prepared to back me and mine to the tune of five big ones but let me assure you all, there's no possibility of my revealing my most private personal possession to compete with anyone here.'

There was a respectful silence.

Then Burns said, 'Aw, go on, Milton. Take out just enough to win.'

Later that same evening Berle, concerned for my English susceptibilities, said he hoped I hadn't been offended by the subject matter of the argument.

I told him no, I'd remembered a similar challenge just a few years earlier between the boxer Ted 'Kid' Lewis and the musical comedian Stanelli.

Stanelli had been booked to entertain from the boxing ring during the interval at a Gentleman's Charity Evening in London's Connaught Rooms. He wore white tie and tails, spoke with a throaty cultured voice and his act consisted of telling slightly spicy anecdotes and playing his Hornchestra, a wheeled chromium framework bearing twenty-five motor horns. While his accompanist thumped out the melodies, the wavy-haired comedian would squeeze rubber balls and poke buttons with nimble-fingered proficiency to produce a comical version of each tune.

I was the youthful guest of the elegant bandleader Sidney Lipton that evening and it was he who told me that one of Lewis's handicaps in the ring was the disproportionate size of his genitals. Sidney had such a grave and stately way of speaking that it seemed very funny to me to hear him talk about such a matter without any trace of humour.

'He's a small man with a lot to take care of, d'you see. That's why he wears such large, loose shorts. It's all tucked up in there out of harm's way. It's not a subject for discussion in mixed company but amongst men there is nothing improper about mentioning it since it may affect the betting. Of course, it's only a coincidence of course, but it's understood that Stanelli is the same. A whatsit that has to be strapped in apparently.'

Now I already knew about Stanelli from Ted Ray who had toured the variety theatres for years and said the man's outsize reproductive equipment was a legend among landladies from Scunthorpe to Cockermouth. 'Every time old Stan gets pissed, out it comes,' chuckled Ted. 'Like a child's arm holding an apple.'

During the first few bouts I looked around the hall. At twenty-five, I was the youngest man present by about fifteen years. Men grew old sooner in those days and even those in their forties were florid, pot-bellied or desiccated, white-haired or bald with the pompous gravity of old fogies. Dirty stories were exchanged out of my earshot in billows of cigar smoke but I soon gathered from snatches of chatter that some of the senior figures had agreed to approach the star boxer and entertainer with a betting proposition based upon a private viewing of the items of male anatomy in contention.

The interval came, Stanelli told his tales and hooted his horns, Ted 'Kid' Lewis fought and won and an elderly man with medals on his dinner jacket came over to whisper in Sidney Lipton's ear. Sidney nodded and the old boy left to join a select group of wrinklies who were crowding into an anteroom just off the main hall. I could see the two smiling protagonists being ushered in through this élite with much masculine laughter and backslapping; Lewis sweating in a blue silk dressing gown; Stanelli carrying his overcoat, top hat and cane, ready to reveal himself, collect his extended fee and vanish into the night where his pianist waited with the dismantled Hornchestra bundled into the boot of the star's Armstrong-Siddeley Sapphire. 'They've come to an arrangement,' Sidney explained to me in his low, earnest tones. 'Cash. I'm expected to attend. I'm afraid I can't take you in with me. The chairman thinks you're insufficiently mature.'

That last line was the one that made Milton Berle laugh loudest of all.

When the US Polaroid Corporation decided to launch their photographic system in Europe, Berle was a friendly broker in getting me the job as their British spokesman. I had made six different TV ads over two years when the company invited all their national presenters to gather at the Cinecitta Studios in Rome for what they called 'a pan-European super-commercial'.

I checked into my hotel on the Via Veneto and the limousine that had collected me from the airport took me on to the film studio where a welcoming lunch had been set up for fifty, including the company's advertising executives, the movie makers and us, the TV hosts who demonstrated the cameras to our audiences in France, Germany, Greece, Belgium, Holland, Denmark, Norway, Sweden, Austria, Switzerland and, of course, the UK. Scripts were distributed in which each of us had to speak one promotional line in our own language. My line described the simple action of removing the exposed film from the camera after a picture had been taken, peeling off the protective paper cover and seeing the image appear as you held it in your fingers.

The actual wording was, 'You pull it out, peel it back, hold it in your hand and it develops in thirty seconds.'

Somehow it put me in mind of Milton Berle and Stanelli.

After a day's satisfactory shooting the company played host for everyone involved, escorting us to a huge new disco called The Piper which was all the rage among young Romans in 1964. It appeared to be a converted warehouse decorated in a dozen shades of green and pale blue. The outstanding feature of its interior design was its varying levels of dance floor, all on differently sized blocks made accessible by inter-locking stairs. One dance area might accommodate thirty dancers while the next had room for only six. There were few handrails and the entire idea seemed to me like an impractical designer's dream and an eventual deathtrap.

We sat in a roped-off dining area a few feet higher than the highest dance floor looking down at about three hundred devotees of what passed for La Dolce Vita. Waitresses were dressed as American teeny-boppers with white bobby socks, black patent shoes, short plaid skirts and tight angora tops above bare midriffs. They took orders for drinks and food by scribbling them down on the green paper table coverings and tearing off a strip. It was meant to be stylish and perhaps it was. Discos aren't really my scene but I'd put in an appearance, intending to leave as early as seemed appropriate, have an early night and catch the first plane back to London. I hadn't reckoned on meeting Lisa Castle.

Lisa Castle isn't her real name, of course; where a lady's reputation is concerned, I'm a gentleman. And, more to the point, so is my lawyer. The name that you would recognise wasn't her real one either. Hollywood has given her that. She'd been christened by her European parents with what the studios considered an unsuitably alien moniter for a movie star, one I'll never forget because she insisted on writing it on my right forearm in ballpoint.

We met in a way that was quite unusual for me but I suspect almost normal for her. Her partner for the evening was the assistant director of the film in which she was starring. He was a friend of the couple I had latched on to, our English-speaking camera operator and his attractive American girlfriend. Lisa decided that he was paying too much atten-tion to us so she set fire to our tablecloth.

By the time the flames had been doused with beer Lisa had taken me by the hand and led me to a vacant table. She sat down and stared at me without speaking. I had seen her in movies and had thought her extra-ordinarily lovely but the camera had been unable to record the delicacy of her beauty. She had the enchanting fragility of a perfect orchid.

She was thirty years old and was better known for her off-screen romances than for her acting ability. I had glimpsed her only once before when she came to England to co-star in a sea-going adventure. I was filming a Rice Crispies commercial and she'd come bouncing past my table in the studio restaurant, laughing as she turned to gaze bewitchingly at the handsome Hollywood leading man whom she briefly married. Now this incredibly beautiful and previously unattainable lady was staring into my eyes at a table for two in the world's most romantic city. It couldn't last so I relished the moment.

'I'd like to go home now. Will you take me home?'

'Yes, I'd be happy to do that. Where do you live?'

'I have no idea. My daughter knows. I must find her. Wait here.'

She rose quickly and ran down some wide steps into the mêlée of dancers below. I waited about ten minutes but she didn't return. On the off-chance of finding her, I followed the direction she'd taken. Twisting and turning my way around the awkward floor levels, I suddenly spotted her through the dancing crowd, sitting on the floor in a corner beside a man who had his head in his hands. As I moved closer I could see he was in green overalls, a middle-aged workman who appeared to have collapsed in tears.

Lisa looked up at me.

'Bob, this is Halgo. He must come home with us.'

'Why?'

'Show some compassion. He is like me, a refugee from Israel. His wife has thrown him out and he has no place to go. He's an electrician here but the manager just fired him for drinking. Come!'

She stood and raised the electrician to his feet. He stared at me through tear-filled eyes and the oily black hair that fell across his seamed face, an attempt to smile humbly revealing his ugly teeth.

'I must find my daughter. She knows where we live.' And Lisa vanished into the mob again leaving me with Halgo and a feeling that things weren't working out as I'd dared to hope a few minutes earlier. The man was swaying and seemed ready to crack up again so I helped him over to a ledge in the wall. He was half-sitting and whining incomprehensibly when Lisa returned with a fair-haired, dark-eyed child as stunning as herself in tow.

'Oh, mummy, more lame dogs!'

'Really, I'm not a lame dog,' I protested politely. 'Your mother asked me to see you both home.'

We left the noisy club and immediately found a taxi driver who understood Tara's directions. The journey took us uphill into a suburb where the film company had hired a furnished home for Lisa and her daughter. All the way there Lisa kept up a non-stop barrage of complaints about Italy in general and Rome in particular.

'I've lived all over the world, Bob. I grew up in Venezuela, South Africa, Holland, Switzerland . . . oh, my dear, I know about men of every kind. My father was Belgium, you know. He was a diplomat so we travelled wherever his work took him. When I was ten years old I was as beautiful as Tara but the only men I had to fight off were Italians. They didn't care how young I was. Englishmen like you make the most considerate lovers. I met so many charming Englishmen when I worked in the offices of the British Embassy in Tel Aviv.'

Aha, so much for being a fellow refugee of Halgo's. I warned myself not to take everything the lady said as unalloyed fact. My hopes of a romantic outcome to the evening were slightly buoyed by the urgent grasp of her right hand on my left thigh as she talked. Halgo sat asleep on her far side while Tara was in the front passenger seat, guiding the driver. Suddenly we drew up and I found myself left to pay the fare.

'Let him go!' called Lisa as she opened her front door. Yes, I thought, I just might be stopping for the night. I let him go.

As I entered the dark, ornate interior of the old house I felt as if I'd stepped into a film set. The richly decorated hallway opened upon a split level sitting room that would have seemed overelaborate as Norma Desmond's home in 'Sunset Boulevard'. Fussy swags and drapes festooned every corner with gold and silver tassels, no item of furniture was without embellishments, an ancient piano and ostentatiously carved mahogany antiques crowded the walls and dim crystal lamps completed the suffocating effect.

Tara had gone on into the brightly lit and austere kitchen beyond the shadowy hall with Halgo shuffling behind her. Lisa was nowhere to be seen although I thought I could hear water rushing upstairs as though a shower had been turned on.

I sat on the end of a chaise longue for the next twenty minutes pondering on my situation. It was past midnight and I was a long way from my suitcase and air ticket. Was it really worth all this lunacy for the sake of some remote chance of having sex with a fantasy? The mere thought stirred my thirty-six-year-old loins into an affirmative response. Then a scream came from above and, as I reached the foot of the staircase, a cascade of water shot over the top step and began gushing downwards over the brocaded stair carpet. Tara ran past me and up the stairs, splashing as she went and meeting her mother at the top who was nude but for a small patterned towel.

'The tap's come loose and the tub's overflowing! Do something!'

Ten minutes later we had the plumbing under control but water was still pouring through the kitchen ceiling and the hall carpet squelched underfoot. Lisa now wore a thin housecoat and a bra but that was all. While I appreciated the sight of her superb figure and Tara seemed indifferent, old Halgo sat eating the cheese he'd been given and leering openly as Lisa mopped up water with bedsheets and a lace tablecloth. She sang as she worked in a cheerful manner, apparently enjoying the little drama. Tara left the kitchen, then reappeared to hand her mother a pair of peach-hued silk knickers, the wide legged kind with a lace trim. Lisa took them from her absently and used them to wipe the top of the fridge.

Satisfied that the drying process was as complete as it could be, she sent Tara for blankets and settled Halgo on a high-backed settee in the dusty conservatory that divided the main sitting room from the overgrown back garden. I'd returned to my previous perch, awaiting developments. Lisa eventually joined me carrying two glasses and a bottle of Valpolicella.

'Tara's gone to bed,' she said softly. She snuggled beside me and put the glasses on a low table, pouring the wine. 'First, you must know who I am.' She plucked a ballpoint pen from her bra. Biros were an expensive novelty then. They could write underwater, upside down and on human skin.

Carefully, frowning prettily with concentration and writing like a schoolgirl, she inscribed her real name, place and date of birth, on the inner part of my right forearm. I felt it was something she had done many times.

'There! Now that is who you will make love to. Shall we light a fire?'

The night was warm but she seemed keen on the idea so I did my best to set light to some curious little bundles of straw in the large wrought-iron hearth. They smouldered and began to fill the room with stale-smelling smoke.

I found two large sheets of newspaper employed as dust covering inside the piano and tried holding them over the fireplace to create an updraft to burn off the choking fumes but the chimney wouldn't draw. One of the dry old papers caught fire and the next thing I knew Lisa had thrown the contents of a Chinese vase over my shoulder on to the grate, all yellowed water and withered flowers. Half of it splashed back on to me and steam was added to the smoke that belched from the incendiary straw bundles.

We had difficulty in opening the windows, two of which were

painted shut, so I let the doors to the glassed lobby and the street stand ajar till the worst of the smoke cleared. As I returned, Lisa was standing in the middle of the room with her fists on her hips.

'This is not the right place to make love,' she announced.

'Let's go upstairs,' I murmured.

'No, I make a lot of noise and we'd keep Tara awake. Besides, it's not risky. I like somewhere risky. Let's look for a car.'

She walked out into the silent suburban street in bare feet and looked up and down the parked cars in the bright moonlight. She turned to me, resembling a dishevelled angel, and said, 'Leave the door on the latch and come along.'

I followed uncertainly as she tried the handles on six cars before finding the seventh, a Volkswagen, unlocked. She scrambled into the front and I slid behind the steering wheel.

I said, 'Wouldn't there be more room in the back?'

'We don't need more room. Kiss me.'

I kissed her and she unzipped my trousers. A dog barked.

'Someone might come along at any minute, the owner of this car maybe.'

'That's the whole point,' she giggled. 'Take the brake off. Let's do it while we're moving.'

I hesitated.

'Do it, do it now! Before I lose the mood!'

I eased the handbrake off and the car immediately rolled forward. Having no way to start the engine, I had to wrench the wheel toward the road to avoid hitting the Fiat parked in front while pumping the footbrake to control our speed. All this effort had a discouraging effect on my tumescence.

Lisa noticed my flexibility. 'What's the matter? Don't you want me?'

'Yes but I can't do anything while I'm trying to control a stolen runaway car on a steep hill.'

'Pull over. Look, there's some waste ground. Steer on to that.'

We trundled across the kerb, over some flattened fencing and fetched up with the bonnet nudging a great pile of abandoned barrels, boards and tyres. Lisa jumped out of the car and ran round the other side of the heap of rubbish where I couldn't see her. I trotted in pursuit and found her wildly tugging at an old mattress which was half trapped under a rusty mangle.

'Help me! We'll drag it into the road!'

'We can't have sex in the bloody road, Lisa, we could get run over.'

'Yes! Just think of it! Help me pull this out.'

A gruff voice called out, 'I help.' Around the garbage pile walked Halgo, breathing heavily. 'English scared. I do it. Then you, me, we fock.'

Lisa froze. 'Go back to the house, Signor Halgo.'

'Why? I got same as English. Bigger! I show you.'

'Mr Halgo,' I said with all the self-assurance I lacked at this moment. 'This is a private matter between Miss Castle and myself.'

'Me too.'

'No, not you too. You were only offered food and shelter.'

'You got bigger than me? Let lady see who got bigger, lady choose.'

So here we were back at the ultimate male challenge, the measuring of the meat, the todger tournament; I couldn't believe it. What the hell was Lisa thinking? I looked back at her where she stood in the last of the moonlight, her exquisite profile etched in the fading silver while the outline of her back was touched by the faint pink of dawn. I've never seen anyone so desirable, a lovely idiot gazing down the hill toward the city that lay asleep and oblivious to my mischief and my frustrated lechery. Then I realised that she was watching a headlamp approaching.

Halgo caught on first and moved out of sight behind the dump. Then Lisa turned her head to me and said without expression, 'Police.'

The officer's motor scooter buzzed up to the pavement, he propped it up and loosened his truncheon, then crossed the fifteen feet of waste-ground to stand before us silently with his arms crossed. From the angle of his approach he couldn't see our stolen Volkswagen or Halgo.

'This must look rather strange. Do you speak English?' I ventured but he wasn't looking at me.

'Signora?'

'Officer, I'm an American. I'm staying in a rented house a little way up the road.' She added a few words in Italian that included her famous name. He gestured at her and spoke our language haltingly. 'Why no clothes?'

'We . . . er . . . had a domestic argument. A fight. I ran out of the house. He ran after me to apologise.'

'You wife of him?'

'No.'

'You want to go back to house with him?'

'No.'

He looked at me and pointed his finger first in my face then towards the city centre, 'You can go.'

'Go?'

'Go away.' He paused to see if I intended to object then, satisfied, turned to Lisa and touched his cap. 'I see you safe.'

She looked him up and down and combined a tiny shrug with a smile.

The last I ever saw of Lisa Castle was her back as she rode away up the hill on the back of the policeman's blue-and-white scooter. I wondered if she'd remember which house was hers. My wristwatch showed 4.35 a.m. I heaved a sigh and stepped out for the long hike back to my hotel. I'd walked about six hundred yards when I heard a car trundling along behind me. It was Halgo in the Volkswagen.

He braked beside me and shrugged. I got in the car and together we rocked and rolled all the way down the long road into Rome.

I didn't care about the size of other men's endowments. I felt the biggest prick in the world.

## Sunday, 1 June – Tuesday, 24 June 1997

Today I awake to my sixty-ninth birthday and open one eye to see the faint light from the bathroom outlining the plush furnishings of our suite in the Sutton Place Hotel in downtown Vancouver. A lifetime of living in hotels has inculcated a few travellers' tricks like that one. When you waken in an unfamiliar and pitch dark room, especially after wining and dining well before you slept, your stumbling path to the loo is an obstacle course of potential toe stubbings. I've learned to leave the smallest light on, sometimes the shaving mirror, sometimes the medicine cabinet, nothing too bright. It will guide your way to that all-important 4 a.m. pee.

This is the first day of our holiday in Canada and the Pacific Northwest of the USA. I ease myself out of the large double bed so as not to shake Jac awake and pussyfoot to the next room with its huge shop-window view of a perfect dawn.

Last night on TV they had warned us of forthcoming rain and thunderstorms but that meant nothing. Vancouver's weather forecast has to be revised every fifteen minutes.

Now I'm looking at a sunny, cloudless sky with air so crisp and dry that if you snapped your fingers it would ring.

An hour later, over a room service breakfast of fruit and coffee, we plan our day without planning anything. Organised tourist behaviour can wait until we've got our bearings and taken a random sampling of the city and its charms.

We begin by exploring the shops of Robson Street, all glistening brightly in the glory of one of those rare days that seem to step out of the calendar wearing tap shoes. Weaving our way with care along the crowded sidewalk, we can see why the city has been dubbed 'Hongcouver'. At least a quarter of the faces around us are Chinese or Japanese and every restaurant offers sushi.

We settle for an outdoor brasserie, the Monterey that provides a strictly North American menu and have our first ecstatic taste of Copper River salmon. I thought I'd eaten great salmon before but the memory of a thousand pink platefuls surrenders and fades away as I discover the glorious texture and flavour of that heroic fish whose final journey upriver to its birthplace of seven years earlier has been unkindly curtailed for my delight.

In such balmy air as this a stroll in Stanley Park seems irresistible. It's a vast area of lawns and lakes and forest where bold racoons in burglars' masks line the pathways demanding food without menaces. Signs advise against feeding the wildlife, especially coyotes who can be stroppier than the jet black squirrels who sit up and beg very appealingly. My small bag of peanuts, in my pocket since yesterday's flight, doesn't go very far.

Our little map tells us that we are circling the Lost Lagoon but we are venturing quite a bit further than we'd first intended. Other visitors have been left behind and, as we cross a wooden bridge, the view across the huge expanse of the lake makes us realise how very far we've walked.

'Shall we carry on or retrace our steps, Jac?'

'Mmmm?'

She's looking at the mountains that crowd the inland horizon. From behind their niveous peaks a cloud is boiling up into the sky with all the speed of steam from a locomotive. Sparkles dance within its fast-growing inflation and it takes us a moment to twig that this is lightning. We stand transfixed by the sight of the cloud's rapid pullulation, baby clouds sprouting from it and immediately giving birth to more, the crooked rods of lightning seeming to galvanise the process into greater urgency.

By now only half the sky is still blue, the other half a stormy mantle of grey. The first clap of thunder shakes us into action.

'Let's get going before it reaches us!'

A sign on a tree says TO THE BOATHOUSE and urges us to go forward in search of shelter should we need it. We are walking quickly now but the fury that is filling the air above us is far quicker. The bright sunlight of a few minutes before has departed and we're half trotting through twilit pines. With the darkness comes a deafening crack and, as we cross a clearing, a violent rush of rain hits us hard. The raindrops are big and icy cold and we are soaked in seconds. Some thickly clumped trees invite us to find refuge and we scurry beneath them. That's a bad move.

We're instantly covered with the muck of dead grubs and insects that's washed from the branches by the downpour. As if to indicate the danger of standing under trees in a storm, a ragged bolt of lightning zaps into the woods behind us and we start running.

At first we try to protect our heads with newspaper but it's beaten to pulp at once. Our hair is flattened, clothing saturated and our shoes are full of rainwater. Visibility is down to about three metres but we can make out another sign: BOATHOUSE CLOSED.

We run past the dark bulk of the shuttered boathouse and up a path that's become a rushing stream down to the now invisible lake. At its crest the path joins a tarmac road and we can see cars swishing by, headlights full up and windscreen wipers lashing uselessly at the blinding gush. We try waving down a passenger car but it seems the drivers either can't see us or don't want to stop. Holding each other's hand, we keep running along the road which is giving us harder footing than the soil but wet leaves are a frightening hazard. A twisted ankle out here would be a hardship too many.

Five minutes of this and we're breathless and exhausted. The stunning din of wind and the torrent it drives has us deafened and our running has slowed to a progress that alternates between jogging and a dogged plod.

No more cars have passed since we tried hitching and it seems that we two are alone in an unceasing monsoon, bitterly cold and battered by a million watery bullets.

At the top of a rise the road slopes sharply downwards and then veers left. Halfway down this descent, the racing flood covering our sodden shoes and tugging our feet, we lose our balance and fall on our backs. The ground is slick and we begin to slide forward helplessly to where the waters are rushing, a gaping storm drain. Its mouth is high enough and wide enough to swallow the two of us with ease. We are being sluiced to our deaths. Jac grabs at me and yells above the racket of the storm, 'Roll!'

She flings herself to the left and, grabbing at my clothes, tries to roll sideways. Getting the idea, I attempt the same thing.

We've already skidded several feet towards the big drain and we're still sliding but the action of rolling increases our traction on the road surface and the sheer terror of being sucked into oblivion energises our efforts.

After some difficult and painful effort, with aching limbs and sore elbows and knees, we lie heaving with exertion on the road out of the strongest pull of the teeming current.

Coughing, I say, 'Turned out nice again!' and sheer relief makes us laugh.

Once we've started up again and taken the left curve of the road, we can make out a castellated wooden structure on a small hill. Its imitation battlements lead along balconies where timbered walkways run up from our road and down to the lake beyond.

'Let's try it,' says Jac and moments later we're hammering on a door and calling out our hellos till a worried face appears at a window, a lock is opened and we're allowed to stand inside the office of the Vancouver Rowing Club, leaking gallons on to its worn lino.

The sympathetic couple in charge phone our hotel for us and a limo shows up ten minutes later. As we totter into the hotel foyer, the storm has blown itself out and the sun is putting a shiny touch to the end of an unpredictable day.

Jac showers herself warm and I opt for a long hot soak in the tub. It takes three days for our shoes to dry. A large bunch of flowers is on the table, compliments of the manager.

The card says, 'Welcome to Vancouver! Have a nice day.'

That same evening we venture out, but not too far, to find a superb dinner at Cin Cin on Robson Street. (If you're ever in Vancouver, go there; it's pronounced Chin Chin.) We're in bed by eleven as we have to be up to catch the tour bus at 8.15 a.m.

It takes about an hour to reach the ferry which churns its way down the Howe to Vancouver Island for two hours more. Then it's back into the coach for a forty-five-minute drive to Victoria, the very English capital of British Columbia.

In sunny, blustery weather that we don't trust one little bit, we explore the shops and lunch at 1218; delicious. There's an intriguing display of Canadian native art and sculpture in the imposing Empress Hotel where afternoon tea is a must for anyone who yearns for the atmosphere of pre-war Eastbourne.

The coach takes us to the famous Butchart Flower Gardens but we really aren't impressed. The range of blooms seems curiously narrow and the layout of the flowerbeds too rigid and unimaginative. Not that I'm much of a gardener. When I plant my vegetable garden I'm always careful to save the little seed packets. They come in handy later for storing the vegetables in.

We get back to our room shattered at 9.45 p.m., too tired to do more than use room service. The weather forecast says rain all tomorrow.

Sure enough, it's blazing sunshine, perfect for elevating to the 42nd floor of the Landmark Hotel and viewing the city from its revolving restaurant. Just right too for a return to Stanley Park, this time attracting funny looks because we're carrying umbrellas.

Playing our part as tourists to the full, we ride around the splendid gardens in a horse-drawn trolley. It's a charming trip but we can't suppress an involuntary shudder as we pass one memorable corner below the Vancouver Rowing Club. It's where we nearly went down the drain.

Next day we catch the steamship *Britannia* and chug out in stately fashion for three sunkissed hours, sitting on the top deck and going popeyed at the scenery, steep verdant elevations rising all around us like a thousand Bali Hai's. Atop these remote and apparently inaccessible heights are isolated homes, some with a simple backwoods look and others like opulent mansions built for helicoptered zillionaires.

We terminate the voyage at Squamish, a logging town from whose docks countless pine trunks spread along the bay and float with the current to their destinations. The little community is well blessed with inexpensive restaurants and we have a simple but excellent Greek lunch.

The friendly proprietor tells us proudly that he comes from Mykonos where they have 365 churches, one for each day of the year.

I can't resist saying, 'I bet they can hardly wait for Leap Year so they can have a lie-in.'

He seems a little less friendly after that.

An hour and a half later we board the Royal Hudson choo-choo and puff along the coastline back to Vancouver.

The glorious weather continues as next morning we meander down Thurlow Street where a small ferry takes us across to Granville Island, an exotic conglomeration of touristy shops and bountiful food centres heaped with enough fresh edibles to fill an army of Pavarottis. After a fine fishy lunch in the open air at the Bridge, we take the bus to Gas Town, off Water Street, where everything quaint is normal. Truly weird stuff is available to buy, from dog polishers to fur sinks. We move on to the immense Canada Place complex with its singular rooftop of wind-filled sails making it appear like a gigantic moored schooner. It's a port terminus with hotel and entertainment facilities so we stay to eat dinner at the Prow overlooking the bay and to visit the Imax Cinema where the enormous screen was filled with heart-lifting panoramas of Alaska. It's so real the people in the front row get treated for frostbite.

Our concierge recommends a visit to Lonsdale Quay in north Vancouver. It's packed with locals and even more fantastic foodstuffs: game, venison steaks, exotic pastas, oysters, delicious North Pacific halibut, Chinese delicacies, rare wines, delicately decorated cream cakes and sweetmeats. My mouth waters so much my teeth go down for the third time, but we grab a light lunch in a hotel roof garden and are glad we did because dinner at the Piccolo Mondo turns out to be sumptuous. I'm glad the scale in our bathroom isn't working.

On Wednesday, 11 June, we bid Vancouver a reluctant farewell and limousine our way for 130 miles down the coast to Seattle where it's famous for its constant rain. Instead it's basking in a dry eighty-five degrees. We check into the Alexis and promenade along the colourful front before taking a cab to a converted private house on the outskirts of the city to enjoy a five-course gourmet menu at Rovers. Our waiter is a middle-aged man with a dry wit. Asked to recommend other restaurants in the area he suggests Green World.

'That sounds vegetarian.'

'It's not exactly that, more environmentally friendly.'

'What does that mean?'

'I'm not sure, perhaps their pork chops come from pigs who volunteered.'

Hayley Mills is staying in our hotel and she arranges good seats for us to see her in *The King and I* at Seattle's publicly funded theatre. That will take care of Saturday evening, so we get on with our temperate Thursday, popping into the seafront Aquarium to laugh at the otters, lunching in Ivars, a traditional joint that boasts 'Acres of Clams', and then joining the throng of tourists in Pioneer Square for the 'Underground City Tour'. Present-day Seattle was built on top of the old town and subterranean passages lead to the long-buried secrets of its complex hypogea. Unfortunately, the tour guide thinks she's a stand-up comedian and after twenty minutes of her preliminary address we cop out. Her act should be buried along with the hypogea.

After dining at the highly recommended Reiners, we too can offer a recommendation. We recommend that you don't go there. Too late, we learnt of a very recent change of management.

Friday is the sunniest day yet and so hot I work up a sweat just spraying on my anti-perspirant.

We have nosy fun poking around the Pike Public Market on the waterfront. A complicated maze of shops at different levels sell everything you can think of and a lot you'd never dream of.

We lunch al fresco in a pretty Italian café called the Pink Door which provides us with two favourite dishes, a Canneloni Ripieni for me (that's the one with the filling of diced veal and chopped button mushrooms) and for Jac, Fettucini alla Capricciosa (nicely *al dente* and

4 September 1995 – 1 June 1998

smothered in a red wine sauce of finely chopped veal, peas and sliced mushrooms). It's amazing how we can both eat as much as we like of high-calorie food like this and yet remain really fat.

We try to walk off our intake by marching around Bon Marché and all the other elegant shops that line Pine and Union Streets. We buy more gifts for friends, consume a big beefy dinner at the smart and noisy Union Square Grill (if you order the large steak, have the waiter remove the horns), and drop into the civic theatre to marvel at the juggling skills of the Brothers Karamazov who are recreating the Marx Brothers movie *Room Service* as the stage play it originally was. They're good but I'm still a loyal Marxist.

It's quite a walk back to the hotel but the night is so balmy that we navigate Seattle's safe streets feeling nothing but happy.

After Jac has a Robert Leonard hair-do in the morning, we ride the high-speed lift to the top of the Space Needle where the views are glorious even if the lunch isn't. The Saturday crowds in the surrounding funfair and exhibition halls mean pushing our way everywhere. I try to put my hand in my pocket and have to wait my turn. So we jump aboard the monorail which takes us to more shops on Westlake Street, dine well at Shuckers outside the Four Seasons Hotel and go to see Hayley as Anna. She deserves her ovation.

There's an extraordinary spot to watch hundreds of boats working their way through dramatically varied water levels called the Ballard and Chittenden Lock. You can snaffle some great grub off the buffet tables at a nearby eaterie called Pescatore and then wander around these titanic locks as the swarming yachts, ketches, sloops, fishing boats and the occasional barge queue up to drop or rise fifty feet in the massive chambers beneath the walkways. A military band situated in an adjacent park belts out Glenn Miller medleys to fill the warm air with that famous, lilting sound. We love it.

For our final Seattle evening we've saved the best till last and Chez Shea doesn't disappoint. No wonder 'Frasier' eats there.

We've decided not to go directly to San Francisco as originally planned and, on the spur of the moment, have booked a suite at the River Place in Portland, Oregon. It's a smooth motorway ride and our hotel windows look out at a picturesque vista of the bay and its impressive bascules and swing bridges. We get lucky again with our dinner restaurant, Wildwood on 21st Street, serving cuisine to make Marco Pierre turn White.

Downtown Portland is good-looking but its air of sophistication seems somehow recently adopted. You feel as though, had you arrived a year earlier, you'd have caught them dismantling a frontier town to build the new one.

One of only three widely spread off-licences, the one in the middle of town sells a wider range of fine malt whiskies than you'd find in Aviemore. Cheaper too.

Although Piatti does a lovely light lunch (try the Trenette con Pesto with Romano or Pecorino cheese instead of Parmesan), don't dine at Zefiro unless you like eccentricity on your plate. Sardine-stuffed lemons are fun but not comfortably served alongside venison stew.

We spend Wednesday sailing on the swollen Willamette aboard a luxuriously appointed cruiser, *Spirit of Portland*, sympathising with riverside home-owners whose sunken gardens are more deeply sunk than they intended, chuffing round the local zoo on a steam train and wandering in the extensive Rose Garden where we spot roses named Nicholas Parsons and Angela Rippon. What these names mean in Oregon we can't imagine. We see a large red rose named after President Clinton and wonder if Saddam Hussein has a bag of manure named after him.

Dinner is at another out-of-town house conversion named Genoa, five courses served unannounced and virtually unseen since the room has as much illumination as the Black Hole of Calcutta.

Thursday sees us on the plane to San Francisco and checking into the Royal Suite (1607) at the Mark Hopkins. It's magnificent.

Taking full advantage of the consistently shiny weather, we go to Pier 39 to find that Fisherman's Wharf has expanded enormously in the three or four years since we were last here. We lunch at Neptune's Palace where the terrific fresh halibut is cooked in a simple way because it can't be improved upon. Walking back all the way through Chinatown we see the sign AUTHENTIC CHINESE EATING and wonder if that means that you have to drink your alphabet soup from right to left.

Later that evening we visit the acclaimed Tommy Toy's where a per-suasive head waiter advises us that wise diners choose to have the set dinner. We follow his tip. In rapid succession the courses arrive: squab in lettuce, soup in a coconut shell covered in pastry, lobster, crispy duck in a sourdough roll, beef in oyster sauce and peach mousse. We look around us. The place is packed and everybody is eating the same dishes. We've all been talked into ordering the set meal.

We feel rather like battery consumers on a production line. I wonder if, when some awkward customer refuses the table d'hôte and orders other dishes from the menu, they have to send out to another restaurant to get them. The bill is presented as the final spoonful goes down and we're out of there and on the street in just forty-five minutes. Very efficient and smart but quite the most soulless of our gustatory tour.

The most soulful comes next day with the best Linguine Vongole I've ever eaten, a dish made with impeccable skill and love by the chef in Kuleto's, Union Square. We shop for clothes, books and recordings and, to my delight, Jac reluctantly allows me to talk her into letting me buy her a ring. She doesn't really want it, she feels she has quite enough jewellery, thank you very much, but I use the Chinese head waiter's technique.

We give a handful of Michelin stars to Charles, partly for its top-notch dinner and partly in recognition of the charm and humour of greeter Evan and two Joes, waiter and bartender.

Under an unblemished hyaline azure, our limo slides us quietly through the greenly vined slopes of the Napa Valley and our Sunday is blessed by a visit to the exquisite Auberge du Soleil in Rutherford. A hillside of olive trees descends to a mosaic of vineyards, a setting that in 1981 inspired Claude Rouas to open this hospitable haven perched halfway up one of the eastern hills. It's full of earthy tones, bare woods, fine sculptures, monumental wall sconces and cheery fireplaces blazing away. The greeting is gracious, the service is perfect and the wine list requires a bank loan. Ah, but the food! Andrew Sutton is the chef and he bids fair to challenge a Nico Ladenis or Raymond Blanc in his flair and accomplishment. Who else would create a starter of oven-roasted lobster sausage?

His sautéed Petaluma Exotic Mushroom starter includes wild matsutake, pompoms and oyster mushrooms, served with a chive waffle, sautéed onions, watercress and coarse black pepper bits. We drink water with that. Those pepper bits explode like grenades. While I opt for the thyme-roasted pheasant with sunchoke ravioli and those craterellus mushrooms that look like black trumpets, Jac chooses a veal loin char-grilled and then sliced, the strips laid on to a mildly spicy sauce with polenta gnocchi and a tomato-and-artichoke ragout. How the hell we find room for 'chocolate indulgence' and a mango-lime brûlée I do not know, but we do.

Our chauffeur takes us to two major vineyards, Beringer and Mumm's, where we sample the newest vintages of Chardonnay, Cabernet Sauvignon, Zinfandel and champagne. When we regain our hotel suite we put on a video of Clint Eastwood in *Absolute Power* and, I'm proud to say, are able to follow the entire plot for nearly fifteen minutes.

On our last day in SF, I go looking at artwork in the galleries and boutiques while Jac packs for our long trip early on Tuesday morning. We'll fly out at 7.10 a.m., arrive in Miami at 3.25 p.m. (there's a three-hour time difference), depart at 4.45 and land at Barbados at 8.35 in the evening. We're knackered but it's a trip I'd do again. If you fancy trying it, take this book. It's not a bad guide to increasing your shadow in style.

But if you go to Stanley Park on a sparkling sunny day, take a tent.

### Thursday, 26 June 1997
I was very sad when Charlie Chester died today aged eighty-three.

I loved Charlie in my early years writing and performing on radio. He was always so encouraging and helpful. I remember being his guest when the Grand Order of Water Rats made him King Rat in the 50s. They used to drink a lot at the meetings in those days and Wee Georgie Wood, a pompous midget, had the nasty habit of going to the lavatory and leaving the door open.

In committee, Charlie said, 'I'd like to propose a new rule that Georgie Wood must close the door when he's sitting on the loo.' And, turning to Georgie, he added, 'In all fairness, brother, no one wants to see a little shit *having* a little shit.'

### Friday, 27 June 1997
A newsagent named Mr Patel (I'm serious) now delivers the newspapers from England here in Barbados only one day late and today's delivery carried a story about our comedy chum Eddie Large, two-thirds of the team Little and Large.

According to the reporter, Eddie and a neighbour had a dispute over right of way for their cars on a narrow country lane near their homes.

With their motors nose to nose, like Robin Hood and Little John neither would give way.

Something unusually infuriating must have provoked mild-mannered Eddie because he took a golf club to the bloke's Range Rover and whacked seven bells out of it.

Our mutual agent and manager Peter Prichard asked Eddie, 'What did you use to smash up his car with?'

Eddie said, 'My putter.'

'You must be mad,' said Prichard. 'Everyone knows you need a five-iron for a Range Rover.'

### Thursday, 31 July 1997
I'm excited today, driving to the Church Hall, St Augustine's Priory, Fulham Palace Road, Hammersmith. It's not only my granddaughter

Megan's second birthday but the day when fifty people are convening for the read-through of a script in the BBC 1 comedy drama series 'Jonathan Creek'. It's the third episode in the second run and the writer is the brilliant creator of 'One Foot in the Grave', David Renwick. He's invited me to play the role of the villain, a snobbish theatre critic named Sylvester Le Fley.

I enjoy straight acting enormously although my raw early efforts in black-and-white, low-budget feature films are something I try to avoid watching. There was only one movie, made around 1961, in which I thought I did a fair job and it seems to have disappeared; a shame because it got good reviews at the time.

*Weekend With Lulu* had me as a London chancer who accidentally drives an ice-cream van on to a cross-Channel ferry and gets mixed up with the *Tour de France*. Also in the van were Leslie Phillips, Irene Handl and Shirley Eaton and it was directed by the man who had won my lasting affection for making *The Chiltern Hundreds* with A.E. Matthews.

On first acquaintance John Paddy Carstairs seemed quite a nondescript little chap until, quite suddenly, he'd give you a shy, sly grin from beneath his film director's cap and switch on some sort of illumination behind his gaze. That's when you understood how this small man's reputation as the successful seducer of Britain's most desirable movie actresses could be true. His smile had the radiance of a rapacious angel.

During breaks in filming he told me stories of his conquests.

One lively night he'd managed to talk a gorgeous graduate of the famous Rank Charm School into bed and during the next two hours made love to her four times. As she finished dressing and prepared to leave, he was vaguely piqued at her failure to comment admiringly on his virility and was unwise enough to ask, 'What did you think of my performance?'

'Not bad,' she smiled as she moved to the door. 'Although I'd print only takes one and three.'

Paddy had a reputation for appropriating items from the films he was directing. It was wickedly rumoured that his home had been largely furnished in this way. No sooner had a scene been completed than someone would report seeing Paddy in the car park loading up his car with an oil painting or a Chinese rug or even clothing that was no longer needed for the film.

When he was setting up a low-budget war movie for Nat Cohen, the boss of Anglo-Amalgamated kept a wary eye out for Paddy's acquisitive ways. One day he found the reputedly light-fingered director leaving the company's production suite in Wardour Street with what appeared to be a folded suit-bag under his arm. Nat took Paddy's arm and propelled him into his small office.

'Have you got a suit from our movie in that bag?' demanded Nat.

'No,' replied Paddy. 'I've got a boat for the six frogmen to escape from the Nazi submarine pens.'

'One more smart remark like that and you're off the picture!' growled Nat. 'Now let me see what's in the bag!'

In answer, Paddy pulled open the flaps on his package, turned a valve on the gas cylinder inside and scooted out of the door.

The inflatable boat billowed up to its full size within seconds, pinning Nat behind his desk so securely that eventually the fire brigade had to be called in to assist his escape through the window.

## Saturday, 9 August 1997

Occasional edicts circulate at the BBC TV Centre forbidding this or that as a topic for comedy. Earlier in these memoirs I told how, after I burlesqued Robert Maxwell on 'Noel Edmonds' House Party', a memo went round the Light Entertainment Department warning that further fun-poking at the cancelled Czech would not be prudent.

My favourite admonition came after I had delivered a comedy routine about people who can't spell very well. The notification read (I have it before me as I write), 'Following a number of telephoned complaints, all programmes must avoid joking references to dyselxia'.

There are a lot of things you can't say or do on television without attracting a logjam of complaints. Obviously libel is out. Not that it's as easy to offend with disparagement as it used to be.

Call someone a 'lying scumbag', as the *Sun* newspaper characterised Jonathan Aitken MP, and like as not it'll qualify as fair comment. All publicity is good publicity, they say. These days, if you accuse some celebrity of being a coke-snorting nymphomaniac who robbed her blind father, she'll thank you for reading her autobiography so attentively.

Now I invite you join me in a matter of judgement. Here is the topical monologue I delivered on 'The National Lottery Live' on the date above. Can you identify the two gags considered so outrageous that they were the subject of an official complaint?

*Thank you. No one trousered the Wednesday night seven-figure fortune so it's time to roll 'em over, pay your pound and do it again!*

*Which makes this a pretty hot show for a pretty hot day. Hot? Today it rose as high as ninety-four degrees and that's not bad at my age.*

*Hot? I saw two dogs pretending to mate just so someone would throw a bucket of water over 'em.*

*Great news, the football season started today which meant Fash, Segers and Grobelaar were let off just in time to get a bet on.*

*Liz Hurley says she's getting fed up with her skinny, boyish bum. So much for Hugh Grant.*

*Robin Cook's been having an affair. Well, he might as well put it about before his looks start to fade.*

*They do say he won't resign because he likes his position in the Cabinet. Although she prefers it when he's swinging from the chandelier.*

*The Archbishop of Canterbury has said that Charles shouldn't marry Camilla, and thank God. Who'd want to lick a stamp with her face on it?*

*According to a psychological study this week, women go out and buy things to make up for a dull sex life. I wanted to ask my wife what she thought but she'd gone shopping.*

*The world's oldest woman has just died six months after celebrating her 122nd birthday. It's a tragedy really because they were only halfway through giving her the bumps.*

*She's left all her cash to charity, her organs to medical science and her skin to World of Leather.*

*And finally – this week Mike Tyson became the father of a baby boy. The kid's got his daddy's eyes, his mummy's nose and Evander Holyfield's ears.*

*If the kid takes after his dad I'd advise against breast-feeding.*

*Four girls came up to me today and said, 'I know where it's at' and I'd have let them show me too but my pension only stretches so far. Turned out they were telling me the title of their new single, 'I Know Where It's At' and I know where they're at – at a TV set near you – Melanie, Shazny, Nicky and Natalie – All Saints!*

Are you thinking that there's nothing in that lot to offend a reasonable adult? I'm not claiming that any one of those jokes is a masterpiece of comedy but you should bear in mind that I'm out to get laughs from 250 people in the studio for whom the wit of Oscar Wilde is a vague rumour.

Nevertheless, on 14 November the Broadcasting Standards Commission under the chairmanship of Lady Howe issued a finding concerning this evening's show saying that two viewers had complained about offensive jokes concerning public figures. Two! It summarised a statement from the BBC in which it was said that I began each edition of the show with topical jokes in which figures in the public eye, including politicians and royalty, were fair game. The BBC's statement had continued that these jokes 'lampooned prominent people, including their personal appearance. This was a time-honoured feature of British humour. Although the lottery programme was one of the most popular shows on the BBC, attracting regular audiences of nearly 11 million, only a small number of viewers had written to or telephoned the BBC to express concern.'

This report of the BBC's justification concluded, 'The broadcaster did not believe the tone and content of Bob Monkhouse's introduction in this edition were any different from other programmes in the series to which viewers were accustomed. It also considered that such an approach to humour, which included an element of innuendo rather than being explicit, was acceptable at that time of the evening.'

Despite this defence, the BSC's finding read, 'A Standards Panel watched the programme and noted the comments in question. While it acknowledged that viewers were unlikely to object to light-hearted ridicule of prominent public figures, it considered that, on this occasion, *the remarks went beyond acceptable limits. The complaints were upheld*' (my italics).

This prompted Paul Jackson, Head of BBC Entertainment, to wonder what on earth I could have said to cause this decision.

The producer of the programme, a fair-minded and very experienced man of integrity named Peter Estall, duly reported back with the details and a tape of the show, adding that he would be intrigued to know the date of the complaint since, in the past, two of my regular targets had been Charles and Camilla. For obvious reasons, this stopped at the end of August with Princess Diana's death.

Paul Jackson decided that he wanted the matter of the upheld complaint to be pursued vigorously. He found it difficult to understand, either from the full text of the initial complaint or from the actual text of the BSC's finding, exactly what the nature of the objection was. Having studied the transcript, he could find nothing of an offensive nature, believing that the references to Mrs Camilla Parker-Bowles and Robin Cook fell well within the boundaries of acceptable comment as he understood them. He thought that simply accepting this ruling would be dangerous and, although well aware that BSC decisions were final, he saw no reason not to question them when they were plain stupid.

Even if there was no hope of a technical argument that the nature of the complaint fell outside the BSC's remit Paul felt that it was important for the BBC to register its disappointment at, and total lack of understanding of, this particular ruling.

Nicolas Moss, Head of Policy Management, BBC Broadcast, reports to the BSC on matters of taste and decency. He stated that there had been a dozen calls to the BBC's duty officer but mostly about innuendo, none about Camilla and only one about Robin Cook.

While allowing that the Parker-Bowles remark was rude, he saw it as being no ruder than other remarks I had made about public figures and certainly in keeping with my well-established style. Although there was now an argument that this finding was on the cusp of the BSC's remit, Moss felt there was little point in writing to them about it. As the BSC's Stephen Whittle had made clear on other occasions, the Commission's decisions are final.

In this case my decisions are final too. But fortunately unprintable.

## Tuesday, 2 September – Tuesday, 9 September 1997

A week of wonderfully sunny weather in the grounds of Loseley House, near Godalming as an episode of David Renwick's acclaimed series of 'Jonathan Creek' mysteries is filmed with me as Sylvester Le Fley, a thoroughly nasty and snobbish theatre critic whose priceless painting is apparently stolen in seconds from a sealed room. Caroline Quentin is Maddy, the woman who embroils Creek in each adventures. Maddy is very similar to Caroline. Comedian Alan Davies plays Creek rather like himself in real life too. It's very effective.

The stand-up comedians who perform as themselves made large are bold. Many funny people, lacking this boldness, just can't go on stage without the mask of an invented character.

For others, the mere assumption of a comic identity is not enough; they need costume, makeup, wigs and props. Like the author who comes to hate his own creation, some comedians grow to resent the very role they've invented for themselves, scorning their public identities much as Baron von Frankenstein rejected his monster.

Occasionally the comedian had no choice.

Nature had decided the matter.

Wee Georgie Wood was British music hall's little boy who never grew up. As himself he was just a very short man with a falsely posh accent and a pompous manner, but as a cheeky schoolboy, straining the patience of his stage mother Dolly Harmer in fifteen-minute sketches, Wood was able to sustain a theatrical career well into middle age.

Lack of height gave a similar professional life to Jimmy Clitheroe, popular in panto and summer shows as the naughty 'Clitheroe Kid' and, aided by listeners' imaginations and his own naturally childish voice, a long-running success on radio.

Born in 1916, the Lancashire comedian never appeared publicly except as a pre-adolescent boy.

I shared a sauna at Grayshotts Health Centre with him once in 1962. As we sat there naked he volunteered that he was unembarrassed by his tiny, hairless body.

'It's been a curse but never a humiliation, not since I mastered it. The trick was in making people laugh at what I did, not at what I was. I feel really sad for circus midgets and such, although most of them are proper men and, of course, I'm not. I don't waste pity on myself though. I listen to the people's laughter and I look at my bank statements and I think, well, Jimmy, you made something out of worse than nothing. Mind you, I don't much fancy living to be an old man. That could look a bit freaky.'

Jimmy died in 1972, just fifty-six years old.

Neither Arthur Askey nor Ronnie Corbett ever allowed themselves to become trapped inside a single characterisation to account for their short stature. Like the American actor/director Danny DeVito, they used it as a wonderful asset. They knew that a funny little man could win far more affection and louder laughter than a funny tall man, notwithstanding John Cleese.

For every single joke it's possible to make about being tall:

*My tailor has to measure my inside leg on a trampoline.*

there are a hundred about being short, as Mickey Rooney, Paul Daniels and Ronnie Corbett have demonstrated over the years:

*It's not my fault that I'm late. I was cleaning out the budgie cage and the door slammed on me.*

*I haven't done badly when you consider that I spent the first six months of my life on a charm bracelet.*

*She's the only girl I know with mud-flaps on her knickers.*

*He paid twenty-five pounds for a big, thick book called 'How to increase your height'. It said, 'Stand on this book.'*

*Short? His passport photograph is full-length.*

*I played a vital part in the film 'The Hunchback of Notre Dame'*
*– they shoved me up Charles Laughton's back.*

and so forth. Corbett's neatness of appearance and precision of gesture give him the air of a mechanical toy. The son of an Edinburgh baker, he was drawn to amateur dramatics in adolescence but had to wait for his RAF service and his appointment as a camp entertainments officer to discover his abilities on the stage.

London's West End kept him busy in late-night cabaret in the 50s, principally with Danny La Rue. They performed costumed sketches crammed with innuendo and puns by their writer, Bryan Blackburn. As Napoleon, Corbett craned his neck to look up at La Rue's high-heeled Josephine. 'I am going to make ze love to you,' he said and got the reply:

*'If you do and I ever find out about it . . .'*

TV bookings on 'The Frost Report' and 'Frost Over England' led to his teaming with Ronnie Barker, another grammar school boy who'd found his way to an actor's life through am-dram.

Twenty-two years of 'The Two Ronnies' followed, the popular mix of jokes, sketches and music establishing Barker as the more powerful character player and Corbett as the better monologuist. His 'Ronnie-in-the-chair' routines – long anecdotes packed with funny *non sequiturs* – were originally scripted by Spike Mullins, a white-bearded cockney wit whose whimsy was perfectly matched to Corbett's amiable air of distraction. Spike's clever trick was to take the surefire punchline of a time-tested tale and decorate its narrative with comic diversions like this one he once gave me:

*Tonight is one of those times I feel I could make an audience laugh,*
*cry or have an early night.*

*I could sit here and . . . well, I could sit over there. I prefer to sit*
*here though, because I'm talking to the audience. If I sat over there*
*I'd be talking to two stagehands and a fire bucket.*

*What was I saying? Oh, yes, I could sit here and . . . if you want*
*pathos, good heavens, I could tell you about my own personal child-*
*hood, how I was found on a doorstep. Well, not really on the doorstep*
*because the door opened outwards. I was found halfway across the*
*road. And pinned to my nappie was a note which said, 'Keep your*
*head down, the door opens outwards. Signed – Mummy.'*

*Oh, yes, I could tell you about how, up to the age of four, my only playthings were a cornbeef sandwich and a picture of Nellie Wallace. Ah, I've got you now, haven't I? Don't hold back the tears – you could get a hernia.*

*I could tell you that I've never given up the search for my real Mummy . . . and I've had some very nasty letters from Sophia Loren and Shirley Bassey.*

*Or I could, if prevailed upon, recount a rather amusing anecdote that occurred after a party at my agent's place last week. He has a little do once a year to celebrate the grand opening of his wallet.*

*I say agent, actually he's more like one of the family. On my wife's birthday last year he sold her a lovely card.*

*His parties are always a bit of a disaster, I'm afraid. He's a do-it-yourself man, makes all his own wine, and when we got there at nine o'clock he was still in the bath . . . treading his grapes. Not a pretty sight.*

*Then he lost the key of the sardines. We had to put the tin in the road and let someone back over it. Again, not a pretty sight.*

*Otherwise it was rather a quiet evening. In fact, it got so quiet the phone rang and a chap with a weak heart had to be taken home. Just between us, I don't think he had a weak heart at all – he'd been there since seven o'clock and he'd lost the will to live.*

*Anyway, on our way home, and this is the exciting bit, we were waiting at Paddington Station when a train pulled in and a chap jumped out, nude! Barefoot to the chin! I thought at first he was wear-ing a blue body stocking. It was a cold night.*

*The station staff were all taken aback. 'Goodness gracious,' they cried, 'Bless my soul!' and 'Who dat dere?' and 'I love you.'*

*Then the stationmaster came over and said to this chap, 'Excuse me, sir, but I think you had better explain yourself as to why you're walk-ing about on my station in your birthday suit causing alarm and con-sternation. What's more, you've woken up the man in the ticket office.'*

*And the chap said, 'Well, the explanation is simple. I was at a house party with some friends in the country and the hostess said, "Why don't we all take our clothes off and go to town?" And I seem to be the first to arrive.'*

That final gag, the naked man who's gone to town, dates back to the 20s when Ben Travers invented it for one of his famous Aldwych farces. That's when the golden age of the comical character actor who was always the same in every production was flourishing, for in those ten years before films added sound, the most popular plays in London were high-speed farces inhabited by human caricatures.

The Aldwych stage company boasted such comic luminaries as Ralph Lynn, a drawling upper-class twit with a monocle; Tom Walls, the lecherous and boozy old scoundrel of the rigged race and fixed fight; bald Robertson Hare, long-suffering and henpecked and fearful of everything; domineering Alfred Drayton – all magnificent ensemble comedians doing credit to the deftly daft dialogue crafted by the prolific Mr Travers. Prior to the coming of radio humour or talkies, his jokes were a new phenomenon.

When 'Bunny' Hare protests, 'I am a man of peace!' Walls threatens, 'Do what you're told or you'll be a man in pieces.'

On a clandestine weekend the vague Lynn is forced to sign the hotel register. The landlady inspects it suspiciously: 'You don't write very clear.' She gets the answer, 'No, I've just had some very thick soup.'

Occasionally, as in *Plunder*, Lynn tries to shake off his languid amiability, his choice of expletive being: 'Rats!'

A police inspector cautions, 'I should advise you, sir, to moderate your language.' Lynn caves in: 'Oh, very well then. Mice!'

In a haunted mansion Walls observes, 'Somebody moaned.' Lynn says, 'I think it was the wind' and Walls replies, 'I don't know the cause of his affliction but somebody moaned.'

Like those of the best French farce writers, the Travers comic plays relied upon the proliferation of misunderstanding while filling the stage with stereotypes: pedantic butlers, Wodehousian aunts, vulgar foreigners, dimwitted constables, gullible clergy, frivolous blondes in French undies, shifty crooks, the ignorant rich and the clever poor.

Unlike Feydeau, the British would-be adulterers never used to succeed in their adultery. Their motives might have been naughty but their eventual morality remained intact.

Ah yes, but that was then, now is now. Today's master of the genre is Ray Cooney and he explained to me how this curiously British need for actual sinlessness in farce has changed along with the moral climate:

'It had to change. Otherwise we'd be stuck in a time warp with yesterday's social standards restricting us. The farces I wrote with John Chapman, they were very much of their time, reflecting the current tastes in the days when we had the Lord Chamberlain to contend with.

'Some of my more recent work like *Run For Your Wife* and *Funny Money* have had the sort of premise that in a normal play would be pretty serious. In the first one, a bigamist runs two homes. Imagine the tragic consequences of that in real life with two families turning up at his funeral. And in the second farce the hero has mistakenly acquired

£75,000 in used banknotes; dishonest loot and he's hanging on to it. Two serious crimes being used for comedy and not black comedy either.

'Now Michael Frayn or Alan Ayckbourn would treat those subjects differently. My way is to keep all my characters upbeat, likeably optimistic, so that no matter what sin they've committed, the audience is on their side.'

'Ray, is there no time for deeper character development in your farces?'

'I've got time to reveal the nature of my characters and that must be done clearly and effectively so that the audience can believe in them and their actions. My principal characters must be convincingly real and their dilemmas apparent. After that it's a matter of building up a credible house of cards, piling one panicky move on to the last. If the hero's caught out in a lie then he'll try to rectify it by telling another and when that backfires, yet another. And with my plays, it's always happening in real time. The first half ends on a climax and when the curtain goes up after the interval, everyone's still in the same crisis.'

'And the characters, must they be stereotypical?'

'Well, there's room for the more significant ones to change and develop during the two hours of the story but supporting roles need to be quickly identifiable and reliably consistent whether they're policemen, crusty colonels or wimps. To laugh at them, we need to recognise them. Most actors know this and will sustain those roles to the benefit of the play. Some comedians – not you, Bob, of course – can undermine the audience's suspension of disbelief by doing unlikely comic tricks to win easy laughs. That's very damaging to any play and it holds true for farce. It must keep in touch with some sort of reality, some commonly human truth.'

I met Ben Travers shortly before his death and the nonagenarian had lost none of his love for farcical situations.

'Life is a farce, dear boy, and the farce is part of life; you can observe it everywhere.'

Then he gave me this example which he swore was true:

'We were touring *Cuckoo in the Nest* and we had a chap named Clancy shifting the scenery and driving it from theatre to theatre for us. Clancy had very long hair which was unusual in the 30s. I made some remark about it one day and Clancy told me he'd had his right ear cut off while he was repairing a circular saw and, by heaven, he showed it to me. He kept it in a matchbox.

'So I says to him, "D'you know we could make a few quid with that?"

He says, "How, Mr Travers?"

'I says, "We go into a pub and I say, "I'll lay twenty quid that my friend here can do something that nobody here can do!"

'Once we've stirred up a bit of interest I'll suggest a whip round. Then, when the landlord says, "Go on then – what can he do that none of us could do?", why, you pipe up and say, "I bet no one here can bite his own ear!" And no one will be able to, d'you see?

'So Clancy agreed and things went exactly as I've just described right up to the point where Clancy had to prove he could bite his own ear.

'Like a magician producing a rabbit out of a hat, he slowly opened the matchbox, removed his ear and brushed back his hair to show how the ear fitted in place. Then, quite gently, he bit his own ear and reached for the cash on the bar.

'Before he could take it, a bony hand snatched it up. It was the oldest inhabitant, who'd come out of his dark corner with his pint. He just winked and he cackled and he took his teeth out and bit his own ear with 'em just like that!'

## Saturday, 4 October 1997

Here's our wedding anniversary again, the twenty-fourth this time. And here's us in the all-white, minimalist honeymoon suite of the Tides, the newest and most fashionable joint on Miami's South Beach art deco scene, owned by Chris Blackwell of Island Records. The CD player is wafting his latest romantic releases around the bedroom.

In case you like the suite's panoramic view of sand and sea so much that you'd like more detail, there's a high-powered telescope on a tripod. My wife kindly trained it on a topless beauty for me. I watched him do a few push-ups, then accepted Jac's invitation to join her in the hot tub on the balcony. She added, 'Bring my book and reading glasses.'

As if I was planning to harass her. I'm not much trouble where that sort of thing's concerned. I read an article in my wife's *Marie Claire* magazine that said the average sexual encounter lasts twelve minutes. Well, I don't want to boast but I think I can cut that time in half.

I make jokes about marriage, and single people think we envy them their freedom but they don't know how great it really feels when you first become a married person.

At last we can be ourselves with none of the single person's 'best behaviour' tension. None of that holding your stomach for the men, women pretending they don't eat much in restaurants – that's all over as soon as you're married.

287

And when you become a dad, the freedom to be yourself is even greater. If you're a dad you can scratch yourself wherever it itches. You can't do this when you're courting but as soon as you become a father, as soon as they say, 'Mr Monkhouse, you've had a baby boy', then it's 'Thank God, I can scratch!'

Fathers just don't care. My father would come to the breakfast table scrabbling at his groin, going, 'Do I smell kippers?' And we'd yell, 'Dad, please, we're eating! Couldn't you at least wear pyjamas or a dressing gown or something?'

I've got a friend, engaged to this woman for four years, finally they're getting married, I said, 'How come?' and he said, 'I couldn't hold my wind in any longer.'

You can't let one go while you're romancing, try to blame it on the dog, it's embarrassing. You're sitting on the sofa with your beloved and you feel that bubble preparing to escape, you've got to do that leaning-sideways-and-sneaking-it-silently-into-the-cushion bit. But as soon as you're married it's 'Open the windows, Stella, I feel a fog warning coming on!' First thing in the morning my father could make them open Tower Bridge.

In the evening, Jac and I wandered down to the Lincoln Mall, a long parade of shops and cafés that stay open late. Half-nude skateboarders and rollerbladers whizz close in both directions but you soon tire of flinching. We enjoyed great Italian food at the Osteria di Teatro on Washington and Espanola 15 Street and went to bed early and Jac immediately fell asleep.

I returned to the hot tub with a large Deanston. I've learned a lot from twenty-four years of marriage. For instance, I've learned that sexually I'm self-sufficient.

## Monday, 13 October 1997

Beryl Reid died today. I first met Beryl when she was a hit-and-miss impressionist doing eccentric versions of Marlene Dietrich, Greta Garbo, Leslie Henson and Popeye. As soon as radio shows began to employ her regularly on the strength of her original character voices, she dropped the dodgy impressions and developed her best inventions, principally the frightfully posh St Trinian's schoolgirl Monica and a much-loved Brummie shopgirl named Marlene.

After one successful career in comedy, she began another as a dramatic actress, winning acclamation for *The Killing of Sister George* on stage and screen.

Those of us who worked with her adored her for her spontaneous wit.

She used words with extraordinary precision and emphasis. Her humour might sometimes have seemed poisonously scornful but for the gurgling pleasure that welled beneath it. She had a chuckle that could melt a snowball and enough charm to coax a headscarf out of a silkworm.

So passionate an animal lover was Beryl that she would go home during the lunch break in rehearsals to change the radio station for her cats. At one time she had eight of them and her furniture bore witness, every piece scored or tattered. 'Claws and effect,' she explained.

It wasn't so much what she said as the words she chose to say it. Commenting on my permanently sunburned appearance, she murmured, 'Your tan would look overdone on lederhosen.'

Some of her 1969 film *Entertaining Mr Sloane* was shot on location in south-east London. Beryl's opinion of the area was not high. 'The trouble with Brixton,' she said, 'is that when you get there, it's there.'

Only once in his life did the penny-pinching promoter Carl Ritchie invest heavily in a stage production. Uncharacteristically he convinced himself that the Christmas musical *Somewhere Over the Rainbow* could make him a millionaire despite requiring a large cast of singers, dancers and midgets. The only famous name on the bill was Beryl Reid, playing Wanda the Wonderful Witch. Even her name couldn't sell enough tickets to fill the large theatre. On the fifth night of the run she was appraising the house through a peep-hole in the curtain when Ritchie asked, 'How is it?'

'A bit better than last night,' said Beryl, 'but we're still in the majority.'

Beryl could be catty more sweetly than any other actress I've known. When playwright Willis Hall married actress Jill Bennett, Beryl enthused, 'What a lovely wife you have now. With those magnificently flared nostrils. You can almost see her clever, clever little brain working away!'

She was fascinated by Dusty Springfield's heavily mascaraed eyes. 'Goodness me, they resemble twin craters, both extinct.'

For some vague reason she took a dislike to a female TV presenter considered by most to be quite beautiful. Beryl gazed at her in apparent admiration and gushed, 'Oh, how I envy your looks. What I wouldn't give to have those thin, *thin* lips!' The poor woman never quite got over it.

In a year when the major film studios were dominating distribution, Beryl was persuaded to attend the première of an independently produced film. Asked her opinion afterwards she said, 'I was told I ought to come along to support the independent producer. Well, I'm buggered if I can see what that producer's got to be independent about.'

In a crowded lift at the BBC Television Centre, Beryl suddenly thrust her hand up above her head, clutching the hand of the man behind her. She called out, 'Does anyone own this? I just found it on my bottom!'

In 1956 I was one of the writers and voice-overs for a series of animated commercials advertising a brand of pickle. Beryl supplied the principal voice, that of a cartoon owl. The account director was fussy and given to verbose interference. He rewrote Beryl's lines, asked her for various readings and expostulated at length about the image of the product, eventually explaining his numerous contributions to the work in hand with, 'You see, Miss Reid, I have to wear a number of different hats.' 'And which of them are you talking through at the moment?' purred Beryl.

Though a quick study with lines, she had extraordinary difficulty remembering numbers. Moving home, she gave her new phone number to a select few. When I called it and asked for Beryl, I found I was talking to a woman who managed a Sue Ryder charity shop in Windsor. I apologised and said I'd contact Beryl through her agent. 'When you do get in touch with her,' said the shop manager, 'could you tell her that her new spectacles are ready at the optician's in East Sheen?'

The last time I spoke to Beryl was on the phone. Her health was worsening and she seemed greatly interested in reading obituaries. 'When I see someone's died who's younger than me, I think "Well, I beat you anyway, cock!"'

Our conversation ended with a typical Beryllism. Her doctor had made some unguarded remark about some of his patients 'welcoming death'.

Beryl said, 'I told him anyone who welcomes death has only tried it from the ears up.'

## Thursday, 23 October 1997

This evening I tape my second appearance on 'Have I Got News For You?' My first appearance on the show three years ago prompted a curious rumour to go round the business to the effect that I had arrived for the cursory 'rehearsal', such as it is, mob-handed with gagwriters to help me through it. Then a hostile journalist printed the tale with a few sneers about my inability to ad-lib. I felt spurred to set the record straight rather than have the readership of the *Glasgow Herald* think me so incapable at my job. 'Dear Mr Jarvie,' I wrote. 'It's said that there is nothing a vulture detests so much as a glass eye. Likewise, I am sure there is nothing a newspaper editor detests so much as a factual inaccuracy. I write to correct one such.

In a recent article headed 'Nice and oh so cheesy does it', the writer offers your readers a 'famous story' which is simply not true. It is said that I turned up for 'Have I Got News For You?' with 'a squad of five gag-scribblers, much to the chagrin of Messrs Hislop and Merton'. I did not. I arrived accompanied only by my wife and relied entirely upon my wits to make what ad-lib comments on the news I could devise. No comedy writers other than myself assisted me or were present.

In the same piece it is suggested that I am the sort of comedian who is 'whatever his writers decide to make him' and that in 'An Audience with Bob Monkhouse' I performed 'a range of material penned by a variety of hands'. Again the writer is quite wrong. All the material used in that programme was my own and no other comedy writer contributed to it. It is quite discomforting enough to be ticked off for one's real inadequacies without having false ones invented by a journalist who prefers to make assumptions based upon fancy in favour of assertions based upon research. A single phone call would have sufficed. Or a closer look at the show's credits. Or an arrogance by-pass.

Yours good-naturedly . . .'

While feeling considerable admiration for Angus Deayton and Ian Hislop, it was to the comedian of this famous triumvirate that I was drawn. All I knew about Paul Merton were a few bare facts that had appeared in the press: that he was born in Parson's Green, south-west London, in 1957, that his dad was a train driver on the Underground and his mum a nurse. They shared a council flat with Grandfather who, when Mother went back to work, looked after Paul and his younger sister.

I'd also read that when Paul was eight, Merton's dad was transferred to Morden where the boy attended Roman Catholic primary school, failed his eleven-plus and moved on to Wimbledon College just as it became comprehensive.

He began his working life at Tooting Employment Office. Undeterred, sometimes inspired by such surroundings, he pursued his ambition to make people laugh and eventually became a stand-up comic at London's Comedy Store. From there he graduated to BBC Radio's long-running comedy panel shows 'I'm Sorry, I Haven't a Clue' and 'Just a Minute', scored consistently on Channel 4's 'Whose Line Is It Anyway?' and made a success of both his own broken comedy show on Channel 4 from 1992, 'Paul Merton, The Series', and BBC 2's topical panel programme, the one on which we were employed this evening. After the taping, I found him easy to talk to in the LWT bar (although a BBC 2 Series, it's taped in the ITV London studios). I reminded him that he'd once said that watching clowns at a circus when he was three years old decided him on his career, and quoted his remark, 'I had no idea that adults could behave like that.'

He told me that he can't remember a time when he didn't want to make people laugh. When he was three or four years old, the games that he played on his own always involved performing to an imaginary audience.

Although he can't remember it himself, his mother tells me that when he was about two she saw him in front of the television with a knitting needle, conducting the Joe Loss Orchestra.

From quite early in life he practised writing his own autograph, 'something I thought everybody did until a few weeks ago'.

He had a great thirst for everything funny. Someone gave him an early reel-to-reel tape recorder and, when BBC TV re-ran Tony Hancock shows, the small Merton would hold a microphone against the speaker to collect the comedy for himself.

Although he had a childhood addiction to 'The Goon Show' and 'Round the Horne' on radio and has fond memories of watching Arthur Haynes on TV, a performer whose belligerent stance might well have affected him, it's Hancock who's persistently suggested as a 'major influence'. *Time Out*'s description of Merton could have been written about Hancock, observing 'his deadpan demeanour, accentuated by a hangdog expression, slouching posture and prematurely pot-bellied physique', adding that Merton 'makes Ken Livingstone sound animated'.

Merton pooh-poohed the Hancock comparison but admitted being able to understand the reasons for it, acknowledging the similarity of his lugubrious, even morose style.

'But he's just one of many people really. And I have no intention of going to Australia.'

In real life, Merton shows no trace of the glum, unsmiling comic persona. 'And I think probably Hancock really *was* like that in real life. That's one of the differences.'

Like so many comic performers, Merton has always been a shy person and was unwilling to push himself forward in school despite his natural gifts. 'My academic career peaked when I was about eight years old thanks to a very good teacher called Mrs Gately who encouraged my interest in English.'

Before long his precocious work was so exceptional that he was giving reading lessons to other children. Then came the summer holidays and a change of teacher, a nun with a strict view of what the children should or shouldn't write.

When the lad submitted his essay on 'What I Did in my Summer Holidays', it was well outside the limits she set. The piece began normally enough but not for long:

'Me and my family went to Littlehampton. It was very nice. A spaceship landed. I got on the spaceship and went to the moon. It was very cold.' And so on into further flights of fancy.

The nun castigated the young author in front of the entire class because, she said, 'This didn't happen! You can't write something which is untrue!'

Rashly, she read the essay to the class. This had an inspiring effect on the other children who all began to write in the same vein, abandoning their tales of buckets and spades on the sands and a day in the life of a penny in favour of wild fables involving dinosaurs and flying carpets.

Two or three weeks later, the nun again had Merton standing before the other pupils, blaming him for this 'new trend' that had been established. There's a sense of residual outrage in his voice even today when he speaks of it.

'It just seemed to me so wrong-headed but, when you're eight years old and there's a nun telling you that everything you feel is right for you is totally wrong, then that is a bit disturbing.'

However, young Merton did end up his education with a bit more than his CSE in ungraded metalwork.

'Ungraded!' he bewails.

There were a couple of A Levels to his credit when, about to leave Wimbledon College, full of baffled admiration and hopeless dreams of comic fame, Merton could see no path before him that could possibly lead to showbiz. How could he go to his careers officer and say, 'I want to be a comedian' in the hope of hearing the reply, 'OK, we'll fix you up with an apprenticeship in the Harry Worth/Petula Clark Show at Paignton'? It just doesn't work like that. So he never told anybody what he wanted to do. He feared the reaction would be the wrong kind of laughter.

As for confiding in friends, that relief was denied him too. For some absurd schoolboy reason, he was sent to Coventry by the half-dozen lads he'd previously looked upon as mates.

For almost his final year at school he felt cut off and, in searching for any kind of kinship, formed a new bond with a boy called John Irwin who shared his love of comedy. Today they script much of Merton's material together, all in carefully considered longhand with little rewriting, but in 1979, when together they bought a ramshackle maisonette in West Norwood, south London, the chance to realise whatever eager plans they made lay over a decade in the future.

Merton worked at Tooting Employment Office for ten years. He remembers it as good fun, but then he was never involved with the disagreeable task of interrogating the unemployed with questions like 'Why haven't you worked for three years?' He says he'd have been useless at acting the hard man.

Part of his happier duties there involved the New Towns Scheme which had been introduced after World War II. Basically the idea was that people who lived in bad housing in London could go to Basildon or Bracknell or any one of the new developments. If they could land a job there, a house came with it. Helping people to a better kind of life pleased Merton and part of the fun was a newsletter called the *Milton Keynes Bulletin* he received regularly and found hilarious.

'This was around the time of the famous concrete cows. A herd of concrete cows in a field! With a concrete milkmaid on a concrete stool! And these cows were made out of bits of builders' rubble so they had square jaws and bent necks, they looked like they'd been in a car accident. And the spokesman said that that was all very well but if you were passing overhead in a plane, it looked like a real herd. It's not easy to write funnier stuff than that.'

Life at the Employment Office neared the end of its natural term. Merton was beginning to realise that if he didn't leave soon, he'd be there for ever. He waited until 29 February so he would never forget the date, but a couple of years were to pass before he actually got up the nerve to do what he had always yearned to do: to try out his ability as a comedian in front of a paying audience.

'The big fear was, well, supposing I can't do it, suppose I'm not very good at it.'

But if he didn't make the leap, then he would never know, so one night in April 1982, he found himself above a strip club in Soho at half-past one in the morning, walking on to a stage in front of a bunch of drunk people.

This was the Comedy Store, London's answer to the legendary comics' graveyard of earlier years, the Glasgow Empire. 'Although in Glasgow, you'd get a certain amount of credence if you were *from* Glasgow. In London, it didn't matter if you'd lived in Stepney Green all your life, they were going to get you if they could smell blood.'

Merton had almost incredibly immediate luck in his choice of material. While his general attitude towards the audience was dictated, as you'd expect, by his desire to have them like him, quite understandably he still lacked what most comedians strive to find over a period of years: a style – a consistent, recognisable tone and technique.

Then, on only his second or third night, he found the dour role that was to inform his comic approach ever since. Adopting an unamused air came smoothly to him because he had never been a fan of anyone set upon being the life and soul of the party.

'I had this thing about comedians who laughed at their own jokes. If the loudest laughs are coming from the comic, then something's gone wrong somewhere.'

With this distaste for the falsely chuckling funnyman, he was ready to be drawn towards finding the vaguely truculent but almost expressionless manner that suits him best. The key to his future style emerged from his portrayal of a constable.

'One of the first things I did at the Comedy Store was this sketch about a policeman taking an hallucinogenic drug. And he starts off in a very policeman-like manner: *I was patrolling along the road on October the 27th* . . . you know, about twenty seconds of that, then he reveals that he's been given this hallucinogenic drug disguised as a Smartie. And he carries on describing his hallucination in the same deadpan way – *while sitting aboard this inter-galactic spacecraft* – and that worked very well because it was the morose policeman in court, being very much a sort of stereotypical copper really, but describing these fantastic things like meeting Marilyn Monroe on top of a bus shelter. It was the contrast that worked, the weird delusions reported in the down-to-earth, no-nonsense delivery of an unimaginative policeman.'

Few comedians have been as fortunate in discovering a lifetime technique contained in a single sketch. And so soon.

'I didn't have an act, I didn't really know what I was doing, but this one night that I did the policeman it was like very dream come true.

'I walked all the way home to my bed-sit in Streatham. I was on a cloud. And that one night got me through every single bad gig after that – and there were a lot of them. I was so lucky to get that encouragement early on. It kept me going over the next eighteen months of just dying the whole time.'

He read *Time Out*, learned of comedy rooms that had recently opened and rang them for work. His open sesame was, 'I've done the Comedy Store.' That was regarded as the baptism of fire.

Some gigs were hostile; others, like the vegetarian curry joint Earth Exchange in Archway, north London, were easygoing and tolerant. In such ambiences as the latter he could explore and expand his range.

If the god of comedy blessed him from the start, other less kindly forces were in charge of his subsequent luck. In 1986, while performing on the Fringe in Edinburgh, he was mugged in the Lothian Road. He'd volunteered to help put up posters for a friend's show.

'There we were at midnight, sticking posters on a wall, and these three guys came round a corner, luckily wearing soft shoes. They were just looking for trouble and I suppose I must've said the wrong thing at the wrong time or whatever and one of these blokes came vaulting over a barricade at me and kicked me in the head. It was dreadful, I had to go to hospital, really badly shaken.'

Then, a year later, 1987 found him in Edinburgh and hospital again. He'd opened in his first one-man show in Scotland, receiving some of the best reviews he'd ever had. GO AND SEE THIS MAN! commanded one headline. Greatly cheered, the next day he went out to play football with a bunch of comedians.

'It's a sort of tradition up there and about as interesting as watching a bunch of footballers telling jokes. And I was running along and I think I fell over my own trouser leg or something because all of a sudden my feet were where my head had been. There was a very loud crack of a bone breaking and that was the end of that show.'

Merton lost the £3,000 he'd paid up front for the theatre and would have been in worse trouble had the Comedy Store not held a benefit for him.

He'd been in hospital for several days with a badly broken leg when he got a severe pain in his side. It turned out to be a pulmonary embolism, the kind of life-threatening blood clot that sometimes forms after a breakage and which can go to the brain, heart or lungs. Luckily, it went to the lungs but, on top of all this, he contracted hepatitis A, 'from the hospital food, I reckon', and, at the age of just thirty and on the brink of major success, his burgeoning career was stymied.

Although deeply depressed, Merton's nature inclines towards finding the positive elements in every setback. Being in hospital gave him time to think and to make an attempt at plotting his future career. It's evidence of his extraordinary determination, tenacity and increasing self-confidence that, ill and defeated by circumstances, he lay in bed considering how to achieve one paramount goal: his own television show.

The next development for a comedian who works hard at his scripts and respects what he's written was the loosening-up process demanded by improvisation. He'd started experimenting with extemporaneous comedy in 1985. Mike Myers (a Canadian actor in Edinburgh who would go on to star in the hit movies *Wayne's World*, *Wayne's World II* and *Austin Powers*) was doing a double act with Neil Mullarkey and, together with American Kit Hollenbach, they were keen to have Merton join them in creating a small company of players inventing unwritten, impromptu entertainment.

At first Merton thought this concept was unworkable witchcraft but, after attending Kit's classes and letting himself adjust to the very different requirements of comic spontaneity, he steadily came to grips with the craft of talking off the top of his head. 'It's like a conversation except that it's got to be funny.'

Most comedians, reliant upon set routines and scripted rehearsals, would agree that conjuring comedy out of the air according to the suggestions of the audience takes a lot of nerve. Is that what it needs, sheer guts?

'No, it takes more than sheer guts or General Schwarzkopf would be doing it. You need all your confidence, that's at the core of it all. And if the first thing you say isn't funny, then you say the second thing. If that isn't funny, then you let the other person on the stage do a bit of talking and you'll come in with something. The thing is never to think, right, I've got to be funny now – here it comes, here's my chance to be funny – oh! I didn't say something funny! That's no good, that's too tense. You just relax into it and it will happen.'

The kingpin of his current popular reputation is the show we've just been doing, TV's hugely enjoyable version of Radio 4's perennial 'The News Quiz'.

But just how ad lib is 'Have I Got News For You'? How much is it over-recorded? How heavily is it edited? We know it's tape the night before it goes out but how much preparation precedes the taping and how much doctoring follows?

'Well, as you could see for yourself, the stuff that Angus does, he doesn't like people to know so it's on autocue. He works with the producer from Monday onwards, writing all those links and doing all the kind of heavy work on it, finding questions and bits of film and all that sort of stuff. And myself and Ian go in on a Thursday afternoon, early evening, like we did tonight, about half-past five, we're there till about half-eight and then that's it for us really.

'I mean, you've got your mind on it all week to a certain extent, eyes open for the sort of headlines that they're likely to pick on, you know, as much as you can afford to do without going potty. And you get a kind of instinct for it after a while. I remember a couple of years ago there was a story, MAN SLEEPS WITH PET PIG. About how he shared the bed with this pig and the wife said, "It's either me or the pig." And she left and he carried on with the pig and, when you see a story like that, you just know that'll come up.'

And post-production adjustments?

'Every week it's pretty much like it was this evening. We only record about forty-five minutes' worth for a half-hour show so, if there's not a good show in there somewhere, we shouldn't be allowed on really, should we? Also, with the nature of this thing, because a lot of it is ad-lib stuff, there's a finite period on it. If you haven't got anything in forty-five minutes, you're not going to get it in an hour and a half because your energy goes down. After all, you're not just reciting lines. You're trying to find fresh stuff.'

He tends to make it all sound easy, almost as if he's funny by accident, but this is due less to pretension than to his desire to avoid it. Asked to admit that it's much harder work than he is suggesting, Merton's honesty comes through.

'Well, no, it isn't all that easy. But the way I can deal with that is based on the fact that I've been performing for over so many years now, improvising since about '85, and I'm in the habit of saying things off the cuff as they occur to me and not being thrown if something doesn't work.'

Merton invariably gets the non-comic guest, the politician or the commentator, on his two-man team. Keeping someone in play who's so inexperienced in the cut-and-thrust of spontaneous comedy can't be easy either.

He says that these visitors generally fall into two camps – either they hardly say anything at all and they're just frozen by the whole thing, in which case 'you just grab at anything they do say and try to turn it into a joke and at least take it on somewhere that will help the show along', or he gets the kind who talk non-stop and none of it is any good. 'So whenever you watch it and you see the fourth member of the panel just smiling at everyone else's jokes and saying nothing themselves, it's either because they didn't say anything at all or they spoke for hours and it was all useless stuff. All yours was very good again so most of it will stay in, same as last time you did the show.'

Merton's indomitably sardonic humour conceals a private sentimentality. When he proposed marriage to Caroline Quentin, he chose to do so in the most romantic place in London he could think of – in Piccadilly Circus beneath the statue of the Greek love-god, Eros (an anagram for sore, by the way). He got down on one knee with all the homeless people and police and Japanese tourists and drunks watching him and popped the question. In spite of this, Caroline accepted after a suitably long and painful pause. After all, she is an actress. Did they make each other laugh?

'Oh, yes, but that's essential in any kind of relationship really, isn't it? But then again, I don't want to paint a picture where, as soon as we got home, we locked the door and laughed uproariously until next morning when we went out again.'

The marriage eventually ran out of laughs and ended. Neither career has suffered.

In spite of his success, or perhaps because of it, Paul Merton eschews self-satisfaction. He recalls hosting a music event just after appearing on Terry Wogan's BBC 1 chat show. Idly talking to the drummer of a small pop group called Voice of the Beehive, he was feeling very full of himself and seized upon some innocuous question to turn it around so as to introduce the subject of his appearance on Wogan the night before. The musician listened civilly to Merton's account of the great event, then sympathised with the stress of it all: 'I had to do some telly for a group I was in.' Asked rather loftily about the name of the group, the drummer answered, 'Madness'.

Merton is still rueful about his unjustified vanity. He says, 'My ego had got temporarily out of control. I was speaking to this guy from Madness who must've done a thousand television shows all over Europe!'

He never intends to let himself think he's better or greater than he really is. I believe it's this commitment to being level-headed that lies behind his great comic gifts and lends them honesty. Truth in comedy with added surreal imagination.

His career continues apace with no fear that the bubble will burst because he doesn't see it as a bubble, a manufactured thing.

He argues that 'Have I Got News For You?' is a success not just because he's on it but because of its combination of assets, although I thought it flagged badly during his absence.

Expanding his activities to writing a book and touring the country with his stage act, these are just parts of the job he always wanted to do. He hopes and believes he'll improve and is relieved that his parents are pleased with his TV appearances as it means they no longer leave newspapers lying around, open at Situations Vacant with rings drawn around suitable opportunities.

They must have concluded, along with the rest of the British public, that their son has job security.

## Saturday, 1 November 1997

This evening I presented 'The National Lottery Live' wearing my second smartest suit. My comedy guest star, Harry Enfield, wore my smartest. It was way too big for him around the middle but he still looked better than he would have done in his own grungy clobber. He'd meant to pop back home to get a fresh outfit but then feared that crowds celebrating an early Guy Fawkes Night in the streets would prevent his returning in time for the live show. Since he was plugging his book sales for Christmas, I persuaded him to run through a brisk parade of his best-known characters and their catchphrases. The studio audience loved it. So did I, partly because Harry makes me laugh more than almost any other comedian of comparatively recent vintage and partly because I sense his humanity. Oh dear, that last phrase has the sound of pseudo-speak. Let me explain what I mean.

In presenting yourself as yourself on television, as in all forms of human contact, sooner or later the impression you make upon others comes from what you are and not from what you pretend to be. Your true self doesn't remain concealed for long. Given enough TV exposure for viewers to form a judgement, your real nature will be detected, your falseness discounted. And so the public gives or withholds its affection according to a sense of discrimination often more instinctive than conscious.

For the comedian who strives to offer himself to his audience as a nice guy, without the comic disguise of some adopted character to mask his real nature, his genuine likeability is a primary constituent of the public's acceptance. Faking it won't work for long. The people soon sense a phoney salesman.

And being a popular individual in your personal life won't be enough to win their fondness either, notwithstanding your talent. If the crowd senses that your performance is a misrepresentation of who you really are, they won't like you for it.

Likewise, a comedian who isn't especially endearing in his private life can fascinate and win over the hearts of the people by simply being genuine. Sixty years ago in Hollywood W.C. Fields exploited his appalling traits of drunkenness mingled with mean-spirited self-interest and rang true as a flawed man who was achingly funny. Today in Britain Jack Dee and Paul Merton are examples of successful comics who allow us to see their surly, disgruntled and contemptuous side with little apparent attempt to charm. But we like that honesty, recognising a kind of integrity in their grumpy comedy.

## Thursday, 20 November 1997

So this is Oxford, City of Spires, home of the sanctum sanctorum for 10,000 students where the Thames becomes the Isis and where this evening I become a target for comic calumny, brickbats and general obloquy from the best wits that the Oxford Union can assemble.

LWT producer Paul Lewis has arranged the taping of a one-hour special called 'Bob Monkhouse on Campus' in which the university's ablest debaters will argue individual contentions with all the fluency and waggishness they can muster while denigrating me as cruelly as they dare. My job? To rise to my feet after each assertion and refute it.

I left Dulwich College when I was seventeen and most of what I learned there has been so eroded by time and indifference that I can no longer retrieve it. I wish I had gone to university. Perhaps my brain would be in better condition now as a result of a few years spent in training, mental discipline and the expansion of knowledge when my youthful ability to store information was so much greater than it later became.

Ignorance isn't bliss, it's like brain death. I can't bear being ignorant of all the things I don't know.

Like – If blind people wear sunglasses, why don't deaf people wear earmuffs?

If the police arrested Mr Bean, would they have to tell him he had the right to remain silent?

Ballpoints, should they be awarded?

If you're born again, can you vote twice?

Why didn't Dizzy Gillespie keep falling over?

How can we expect a politician to believe in the wisdom of the people when he knows it was the people who voted him in?

When a nudist wants to remind himself of something, what does he tie a knot in?

If there's a heaven for atheists, is there anybody there?

Clumsiness, is it catching? Or is it dropping?

Why do we say 'My alarm clock didn't go off' when it obviously didn't go on?

Do crabs think we walk sideways?

Why do they call it 'rush hour' when your car just sits there?

Why do people with no watch look at their wrists when you ask them what time it is? And why do you ask people with no watch what time it is?

Why is it we never see black people playing accordions?

If women were in charge of nuclear defence, would missiles be shaped differently?

Why do they have parking spaces for the disabled at skating rinks?

If your goldfish were incontinent, how would you know?

Why is the word 'abbreviated' so long? For that matter, why is 'dyslexia' so hard to spell? Why does the word 'blind' have one 'i'? And why has the word 'lisp' got an 's' in it? Isn't that unnecessarily sarcastic?

What do gardeners do when they retire?

If we call a fly a 'fly', why don't we call a fish a 'swim'?

Whatever happened to the first of the Mohicans?

If (A) can saw a log in three hours, (B) in two hours and (C) in one hour, why the hell don't they let (C) do it?

If they have no reflection, how do vampires shave?

Why doesn't Superglue stick to the tube?

How did the Phantom of the Opera get his huge organ into that sewer?

What happens when you go up to the Man With No Name and ask for his autograph?

When sour cream goes bad, how do you tell?

Why does a cowboy wear two spurs? If one side of the horse goes, so does the other.

Why do they call it a TV *set* when you only get one?

Do you have to brush your teeth during a fast? And why do they call it a 'fast' when it goes so slow?

When the inventor of the drawing board cocked it up, what did he go back to?

If gay people can't breed where the hell are they all coming from?

Whatever happened to the rest of John the Baptist?

If your name is Samsonite, what do you put on your luggage?

Where do homeless people have 90 per cent of their accidents?

I spilt some stain remover on my sleeve the other day. How do you get that out?

Can a hermaphrodite have a sex change operation? And if so, how and from what to which?

Do illiterate people get the full effect of Alphabetti Spaghetti?

If the formula for water is $H_2O$, is the formula for an ice cube $H_2O$ squared?

People in hell – where do they tell people to go?

What do acupuncturists do when they get an attack of pins and needles?

If New Age Travellers love to travel, why are they always bloody moaning when the police move them on?

Can you use a yo-yo on the moon?

302

How did they describe thick fog before the invention of pea soup? For that matter, how did they describe hailstones before the invention of golf balls?

What do you call a male ladybird?

If they tried to change our National Anthem, would people stand for it?

What did Long John Silver do with his left shoes?

Why can't faith healers do teeth?

How do they make Teflon stick to the pan?

If the pain in your leg is caused by age, how come you don't get the same pain in your other leg? It's the same age.

If you were trapped right up to your neck in quicksand and someone threw a brick at your head, would you duck?

Why can't you tickle yourself?

How is it that the holes in a cat's fur always come exactly where its eyes are?

Why don't they put typewriter keys in alphabetical order? Then we'd all know how to type.

What is occasional furniture the rest of the time?

When you're sitting in the cinema, which armrest is yours?

What is it about being alone in a car that makes men want to pick their noses?

If supermarkets were less crowded, would more people go to them?

Why is it that wrong numbers are never engaged?

Did the Sioux bother with bald cowboys?

How did Adam keep his fig leaf on?

And aerosol deodorants, I'm annoyed with myself for using them because they're dangerous. Have you ever read the label on those spray cans? 'INFLAMMABLE CONTENTS UNDER PRESSURE. IF EXPOSED TO HEAT MAY EXPLODE' – listen, I don't want anything under my arms that's going to explode. Because it sometimes gets really hot under there. That's all I need, I'm on TV sweating under those lights, and boom, boom, both my arms blow off! Probably get a round of applause but what would I do for an encore? I don't know! Ignorance is hell.

## Sunday, 30 November 1997

My agent and manager for over thirty years, Peter Prichard, OBE turned sixty-five today. He said to me, 'I got worried when policemen began to look young to me. Now it's Chelsea pensioners.'

Peter also represents Jimmy Tarbuck, Ray Alan & Lord Charles, and that lovable duo, Little and Large. It wasn't always so. Eddie explained to me today, 'Peter's been fantastic for us but we used to be nervous of agents at first.'

The team had been accepting their bookings direct from the concert secretaries of working men's clubs for years when they suddenly made a hit on TV and found themselves famous.

Everyone told them, 'You must get a press agent' so the boys got themselves a publicity man and signed him up for £100 a week. The first month went by, nothing in the papers, so Eddie called him up: 'What's happening? A hundred quid a week, that's £400 so far . . .'

The press agent said, 'I got 'em talkin' about yer, lads, I got 'em talkin' about yer!'

Another month passed. By now they had paid £800 and they were worried, but the press agent just repeated, 'I got 'em talkin' about yer, lads, I got 'em talkin' about yer!'

The end of the next week came, £900, their life's savings, and still nothing.

The boys walked into the agent's office, angry and feeling humiliated. They demanded, 'What does this mean? £900 and nothing!'

Yet again they heard the same answer: 'I got 'em talkin' about you, lads!'

Sid finally lost his temper. He shouted, 'They're talking about us, are they? And just what the hell are they *saying*?'

The press agent shrugged apologetically and said, 'They're saying – whatever happened to Little and Large?'

## Friday, 2 January 1998

Barbados has us in a social whirl this season. After a riotous New Year's Eve at the Lone Star with a bunch of showbiz boozers, we were out again last evening for dinner at Sandy Lane with Shirley and Don Black (he's written lyrics for countless hit songs from 'Born Free' to Lloyd Webber's 'Sunset Boulevard') and our hosts, Lord and Lady Feldman. Tonight takes us to the home of restaurateur Nick Hudson and his enchanting wife Veronica where we'll dine with one of Hollywood's most employed English actors, Tim Curry. By the end of the evening I am hoarse with laughing. Here are some of the reasons:

Tim tells us he's seen that film *Crash* where a couple becomes sexually aroused by car crashes and jokes. 'They get into a big argument when the man refuses to use an air-bag.'

Nick says, 'I think sex is more like safe driving. You start slowly and gradually increase your speed, making proper use of your clutch and always being prepared to pull out to avoid a child.'

We get on to the subject of the national fondness Americans have for suing each other and Tim tells us that US customers have taken out a $25 million lawsuit against the computer service company called America On-line because they say the company has taken on so many new subscribers that it's almost impossible to get on line now. He says, 'They say many computer users are being forced to go out and get a life.'

During the laughter Nick pours some more wine and marvels that, 'Every Christmas the supermarkets in Barbados are full of Advocaat. How did they invent that stuff?' Jac reckons they must have been thinking, 'Hmmm, I'd like to get a little drunk . . . but I'd also like an omelette.'

The conversation turns to crime in California and I mention that I read where O.J. Simpson's had offers for his estate of $1.5 million more than it's thought to be worth. Veronica says, 'So it looks as if he can get away with making a killing yet again.' And Tim adds, 'O.J. was greeted at the airport with cries of "Murderer, murderer!" but it was only his limo driver paging him.'

We get around to current events and I say, 'You've got to hand it to Richard Branson, he's going to try that round-the-world balloon trip again. What else can go wrong with it?' Tim suggests, 'A hijacking maybe? Can you imagine a terrorist hijacking a balloon? "Look out, he's got a pin!"'

It seems everyone at this dinner party is wittier than the professional comedian. But I'm a terrific audience.

**Monday, 5 January 1998**
It's exactly fifty years since my late working partner Denis Goodwin and I made our first broadcast as a double act.

Though Denis wasn't particularly Jewish in his manner, he delighted in the fact that his attractive mother Evelyn often was.

When Denis told her that he was quitting his job selling radios in a department store to enter show business full time, she was horrified.

'I'm just glad your father didn't live to hear of such a thing! A son of mine telling jokes for a living? What are all our friends and neighbours going to think?'

Denis had his answer ready. 'I'll change my name.'

'Change your name?' cried Evelyn. 'What if you're a success? How will everyone know it's my son?'

**Saturday, 17 January – Saturday, 31 January 1988**
A splendid flight back to Heathrow and thence to Granada's Manchester

studios to start taping five shows a day for BBC 1. It's an elimination game called 'Wipeout', a format I've admired ever since Paul Daniels hosted it on Friday evenings a few years ago. I've agreed to make seventy programmes for Monday-to-Friday transmission in what is now referred to in TV circles as the 'sexy hour' of noon till 1 p.m. The production company is Action Time and its boss Stephen Leahy is quite the nicest and most accomplished light entertainment maestro I know. He believes we'll add a million viewers to the midday slot and he'll turn out to be quite right.

Over dinner at Chez Nico Stephen asks my advice about the series and then wants to know what sage advice has ever come my way. I'm reminded of John Steinbeck's words, 'No one wants advice – only corroboration'. Then I remember Ronald Frankau.

How early in my life I first heard and laughed at Ronald Frankau on the wireless I can't be certain but I'd place it around 1936 when I was eight. Loving wordplay, I relished his broadcasts as I did those of equally literate humorists – Gillie Potter, Oliver Wakefield and, later, Eric Barker and America's Fred Allen. None of these, however, did wonderful comic songs with Monty Crick at the piano. And none engaged in the relentlessly speedy verbal swordplay with so worthy a wordsmith as Tommy Handley, remembered now as the legendary star of the World War II radio series 'It's That Man Again'. I memorised every 'turn' performed under their pseudonyms of Mr Murgatroyd and Mr Winterbottom as best I could and painstakingly transcribed each routine in longhand . . . 'Have you read Hans Andersen?' . . . 'No, they're white, and why call me Andersen?'

When I'd passed my BBC audition in 1947, I quickly exhausted my store of original patter in about two dozen broadcasts. Stuck for a closing gag on a show called 'The Golden Slipper Club', presented to listeners as a cabaret from a West End nightspot hosted by Edmundo Ros, I appropriated a funny story that I'd heard told on the air a year or so before by Mr Frankau. He'd told the audience at Saturday night's 'Music Hall':

'The girls of Hawaii are rather friendly, I believe. They wear grass skirts, you know. My friend went there with a lawnmower. He's an American fellow, name of Buck. Anyhow, Buck arrived in Hawaii and no sooner was he promenading along the sandy shore than a jolly lovely Hawaiian lass stepped out from behind a pineapple bush and gave him the eye. Well, he tapped himself on the chest and said, "Me Buck!" And she tapped herself on the chest and said, "Me, twenty bucks."'

It was quite a racy joke for radio in the late 40s but it got past the censor and I decided I could get away with it too. As I told it:

'The RAF had me stationed all over the Pacific. Once I was in Hawaii where the girls wear grass skirts. You should see them rotating the crops. I was strolling down a dark lane in Honolulu where a smashing girl stepped out of the shadows. I said, "Hello – me, Bob!" She said, "Really? Me, thirty bob."'

It scored a huge laugh and I was well pleased.

A couple of days later the BBC's Charles Maxwell, producer of the hit comedy series called 'Take It From Here', phoned my parents' home in Beckenham and asked for me. 'Ronnie Frankau's been on to me, he wants to talk to you. I gather you've been a naughty boy. You're due here tomorrow for a meeting with Roy Speer. Make it half an hour earlier and be in my office at two – good idea?'

As instructed and feeling guiltily nervous, I went to Aeolian Hall, Bond Street, and found Mr Frankau sitting in Maxwell's office. Maxwell excused himself and left us alone. The great comedian could look benign – I'd seen him on the variety stage at the Brighton Hippodrome and the Lewisham Empire, eyes twinkling beneath his bald dome – but he could also look frightening. He fixed me with eyes no longer twinkling but bleak, a pair of hot poached eggs, and his irregular teeth gave his rather thick and livid lips an angry sneer. He didn't invite me to sit and I remained standing beside Maxwell's desk as he spoke in familiar low, raspy tones.

'Three things, all worth learning if you hope to make a career for yourself in this profession. One, you won't get far on stolen ideas. We tend to close ranks on any outsider who tries that more than once. Two, don't try to run before you can walk. You're a lad, not a man yet, otherwise I shouldn't be dealing with you so politely. You're clean-cut, well turned out, so leave the risqué sort of comedy to men of maturity. When you changed Buck to Bob you made it seem as if you yourself were trafficking with a prostitute. It's unhealthy coming from a youngster. And three . . . come on, sit down.'

I sat in Maxwell's chair.

'Three, well done. I've heard you on the air two or three times now. You're a bit Yankeefied, what I call a bit too mid-Atlantic, but that probably comes from too many moo-oo-oovies and shortwave radio from America.'

He pulled out his wallet and removed a card.

'Here's my address and telephone. If you're short of a good clean

307

story, give me a call. There are hundreds I don't use. That Hawaii wheeze though, that's a regular of mine and now I'll have to drop it for a while. Can't have people thinking I'm whipping my best tales off lads like you.'

He stood up and so did I.

'Registered, have I? I hope so. You've got a brain, so use it. Think up your own patter. Find your own voice, your own attitude. If you're a funny chap, if you make your pals laugh, concentrate on why, on what it is that's naturally funny to you and use it onstage. You see, there are plenty of comic singers besides me. There's Norman Long and the Western Brothers and Jack Warner and Stanley Holloway and Billy Bennett and even poor old Clarence Wright – but we're all different, all individuals. Don't be in a hurry because it takes time, but don't let up either. Don't take the easy way, you'll only fail. Keep looking for your *comic identity*!

'I can see this is sinking in so I'll expand on the subject just a wee bit. In presenting yourself to the public, as in all forms of human contact, the impression you make upon others comes from what you are and not from what you pretend to be. Your true self doesn't remain concealed for long. Given enough radio exposure for listeners to form a judgement, your real nature will be detected, your false display discounted. And it'll be even truer of television when it becomes the prime source of entertainment.

'The public gives or withholds its affection according to a sense of discrimination often more instinctive than deliberate.

'If the crowd senses that your performance is a misrepresentation of who you really are, they won't like you for it. Be yourself, sonny boy, and you'll be false to no one else! There, Shakespeare rewritten!'

He was warm and kindly now and he shook my hand vigorously.

'Never mind me, sounding off like a Dutch uncle. Always have liked the sound of my own voice, y'know. Now run along and behave like a gentleman in future, eh?'

I thanked him – only the second time I'd spoken at all – and ran along. As soon as I got to producer Roy Speer's office I grabbed some sheets of paper and wrote down everything I'd just heard.

I kept the pages for many years, losing them eventually to water damage in my London basement. But by that time, I'd read my notes so often I could hear his voice in my head.

Of course some of Frankau's views have dated pretty badly and much of what he said was more pompous than patronising but I think that along with Jack Buchanan's admonition – 'For God's sake, don't go onstage without pressing your trousers!' – and a master class on comic delivery that Max Miller once gave me in the back of his Rolls-Royce, it's the best advice I ever got from anyone.

## Wednesday, 4 February 1998

At noon today I join a bunch of very lucky people at the National Lottery's Millionaires Luncheon in the elegant Lanesborough Hotel.

I've never been in a roomful of such happy, grateful folk. Moving along them, shaking hands and striking up conversations, I learn a lot about how gloriously a giant windfall can improve the lives of decent families.

In my after-lunch speech I start by saying that I'm sick and tired of reading about big winners who've said the money won't change their lives. I have a punchline to this but the set-up provokes such a roar of appreciative agreement that I abandon the gag and move along to some other apposite anecdotes.

In one of them, I tell them about how, while hosting the Lottery one week, I met a cattle farmer who'd won £7 million. I asked him what he planned to do with such wealth.

'Well,' he said, rubbing his chin thoughtfully. 'I reckon I'll just keep on farming till it's gone.'

One multimillionaire approaches me after the speech. He's a thickset, ruddy-faced character with tufty white hair and a chubby wife in tow.

'Bob, I've got to tell you something. When you said that bit about the money not changing your life, well, my wife and I, we didn't laugh, we just looked at each other; didn't we, Barbara?

'Then you told the yarn about the cattle farmer who said he'd carry on farming till his money was all spent. And me and my wife, we never laughed at that neither. We just looked at each other again.'

He smiles at his wife a bit helplessly and she returns his smile with a shrug and nods at him to continue.

'Well, that's us, y'see, Bob. We're cattle farmers. Last year we won £4 million all but a couple of thousand. We're both in our sixties and our only son's settled in Australia so we sort of carried on, so to speak. Didn't let the money change us. Took a bit of stupid pride in it, as a matter of fact.

'I say stupid because, well, what with BSE and all, the farm's been costing us all we'd borrowed and it'll likely cost a lot more yet.

'So when you said them words you said today, Barbara leans over to me and says, "Ron, we must be bloomin' bonkers!"

'I says, "You're not wrong, Bar, are you? That's just what I've been thinking but I didn't say anything 'cause I thought you didn't want no change, like."

'Bar, she says to me, "But, Ron, that's what I thought *you* wanted!"'

'So we've just this last twenty minutes talked it over and we're going to sell up and go to Australia to see our grandchildren!'

I was lost for words.

His wife stepped forward shyly and took my hand.

'Thank you,' she said. 'Wasn't for you today we could've gone on not understanding one another for heaven knows how long!'

Four months later, one day next June, I'll get a card from Perth, West Australia, repeating their thanks and saying 'we found ourselves a very happy home and family'.

I'll still be lost for words.

### Thursday, 5 February 1998

Today I record a Radio 2 arts programme called '100 Laughs for a Halfpenny', produced by the prolific Roy Oakshott and devised, written and co-presented by my fellow Dulwich Collegiate, Denis Gifford. It's a potted (fifty-five minutes) history of comic weeklies, from their birth in the nineteenth century with Alley Sloper (so called because, whenever he spotted creditors, he sloped up alleys) until the advent of Dan Dare and the *Eagle*. Comical voices are provided by Kate Robbins and Peter Goodwright and the broadcast will attract a huge audience of older listeners whose childhood memories are forever populated by unforgettable cartoon characters like Desperate Dan, Keyhole Kate, Lord Snooty and his Pals, Hairy Dan – 'his whiskers neat reach to his feet' – and Pansy Potter, the Strong Man's Daughter.

That title always bothered me, coupling 'Potter' with 'daughter'. When I first submitted my drawings to the editor of the *Beano*, I felt an urge to correct the faulty rhyme and change her name to Pansy Porter. Of course, my fifteen-year-old's suggestion was ignored. Many, many years later I met the elderly editor at a convention for cartoon collectors like me and asked him why the character's strapline hadn't always been a proper rhyming couplet. The old man answered in a broad Dundee accent complete with glottal, 'It does rhyme, so it does! Pansy Poh'er, Strong Man's Doh'er! Wha's wrang wi' that?'

Childhood influences are strong in all of us, hardship strongest of all, although it can provide the early resilience that leads to future survival and success. It's certainly true for many comedians.

For America's 'Uncle Miltie', Milton Berle, it took actual boyhood starvation and a stagestruck mom. Bill Cosby's springboard was a broken home and poverty in Philadelphia. Comedians as diverse as Charlie Chaplin, Bud Flanagan, Dick Emery, W.C. Fields and Max Bygraves began their lives in a state of pitiable deprivation.

'It's in the lack of money or love or both that a comedian is born,' I was told by an old US vaudevillian named Sam Tinker. I taped an interview with him on a battery-driven reel-to-reel recorder in 1957, two years before his death, and the sound of New York's Sheraton Hotel barbershop is still to be clearly heard in the background. Tinker was emphatic about the connection between a disadvantaged youth and a lifelong search for love and approval through comedy.

'I was four years old when my pa drowned himself. My real ma died the very next day, heart gave out. I was adopted. I couldn't call myself O'Hanlon no more, I was Mrs Tinker's boy. We were living dirt poor in Evansville, Indiana. First shows I ever seen were travelling hucksters, medicine shows with crowd catchers working. I took one look at those jugglers and balancers, boy, and I seen all those people clapping and smiling and getting their dollars out and says to myself, Sam, that's it. And I asked a guy named Dr Striker to take me on and he did. I worked so hard my hands bled. He paid me in food and with teaching me all he knew about magic tricks and holding the folks' attention. We travelled all over selling patent medicines and he drank half of it himself, got drunk and beat me up a hundred times or more. I was just twelve.

'I've known every headliner in vaudeville, I've seen every great comedian from Bill Fields to Jolie, Buster Keaton, Chaplin, Fanny Brice, Clark & McCullough, Joe Cook, Bert Williams, you name 'em. And every single one of them was looking for the love and the luck they never had when they was kids.'

For years it seemed to me that old Sam Tinker was right. So many other full-time funnymen, like me, had undemonstrative parents. Others became class clowns as a defence against playground persecution.

'I remember at school I used humour to avoid being bullied. If I didn't try to be funny, they didn't hit me.'

The gag comes from Gavin Osbon, a comedy writer on many BBC TV shows including two series of mine in the 80s. It's a clever but simple inversion of a cliché. And the cliché is ubiquitous in the childhood histories of those who are funny for money.

Harry Enfield says he was a 'small and fat' child and so was forced to be funny 'to make the tough guys laugh'. He attended public school, Worth in Sussex, for two years of misery before returning to grammar school, where he became a punk. Proceeding to York University, where

311

he got a degree in politics, he then became a comedian on an MSC grant of £40 a week. Would he have centred his life upon this ability to make us laugh if there had been no schoolyard enemies to disarm?

But to every rule there comes an exception to test its truth. And the best example could have stepped from the pages of *Comic Cuts*: Ken Dodd, who believes his doting mother and fun-loving father gave him such a taste for fond admiration that he began to seek it everywhere.

He says, 'I had that much love and affection from my parents that I really thirsted, craved for more and I think that's what all entertainers and performers and actors are really searching for – affection.'

Doddy may spread happiness wherever he goes but the first time I encountered him he spread something far less agreeable all over me.

I was riding high in 1957, a hot new star who was packing them in and putting bums on seats wherever I appeared. One evening I was hired to do a cabaret for a firm called Monk & Crane at a Midland hotel. When I arrived and went up to my room to get ready, the London booking agent sidled in the door after me rubbing his hands together and chuckling falsely.

'Lovely room, Bob my son. Double bed! That do you, my son?'

'Yes, fine, but I won't be staying. I'll do my stuff and drive home tonight. What time am I on?'

'As per our arrangement on the phone, 9 p.m. That do you, my son?'

'Great. So I'm straight on after the coffee and the brandy?'

'Almost. We've got a bit of warm-up act going on before you. He's a Liverpool lad who does a bit of nonsense with a big bass drum and sings "Granada". Not my booking, it's something the managing direc-tor's wife arranged. That do you, my son?'

Why wouldn't it do me? I was a big star so I could afford to be big-hearted. What harm could be done by some amateur opening my show for me? What does it say in the Book of Proverbs? 'Pride goeth before destruction, and an haughty spirit before a fall', that's what it says. But I'd quite forgotten that in my vain self-assurance.

'How long does he do, this Scouse boy?'

'Fifteen, twenty minutes tops. Then, when he's settled 'em down and the waitresses are out of the way, that's when you walk out and murder 'em! That do you, my son?'

About five minutes to nine my phone rang.

'Bob my son, everything's going like clockwork, running exactly to time. I'm just going to put this support act on now.'

'What's he look like? Smartly dressed?'

I was faultlessly garbed and hoped for a contrast.

'No, no, he's a mess. Hair sticking up like a fright wig. Dress suit stolen off a scarecrow. A bit pathetic really.'

Yes, I thought, that will do me, my son.

At ten minutes past nine I strolled downstairs to the foyer.

The banqueting suite was in the hotel's lower ground floor and a carpeted flight of steps led down to the large room, filled with one hundred and fifty guests. They sounded like one thousand and fifty. I stood in the reception area paralysed by the deafening gales of laughter from below.

The rest of my evening passes like a waking nightmare. In this dream state, I slowly edge down the staircase in a disbelieving mixture of shock and mounting anxiety. I'm being careful not to be seen by the audience. I need not worry, the audience's attention is fully occupied by the prancing figure in the spotlight. Up until now I have never heard such screams of joy from any crowd anywhere. The cause of the hysteria is this creature from another planet, a clown escaped from some circus asylum. His galvanic vitality is hypnotic, his lunacy inspired, as he aims his protruding teeth and ping-pong-ball eyes in every direction, his arms gesticulating with oddly splayed hands to emphasise each of his wonderfully inane gags. His behaviour is a mad mix of mischief and baby innocence. Like Puck, he is utterly capricious, thrusting a tickling stick at women who shriek in delight at its suggestive sexiness, then producing a giant version to make the phallic symbolism even greater.

'This is me knockers-up pole! If I can get this through your bedroom window, I'll send you to work with a twinkle in your eye!'

He attempts to play a guitar, which explodes. He switches to a gigantic accordion which unfolds in his arms like a live anaconda. He tells us (I say 'us', for although I'm observing from the sidelines, I'm now a part of his spellbound following) that he woke up this morning with Miss Givings and then describes his visit to a Turkish bath which turned out to be a fish and chip shop: 'I took all me clothes off and a lady looked at me and said, "I'll have four penn'orth".' He piles absurdity upon absurdity, donning an outsize pith helmet and strapping on an army belt decorated with dangling pots, pans and the leg of a shop-window mannequin to sing a bizarrely comical version of 'The Road to Mandalay'. The gags get wilder, the crowd is weeping with helpless mirth, the time is going by and nobody cares, not even me. At the climax of his ninety-minute performance, he sings again but this time in a powerful baritone that has his spectators on their feet, cheering him to the echo. To make an exit he has to push his way through the hotel staff who, drawn by the laughter, are crowding the stairs. I shrink into the shadows.

The exhausted assemblage, now his devotees, are left gasping, some still holding their sides, women wiping their faces and making for the ladies' room to repair their makeup while the men pushing their way into the gents' are still chuckling and repeating favourite jokes. It's coming up to 11 p.m. and a toastmaster raps on the table for attention. Eventually he gets it.

'Ladies and gentlemen, for those of you using the coaches, they are due to depart in thirty minutes. I believe the chairman and his good lady have to be on their way so let us wish them safe home. Will you put your hands together for the chairman and his good lady, thank you! Goodnight, sir, madame, and *bon voyage*! There's no time for dancing, I'm afraid . . .'

Groans of disappointment.

'. . . because now it's time to meet and greet our surprise artiste. From television, Bob Monkhouse.'

The trio plays my opening music and I walk out but the evening is plainly over. The audience is polite but still coming down from the high of a laughing frenzy that ended only a few minutes earlier. I'm getting no laughs at all with my very best material. People are yawning, some whispering to each other, others preparing to leave. I'm contracted to do my full act but it's now a toss-up who's becoming more embarrassed, me or them.

After fifteen minutes that drag like hours, I cue my closing song and, in a voice which seems thin and tuneless in comparison with the full-throated baritone with the buck teeth, I wrap up my dismal little turn.

As I depart to the merest smattering of applause I see in my path the co-conspirator of my humiliation, the booking agent.

He stands at the door, applauding listlessly, and as I pass him I say, not entirely without the merest trace of bitterness, '*That fucking do you, my son?*'

Five years later I was asked if I'd appear in cabaret for the same firm at the same venue. I told the booker, a different fellow, 'I don't think they'd want me back again. I died there in '57.'

He was puzzled. 'No, I suggested you and they were very keen. Said they'd never had you and they'd lay on transport to suit you and everything.'

'Yeah? Who's on with me?'

'That blonde singer, Karen Greer.'

Karen didn't tell jokes or carrying a tickling stick. I took the date and went down very well. It was obvious that no one in the audience remembered having seen me there at their annual function before.

By Jove, I needed that!

**Friday, 20 February 1998**

I am wiped out. Today we taped the seventieth edition – seventy, count 'em, seventy – of 'The Elimination Game' for BBC 1. I thought that it would be interesting to see whether, coming up for seventy myself this next June 1st, I could survive a schedule of making five 'Wipeout' quiz shows a day. The answer is barely but yes.

The programme is computer driven and so subject to technical problems at every turn. Breakdowns sap one's powers of concentration but maintaining the same level of alertness for each programme is essential. Fortunately old pro's instincts saw me through, rallying energy for each showtime as reveille rouses an old soldier; that, plus the unfailing dedication and good humour of producer Jacqui Wilson, director John Rooney, Ged, Andy, Lawrie, Stan, Gloria, Alex, Chris, Jenny, Jane, John, Bob, Col and one of the best-natured crews I've ever worked with.

'Don't worry,' soothed Executive Producer Stephen Leahy. 'We'll get you the same team for next time.'

'Next time, Stephen?'

'This autumn. You're making another ninety.'

My diaries tell me I survived another set of punishing exertions just thirty-two years ago in Aden. Remember Aden? It was a seaport in South Yemen taken by the British in 1839 and one of our crown colonies from 1937 right up until I got there.

We had a lot of troops stationed around this strategically important entrance to the Red Sea and they needed entertaining. Within months of my visit it would become the capital of the new People's Democratic Republic as our armed forces came home but that didn't stop the local rebels from keeping up the pressure in the meantime.

Others before me had volunteered to fly out there to keep up morale. I'd been tipped off by Mike and Bernie Winters about buying duty-free goods in the NAAFI canteens and a reluctant Tony Hancock had come to the phone with the grudging suggestion that I take along an aerosol of bug spray and a bottle of Kaopectate. No one mentioned danger.

Together with Samantha Jones, a bewitching singer with a Prince Valiant haircut, plus musicians and a Combined Services Entertainment officer whose daughter was the teenage Jenny Agutter, I boarded the starkly appointed RAF plane and sat backwards all the way to the far end of the Mediterranean.

An army captain met us at the airport with a jeep and a driver. He conducted us to the kind of accommodation I hadn't seen or smelt since my RAF service. Our first performance wasn't scheduled until the following day at a base named Little Aden. After a dodgy meal and my purchase of an Asahi Pentax camera for a sixth of the UK price, we slept late partly because there was nothing worth sightseeing and partly because of the captain's parting shot: 'Wouldn't advise any of you to wander about the area without a military escort – we're on yellow alert.'

Yellow, a perfect match for the streak down my back.

'What does yellow alert mean?' I asked a sergeant named Albert who came to fetch us in the sweltering mid-afternoon.

'It means watch out for the stills. The nationalists, I should say. We've been told not to call 'em gollies 'cause it's offensive to the locals who're on our side so we don't call 'em gollies no more. We call 'em stills.'

'Why do you call them stills?'

'Because they're still gollies.'


We drove through greenhouse humidity in our three open jeeps until the dusty city and its oil refinery smells were miles behind us. I was surprised at the countryside.

Expecting desert, I saw instead fields of wheat and barley. Cotton was growing in abundance and we passed mills and processing plants busy with the production of sorghum, dates and millet.

'The economy looks healthy enough, Albert.'

'This is all recent, this Arab investment. Most of it's money from Saudi Arabia and it's a long-term strategy. As soon as we've pulled all our bases out there'll be open warfare in all but name between South Yemen and North Yemen. Then, after a few years of border skirmishes, they'll merge into one sodding great republic. I know a local politician, he says it's all in the bag. He says money plus time equals whatever result you want.'

We entered the barracks area and drove to the field where a makeshift stage stood before row upon row of benches and assorted seating, almost all of it already occupied by about 200 men in khaki. They cheered our arrival and clapped enthusiastically as our musicians set up their chairs, music stands, keyboard and drum kit. As soon as the officers arrived to occupy the front seats, we started the show.

Behind the audience the low sun made a perfect amber spotlight for Samantha. It was past sunset when I took over and it would have required a pretty pathetic comic to have disappointed that eager crowd.

I've never really liked performing al fresco but on this evening, pacing the planking with a handheld mike and lit by a searchlight shining from a guard tower, I got laughs that could have been heard across the Gulf in Somalia. I was having a wonderful time, doing gags I'd written especially for this trip. I'd been on for about twenty minutes with every intention of doing twice as long when I reached this joke:

'I used to wonder why they call you the regular army. Now I realise that I'd be regular too if I had people shooting at me every day.'

There was a wave of laughter and crackling.

A whistle blew, the laughter faded away and the crackling was repeated.

Like the parting of the nearby Red Sea the audience melted left and right, the searchlight on the watchtower swung away from me and out into the darkness towards the perimeter fence. Orders were being shouted and Albert was suddenly beside me on the stage.

'Show's over, Bob. Time to take shelter. Follow me.'

As our entire crew scuttled on to our jeeps to be sped away to safety inside the officers' mess, we heard more crackling gunfire but this time not from afar. Our lads were responding.

The senior officer offered us beer and some very good fresh fish while explaining, 'That'll be half a dozen youths taking advantage of your show to open fire from the trees. They're terrible shots. You weren't in any real peril.'

The following day Ronnie, our drummer, found a bullet-hole in his bass drum.

At Wellington Barracks the next evening the bad guys were at it again. This time they'd blown up the camp's generators so we did our show in the light of the headlamps trained on us by twelve army lorries.

Having no power for our sound system, Sam and I asked the trio to play softly and got sore throats yelling at the crowd through megaphones improvised from strips of linoleum torn off the floor of the sick bay. Every time I breathed in I got a noseful of disinfectant. Still, I thought, it could have been worse.

On our third morning we were given some insight as to the seriousness of a newly arranged orange alert, a notch worse than yellow.

Driving through Aden's back streets on our way to do our final show, as the third of our jeeps passed over it, a grenade exploded. We had extra guards with us because of the increased threat of danger and one of them was a corporal sitting on the back of the third jeep with his backside hanging over the rear edge. He lost most of his buttocks.

With our first two jeeps undamaged, one had to take the injured soldier to hospital while eight of us somehow managed to cling on to the remaining vehicle and proceed to the site of the lunchtime show. Despite the crowding, not one of us allowed any parts of ourselves to protrude over the sides.

As we flew home we knew that our troops would soon be following us, saying goodbye and good riddance to Aden.

Things have worked out pretty much as Albert's politician said they would. There were border clashes between North and South throughout the 70s and then the two halves got together under pan-Arab influences to form their Yemen Arab Republic in May 1990.

Arriving back in England, I carried my duty-free camera through the green channel and the customs officer gave it a pointed stare, then asked, 'Been doing shows for the army out in Aden, have you, sir?'

'And the Royal Air Force.'

'That's voluntary, is it?'

'Well, they invite you. You could always say no.'

'And unpaid?'

'We get transport, food and accommodation.'

'Very commendable. Welcome home.'

And he winked and turned away. That's the only time I've ever had a wink from a customs man. It was gladly received but slightly unnerving.

### Wednesday, 25 February 1998

This evening Jac and I went to the St James Club to join a host of famous folk celebrating the ninetieth birthday of Sir John Mills.

Slim and agile as ever, he crossed the crowded room to sit at the piano and accompany himself with graceful skill as he sang songs from the stage musical *The Good Companions* in which he had starred three decades ago. Without being told so, no one could guess that he is almost entirely blind.

I've known Johnny since 1951 when I wrote a potted radio version of the film *The History of Mr Polly* in which he played the eponymous hero. In the intervening years I have always found him a charming friend, generous with advice but slightly frugal when it comes to hospitality.

I visited him while he was shooting his 1959 film *Tiger Bay* on location in South Wales. The bleak Cardiff docklands were made even less inviting by a steady drift of icy drizzle. After director J. Lee Thompson had wanted take after take of a cold, wet street scene, everyone was soaked and shivering.

John led me to his caravan. Once we were seated inside he kicked off his wet shoes and, reaching into his holdall, produced a vacuum flask.

'I knew it was going to be a freezing day,' he twinkled and patted the side of his nose with his index finger. 'But we troopers, we know the best thing to warm you up in this wicked weather, don't we?'

I was ready to share a bracing drink as he slowly unscrewed the lid of the flask and took out a clean pair of warm socks.

## Wednesday, 1 April 1998

Jac and I have been back in Barbados since 28 March but today seems an apt date in the year to tell you about Neville.

When we acquired the land on which to build Sandcastle about eight years ago it was a derelict lot sloping downwards from the west coastal highway to the beach with only chattel houses either side of it forming an unnamed village where two areas of our St James shire meet, Mount Standfast and the Garden.

Our tall white house in a Mediterranean style took eighteen months to build and has encouraged others to look at the village with a view to developing property.

Last year the handsome film and TV actor Christian Roberts and his shapely wife Christine completed their purchase of the village's abandoned garage and a large adjoining brick structure, and money was no object to their lavish conversion into the Lone Star Brasserie & Restaurant and the Roberts's own tasteful home. With seafront land no longer being made, it's attracted speculative attention to our stretch of sand and palm trees.

This week the *Nation*, one of the island's two daily newspapers, reported that another would-be purchaser had been scouting the area and we were amazed to see a full front-page picture of our next-door neighbour. In the story he claimed to have turned down an offer of US $4 million for his wooden house, land and interest in a small water sports operation that uses his beachside yard. Allowing for exaggeration, it puts a historically high value on every square foot adjacent to our home, but with Neville you can't be sure of anything.

Every village has a character. Neville is ours.

He keeps some dogs that think barking is as essential to life as breathing while he himself maintains a pretty continuous racket with a hammer, mending his house and kennels and patching up a glass-bottomed boat that's often brought ashore for repairs. We're used to Neville's noise but it sometimes reaches a frenzied level of banging and pounding that's quite incredible to our house guests. It seems as if he can't carry out any handyman work without his hammer being involved. Last Monday, with Neville's unseen battering din at its loudest ever, Dave Ismay remarked, 'And he's *painting*!'

Neville also provides the village with a regular cabaret act. This happens about every three weeks and takes the form of a loudly delivered

and only partly articulate rant about some fancied injustice he's suffered, shouted to everyone and no one. He strides around outside his
house, gesticulating wildly and giving vent to every expletive known to
troopers, quite regardless of the God-fearing congregation that's often
filing into or out of the Seventh Day Adventist church immediately
opposite us.

Yesterday he'd been at it for quite a few hours when at sunset he
seemed to tire and close down for the night. Then at midnight a full
moon rose and so did Neville.

No sooner had he started bawling his troubles to the stars than, to his
amazement, he found himself being out-raved by one of the diving team
from the water sports outfit.

This loon now woke the deeper sleepers of the neighbourhood by
slamming his head against a parked station wagon over and over again.

Now Jac and I sleep at the very top of our house, tucked well away
from external sounds, but the guest bedroom isn't as lucky.

Dave and Dodie had been lying awake waiting for Neville's profane
fuming to run out of steam when the diver started head-butting the car.
Now Dave had endured all he could bear of this double assault on his
senses. Long before he took up being a professional comedian and cor-
porate consultant, he was for a while a police officer so, whenever he
doesn't like the look of things, he tends to take charge of them.

By the time he'd got out of bed, put on a robe and shoes, and rushed
out into the street, the diver was pummelling the windows and panel-
work of the vehicle with his head, fists, elbows and feet. He was actually
wrecking the car using only his body parts.

Then he ran across the road to the church and flung himself into battle
with the chain fence, winding it round his neck and torso.

Dave came back into our house and phoned the police station. With
the vague promise of a patrol car from a yawning desk sergeant, he went
back outside to find the street filling with onlookers in various stages of
night attire, roused from their beds to watch the entertainment with
Barbados-style detachment. The few cars that chanced by also stopped
for casual observation.

By this time the diver was energetically wrenching at the church's
swing gates, yelling scrambled obscenities as he yanked them to and fro
on their rusty hinges. With some amusement, Dave spotted the vacant
face of Neville, staring from the watching crowd and shamed into
silence by a superior brand of nuttiness.

Purely by chance a passing police van from another district drew up
and a very large police sergeant stepped out. He leaned on his vehicle

for a while, watching the diver rolling about on his back in the road, struggling with the church gate he'd managed to pull from its moorings.

Then, slowly and deliberately, the big policeman walked round to the back of his van and, after rummaging inside, brought out a three-foot nightstick. He strolled very casually over to the cursing diver, glanced around indifferently at the half-naked spectators and then, choosing his spot with care, gave the diver's skull an almighty crack with the truncheon.

The diver, suddenly sobered, looked up reproachfully and howled, 'Ooh! Dat hurt, man!' Unwisely, he tried to stand up. For that move he received four more stunning whacks on his bonce and offered no resistance as the sergeant enlisted Dave's help in wrapping the diver up in some heavy-duty adhesive police tape.

When the sergeant was satisfied that his prisoner was properly trussed, he hit him once more for good luck and then lifted him up into the back of the van, pulling out a thick blanket and again indicating that he wanted Dave to assist him. Carefully, almost tenderly, he tucked the blanket around the semi-conscious diver.

As he followed the sergeant's example, Dave asked, 'Why the blanket?'

The sergeant shrugged.

'Make him safe when de van hit de potholes, sah. Don't want de poor fool hurting hisself.'

And it's All Fools' Day in Britain.

## Tuesday, 28 April 1998

Today I meet with my friend, the witty wordsmith Neil Shand, to plan an ITV special called 'Oh! What a Drag!', sixty minutes all about male entertainers who dress as females.

As a rule, men pretending to be women are funny; women pretending to be men are not. By the same rule, effeminate men are funny because they seem harmless and vulnerable; masculine women are not funny because they seem overbearing and threatening.

Some of the comic success of *La Cage Aux Folles* in its various forms – French film, stage musical, Hollywood film – lies in the gender confusion it causes in its audience. Men are subconsciously excited at the discovery that beautiful dancers who attract them one minute turn out to be male the next. Women share this mild hysteria when identifying with the wifely/motherly gay partner's suppression of all masculine characteristics. Our laughter is more explosive than the jokes merit because it's tapping our deepest sexual emotions. The two greatest exponents of cross-dressing that I've ever seen are the late Arthur Lucan and Danny La Rue. Their female roles weren't superficial.

The greatest dragsters have far greater depth than mere makeup and rubber boobs. When Lucan transferred himself into Old Mother Riley his audience virtually forgot that they were watching a man. The Irish washerwoman was broadly grotesque but utterly convincing, 'realistic acting with excursions into slapstick', as the *Liverpool Echo* put it in 1935. It was an outrageously eccentric characterisation of a hard-done-by backstreet harridan underpinned by subtlety, sadness and truth. There was never any question of a woman playing such a caricature.

When I played Buttons in *Cinderella* at the Manchester Palace in 1958–9, Danny La Rue was one of the Ugly Sisters, a lovely absurdity given his dazzling beauty. His ugly Ugly Sister was Alan Haynes. A drab wee man we only knew as Appleton became a stage door Johnny for Danny's on-stage creation. Arms full of flowers, he'd wait for her to come out of the theatre night after night, brightly asking the departing cast members, 'Will she be long?' When Danny came through the door, Appleton used to look at him shrewdly but say nothing.

After a couple of weeks, he watched Danny leave as usual and then stopped Alan. 'That chap, he'd be her brother, by my guess. Would he know where she goes at night?' Alan replied, 'You're wasting your time, mate – he and she sleep in the same bed.' Appleton shrugged cheerily. 'Show people!' he said. 'You're a law unto yourselves, bless you!'

## Tuesday, 10 March 1998

As I walk out on to the Intercontinental Hotel's cabaret stage this evening to perform for my friend and fan Piers Pottinger at his grand function for Low-Bell, Lady Thatcher changes her mind about making an early exit and stays to join in the laughter together with Tory leader William Hague. Lord Archer walks out.

I'm reminded of the night of the Conservative Party's greatest general election victory under Maggie's leadership. In the preceding months Jeffrey Archer had become the hero of every comedian whose stock of topical jokes was growing stale for lack of a good scandal.

Out of the shadows of Victoria Station stepped Monica Coghlan, lady of the night. It seemed that Jeffrey had bunged her £2,000 and his explanation seemed a bit unconvincing to much of the British public. In court he denied any sexual relationship. The jury found in his favour.

At the height of the story the gags on the topic didn't have to be all that good. The mere reference to the case had audiences hooting.

Adrian Walsh joked, 'Isn't it ironic? Archer's got into all this trouble for *not* doing to the girl just what he'd been doing to the Tory Party for the last three years!'

Ben Elton told us, 'Chancellor Nigel Lawson says Jeffrey will have to go. I mean, we can't have Tories giving away money, can we?'

Jimmy Tarbuck cracked, 'If you missed Jeffrey's statement to the House, he'll be signing copies of it at all good bookshops over the next few weeks.'

Naturally I jumped on the bandwagon with a few lines of my own. A tape recording of my cabaret act at that time reveals that no less than ten minutes of it were devoted to the Archer scandal, stonking laughs all the way through.

Jac and I had also been invited to Conservative Party Headquarters to celebrate the expected triumph. When we arrived it was chaotic. The heaving mass of excited celebrants was in ecstatic mood, all the results coming in indicated a Tory landslide and champagne sparkled in the very air. I turned to survey the room and found myself face to face with Jeffrey Archer.

'What a jubilant night!' I said brightly.

'*What*?' he spat.

I was disconcerted. 'Er . . . I said what a night for jubilation!'

'You *dare* to speak to me?'

'I'm sorry?'

'You have the *damn nerve* to speak to me?'

He was pink in the face and trembling with poorly suppressed fury.

'Have I said something to offend you?'

'Just go away, just leave, go now!' he snarled, turning away and pressing his way into the throng of merrymakers.

You'll probably think me naïve but I was bewildered. I couldn't think why Jeffrey Archer should waste his hatred on me. Finding Jac, I told her what had happened.

'What a twit!' she said. 'Someone's told him about what you say in your act. Obviously he can't take a joke.'

'Of course, you're right! Perhaps I ought to apologise to him.'

'Nonsense. He knows you're a comedian and you do topical material. If he can't handle being kidded, let him stew.'

Still, it bothered me. I've never wanted my comedy to cause anger or hurt and, so far as I know, I've only ever annoyed viewers who find me annoying generally not specifically.

The party spirits, already high, rose even higher when Mrs Thatcher arrived, the clamour intensifying and making it hard to talk.

'Let's go,' said Jac and we went to get our coats.

In the men's cloakroom was Jeffrey Archer.

I collected my coat and started to leave. He was holding a glass of champagne and staring at me blankly. I decided to try to make my peace with him.

'Look, whatever I've done to offend you . . .'

'I don't believe this! You've got the impudence to speak to me again!'

I tried to estimate how inebriated he was and took a chance.

'Perhaps you're mistaking me for my brother, Bob Monkhouse.'

'What?'

'People often do. We're not twins but we're very alike. I'm Bob's older brother, John.'

There was a pause while he decided whether I was kidding.

'You're not Bob Monkhouse?'

'No.'

'You're his brother?'

'That's right.'

He took a sip of his drink and thought about it.

'Well, if you're his brother, tell him never to speak to me again.'

'I'll make sure he doesn't,' I promised sincerely and left.

## Thursday, 14 May 1998

Frank Sinatra, an Oscar-winning actor whose unique vocal style and personal celebrity extends from World War II into the 90s, died today of a heart attack. He was eighty-two.

Sinatra was in every way a phenomenon. Linked to presidents and mobsters, the unstinting philanthropist could be an ungenerous woman-iser and, as intrusive reporters soon discovered, a public brawler.

His career had its crests and dips and it was in one of its early low stages that he came to London and I had my encounter with his variable nature. I was scripting and co-presenting a long-running radio series featuring the BBC's Show Band under the direction of Cyril Stapleton. By all accounts, Sinatra had enjoyed his broadcast with the band the previous year and was 'tickled pink' to return. Just how pink, I was soon to see.

Cyril, producer John Browell and I kept our appointment to meet the star in his hotel suite. We waited in the drawing room for two hours until John had to leave to attend another meeting elsewhere. Cyril too was restless.

'Look, Bob, you'd better see him on your own. We've got all his arrangements so there are really no musical problems for me to sort out. What he wants to do with you, comedy lines and such, that's entirely your province. Apologise for me and tell him I look forward to seeing him next week.'

And there I was, alone, looking at the doors and bursting for a pee. I knew which door led to the corridor because we'd come in that way. A second door revealed a small kitchen. There remained only a third door that had to lead to the rest of the apartment and, putting my ear to it, I could detect no sounds.

Gingerly I eased it open and peered round it. A small hallway had three further doors, one leading to the outside and I guessed the other two to be bedrooms with bathrooms *en suite*. I tapped on the nearer door softly, then louder, and heard no reply. In I went.

The bed was unmade and the wreckage of breakfast remained on a room service trolley. The occupant appeared to have gone.

I did a full-bladder walk to the bathroom door and opened it. As I crossed to the lavatory bowl and began to relieve myself, I heard a snore behind me. I turned, still peeing, and saw Frank Sinatra lying asleep in a bathtub full of water. Completing my business, I rinsed my hands at the handbasin and started to tiptoe out as quietly as I could, but not quietly enough.

'Hey!'

As I turned, a cake of soap hit me in the face.

'Get the fuck outa here!'

'S-sorry,' I stuttered. 'I had to use the toilet.'

Sinatra grabbed a towel and hurriedly arranged it round him as he rose to his feet, saying as he did so, 'I don't know who let you in here, fella, but some security guy is sure going to show you the way out.'

As he appeared to search for a non-existent bathroom phone, I backed out apologetically stammering something about waiting outside. In my confusion I mistook the second bedroom door for the one leading back to the drawing room. Standing in the doorway getting my bearings I became aware of a lovely young woman in a flimsy négligé sitting at a dressing table and regarding me coolly.

'Don't you knock?'

I gulped and shrugged and goggled at the one bare breast she was failing to cover. She was very beautiful and I recognised her. Now, as she looked at me, the recognition became mutual.

'My God! You were the compere!'

I would have answered but I had no chance. Sinatra's left hand was on my right shoulder and as he swung me around he punched me. Since I'd swung further than he expected, the punch landed on the left side of my neck and I fell against the door frame and slid to the floor.

'Pick up the goddam phone and call security!' shouted Sinatra.

But Miss Great Britain did no such thing.

'Frank! I know this man! We don't need him telling the world about us!'

Of course she knew me. I'd emceed the contest to find the most beautiful girl in the land only five weeks before. The winner was this drop-dead gorgeous lady who was now attempting to calm down her pugnacious paramour and explain to him who I was. I, playing safe by staying on the floor, chipped in with why I was there. Sinatra took his time about coming round.

Then he nodded acceptance of the situation, extended his hand and helped me to stand up.

'You know this lady, huh. Huh?'

'I do.'

'Now listen up. This situation is private, *compris*? You tell no one.'

'Certainly not. I mean, certainly. I mean, it's none of anyone's business but yours.'

'OK, go.'

I moved towards the exit and then turned. Sinatra was looking at me from the bedroom doorway wearing nothing but a towel while behind him Miss Great Britain was smiling and showing the other tit.

I smiled hopefully.

'I suppose you don't feel like discussing jokes for the radio show?'

He tilted his head forward, widening his eyes in disbelief and pointing a finger.

'I said go. Go now!'

I went.

Sinatra barely acknowledged me when he arrived at the BBC's Lower Regent Street basement studio. He rehearsed impatiently, sat silently with his manager until showtime, sang superbly and performed all the comedy continuity with me with effortless ability.

He departed without saying goodbye to me but as he mounted the stairs to his waiting limousine, his manager ran back to where I was standing and pressed a small box into my hand.

'Frank's little apology,' he said.

Inside the box was a gold Rolex.

## Monday, 18 May 1998

It's an honour to be asked to host BAFTA. That's my job this evening, acting as host for the awards ceremony that celebrates the best in British television. During the day-long rehearsals my carefully scripted quips get great laughs from producer John Kaye Cooper and his crew, always a danger sign. Sure enough, the black tie crowd who fill the Prince of Wales Theatre at 7.30 p.m. listen to me like an oil painting.

I'll be congratulated afterwards for my composure and professionalism under duress. The ITV transmission of the programme tomorrow will be fine, the thin nervous laughter from my jury having been enhanced by sound magnification of the subtlest kind.

Comedians often refer to their stand-up routines as monologues but, in performance before an audience, they become dialogues.

The man in the spotlight plays the principal role but the part played by the audience will determine the main elements of that particular performance – how fast or slow, how subtle or broad, in fact how successful the entire exchange will be.

Like the congregation's responses to a holy roller in a religious meeting, certain laughs can usually be anticipated with confidence. Others are less certain and may vary in nature from audience to audience.

One crowd may be quiet, thoughtful, appreciative of finesse, while the next is noisy, unthinking and happier with the obvious.

While the comic is the conductor of this chorus, he must also be willing and able to adapt to its moods and preferences as the give-and-take process works out. It's a two-way deal unless, for whatever reason, the audience won't do business.

During an interview I taped with the delightfully bellicose Arthur Haynes during his 1961 summer season in Great Yarmouth, he remarked that you must never let a bad audience know that it's bad.

'There's no need of it. Why let them go out feeling that you didn't like them? It's up to you to make them feel as if you loved them. After all, you're in control of the situation. It's not like giving a party that goes wrong. An audience isn't sitting around in twos and threes going, "This is bloody awful, let's leave." There's only one star and when I'm in charge, then it's up to me to set the pace and the mood of what I'm doing according to requirements. A big, friendly lot is no easier for me to deal with than a small one that's quiet.

'The bigger crowd's more fun, yes, but I use just as much effort in scaling my act down to suit the smaller crowd. It needs more intimacy, more concentration. You haven't got the long, rolling laughs that give you time to lean back on your heels and relax. You've got to be nice to people from the stage, even if they're not being all that nice to you. They don't know, do they? And they'll never know they weren't wonderful if you've made out that they were.'

Larry Grayson, back in the days when he worked as Billy Breen, once told the then inexperienced Dave Ismay, 'Never insult those lovely ladies and gentlemen, even when they're crap. Tell them they're gorgeous. Chances are they'll believe you.'

The beloved American clown Red Skelton wrote that, in sixty years of making people laugh, he'd 'never met a *bad* audience, just one or two that weren't very pleased'. He reasoned, 'These folks didn't have a meeting just before the show and plot your downfall. Maybe they just ain't in the mood. I figure it's my job to get 'em in the mood if I can and, if I can't, it's so long, no hard feelings, let's all move along, may God bless us.'

That each audience has its own personality, there's no doubt. The better comedians can weigh up that group personality within a few moments of taking the stage. Sometimes it's even possible to form an opinion before that, either by watching their reaction to a previous performer or simply observing their general demeanour as they sit waiting for the show to start.

Then it's the entertainer's job to match his attitude, material and delivery to his evaluation of his spectators; in short, to give 'em what they want.

'Some nights you can do the show like a kick-about with your pals, everybody joining in and having a good time,' says warm-up specialist Bobby Bragg, putting his skew on a similar view. 'Other nights it's more being on the playground with a bunch of kids that just don't want to play. Basically, though, you've got to treat both the same, as if they're the nicest lot you could wish to meet. After all, the naff audience never saw the good one, did they? So they don't know they're naff. You can kid 'em they're great and they won't know any different.'

Of course, these are assessments made philosophically and in tranquillity. Meet a comic just after he's encountered a really tough throng and it's a different story.

Roy Castle remembered a grim week in his early variety years, doing his level best to get a smile or two out of an unimpressed gathering in the chilly vastness of the Birmingham Hippodrome. After concluding his best routine to total silence and during his ill-judged pause, a voice from the far right in the circle shouted, 'Turn the light out, I'm trying to sleep!' From the far left came another call, 'Don't do that, I'm reading!'

328

It's funny now. It was funny then. But, although Roy took it well, it shattered his confidence for days.

Dave Ismay, one of the most self-assured and caustic of comedians, recalls a cheerful and popular tour with the glamorous black pop group from America, the Three Degrees. All was roses till they hit the Apollo, Glasgow. Dave had the first spot and then, after a ten-minute interval, the girls and their musicians supplied the entire second half.

'The people came to see Sheila Ferguson and her partners, not me. So, of course, I had to work hard to make my mark. But the girls were very big that year and they were attracting the sort of crowds that I liked and which, up until Glasgow, liked me too.

'Well, first house at the Apollo was like the Dead Zone. They tolerated me. Good gags went belly up. I was cheeky in those days and anywhere else I might've teased them a bit, you know, stuff like, "You're a Polaroid crowd, aren't you? It takes you a minute to get the picture" – but, young as I was, even I knew an English comic didn't chance his arm in Glasgow.

'Then comes second house. My announcement is made and I walk out to nothing and stand there doing my usual stuff and they're taking no notice at all. They're talking and arguing and gossiping and generally behaving as if I don't exist. My throat's drying up and I can feel my bottle going. Then the noise level starts rising and rising and people are shouting and cursing and I'm sweating and I hear one piercing voice cutting through all the deafening babble that says, "Ge' yon English bastard off!"

'Everyone suddenly goes threateningly quiet, like a lynch mob in a movie, every unfriendly face turned to me. And I hear myself say, "Now listen! I may be English and you may think I'm not funny but until I finish what I'm paid to do, the Three Degrees won't come on, get it? So if you want to see the girls, you'd better let me finish this *in peace.*"'

Not many comedians beg an audience for *peace*. To his great credit, given their surly OK to do so, Dave did finish his spot, although he admits, 'I crammed the last eight minutes into ninety seconds. Laughter free. Just a threatening silence. It seems like nothing now but the psychological blow I took from the sheer hostility of that gang put me into shock. A comedian is Mister Nice Guy, Uncle Jollity and all that, you become accustomed to being liked. When you run into a solid wall of ill will like that, it rattles your brains. I couldn't help retreating into a numbed depression.

'I stayed like that until we were all on the coach the next day and the girls and all the musicians started taking the piss out of me. I sniped back at them and they all went, "Oh, that's done it! Ismay has been returned to us!" But since that night, I've never *assumed* that I'll be accepted by the audience as a friend. I've been aware of that horrible possibility – the no-win situation.'

In a two-way interview with me on Liverpool's City Gold Radio, Pete Price talked about the comedian's need to dominate every kind of audience.

'It's partly selfish. While I'm on stage, it's my world and I'm boss. I've got the mike to prove it. I had some drunk snatch the mike off me once and it was like losing my willie.'

Although the assertion of amplified authority over the scene of the entertainment is an act of domination, Pricey insists it can only be maintained for the necessary length of time if most of the audience likes him.

'If I'm heckled, I've got to pull out all the tricks to keep the majority on my side. I'll do mock despair, defiance, throw a little tantrum, appeal to God to make me funny, clown about as if it's all part of the fun. Women love it when I make myself look stupid. The women'll go, "Shut up, you lot, and give 'im a chance!" Men'll shut up if they think they're going to get frozen out in bed later.'

When an audience is unwilling to be wooed and won, the problem may lie in their reason for showing up in the first place. In certain circumstances the comedians find themselves unwelcome impediments to the aims and aspirations of those who have come to talk, drink, dance and get lucky with a good-looker.

It happened to me at Bailey's, Watford, in 1977. As a result I broke the comedians' code of honour and got a standing ovation I'm thoroughly ashamed of.

Originally serving the area as a dance hall under the once-popular Rank Suite name, it had been converted into a cabaret venue with no little difficulty. To accommodate those with no wish to dine and see the floor show in what was once the main ballroom, a disco had been incorporated on an upper floor but it wasn't working out well.

The teenage trade didn't like being tucked away upstairs while the grown-ups watched the pop groups and recording stars.

One of the Bailey Organisation's chiefs, Stan Henry or John Smith, came up with an experimental idea: divide the ballroom floor into two halves with accommodation for the diners filling one side and a flashily lit dance floor on the other.

The view from centre stage was distinctly odd.

As you stood at the microphone stand, you looked down and left at a seated audience, sipping drinks at their tables.

Across the centre of the room, starting just below your feet and stretching away thirty yards over the floor, ran a three-foot-high partition of wrought iron topped by a smooth wooden rail.

To the right of this division was the disco floor, filled with young people who wanted to dance and pull one another.

When musical entertainers provided the cabaret, there was no problem. The older half of the audience sat watching on their side while the kids could still move rhythmically and do their thing. But when a comedian took to the stage for an hour or so, teen tolerance was severely strained.

I walked on to a fifty-fifty situation, half pleased to see me and half not. The sound of the applause was as if the right speaker on your stereo had cut out. I managed to deal with this awkwardness from Monday to Friday but Saturday night was pretty full and very noisy.

I was twenty minutes into my act, scoring well with the seated audience on my left, doing better than hoped with the young standees on my right, when one scarred hooligan decided he'd heard just about enough out of me.

The black-leather-clad troublemaker leaned on the central rail about fifteen feet in front of me and began to chant, raising two fingers at me rhythmically as he fixed me with his aggressive glare, made all the more malevolent by one of his eyes being an opaque blood-red. Like the two-note siren on a police car he intoned an incessant wail of, 'Fuck off! Fuck off! Fuck off! Fuck off!' on and on and on.

Now there are lots of ways of coping with hecklers, some of them explored elsewhere in these pages, but for a situation like this you need a bouncer. There was none to be seen. I tried my best to make myself heard, even cued the resident pianist to cut to my first song but had to abandon it after a few bars because the lyric was meaningless against the persistent screaming of the two-syllable taunt.

It was becoming impossible to continue and yet I felt a rising sense of outrage that I could be driven from the stage by this noisy brute.

The surge of anger suffused me as I have seldom known it. The piercing incantation seemed to be getting louder with every repetition. Calls of 'Be quiet!' and 'Stop that!' from the more civilised half of the ballroom were having no effect. Indeed, the hooligan seemed encouraged by them.

Provocation finally overwhelmed my self-control. The last thing I can clearly remember saying was, 'No more!' – then I experienced some sort of blackout and, unaware of the passage of time, I came to, still standing at the microphone but breathless, with the entire audience, both halves, applauding me enthusiastically.

I looked for my tormentor. He was flat on the floor, unconscious.

Mystified by what had taken place, I covered the situation as best I could by taking exaggerated bows, inviting the audience to call out suitable music for the band to play. Suggestions included 'You Go to My Head', 'I Get a Kick Out of You' and 'Hit the Road, Jack'. I still didn't get it.

I carried on with my act with much greater success, the youngsters on my right now crowding forward to the stage and clapping every joke as if I had mysteriously become their hero. Because they now obscured my view I never saw the going of my adversary, whether he was ushered or carried out, but I didn't care much. I was riding high.

When I'd finished my seventy-minute spot to sustained applause, I came off stage filled with curiosity. The manager, Mike Payne, greeted me with a congratulatory handshake, an apology and an explanation.

He had seen me struggling against the insistent cat-calls for several minutes while he attempted to round up the missing bouncers who'd sloped off for a fag outside.

As he returned to the hall he saw the incident happen of which I had and still have no memory.

He said, 'You sort of flipped. You said, "No more!" in a bright sort of way, like an order. Then – and this was unbelievable to watch – you ran along the railing! Like a bloody tightrope walker on speed! You just skittered along that handrail all the way up to that young thug who was paralysed by the surprise. Then you bent your right leg up high and slammed your heel down on to his head! He hit the deck like a dead weight and you, you just balanced there for a second, teetered a bit, and then you spun around on your toes and danced back along the rail as if you were Gene Kelly. No wonder everyone cheered you. It was quite fantastic! Acrobatic!'

His expression changed from cheerful to concerned.

'Now we'd better get you escorted to your car. That bloke you kicked unconscious is a violent bastard. If he's pulled himself together by now, he could have rounded up some pals to do you over.'

I've never left a club so fast. Thank heavens it was Saturday night. I didn't have to come back.

I've often imagined being asked, 'What do you do?' to which I'd reply, 'I'm an entertainer.'

'And if they don't want to be entertained, what then?'

'Oh, I just kick them in the head.'

**Sunday, 31 May 1998**

Jac and Dave Ismay have been plotting for weeks. All I know about tonight's birthday party is that they've booked a big marquee that's been grafted on to the picturesque Paris House restaurant in the grounds of Woburn Abbey. The rest of tonight's event will come as a series of happy surprises.

My inventive tailor has designed a sleeveless dress suit for me and, considering I'll be seventy at midnight, I appear moderately presentable in it if I say so myself. Jac's in a classic white gown and looks radiant. Robert Purdie arrives early as usual and drives us to the venue, past grazing deer and up the sweeping drive to the unique black-and-white patterned building that was built for the Paris Exhibition of 1878 and imported brick by brick by Hastings Russell, the ninth Duke of Bedford. The gifted chef/proprietor Peter Chandler and his pretty associate Gail Baker greet us on the smartly tented terrace and I review the troops: twenty-three young waiters and waitresses recruited for the occasion. They look as excited as we are.

The wines are set out attractively. We'll drink our way through fifty bottles of champagne this evening together with forty-two of Pinotage, four dozen of Penfold's Chardonnay, forty Palliser Estate Sauvignon Blanc, eighteen of Peter's House White and, more surprisingly, sixty bottles of water. Flower decorations and centrepieces glow in the flattering theatrical lighting and Laurie Taylor's straw-hatted oompah band is warming up to welcome the first arrivals.

Among our 120 guests are Des O'Connor with his stunning lady Jodie, Joy and Ronnie Barker, Kate Robbins with her musician husband Keith and her actor parents Liz and Mike (he and I have the same birth date), David Jason with his lovely companion Gill, Anita Harris and her inspired artist husband Mike Margolies, Les Dennis and his far-too-pretty-for-him actress wife Amanda Holden, Sue and Jeremy Beadle, Avril and Denis Norden, Hazel and Jasper Carrott, Stephen Leahy, Annie and Vince Hill, Irene and Michael Aspel, Cleo Laine and Johnny Dankworth, Lord and Lady Feldman, Pat Coombs, John Junkin and his family, Marion Montgomery and Laurie Holloway, Sue and Lionel Blair, Pete Price, Neil Shand, Colin and Kathryn Edmonds, Marianne and Dave Lee Travis, my daughter Abigail and husband Mark, Moya and George Layton, and my agent's new partners Mandy and Laurie Mansfield.

Top alternative health journalist of the year Hazel Courtney is also on hand in case I'm overcome and need St John's Wort administered.

A starter of lobster, smoked salmon and prawn salad is followed by Spatchcock Poussin 'Bourguignonne' while Jimmy O'Brian plays the piano and close-up magicians work their wonders around the tables and a cameraman records memorable moments. These pop up between courses when Dave takes the microphone and announces our surprise speakers. Spurred on with bursts of my singing voice booming out some embarrassing old recordings, some of my oldest friends get up to insult me superbly. The exceptions to the ragging process are Peter Prichard who tells a story he's appropriated from my autobiography, making it sound more impressive than when I wrote it; Jasper relates a funny but flattering account of a charity performance I gave for him many years ago; and, not sparing my blushes, Jeremy pays me a very sincere and generous tribute. During his kindly praise, he makes a point that has cropped up several times in this journal.

'Making people laugh is a lunatic business. If you're successful the press reviles you, you gain uncertain celebrity, your contemporaries are jealous of you and the public defies you to do it again. You are stigmatised for success. So what motivates a comedian to risk all? Glory, approval, admiration? No, quite simply, it is to achieve that sublime feeling that you are responsible for happy laughter. And what finer profession can there be than to allow people some fleeting freedom from the pressures and pain of normal life into a brief world of pleasure and release?'

Les Dennis scores big laughs with his talk as does my old chum Mitch Murray, once the writer of hit records for top groups, now a sought-after speechwriter. He roasts me royally:

'Bob is the sort of friend who's always there when he needs you. And he's the sort of comedian who leaves his audiences gasping for less.'

Denis Norden speaks brilliantly as always. He recalled my first broadcasts in 1947:

'One thing I remember to this day about his act, apart from its trenchant blend of King-Farouk and Stafford-Cripps references, was that he did the whole thing wearing his RAF corporal's uniform. Because, of course, he was still serving his country out there in the hell they called Cleveland Street.'

He welcomes me to 'The Wonderful World of Seventy' because 'though it may not be immediately discernible, I too have reached what you might call "The Oat Bran Years".

'If Bob wants to know what living in "The World of Seventy" is like, well, despite certain disadvantages, like you start to have trouble with the coconut ones in Liquorice Allsorts; bending over becomes a major decision; you can't count the number of times a day you find yourself moving in one direction when you should be moving in another – despite all that, seventy does bring with it certain advantages.

'For one thing, it's true that you now only seem to need four hours' sleep. True, you need it four times a day, but . . .

'Something that's really on the plus side is a recent medical report that establishes once and for all that the human male is physically capable of enjoying sex up to and even beyond the age of eighty! Not as a participant, of course . . .

'But then no decade is *all* gravy. And there's always the other pleasure particular to those of us who are reaching the end of our warranty period: reminiscing, an activity somebody once described as "the most fun an older person can have without actually having much fun".

'But what's for sure is that, with that 50-megabyte memory of his, nobody could be better equipped for reminiscing than this one-man resource centre.'

Denis concludes his droll address with an appeal to my better feelings: 'As someone who has known you as a teenager, as an adult and as an OAP, sometimes all three in the same day, may I be the one to make a final heartfelt entreaty? Please, Bob, please, give up this crazy idea of retiring! I promise you, there still could be work around for you. Jeremy there, he's got these circus connections, he'd always put a word in with Gerry Cottle. And Brian Tesler, not heading up LWT any more admittedly but he's still got a bit of clout, I'm sure he'd find you an occasional "Standby Relative on This Is Your Life". And as all of us saw a couple of weeks back on the BAFTAs, that dinner jacket has got months of wear in it yet.

'So, please, Bob, stay up there for us!'

Of all the marvellous birthday presents I receive, Denis's speech is one of the most deeply appreciated. So is Dave Ismay's masterly display of ad-lib wit as the evening's host.

For our midnight cabaret Dave has booked my favourite singer/songwriter, Beverley Craven. This evening it appears that she's everyone's favourite.

As a huge birthday cake is wheeled out, Peter Chandler lighting its seventy candles with a blowtorch, I see that it's intricately decorated with the titles of every TV show I've ever done while in the centre my five-inch figure stands holding a script and hogging a TV camera. Jac has thought of everything.

Des leads the congregation in the inevitable Happy Birthday song and I deliver a boozy but adequate speech of thanks which I can't remember doing, even when I see it days later on the videotape.

Fabba, the peppy group who specialise in Abba songs, round off the evening's music and guests begin dancing. It seems that no one wants to leave, including me.

By the time I get to bed I've been seventy for four hours already.

## Monday, 1 June 1998

This morning I'm hazily hungover but happy. Peter Prichard phones his thanks for last night's bash and brings me news of a BBC TV Special to mark my seventieth. Can I get it together in three weeks?

'Call it "Over the Limit", guv'nor. Nice plug for the book. They'll put it out early August on a Saturday evening.'

'Great. I'll call Neil Shand and Col and see if they'll work on the script with me.'

'And Carlton TV's been on. They want you and the people at Watchtower to make three more editions of "What a Carry On" . . .'

'If you mean the programme I did last year for Watch*maker* about camp comedy, it was called "What a Performance!"'

'That's it and they need the first one taped by the end of this month.'

'That's a bit soon. But I suppose we could do the next one on comic battleaxes perhaps and . . .'

'That's up to you, guv'nor. You talk to Watchtower about that. I've also got some cabaret dates and a few speeches for you and, oh, Stephen Leacock's calling you this afternoon.'

'Peter, Stephen Leacock is a dead Canadian humorist. Do you mean the chap who was at the party last night, Stephen Leahy?'

'What a nice man. He's talked to BBC 1's daytime boss and they've confirmed that they do want another ninety editions of "Wipeout".'

'Ninety? When?'

'A.S.A.P., but I've told them you can't start making them till August, OK?'

'But I need to work on the scripts.'

'Right. You've got your holiday in July for that. Give you something to do in Bermuda.'

'Barbados.'

'So that's all for now. You're going to be a busy boy, aren't you?'

Yes, thank God, I am. It's wonderful to me that I can work as much as I do. Don't imagine I don't know how lucky I am.

I take inspiration from that wonderful Scottish actor, Finlay Currie. Shortly before he died at the age of ninety, he appeared on a TV chat show where he was asked if he'd ever played a romantic lead.

'Not yet, laddie,' he replied. 'Not yet.'

Is seventy-five too soon to write another set of memoirs?

# INDEX